Other books by Kitty Burns Florey

FICTION
The Sleep Specialist
Solos
Souvenir of Cold Springs
Five Questions
Vigil for a Stranger
Duet
Real Life
The Garden Path
Chez Cordelia
Family Matters

NONFICTION
Script and Scribble: The Rise and Fall of Handwriting
Sister Bernadette's Barking Dog: The Quirky History and Lost Art of Diagramming Sentences

The Writing Master

The Writing Master

a novel

Kitty Burns Florey

White River Press
Amherst, Massachusetts

The Writing Master

A novel by
Kitty Burns Florey

First published by White River Press 2013
www.whiteriverpress.com
ISBN: 978-1-935052-65-4

Ebook published by Armory New Media
April 2012
www.armorynewmedia.com
ISBN 978-1-935073-28-4

www.kittyburnsflorey.com

Library of Congress Cataloging-in-Publication Data

Florey, Kitty Burns.
The writing master : a novel / by Kitty Burns Florey.
pages cm
ISBN 978-1-935052-65-4 (pbk. : alk. paper)
1. Penmanship—Fiction. 2. Murder—Investigation—Fiction. 3. Connecticut—History—1775-1865—Fiction. 4. New Haven (Conn.)—Fiction. I. Title.
PS3556.L588W75 2013
813'.54—dc23
2013011463

This book is for Genevieve F. Hunt

The Writing Master

Chapter One

"Dear Sam."

The man spoke through a short black beard that densely covered his cheeks and jaw. He looked rough, his clothes were ragged and not clean, but he spoke like an educated person, and Charles wondered why he didn't have the skill of writing.

"Go on."

"You have your wish," said the black-bearded man. "The object is in my pocket. I shall be on the road soon."

Charles held up a hand. "I don't write as quickly as you talk."

"Don't make it fancy."

"I am not making it fancy." He dipped his pen. "This is the way I write. *On the road soon.* Is there more?"

"It might take me several days because I'll stop along the way. You know the road I will not be taking."

"The road I will *not* be taking?"

"That's right. *Not.* And after that, write: We will settle up as discussed."

"Signed?"

"Signed nothing. That's all." Then he grinned. His teeth were small and yellow, a front one half gone. "No. Sign it *Your dutiful brother.*"

"Name?"

The man looked blank.

"Your dutiful brother Henry? Thomas? Alexander?"

"Just what I said. *Your dutiful brother.* Nothing more."

Charles wrote the words with a flourish. The man reached for the paper. Charles blotted it carefully, handed it over, and said, "That will be ten cents. If you want an envelope to mail it in, another nickel."

"Of course I want an envelope to mail it in. What do you think I had you write it for?"

"I have no idea," Charles said coolly. He opened his portable desk and took out an envelope. "Address?"

There was a pause. Charles looked up. The man was squinting into space.

"Address?"

"Wethersfield."

Charles waited, staring off into space himself. They were on the town green in New Haven. It was a sunny day, cool for the seventh of May. Charles looked over at the row of elm trees that had just come into leaf, a yellow-tinged green haze over Temple Street, obscuring the steeple of Center Church. He had had no midday meal, and tried not to think about how much he would like a cup of tea and a hunk of bread and cheese.

Two women sauntered by, in close conversation. One of them was red-haired, wearing a flounced blue dress, and when the breeze lifted her skirts he could see low shoes, white stockings, a trim ankle. She was very full-breasted. Both men looked at her, and then Charles dropped his eyes and asked, "Address?" No reply. "Sir? What address?"

The bearded man kept his eyes on the two women. "Put it to S. Chillick. And the address is Colman Street, near Broad."

Charles dipped the pen again and wrote. "Wethersfield?"

"That's what I said."

"Coincidence. I'm on my way to Wethersfield myself. I could almost deliver it for you."

"That will not be necessary."

"I was joking. Delivering letters is not part of my job."

The man looked at him sharply. "You live up there?"

It seemed a good idea, somehow, to lie. "No, just visiting."

No reply, of course. No *Hope you have an easy trip*. No *Enjoy your visit*. The man held out his hand for the letter and the envelope.

"No return address?"

"No return address," he said, as if a return address was a foppish affectation instead of a postal regulation.

Charles shrugged. "Fifteen cents."

After a lot of digging, the man brought up a handful of small change from his pocket and picked out a dime and five coppers. He dropped them into Charles's hand, not actually touching it, for which Charles was grateful. The hand that dropped the coins was filthy, the nails broken, and Charles saw then that the man's other hand, the right, was worse than filthy, it was as black as coal and bore the remains of what looked like a grimy bandage. His writing hand, no doubt. Hence Charles's fifteen cents.

At close range, the man stank of sweat, soot, and — something else. What was it? Something bad and not unfamiliar.

Charles stepped back and added, "You'll need to put a three-penny stamp on that." It was something he always said, because the practice was still new.

"You sell stamps, too?"

"Only the U.S. Post Office can sell you a stamp," Charles said.

If the man had been more polite, Charles would have directed him to the post office, on Union Street. But he thought: *To hell with him, let him find it himself.* The man went over to a bench and folded the letter clumsily with his good hand, stuffed it into the envelope, tucked the flap under. A haphazard mess. As he walked away, he approached the red-haired woman and her companion, passing much too close to them, which made the women step back, drawing their skirts about them, their hoops arcing behind them. The man raised his hat, and Charles heard him say something and laugh. Then he was gone down the path toward Chapel Street.

The two women sat down on a bench. It was getting late in the afternoon. An hour ago, there had been a short queue of people awaiting Charles's services, but there were none at the moment. On an impulse Charles capped his inkwell, packed up his desk, and walked over to the bench where the women sat. They were talking earnestly, and he stood before them until they looked up.

"I beg your pardon." He lifted his hat. "I hope that fellow didn't annoy you."

The redhead looked, for some reason, amused. "No, not at all," she said. The other woman sat glowering in silence. She was older, and taller, and, bonnet to shoes, she was dressed entirely in black. Her eyes and hair were so dark he thought she must be Spanish, maybe a gypsy.

The younger woman continued to look up at him expectantly, and Charles felt compelled to say more. "He seemed a disagreeable character."

"One does occasionally encounter one, even on the very respectable New Haven Green." She spoke with a smile. "But one does not allow them to ruin one's pleasure in such a lovely day."

The other woman spoke up. "Nor to interrupt one's conversation."

Charles took the hint. "Forgive me." He tipped his hat again, feeling like a child who has been reprimanded by a schoolmistress. He was on his way back down the path when the younger woman called him back. "You are a penman, sir?" she asked.

"I am." He turned, and held up the little desk, which he carried like a suitcase by a leather handle. There was also a longer strap, curled around a spool on the side, which he could sling over his shoulder if he needed both hands free. He had made the desk himself in his woodshop, and sometimes thought he should get a patent on it, go into the manufacturing business. Not that there was much call for such things any more. Itinerant penmen were a dying breed.

"Professional? Trained? Do you teach?"

"I have a position at the business college in Hartford. I supervise the teachers and oversee the curriculum, and I also teach bookkeeping, business mathematics, and fine penmanship. But at this time of the year, the school is not in session. Not until the fall."

"And so why are you in New Haven with your desk, writing letters for rude black-bearded men?"

She had noticed him, then, as she passed. He ignored her companion, who was glaring at him, and sat down on the bench, the desk on his lap. "I was a kind of traveling writing master when I was younger," he said. "There are not many left. But there is still a need. I like to set up here on the Green when I'm in New Haven. Some of the people who seek my services have known me for six years or more."

"Do you travel here regularly?"

He was charmed by her curiosity. "I'm passing through on my way from Pennsylvania. My mother lives there, in a German community that uses my services for records. Entries in the family bible. Certain letters and certificates. I have friends here that I always stop with on my way back home."

Her coloring was unusual: hair lighter than auburn — an usually brilliant light red, gold where the sun touched it — and skin that wasn't pale like that of most redheads but had a warm, honeyed tint to it, as if she had spent time in the sun.

Impulsively, he asked, "Would you like to see one?"

"Oh, very much! I have an interest in fine penmanship. Not that I can produce it. My hand is legible, but not what anyone would call pretty."

"That's true of most people."

"Many people, it seems, can't write at all."

"That's a fact. Most of my German relations were never taught that skill. Reading, yes. They read their Bibles daily. But some of them can't write even their names."

"They sign with an X?"

"They do. And some of the X's are none too legible, either."

As he talked, he rummaged in his desk for an ill-fated birth certificate he had engrossed only a few days ago. A pair of birds, a trailing vine, and the child's name, with the date and place of birth: *Otto-Heinrich Gruenewalder, 19 January 1856, Manheim Pennsylvania.*

She removed her gloves and examined it carefully, holding it by her fingertips. "But it's exquisite," she said. "A work of art. Was this not acceptable? Is it flawed in some way that I can't see?"

Charles hesitated. Otto-Heinrich Gruenewalder was the newest son of his second cousin Wilhelm on the Legenhausen side of the family. Usually, his relatives in Lancaster County preferred lettering in the angular German style, but Wilhelm liked to think of himself as modern, so he had requested the highly flourished style that Charles himself preferred. And then Will had refused to pay up. First he said he didn't like the birds. Then he said the lettering was hard to make out. Finally, he said he thought Charles would only charge him half because the modern style was simpler and quicker to execute. Charles had made it clear that his price didn't change.

"Look at it this way, Will," he said. "If I had to count every stroke and price my work accordingly, I would charge you extra for the length of your son's name."

"Can't you be kind, Charles?" Magda, his mother, had been unable not to enter the argument. Will and Alma were struggling, she said. The glass factory was threatening to close, and little Otto-Heinrich — a bald and stolid creature lying peacefully in his cradle — was their seventh child, after all.

"The glass factory is always threatening to close," Charles said, "and it's hardly my fault they have more children than they can support."

His cousin Will had tried to punch him, but he was restrained. Alma had cried, his mother had scolded. But Charles took the certificate away with him.

"I'm not rich, either," he had said to his mother when he left the next morning.

"You don't have a wife and children to support."

"That's not my fault."

"Isn't it?"

She usually gave him a packet of sandwiches and a chunk of *kuchen* to take with him, but this time there was nothing. He wouldn't have taken it even if she'd offered it: the bad will his mother generated had a way of infecting everyone who came in contact with it. She stood there with her arms folded. Charles left with a slam of the door. He traveled to Legenhausen territory twice a year, to deliver money from his father. And that was more than enough.

"Rejected? Well, in a sense," he said.

"I can't see why anyone would reject it. It looks perfect."

"It was for an unreasonable and hot-headed cousin of mine who didn't want to pay me what I asked."

"And what is that?"

"For this style, with this information, twenty-five cents. If I add the names of the parents, the price goes up to thirty-five cents. With more embellishment, it can cost as much as a half-dollar, sometimes more."

He was trying to impress her — only once had he charged more than a half-dollar for a certificate — but she had stopped listening. She stared at the paper in her hands for a long moment, as if she was memorizing every flourish, and then she said, "Could you make one of these for me?"

The dark woman stirred and said, "Lillian."

"It's only a quarter, Elena! It's not one of what you call my extravagances. It's a worthy project."

"It is not a worthy project." The dark woman spoke with an accent: *warethy*, she said, and rolled her *r*'s slightly, but her English was surprisingly fluent. Her eyebrows were like two moustaches on her forehead. She must be in mourning, Charles realized. Even her gloves were dull black leather, and a gauzy black veil was pushed back from her bonnet. "There is no time for this nonsense. We should go."

The woman named Lillian laughed. "There is, and we should not! And nonsense is entirely the wrong word for it!"

"It is a mad idea."

"It's my idea, and I'm not mad. I'm perfectly sane!"

"Not everyone would agree."

Charles cut in. "I would be happy to do it for you," he said, and the woman looked at him gratefully. Her cheeks had become pink during the argument, and he noticed a scattering of freckles across her nose and on her cheekbones. He tried not to stare in the direction of her breasts.

"All right," she said, and opened her netted coin purse. "Here is twenty-five cents."

"Wait until I'm done. If you don't like it, you don't have to pay."

"I want one exactly like this," she said, "and I promise you I will not reject it."

She looked at him expectantly, but Charles said, "I can't do it here, on the fly. I'll have to take it away with me to engross it properly. I could deliver it to you tomorrow."

"Lillian," the dark woman said.

"Elena," Lillian said in the same tone, and laughed again. "We could meet on this same bench tomorrow. At exactly the same hour." She squinted up at the clock on the Exchange Building. "I can't see that far. Can you tell what time it is?"

Charles took out his gold pocket watch — still trying to impress her, he knew that — and flipped up the cover. "It is exactly twenty minutes past two," he said.

"Then that's the time we shall meet. Will that do for you?"

He would rather have delivered it to her home than hand it to her on a bench on the Green. But her disregard for convention delighted him. "It will be fine."

"All right, then." She clasped her hands under her chin and smiled. "It must read like this. Baby's name: Prudence Anne Prescott. Anne with an e, Prudence like the virtue."

Charles had his pencil out, and wrote it down carefully. "And the birth date?"

"The ninth of March, 1856. She is two months old, and it is high time she had a pretty birth certificate."

The woman at the end of the bench exhaled through her teeth, the universal sign of vexation.

"Place of birth?"

"The lovely port city of New Haven, Connecticut. A haven indeed."

Charles didn't comment, just read the information back and, when she had approved it, packed up his desk again. He would have liked to prolong the encounter, but he sensed he would rise in her opinion — and certainly in that of her companion — by staying businesslike and not lingering. He bowed deeply from the waist to each of the women in turn, like Uncle Stan Legenhausen, Aunt Mina's husband, who had been a count in the old country. Supposedly.

"Until tomorrow, then."

"Twenty minutes past two, sharp."

"My name is Charles Cooper."

"I am Lillian Prescott, but I am called Lily." A smile pulled at the corners of her mouth. "By most people."

∂∽

Charles went immediately back to the Gaudets' house on Bradley Street, to the apartment over the stables where he stayed, and set up his materials. He forgot he was hungry — he couldn't wait to get to work.

The apartment was small, but bright and airy, with a skylight, and neatly fitted up for visitors. A perfect place to work. From the window by his desk Charles could see as far as the corner where Bradley Street met Orange, and beyond to what used to be Mr. Bishop's farmland when Charles first visited the Gaudets. He used to stroll there with Sophie, watching the cows swaying slowly toward the barn where, now, there was the daily sound of hammers and saws, the shouting of men, the clatter of carts hauling stone and brick. Mr. Bishop had sold off his cows and was building houses instead.

Charles's in-laws' imposing brick-and-granite Greek Revival house was one of the grandest in this part of town. The Gaudets were a well-to-do Anglo-French family with deep roots in international banking and a side interest in a large cotton mill in northern Connecticut. Bernard's branch of the family had seen heavy losses in the Panic of 1837, when the price of cotton worldwide plunged and several of their banks failed in New York and Paris.

But that same year, old Mr. Ingersoll — Emily's father — died, and she and Bernard inherited his brickyard just north of New Haven. Until bricks came his way, Bernard Gaudet had been an idle, wealthy dilettante — he admitted it himself — whose main interests were wine vintages and the cut of his waistcoat. "And Emily and the children, of course," he would always add — Sophie, born in 1830, and Philip, 1836.

Brickmaking was a risky, grueling, and inconveniently seasonal business, but to his surprise Bernard found he had a talent for it, and what began as a practical necessity, a way to support his family, quickly became a deep attachment to the process of making bricks. He learned the operation from the bottom up, driving the clay wagon to the pit, molding the bricks, and firing the kilns — learning clotting and stacking and edging — everything but kneading the clay with his feet alongside his men, which Emily forbade as undignified. Bernard turned the failing factory into a prosperous establishment that shipped bricks all over New England and New York. He was known for treating his employees well: he gave them a half-hour for their midday meal, he refused to hire children under the age of twelve, he gladly employed Irish workers, and in the winter, when the clay froze and the brickyard closed down, he found his men employment at the ice houses on the ponds nearby, in which Bernard soon had an interest.

Running the factory gave him a respect for people who worked for a living, and when Sophie fell in love with a writing master whose father was the proprietor of a general store, Bernard could not have been more delighted. Even now, with Sophie gone, the Gaudets' house was his second home.

Charles set up a sheet of creamy parchment, drew light pencil lines, sketched out the words. Below his window, Joshua was in the stable yard, sitting on a stool mending a harness, and Hester was unpegging the kitchen laundry. He watched them as they worked, Hester turning her head to laugh at something her husband said as she shook out a napkin and folded it. He always noticed Joshua and Hester, not only because they were black and because it was not the custom to employ a married couple together as servants — the Gaudets were unusual in many ways — but because of the obvious depth of their contentment together. They weren't young, probably well into their forties, had no children, of course, but they seemed as much in love at that age as he and Sophie had been in their early twenties.

Emily always said that Joshua and Hester were like family members, and Sophie had once whispered to Charles, "Yes, except that they sleep in the attic and eat in the kitchen."

Sophie. In Wethersfield, except for his nightmares, he might forget her for days at a time, but she was always vividly present to him when he came down to New Haven, where they had lived in such felicity for two and a half years. And she had been in his mind, he admitted to himself, because Lillian Prescott had reminded him of her. Not that Sophie was red-haired or brown-skinned or voluptuous. She was a tiny flaxen-haired woman, with skin like milk, a nose that turned up, thin lips, pale blue eyes. But something was the same — he hadn't yet figured out what it was.

Not that it mattered.

He found the paper he had scribbled on and smoothed it out on the desk. *Prudence Anne.* Why had she given her baby such a prim and old-fashioned name? For, although Lily Prescott appeared strong and healthy only two months after giving birth, he was sure Prudence was her child. He wondered why her companion had been so odd about it. What was *mad* about a fancy birth certificate?

He dipped his pen into the inkwell. The serene silent world that was created when he was writing settled around him. Here was something he did well, with ease, and as he formed the letters — the floating tails of the P, the generous curves of the E — he became oblivious to everything except the relation of line to loop, angle to curve. It was like art — it was as much art as he could manage. When he was younger, he had taken painting lessons from an artist in Wethersfield. He had produced a stack of barely competent watercolors and a few disastrous oils. One of them, a painting of their barn, had been a present for his father. Matthew hung it in the parlor over a maple table Charles had also made, with legs he had turned himself. The table was fine, but as time went by Charles cringed every time he looked at the painting.

It was his older sister, Tamsin, who had the real talent. She had never taken a lesson, and yet she produced delicate, sensitive watercolor sketches of the barn cats, two pears on a table, a picket fence in the snow — "just any old thing," she said, "is what I like to paint." Charles made frames for many of them, and they hung all over the house, luminous bits of color and line that told Charles he would never be a real artist.

But as soon as he had a pen in his hand, everything was different. Pen and ink, and the letters to provide a foundation. The letters meant it was already half done, and the changes he worked on them were what constituted his art — the useful art of taking the ordinary and making it beautiful.

He gave the certificate a few more embellishments than fifteen cents would usually warrant — a flowery half-border, a bird holding in its beak the end of a banner with the words *Certificate of Birth* — and when he was done he looked at it with satisfaction. Occasionally there were small flaws in his work, some minor infelicity of space or proportion that only he could see. He was always on the trail of perfection, and he was perpetually dissatisfied. *It's not art*, he would say to himself then, angrily. *It's only letters*. But this had come out well.

Prudence Anne, born on the ninth of March. His son Charlie had been born on the twelfth, four years ago, right here on Bradley Street, in the back bedroom of the main house. When her pains began, Sophie wanted her mother, and Charles had been glad of it. His wife was so tiny, her screams and moans so horrifying. Bernard had had to take him out, walk him downtown and back, give him a dose of brandy. And then, suddenly, all was well, and he had a son, and a wife who gripped his hand tearfully and kissed it, and a gold pocket watch from his father-in-law.

He set the certificate aside. He would have framed it, if he'd had the materials with him. But it was just as well. That would probably be going too far. He left it spread out on the desk and went down the stairs and out to where Joshua was still working. Hester had gone inside with her basket of towels and tablecloths.

"Joshua! Good afternoon."

"Mr. Charles." Joshua looked up with his grave smile. He was a little balder every time Charles saw him, and he was getting stout around the middle, but he was a handsome man, with a strong chin Charles envied. Charles had an uneasy memory of the night he had wept, out of control, in Joshua's arms, and he always wondered if Joshua remembered it, too, and thought less of him for it.

"How are you keeping?"

"I'm very well, sir. Hester was down with a bad case of the ague over the winter, but I didn't catch it."

"My father caught it too, up in Wethersfield. I was bringing him broth and negus in bed for nearly a week."

"Negus. Now there's an old-fashioned remedy. I haven't heard of anybody taking that since my mother died."

"I don't know what kind of cure it is, but it did guarantee that he got plenty of sleep."

Joshua chuckled. "I know what kind of sleep that is!"

Charles headed for the main house. In the kitchen, his mother-in-law was drinking a cup of tea and reading. "I knew I'd find you here, Emily."

She put down her lorgnette and beamed at him. "Stay and have a cup, Charles dear. You've been up in your room working, have you not?"

"I got a commission when I set up my desk on the Green, for a birth certificate, and it has to be delivered tomorrow."

"Boy or girl?"

"Girl." He pulled out a chair and sat. "Prudence Anne."

"I like it — a plain old-fashioned name." She poured him a cup. "Do you enjoy that? Setting up in public and talking to complete strangers?"

"I do. Very much. Why do you ask?" The tea was over-stewed and lukewarm, but it tasted good. If Bernard had been home, there would have been cake or sandwiches, but Emily seemed to be able to exist on tea. "Because you would hate it yourself. Is that right?"

"You know I would, Charles. I'd be much too shy. I'm happy here in my kitchen, kneading bread with Hester, and listening for Bernard's carriage turning into the drive."

"You're like your daughter that way," Charles said. "What she liked best was to be home, to be quiet."

He knew Emily liked to talk about Sophie — not too much, or she would start to cry. A word or two. She had only recently stopped wearing mourning, but her dress was still somber — shades of brown striped with gray. Bernard had given her a gold mourning ring with Sophie's initials and dates engraved into it.

13

He said, "Sophie would have been curled up with a book on a day like this, with her legs hanging over the side of a chair, completely oblivious to everything."

Emily laughed. "That's a perfect picture of her, Charles."

He said, "She has been in my mind today."

"I like knowing that," Emily said. "We have a duty to the dead, to keep them alive in our thoughts. That way, no one ever really dies." She reached across and put her hand briefly over his. He could make out part of the engraving on her ring: *1830-1852*. "Give sorrow words," she said.

Charles knew the line was from *Macbeth* because Emily had quoted it to him after the first extremity of her own grief had passed. *Give sorrow words: the grief that does not speak/Whispers the o'er-fraught heart and bids it break* — spoken to MacDuff, whose family has just been slaughtered. Charles had stayed with his in-laws after Sophie and the baby died, while his own house with its burned-out back rooms was being repaired and then sold. He had spent weeks just lying in bed, weeping until he had no more tears, unable to sleep, waking up screaming from nightmares — in the grip of a devastation made up of sorrow, guilt, and the overwhelming desire to be dead himself. Every day, for their sake, he tried to get out of bed and take up his life again, and every time he broke down. Finally, with Emily's gentle presence at his side, he was able to talk about Sophie and Charlie and what had happened, and to be able to forgive himself and Fate. He'd been built up again by Hester's cooking and Joshua's silent strength and the Gaudets' refusal to allow him to blame himself for what had happened. Those weeks had bound him to Emily as he had never been bound to his own mother.

At some point in his convalescence, he had found *Macbeth* in Bernard's library and read it. He could still remember some of the lines from MacDuff's response, but he had never spoken them aloud. They were words he could scarcely bear to run through his head: *All my pretty ones? Did you say all? What, all my pretty chickens and their dam at one fell swoop?*

Charles wondered what Emily would say if she knew what had occasioned his thoughts of Sophie on this particular day: a conversation on a bench with a pretty woman. Not that Charles didn't sincerely mourn his dead wife, and not that he had forgotten his promise never to remarry, never again to have a child. But there were times that he was aware, hazily, of a wish ripening in some distant corner of his mind: a wish that, after nearly four years, he could stop being quite so true to the guilt that consumed him, and in his angry moments he sometimes thought: *If Sophie had any faults, her death by fire at the age of not quite twenty-two effectively rubbed them out.* Then he would think of little Charlie, so blameless and innocent, or of his wife's face, and the way she looked with her pale hair spread out around her on the pillow. He did that now, sitting over tea with his mother-in-law, to keep himself from looking forward too much to his appointment tomorrow afternoon with Lillian Prescott. Lily.

Finally he had to ask, "Emily, is there a crust of something I could gnaw on, do you think?" His stomach was making noises. "I'm having trouble waiting for supper."

"Charles! You know where the bread is. And the butter, too." She watched him with amusement as he cut a thick slice, got the butter from the crock and smeared it on. "You needn't ever ask, my dear. This is your home, and you can treat it as such. Always."

Always, he thought. Would his life, then, move along in the same groove forever? He had not thought of another woman for all these years, had scarcely talked to one. He had kept the old familiar grief at bay by concentrating on his profession, his aging father, the store, the large and small responsibilities of his life. But it was there just the same, his stalwart companion. And now he could not escape the thought: Is this the only companion I will ever have?

Hester's bread was delicious, as always, but he had trouble getting it down.

He saw her when he turned off Church Street onto the Green, sitting on the same bench. There was no sign of the dark-browed Elena. His heart lifted.

She was watching him coming down the path. He remembered that she was short-sighted, and raised his hand in a wave.

"Good afternoon, Mrs. Prescott," he said, and wondered why he hadn't noticed the curious greenness of her eyes. Maybe the light was different today. The color was singular but very clear, and the iris was edged in black.

"Miss Prescott."

Her smile didn't waver, nor did his. "Miss Prescott, then." He set his desk on his knees and opened it. "One certificate of birth, for Prudence Anne Prescott," he said, and drew it out. "Delivered as agreed, at twenty minutes past two."

She removed the glove from her right hand, took the certificate and studied it. For perhaps half a minute she didn't speak, and he wondered if she was disappointed. He craned his neck at it. Had he misspelled something? Should *Prescott* have only one *t*?

"It is beautiful," she said finally, looking up at him. "Exactly what I wanted. I am more than pleased, and it looks like it is worth much more than a quarter. Twenty-five cents!" She laughed — three notes, rising. "So many inferior things can be bought for a quarter. A yard of cotton. A newspaper full of tedious politics every day for a month. A slab of very greasy bacon that some ignorant butcher hacked off the haunch of a poor pig. I would much rather have this."

He was charmed by her grasp of practicalities like the prices of bacon and cloth. She seemed so exceptional in her beauty — so goddess-like — and yet here she was bemoaning the quality of the New Haven penny newspaper. "You are very kind."

"But look at the artistry! These perfect birds, made with only a few pen strokes! And your capital *A* is a work of art. You should ask at least a half-dollar for something like this, Mr. Cooper."

"Twenty-five cents will do fine."

She brought out three dimes from her small string bag. "Take these."

"I will give you five coppers."

"I don't want your five coppers."

Suddenly he felt foolish, haggling over pennies with a woman he had met on the Green. He had far too many moments when he felt like a doltish boy in a world where everyone else was quicker and cleverer and more worldly. He wished he had never entered into this transaction. "I insist," he said shortly. He found the coppers in his pocket and put them into her hand.

She narrowed her eyes. "You'll never get rich that way."

"Most writing masters are not rich. But nor are they usually poor. I am lucky to have a regular position at a very fine school. This sort of thing I do as a lark."

"Do you ever give private lessons?"

"I do."

"Can ladies learn this writing? With all the frills and flounces?"

He looked at her with renewed interest. Was she flirting with him? "You make it sound like some kind of garment."

"You know what I mean. This script that flows like a stream, that looks as if it was penned by a celestial spirit, an angel."

He laughed in spite of himself. "It's called Ornamental Penmanship, Miss Prescott, but it's not so different from what is taught in schools to young men who wish to go to work in business offices — none of them, most likely, spirits or angels."

"Cherubs and vines are not part of business writing. I have never seen even a glimpse of one on a bill of sale or a tradesman's receipt."

"You might have, a quarter of a century ago. But the world has speeded up. The pace of life has become as fast as that of a steam locomotive!" It was a subject close to his heart. "Basic penmanship has become simple and spare to the point of monotony. What's important in the world of commerce is speed and legibility above all. Beauty and elegance are no longer prized." He knew his passion could easily spill over into pedantry, so he stopped.

"And so what sort of penmanship do you teach?"

She seemed to really want to know. "In my classes at the college — my bread and butter — what passes for penmanship now is called the *running hand*, and with good reason. You never lift the pen, you just keep going — like a horse in a race."

"Well! Your ornaments may not run, Mr. Cooper, but the writing soars. It is like a flight of birds across the page."

"This kind of ornamental penmanship is old-fashioned and rare, and that's why people like it. I teach that as well, when I get the chance. This is the script they wish to see on a certificate, or on an important document. What has always fascinated me is that it doesn't even need letters. Flourishing, especially, is all about the design of a thing, about learning to form a graceful line, about shading. If you have an artistic gift, it's all in the kind of nib you use, and the way you hold your pen. And if you lack a natural aptitude, you can be taught. Anyone can learn it by simply tracing the letters in a workbook with a broad-nibbed steel pen."

"And after a mountain of paper and an ocean of ink, one's little stream of letters would flow like yours. Perhaps."

"Yes, it would, and it would not take that long." He smiled. "A hill and a small pond, perhaps."

"I would love to learn."

"I would gladly teach you," he said.

"Would you?"

He tried not to stare at her as if she was an exotic tropical bird. He knew red hair was considered disagreeable by most people — there was a girl he'd known as a child who was always called Carrot-Top and teased until she cried — but he had always liked it. Miss Prescott seemed proud of hers. She wore — against the fashion — only a small straw hat perched forward, and her hair was swept off her neck and wound into a bun at the back, shining red-gold in the afternoon sun and revealing the warm pale brown skin of her face. Such colors, he thought. She would glow even in the dark. He wanted to press his lips to her smooth, bare forehead.

He took a deep breath. "I am here for only another day. I'm on my way back up to Wethersfield."

"That is a pity."

"I'm sure you could find a teacher here in New Haven. There are probably a dozen of them."

"But it's you I would like to have for my teacher."

He had no idea what to say. For a moment he couldn't speak at all. Then he said the first thing that came to mind. "Is your family from New Haven?"

"My father's people are originally from Boston, but have been many years in New Haven, yes. Too many, perhaps. Such a tiny city! And everyone knows everyone."

"I have always loved it," Charles said. "I like the way it sits cupped between the two rocks, East and West, like a jewel held in someone's hand. And with the harbor to the south." He smiled. "And of course Wethersfield to the north. I'm probably talking like the provincial that I am."

"Forgive me. Of course New Haven has its beauties! I've been in Rome too long. My —" She stopped, then went on. "My companion, Signorina Zanetti, is Italian. She and I made the voyage here from Southampton only last November."

"But your people are here?"

"My family life is rather complicated. My father is in Italy but keeps a house here. He has always traveled extensively — he used to live in Florence and then in Rome, where he met my mother."

"She is Italian?"

"Was. She was half-English and half-Italian. She died of Roman fever when I was four years old. I traveled with my father when I was small, in those first years after her death. He seemed not to want to let me out of his sight."

"You must be very close to him."

"I was. Until six months ago when he disowned me."

"Disowned you!"

The speedy intimacy of their conversation seemed highly peculiar. Had he ever talked to a woman with so much freedom on only a second meeting? To anyone? But it also seemed entirely natural. It was as if they were old friends.

"Well — maybe not. Not really." Her face had grown solemn, but now her eyes twinkled at him again. "Sometimes I embellish a story the way you embellish the capital *A*, Mr. Cooper. I should not do that. Elena constantly tells me I should not do that, as does my father." She turned away, and the brim of her hat shadowed her face. "He is angry with me, and I'm not sure when I'll see him again. I am back in New Haven, and he is in Rome, and I think this time he intends to stay there."

"I am sorry," Charles said.

"My father believes himself to be a Bohemian, tolerant of all things, a supporter of women's rights and abolition and even of dress reform — he favors trousers for women and disapproves of the corset. He wears Turkish slippers and refuses to own a top hat. He usually keeps a mistress in a villa on Lake Como that came down to him through my mother's family. But he wants nothing to do with me."

"Because —?"

"Prudence Anne Prescott."

"You are — a widow?"

"If I had a husband, I would be a widow. But I have never had a husband."

What to say to such a confession? The child was born out of wedlock. Was he shocked? Yes, he was shocked, though he also felt that if Lily Prescott had had a child out of wedlock, there had to have been a good reason, or even that it had to be all right, somehow, to bear a child under such circumstances. And yet he hardly knew her. What reason did he have to think this, aside from his fascination with her skin and her hair and her green eyes?

She noted his silence. "This, Mr. Cooper, is where a certain kind of person would say *I see*. Or, if he was English, *Quite*."

Charles said, "Well, I don't see. Quite."

She laughed. "I'm sure I've shocked you," she said, as if reading his mind. "And probably horrified you, too."

"My family has its own complications. Perhaps everyone's does."

"I've told you one shocking thing. Now you tell me one."

He thought for a moment. "My parents don't live together. They are separated. My father lives in Wethersfield, where he operates the general store, and my mother lives in Pennsylvania among her relations."

"That's more irregular than shocking, Mr. Cooper. Tell me something shocking — about yourself, not your parents."

He felt, suddenly, the heat of the sun beating down on their bench, and the sweat forming in his armpits and at the back of his neck. He looked at the lift of her eyebrows, her small ears, her golden hair smooth beneath the little hat. He gasped, as if all the air had gone from the New Haven Green. "No," he said. "I don't think I will."

But she seemed not to hear him. She had jerked her head upwards. "Mr. Cooper!"

It was a flock of pigeons, wheeling in synchrony above the new green of the trees. "We were talking of birds, and look! Like a dance! How miraculous that every single one of them knows how to do it!"

Charles glanced up at the pigeons, and then at her face. She was gazing wide-eyed at the sky, her mouth slightly open. Her ungloved hand, fine and delicate, with tapered fingers, lay on the gray cloth of his coat.

Chapter Two

9 May, Friday. I am driven to write here partly because I have decided to practice my penmanship, but also because I have no one to talk to. I so very much wish I had a real friend. I wish Aunt Julia were not cowed by my uncle. I wish James would answer my letter. And despite my loneliness, I regret every day that I brought Elena back here with me as my — what? Companion? Duenna? Nursery maid? I don't pay her — I just *keep* her. She has been in service since she was a child, & yet her life with me in New Haven is almost one of a lady of leisure. She helps me with Prudence. She does the marketing & some of the cooking. She takes over for Dora on her half-days off. She accompanies me when I want accompanying & is learning to leave me alone when I don't. But she has a great deal of time to herself, & is often not at home. This suits me very well, though I cannot imagine where she goes, wearing her black shawl & her determined expression. But sometimes she comes back looking positively light-hearted! I suppose the exercise does her good.

She is so large, so black-browed, so silent in her disapproval, so disapproving in her silences! So watchful of me! So strange the way she stares when I feed my baby. So scornful of my decision — no, my need! — to feed Prudence Anne myself.

She likes to enumerate for me, whether I am listening or not, the mistakes I am making with Prudence. It began when I not only refused to have her christened but gave her the heathen name of Prudence. In the pantheon of minor gods & goddesses that Elena's religion calls saints, there is no Saint Prudence. E. favored Frances, after some Roman saint whose feast day falls on March ninth. I told her Frances was a name for someone's dried-up old prune of a maiden aunt. Then she urged me to at least tack Anne on to Prudence. I did because I like the sound of it, not because E. suggested it. When I hear her call the baby *Anna* when she doesn't know I'm listening, I think it was a mistake. *Ah-nah*, in her Italian way. It is very pretty but not her name.

Also, a baby's ears should be pierced before she is eight weeks old, says E. Before she can feel pain. This is so absurd I don't even respond! Sometimes talking to E. is like trying to talk to my stays. She showed me pair of small, hopeful gold hoops — for someday, she said. *Qualche giorno.* For when she is seventeen, I replied — *maybe.* Elena flounced off in a sulk. She keeps the earrings wrapped in silk in a blue enameled box in a drawer of the big wardrobe in her bedroom. I know this because I have snooped through her things, not because she interests me but because I need to be aware of what she is about. Now I know that she has a lock of someone's coarse black hair pressed in her Bible, she keeps a gold St. Anthony medal under her handkerchiefs, she uses something called Recamier Facial Bleach on her dainty moustache, & she wears red chemises & drawers under her endless black — I think to ward off the *mal occhio*. And she is embroidering for Prudence a long & elaborate white dress, all tucks & smocks & beautifully worked designs — no doubt a christening dress, for some future day when she will spirit her away to the Papist church so a priest can pour water on her & mutter in Latin.

E's favorite piece of child-rearing wisdom is that Prudence should have a wet nurse. Of course, she has ferreted out the perfect milker on her long walks into the nether parts of town. Or on the Sunday mornings when she flounces off to church to gather with the other black-gowned, black-bonneted biddies. What do the Irish ladies at St. Mary's make of her dark skin & her accent? E. is still a moderately young woman, just past thirty, though you would never suspect it from a distance, or to hear her talk — she is all lumpy black crape & bombazine, all gloomy observations about the weather —

too hot, too cold, too wet. Only up close can you see how fine her skin is, & how silky black the waves of her hair — done though it is in that ridiculous way that she perceives to be fashionable: bundled up on either side of her head into two awkward parcels, each dangling a ringlet.

From certain angles, she looks like Tomasso.

So far, Prudence resembles neither of them. She is the picture of my father, with his round face & pink cheeks & dark blue eyes, & with browner hair than mine — what wisps of it she has. There are times I can almost forget that my daughter is half a Zanetti! E. doesn't forget it, needless to say. She dotes on the child, & is never happier than when she can hold her, & sing off-key Italian lullabies, & touch her little chin to make her smile. Only once has she dared refer to herself as Prudence's aunt. As if this gave her any authority! Aside from the fact that I forbade her to do this when I agreed to let her accompany me.

If she croons to her in Italian, calling the baby *mia nipote, la figlia di mio fratello*, & probably slipping in an *Ah-nah* now & then — well, I am not aware of it. And she had best not let me hear her.

I have not told Elena, but I have certainly not forgotten, that it was her own mother who came to my bedroom, in her blackest gown & whitest apron, her face a wrinkled map of misery, to mumble about *il dottor Campanaro. Il bambino.* Sad *arrividerci* gestures with her hands, like sweeping. She could take me to him tomorrow, if I wished, to that narrow bit of a street near the basilica. Or there was the *strega*, Luciana — *Tutti sanno lei, signorina!* — the ancient woman who lived down by the river. Failing that, the convent of Sant'Onofrio, where they pack you in rock salt for nine months & turn the babies into nuns & priests. I threw a shoe at her & told her to leave me alone. *Basta! Silenzio!* I did not want her *aiuto*. I told her never to speak to me again.

But it was not poor Angelina's fault. She was sent by my father, I have no doubt, to have their grandchild disposed of. It was what one did, in my father's circle. In Angelina's too, for all I know. But I did not do it. And so I have my Prudence Anne.

24

Elena is always recommending a tonic to me, something Mrs. Duffy from her church cooks up, a friend of Mrs. McAlmond, the midwife — another of her Irishwomen from Little Dublin, by the river. But E. says Mrs. Duffy makes the tonic of Chinese herbs & medicinal plants. E. swears by the stuff, though I have never seen her actually take it, just noted the evil-looking brown bottle on the stand next to her bed.

Today was Dora's half-day — Friday this week instead of Thursday, so she could go with her sister to her mother, who lives in Southbury, where she used to work at the woolen mill but now is ailing and is staying with her grandmother, or her godmother — I never have Dora's complicated family arrangements straight in my head. I did not like leaving Prudence with only Elena. But she was having her nap, peacefully asleep in her cot, & so I did, & walked out to pay my quarter to Mr. Cooper, who had written out a lovely certificate of birth for her. But Prudence slept the entire time. She slept, in fact, until nearly four o'clock! (I can't help wondering if E. gave her some concoction.)

I suppose Papa meant for me to live here in shame & seclusion, with only Elena for company. He has not even arranged for me to have at my disposal the rather grand brougham he acquired a few years ago. It is kept at Mr. Moore's livery stable. I could send a note to Mr. Coakley, but it would be mortifying if Papa has written him I am not to have it. Would he do that? It is one more thing I do not know, & so when I need a carriage I hire one.

I can imagine Papa's dismay if he knew that I do not stay at home, & mope, & repent. I have not yet taken Prudence out for an airing, except into our garden — I so wish I had a pretty little carriage for her! But I make it my habit to stroll across the Green to Hillhouse Avenue, or down to the old canal, not every day but often enough, & not always with E., though usually. I love to use my legs to go somewhere besides bedroom, table, & chair. And to see the world — a world that is so far inferior to the world I left behind, but still a very nice world sometimes.

If I did not walk, I would be like a bird trapped in this house, beating my wings against the walls, banging into furniture.

And what if I did meet an old acquaintance? Papa & I have always been such wanderers, but there was a time, not so long ago, when I had friends here — Lizzie Dale, & Margaret Brock, & the entire Carlisle family. What would Lizzie say if she saw me wheeling my baby down Temple Street? How long would it be before the Dales & the Carlisles get together over the tea table for a shocked & delicious gossip? Ten minutes? But maybe not. Maybe they would remember that they liked me, & invite me to visit & to bring Prudence. Maybe they would want to hear my story, & would sympathize. What bliss it would be to talk to someone, honestly & openly. To tell someone of my foolishness & have them say, maybe, that I was not so foolish, that I only did what anyone might do, that I have been not stupid but unfortunate.

What a dream. I have been here six months, & no one has called on me or even left a card, though it is not hard to see that our house is open & occupied. But New Haven, for all its supposed importance, is like a small town, & by now I'm sure that there are few of my acquaintance who aren't aware that Lily Prescott is back & she has a baby with her. The servants gossip unmercifully. I am fond of Dora, she has been with us, on & off, for nearly six years. Before Dora, we had a series of girls from the country — one of them could not properly clean a carpet because she had never seen a carpet before! Dora was a gem, & became quite a member of the family, & I am very fond of her, but Prudence is news she could not keep to herself, & I wouldn't blame her. She sees her sister Sue, who works at Mrs. Wiggins's house on Crown Street, almost daily. She is always in our kitchen, or the two of them are sitting out on the steps in the alleyway. Sue is a chatty little creature, not nearly as bright as Dora but much more sociable. Not too many years ago Sue worked at the mill with their mother, but as soon as she was old enough to go into service Mrs. Wiggins snapped her up, though I know she really wanted Dora. So far, Dora has been content to work for us when we are here, & when we are not, to go back to the mill. But she is an honest & hard-working girl, & I fear every day that someone will lure her away. Her wages are taken care of by Papa's banker, Mr. Coakley. I hope he is paying her well.

I should go to see Mr. Coakley. It is one of many things I should do. I should send to Papa's gardener & have him clean up our back yard — trim things & pull weeds & rake up all the old leaves & — oh, I don't know. I've forgotten his name — Jeremiah something or other. I could ask Dora but I don't. Nor do I go over the books as carefully as I should. I did at first, scrutinizing every delivery of wood & dealing myself with the boy from Zunder's Market. The cares of keeping a house are many, & I'm not used to them. I gave up out of boredom & a general feeling of ineptitude. I would rather do things I'm good at.

And what would they be, Lily?

When I got home this afternoon, while the baby slept, I went upstairs to the studio & rummaged around for a frame. How the smell of paint & turpentine brought Papa back to me! At the far end of the room is his high carved bedstead. Dora keeps the linen fresh for his return, which I haven't told her may never occur. I sometimes have an urge to climb into it for comfort. Beside it is a matching carved table, & on top of that a brass-trimmed wooden box in which my father keeps a few trinkets that belonged to my mother. One of my occupations is to take them out & look at them. A heavy silver bracelet, engraved with a garland of looped roses. Some thin gold bangles. A cameo ring that looks very old — slightly chipped. The small soft-leather case in which she carried her calling cards — empty now. An enameled miniature, hung on a ribbon, that I think is a picture of her mother, my grandmother, a long-necked woman with coiled-up hair & a nose that's something, I fancy, like mine. I don't know if these are keepsakes he has forgotten about, or things he has stored here because they are dear to him, or whether he meant them for me. All the months I have been back here, I have wanted to take these objects for my own, or even one of them — the bracelet, or my grandmother. But I do not dare. Why? Papa will never return. Who is watching me? I suppose it's a superstition. I'm as bad as Elena.

Mama's jewels are in Rome, supposedly for me to have when I marry. And everything I own of hers is there, too. Here I have only the pearl necklace I wore when I left, & a matching ring that is so tiny it almost doesn't fit me. And that's all, except a dim & beautiful memory of her, wearing one of the slimmer dresses of fifteen years ago, in a garden with a basket for cutting flowers, bending down to hand me a blossom. But perhaps this is something I saw in a book, or a painting in some artist's studio. I wish so much that I had an image of her — anything! a pencil sketch! She died before there were photographs, & Papa never painted her — or, if he did, I am not aware of it.

But he was never renowned for portraits, only landscapes & large, impressive buildings. Some of his sketches are here in the studio, mostly in pencil, some in charcoal. A bridge over a stream, cypresses, a view of hills. A crumbling, particularly picturesque stone wall that is, I think, a study for the large oil that hangs over the sideboard in the dining room. Orlando Prescott's subject matter is very conventional, which is no doubt why his pictures sell for high prices.

It didn't occur to me until I had returned to N.H. — during the months while I waited for Prudence Anne to be born, mostly spent sprawled with my big belly on the window seat in the parlor, stitching tiny garments & watching the horses pass & the snow fall & the pedestrians shiver & the boys from Yale careless in their long scarves, and thinking thinking thinking — that my father took me to Rome last spring, when I had just turned eighteen, for the purpose of getting me away from James Davidson, my professorial friend, whom my father always described as *flimsy*. The point was to find me a wealthy husband. Preferably an American, but Papa would not have been averse to marrying me off to some count or other. Someone as un-flimsy as possible, meaning a man of substance who had not a moth collection & a head full of Greek & Latin but a large bank account & a thriving business in something or other that people pay for. He always had in mind his friend Signor Felice, the art dealer, who is both rich & (I must admit) handsome, though of course rather old — close to forty, I'm sure. Or the dim young

American who bought three large & expensive oils as a wedding gift for his sister back in Poughkeepsie. Or the stout, short, jovial, & almost entirely bald man — Austrian? — who once dined with us at Villa Fraguglia. It would have been interesting, in a way, to wake up every morning to the perfect pink shiny roundness of his head, like an enormous billiard ball.

What a disappointment I was to Papa, dallying with his groom instead. Worse than dallying. And worse than a groom: *my stableman*, Papa spit out.

Ruining, to put it mildly, my chances.

I never did things like that in New Haven. Something happened to me in Rome. The elastic that held me in check, that kept me a prim girl with downcast eyes who read too many books & scarcely knew where babies came from — it began to fray, to stretch, in the hot Roman sun, & in the radiance from Tomasso's golden-brown eyes, until at last it snapped, & released me into what may have been my real nature. Wanton, harlot, strumpet, *putana*. All those bad names.

And here I am in N.H. again. I still read a lot! And I surely do know now where babies come from — & how they get in there, too. But who am I now, Papa?

Among other things, I am the mother of your granddaughter.

Among other things, I am someone who sorely misses the *stradas* & statues of Rome but tries not to think about them.

A flock of birds that I saw on the Green, rising and swooping over the churches, brought me almost to tears. Something about birds, their freedom, my longing for it. A song I learned from my old governess floats through my head, one of those tunes that will not leave no matter what you do. "Flee as a bird to the mountains, thou who art weary of sin...." An old hymn she picked up from a previous governess position in a family that went in for such things. Her voice was true but quavery, & she had a dreadful accent. The song was like a dirge, but very stirring, & I loved singing it with her. She would gaze into space & clasp her hands at her chest, & I would do the same. Papa heard it once as he passed the schoolroom & came in & made us stop. "We do not teach this child this sort of nonsense." Mademoiselle Lefèvre disliked him because he was scornful of Papists & because he became annoyed when he could not understand her English. But she loved me, & called me her *petite princesse*. I always tried to like her better, but she was not pretty, & she was always wanting to smooth my hair or stroke my arm. I was not unhappy when she left and I began going to Miss Derrin's with Margaret and Sally. But the song has stayed with me, along with an occasionally useful grasp of French & a taste for café au lait.

I found a gold-leafed frame with only one tiny corner of its glass chipped away. The certificate fits almost perfectly. I had to trim the stiff parchment, but not very much: I made no incursions into the flying birds or the fancy letters. It sits on the shelf above the baby's cot, where I will see it every morning when I hear her tiny cooing sounds & get up to feed her. The date is beautifully inscribed: *9 March 1856*, the *M* especially exquisite, flags flying from graceful pillars.

My own script looks clumsy to me now, the writing of a school-girl. I continue to write with a quill. I mean to start using a steel pen, though they always seem to scratch the paper. I read somewhere that Mr. Dickens, who could surely afford the finest of metal pens — a gold one if he wished, encrusted with jewels! — writes nonetheless with a quill. All of *David Copperfield*, with a feather plucked from the wing of a goose!

Prudence's certificate brings the day she was born back to me as vividly as a scene in one of his books. The ninth of March, a chilly, wet Sunday. A troubled sleep & then I woke, shaking with cold, to soaked sheets. I had not known about the water! While Elena was building up the fire, the pains began. The intensity of the pain, the awful pressure of the baby, & then the feeling of being ripped in two, over & over & over & over. My howls on that quiet winter morning were terrifying even to me. The agony went on for hours — but I could sense, I know not how, that it was going well, that it was not an extraordinary birth, & that I should not take the laudanum Dora kept twittering about. I know I screamed out vile things, & I know I cursed Tomasso at the top of my lungs. One more reason for E. to disapprove of me, but she sent Dora quickly for the midwife &

kept the fire going, fetching the wood herself, staying out of the way when Mrs. McAlmond took over. And when it was peaceful again, she tended me well.

But I hated the intimacy of it. I hated that she cleaned up the blood & changed the linens, that she swaddled my baby & brought her to my breast & helped encourage her to fasten on by smearing a little honey on my skin. But she did her duty, & she has been good to me, in her way, & good to Prudence.

Prudence is my punishment for what I could not help, for giving in to a feeling wholly new & unexpected, as unstoppable as anything I can think of — as childbirth! An avalanche! Impossible to fight against it. And now as I hold my darling child & smell the sweetness of her scalp & feel her fine light hair against my cheek, I see it was all a blessing. It was good. It is good.

If only Elena were not here!

There has been a murder in town, Dora told me — a young woman brutally killed. She does not know who or how or where. Somewhere to the north, out by the gun factory, she heard. I hope she is right & that it did not happen near us. I think of Tomasso, & I know E. does, too — though rather differently. She sincerely mourns her brother. He was Angelina's youngest, she the oldest. I mourn him, too, I suppose. I mourn those hot nights in Rome! But I also burn with anger.

I like writing here. If nothing else, it is something to do, but it also gives my empty days some importance. And I have forgotten to say that Mr. Charles Cooper, the penman, is not without interest. A nondescript fellow, a bit stoop-shouldered & just my own height. He has sparse brown whiskers & not much of a chin, but such kind eyes! And a smile that lights up his face. I keep the idea of Mr. Cooper lodged comfortably at the back of my mind.

Chapter Three

Charles had breakfast with Bernard and Emily the next morning before he left for the station, the three of them at one end of the table in the dining room. There was Hester's excellent coffee in the French silver pot with its jutting handle of turned black wood — this had been, Charles knew, a wedding present from Bernard's *tante* Elise in Paris. He also knew that the rose-sprigged breakfast china was from Emily's family, the Ingersolls, and that the embroidered napkins had been part of her trousseau, lovingly washed and ironed for nearly thirty years. The green velvet drapes were put up just a year ago, replacing the rose satin that had been installed when the Gaudets moved into the Bradley Street house as newlyweds. The rushed seat of the armchair Charles was sitting in had been repaired at the same shop in Cheshire that it had come from twenty years before. And Bernard's frock coat had been made for him the previous winter by his English tailor on Church Street, Mr. Tobias Howe.

Charles knew all these things because he was, as the Gaudets kept assuring him, like a son to them. He was aware that his connection to them seemed simple to his in-laws; to him, it was infinitely complicated, even troublesome. And yet he loved them both dearly and didn't know what he would ever do without them.

The problem was that every room in the house, every detail of their existence, the sounds and sights of Bradley Street all reminded him of his dead wife, who had lived there all her life until she moved half a mile away to live with him on Wall Street. Just sitting across the table from her parents could be like a knife in his side. Sophie had managed to resemble both of them. She had Bernard's tilted nose and Emily's blondeness and small pink lips, bowed in the middle in exactly the same way. *Lorelei*, Charles had called her, after the maiden in Heine's poem, which he'd memorized when, because he liked the sound of the words and because his mother nagged him, he had thought it a good plan to learn some German.

Ihr goldenes Geschmeide blitzet, Sie kämmt ihr goldenes Haar. It was nearly all he had left of the poem — the woman with her golden jewelry and golden hair. The lines had come back to him one day when he watched Sophie at her dressing table wearing just her chemise and combing out her hair. She was not beautiful, but small, quiet, neat in her ways — these qualities were what had drawn him to her. After the chaos of his parents' life and the breakup of the household, the departure of his mother and then, abruptly, his sister, he looked to marriage to help him make sense of his existence. Family, house, calm, peace, a reason to get up in the morning: Sophie had embodied all that.

Sometimes a stay at the Gaudets' brought on his peculiar nightmare — the nightmare that was not really a nightmare — it was all in the waking up. The dream was that Sophie and Charlie had survived the fire, they had hidden in a secret room, or escaped to the cellar, or run out the back door, and now here they were — missing all this time, but miraculously found. In the dream he clasped Sophie to him, the baby between them, and they laughed, laughed, they could not stop laughing, to think he had thought she was dead, and now here she was, here was Charlie, here was their old life together, restored, intact....

Then he would awaken, and the nightmare of their deaths would be with him, harsher and more vivid than ever.

On this visit, he had not had the nightmare. He had slept soundly and woke up hungry. He could have used a plate of Annie's eggs and bacon, but breakfasts were simple at the Gaudets'. For her health, Emily ate little cakes of baked wheat that she crumbled into a bowl — something Hester concocted for her — and on which she poured a weak mixture of milk and water. Bernard ate bread and butter with several cups of coffee.

Emily poured coffee for Charles, cut him a slice of bread, passed the cream and the butter.

"Joshua can drive you to the station," Bernard said, spooning jam thickly onto his bread while Emily looked on with vague disapproval. Her dish of wheat flakes resembled the dustings from the floor of Charles's carpentry shop.

"That would be nonsense. It's but a step."

"Charles." Bernard took a bite of bread and looked at him gravely as he chewed. His face was florid against his old-fashioned high collar. His moustache and hair were snow white, and had been since his thirties, but his eyebrows were jet black. He kept his eyes — blue like Sophie's — on Charles as he finished chewing, and took a sip of coffee. Then he said, "It's well over a mile to the station, and you have your bags, which I know are heavy. Joshua will drive you in the trap."

"But don't you usually take the trap to the brickworks?"

"I can drive out with Joseph Dickerman."

"Then you can bring me all Mr. Dickerman's gossip, Bernard," Emily put in, as if to show Charles that there was a bright side.

"Would you not rather drive in your own carriage?"

"Oh, don't be a martyr, Charles!" Bernard set his cup in his saucer with a rattle. "I repeat: it will not hurt me to drive with Joseph Dickerman, and Joshua will take you to the station in the trap."

Charles looked at his plate with its half-eaten slice of bread. "I'm not —" he mumbled. "I'm just —" *I am having trouble accepting your kindness because the thought of a woman I met two days ago is filling my head.* He let out a deep breath. "I don't mean to be a martyr."

He could feel the Gaudets looking at each other across the table. Then Bernard said, mildly, "I hope not, my boy."

"You know how much this family cares for you, Charles," Emily said.

"This family? Philip too?" Sometimes their unfailing pleasantness and understanding angered him instead of making him grateful. Sometimes he couldn't help injecting a note of conflict. "Should I stop and call on him on my way to the station?"

Bernard pursed his lips. "Philip remains Philip."

Sophie's brother was in his final year at Yale College, bound for the Divinity School in the fall. He lived in a rooming house on Elm Street, and he often came home to have supper with his parents — but never when Charles was there. Charles had not seen him in more than three years.

"I've tried to talk to him," Emily said hesitantly. "We hate this as much as you do."

Charles knew he was being perverse. His saintly in-laws could not be held responsible for the behavior of their son, and their gentle Quakerism had nothing to do with Philip's fanatical righteousness.

"Forgive me," he said. He threw down his napkin, stood up, and went around the table to touch Emily's shoulder and kiss the top of her head. Her lace cap was stiff and starched against his lips. He knew his gesture would make her smile, and it did. He said, "I'm sorry if I'm being difficult this morning. It's always hard to spend time with my mother's people. I've been away from home for two weeks. I think I'm a little homesick." He took a final sip of coffee and pulled out his watch. "I'll gladly accept your offer of Joshua and the trap, Bernard. And if I'm going to catch the train that leaves at 9:30, I'd best be off."

"You will not stop another night, Charles?" Emily asked. "And go to meeting with us?" The Gaudets had become Quakers after Sophie's death.

"I promised my father I would see him Sunday."

"Your earthly father," she said.

Ill temper threatened again. "Yes, my own dear father in Wethersfield, who is far from well and who needs me at home."

"Don't nag the boy, Emily." Bernard held out his hand. Charles grasped it, and then Bernard caught him in a brief embrace. "Give my best regards to your father. I hope this summer will see his health much improved. And come and visit us again when you can. Your room is always ready."

"And write!" Emily begged. "Don't neglect to write to us! How I love seeing your beautiful envelopes in the post."

He promised, kissed her again, put on his hat, and was out the door, calling for Joshua and the trap.

❧

As the train chugged northward along the river, Charles indulged in a silent monologue, half-directed at his mother-in-law, half at the trees speeding by out his window. *What kind of god is it, may I ask, who demands to be worshiped? Is that not the deadly sin of pride? Is that not arrogance? And what kind of god is it who would* call home *a vibrant young woman in the prime of life? What did this god want Sophie* for, *exactly? To rub his back when he had been too long at his desk? To lie beside him in the night and tenderly undo his buttons? To guide his hand between her legs and catch her breath with pleasure?*

And a baby barely three months old who lived only for milk and his parents' smiles and a soft sleep in his little cot?

God wanted them, Charles. Emily was a sensible, intelligent woman, Charles had a deep respect for her, and yet she had said such things in the weeks after Sophie died. *He wanted them, it was their time, He called them home to himself.*

And in such a way. If he wanted them, could he not have given them influenza? Did he have to burn them to death? Did Sophie have to die screaming?

He had not been there to hear her screams. By the time he arrived she was charred and silenced. But her voice echoed in his dreams and sometimes, still, disturbed his waking hours.

Thinking of this in the railway carriage, he realized suddenly what it was that he had smelled when the black-bearded man on the Green took his hand out of his pocket: the rank odor was the smell of burned flesh.

Chapter Four

12 May, Monday. E. worries me extremely. It is more of a feeling than any fact I can point to. Her position here is without definition, & I don't know how far to let her go, when to rein her in, when to tell her to be quiet & leave me, when to ask her for help.

She is a Roman *domestica*, a *governante* who came to America with the daughter of her employer who has given birth to the child of her brother who was stabbed to death in a brawl in a tavern before the baby had even begun to kick. What does this make her now that she is here? Who is Elena when she has been transported out of Rome, Italy, to New Haven, Connecticut?

She has, in fact, been very sweet to me these last days, making an effort, it seems, to be a real companion instead of just a dark, disapproving presence. A *sister*, she said once, before I made it clear that this is not an appropriate word — worse than *aunt*. Whatever else she may be, she has not come here as my relation! What a thought.

She brought home two books from the lending library. She thinks it would be good for us to take turns reading aloud to each another in the evenings, & I quite agree. I am tired to death of needlework! Elena has made me an étui, I have made her a bookmark. Now we are each embroidering a pillow cover — what to do with them when they are done? And the spinet needs tuning, so though I would rejoice to hear a little Mozart, a Bach minuet or two, I do not play. Elena wants to improve her pronunciation of English, which is already quite good, thanks to her years with various Mrs. Things of Mayfair & Rome. And I want to be entertained.

I suggested to Elena that we ask Dora to join us if she has finished her evening chores. She is a decent girl, & always cheerful — or appears to be. What do we know of our servants? I hate to think of her alone down in her dingy room off the kitchen. Doing what? I don't think she is entirely literate, so she does not read. Maybe she sews? Or maybe she is just so tired after her long day that she drops into sleep instantly. It's that strain of American democracy, I suppose, running through me despite all my time away, that wants her upstairs with us. And I want to please Dora, to keep her on my side.

But Elena, who perforce lacks the democratic spirit, was violently against the idea. Her own position here is so undefined, I can see that it's natural not to wish it threatened. And to be entirely honest perhaps I felt some relief, & that prompted me to give in to her. Dora herself might have been horrified.

Despite her accent, Elena reads quite well — with expression, but not in an exaggerated way. In another world, she might be an actress. (What a thought!) We started with stories in magazines, but soon realized we would rather read books. We began with the first volume of *Bleak House*, but Elena refused to continue after a few chapters, she said it was too tedious. She likes only books that have love affairs in them, & they had better begin within the first twenty pages or she will pronounce the book *tedious*, a word she is enamored of. I suspect she would apply some nicer adjective to dime novels, penny dreadfuls, the yellowbacks they sell at the railroad station. But she has probably never seen one, & would never admit it if she did. Above all, Elena wishes to be a proper lady.

We have begun another, called *Westward Ho!*, which contains a good deal of both description & history (Elena approves of both) & takes place in the time of Queen Elizabeth. Her reading is lively, when she is not distracted by the great furry moths that flutter in through the window & fling themselves against the lamps. Elena normally has nerves of steel. On the boat coming over, she minded nothing — not the vomit, not the moldy bread & the occasional maggot, not the vulgarity of some of our fellow passengers, not even the pitching overboard of one of them before our eyes. What a bulwark she was! But she is afraid of moths.

She is always especially attentive to my little Prue, & worries constantly that she is not getting sufficient milk. I am sure she is. She is fat & happy, & if she frets it isn't because of my milk but because — babies fret! The truth is that Elena disapproves of mothers nursing their own babies. (She has so much disapproval at her disposal! It must have an outlet!) Upper-class women in Italy, she says, do not do so, they send the child out to a wet nurse. Also in France — though it's a mystery how she knows this, she had never been out of Rome until we got into the coach for Southampton. In the grand *casas* where she worked as a housekeeper, she says, no lady would ever have deformed her breasts in that way. Signora Somebody said this — & then there is a flow of rapid Italian. And the Principessa Somebody Else — more Italian, more rapid, more vehement.

I tell her I am not an upper-class woman — a term she seems to apply to anyone who is not a servant. I ask her what God gave me milk for if not to use it? Where does she think the word *mamma* comes from? I tell her I love nursing my child, but I also assure her that it will not go on for much longer — six months, everyone says, is the proper time to stop. Still she frowns whenever I open my bodice.

I dwell on Elena at length because I see almost no one else. I have little to write about. And yet I find that I like writing here, wandering through my thoughts to see where they will take me.

Papa: I think about sending him a letter. *Dearest Papa, It is painful to think about what you said to me when we parted, & yet I would forgive you in an instant if you wrote & asked me to. Or if you did, after all, return to New Haven & walk in the front door! I have not given up hope that this will happen.*

That is what I would write, but is it true? Any of it? Do I find it painful or does it make me furious to remember that my father called me something vile? That my widowed & aging father (who — one would think — would cling to the small scrap of family he has left) repudiated not only me but my baby. Would I forgive him? Not without a struggle.

And do I retain a hope that he will return to America & let us be a family again? I suppose I do. What a silly woman I am. What an angry one as well. When I wake up before dawn to feed Prudence, that is the hour of *thinking too much*. In the quiet dark of my bedroom, Elena snoring down the hall, Dora far below in her cell off the kitchen, the house tucked silently around us, there is nothing to distract me but my child's little chirping noises as she nurses, & I think of so many things. I always, without wanting to, go back to Italy. It seems so recently that I was there! That big cool house, the lovely flaking frescoes in the dining room, my father's garden & its stone pots overflowing with tiny roses & the fateful spot where Tomasso first kissed me. It was in the shadow cast by the statue of Persephone, with the moonlight shining down all around us. How blithely I took my chances against the Roman fever & the night air, the *mal' aria*. I think of the row of poplars at the end of our drive, the scent of the tall rosemary plants, the green hills dotted with red roofs & the yellow broom that grows there, with its acrid smell coming in on the breeze. I let it all pass through my head like photographic prints in an album, the images that made up my world for so many years. The swift red lizards, the sweet cats in the stable, & my father's lame hound, Mortimer. I can't think of Mortimer without tears.

And the huge, deformed pine tree that grew outside the window of my bedroom. On the one & only night that I let Tomasso into my bed, wanting to exchange haste & the damp grass for cool white sheets & a sense that the night could go on forever, I watched the tree's skeletal branches swaying in the wind as he lay on me. The branches were black against the white midnight sky, like a monstrous many-limbed animal. An omen. It was that night, I am sure, that Prudence Anne was conceived.

I am not lucky in the men in my life. Sometimes it's only my baby in my arms that keeps me from leaping up & screaming with rage & throwing the chamber pot through the window! Tomasso, who deceived me & then got himself killed. My father, who informed me that I'm a disgrace to the memory of my mother & then sent me away, out of his sight. My old admirer, James, who has not answered my first note or my second. And oh yes — let us not forget Uncle Henry, proprietor of the Blue Hills Auger & Bit Company, who has informed poor Aunt Julia that she must have nothing to do with me.

Screaming is the least of it. I would like to scratch their eyes out!

Tomasso, of course, is dead, & beyond my wrath.

Ah, poor Tomasso. My young, lean, lithe Tommy. His soft eyes, his rosy mouth — & so many lies! I was a fool. I could not keep away from him. The man who took care of my father's horses! Who drove the carriage! What else could one expect of him? But of my father, my uncle, Mr. Davidson who promised to be ever my friend —!

Even Mr. Charles Cooper has gone back to his dreary little town of Wethersfield. I would have liked mastering the trick of transforming mere penmanship into glorious art. But he has abandoned me too.

I am left with Elena, Dora, my darling Prudence. Aunt Julia, who at least sends me a regretful note from time to time. Females all. And there is a lesson in that, I am sure!

Chapter Five

It wasn't until the train approached the station and he was getting his things together that Charles realized he had left his portable writing desk behind. "Damn," he said. The train was crowded, and an elderly man glanced over at him with a frown of disapproval. "And hell," Charles added under his breath.

It was a minor inconvenience, and it should not distress him quite so much. He had a good store of paper and ink at his father's house, as well as his best pens, and he most likely wouldn't need the desk until, in fact, he was in New Haven again. Until then, the desk could gather dust quietly in his room on Bradley Street without inconveniencing anyone.

Still, irrational or not, he wanted it. He knew he had a tendency to fuss over his writing implements, and the neat little desk, with its leather handle and its ingenious compartments, was his pride and joy. Perhaps — and an image of Miss Prescott shimmered into his head — he would have to make a quick trip to New Haven to retrieve it.

From the depot, despite the heaviness of his bags, he walked to High Street. He suspected his father would be there rather than at the store around the corner, and he was right. He found Matthew Cooper on the back porch in a folding wood-and-canvas chair, slumped with his chin on the newspaper, either dead or asleep. Louie, the old gray cat, was on his lap.

"Father!"

Asleep. He woke with a start, and Louie leapt down. "Is that you, Charles? Back so soon?"

Charles sat down beside him, dropping his bags. "I told you I'd be back today. Saturday."

"I meant so soon in the day. Why, it can't be —" Matthew pulled out his watch and peered at it. "Mercy on us. It's well past noon. I thought it was round about eleven. I didn't hear the whistle."

"It's a warm day, Father. The heat makes everyone sleepy."

"I was not asleep," his father said. "Just dozing." A dubious distinction but one he made often. The old man yawned and ran his fingers through his hair, which was thinning but scarcely gray. "So, my son. A hearty welcome home to you! Tell me about your voyage into the depths of Pennsylvania. How is your mother keeping? And your aunt Wilhelmina and uncle Stanislaus?"

"Much the same."

"Is that all you have to say?"

"They are well. In the pink of health. Unchanged. In the town of Manheim, time has stopped dead. Mother seemed glad to get the money."

"And she told you to thank me for it. Yes?"

"No." The two men glanced at each other and chuckled. Charles said. "I had an argument with my cousin Wilhelm Gruenewalder, and Mother took his side, and I left under a cloud."

"The Legenhausens at their finest. They stick together like a sack of caramels on a hot day." Matthew reached out a hand in his son's direction, and Charles clasped it briefly in mid-air. It was as demonstrative as they ever got. "I'm sorry I need to keep sending you on this errand, son. It's just — you know I'm afraid to send money through the post."

"It's all right, Father." It wasn't, really. He dreaded the trips to Manheim, and the week he had to spend with his aunts and uncles and cousins and second cousins — and with his mother, whose caustic dissatisfaction could bring back the turmoil of his childhood with just a word or two. "I can usually find a little humor in it, and I

43

enjoy the train journeys." he added. That at least was true. "I will of course write her a note, apologizing."

"Save your ink. She will not reply."

"Still, she is my mother."

Charles had always been allied with sensible, reasonable Matthew, the calm antidote to Magda's noisy excess, but he couldn't overcome the twinge of disloyalty he always felt when he reported on her and her sour temper. Officially, he knew, it would all blow over. But the harsh words they'd exchanged would attach themselves to the long string of similar squabbles — neither forgiven nor forgotten, just not talked about.

Matthew sensed it was time to change the subject. "Tell me about the New Haven portion of the trip. How is my friend Bernard? How are his bricks?"

Bernard Gaudet and Matthew Cooper had liked each other from the start. Oddly, they shared a birthday and were both not quite sixty, though Bernard was the picture of robust health, and went daily to his office at the brick factory, while Matthew got smaller and thinner every month, and lately lacked even the energy to walk down to High Street and stand behind the counter of his store. They had moved his bed to the back parlor because he could not walk up the stairs without becoming short of breath.

"Bernard and his bricks and his Emily are all very well."

"Did you see Philip Gaudet?"

"I did not."

"That's a relief to me, Charles. I worry every time you go to New Haven. I didn't like his threats."

"Nor did I. But that was a long time ago."

"It doesn't seem that way to me." Matthew sighed. "I've been noticing lately how time becomes more compressed the older one gets. And how it does zip along. Maybe not down where your mother lives, but here in Wethersfield. When I was a boy a day would stretch out like a week. There was time for everything. Now it's Tuesday and next thing I know it's Friday night. This year is nearly half gone, but it seems only a month or two ago we were eating the Christmas goose and lighting the candles on the tree."

"*O Tannenbaum, O Tannenbaum. Du kannst mir sehr gefallen.*"

"Please." Matthew held up his hand. "You know German can bring on a bilious attack."

Charles continued doggedly, *"Wie oft hat nicht zur Weihnachtszeit ein Baum von dir mich hoch erfreut."*

Matthew snorted. "Perhaps this year we can discontinue the Tannenbaum."

"Don't tell that to Calvin. The boy is staunch for the old traditions, whosever they may be. He'd as soon give up Annie's porter cake and burnt cream." Louie jumped onto his lap, but Charles set the cat down gently and stood up. "I'll look in at the store once I've had something to eat."

"Annie will fix you a sandwich. There should be some pork left from last night's supper."

"I can fix it myself, Father."

"And there is a letter from Tamsin on the table with the other mail."

"Excellent."

"You'll find Sarah minding the store this afternoon, and Cal is probably there, too."

"I will have to see how his penmanship is progressing. He has probably reverted to his old hen-scratch without me."

Charles patted his father on the shoulder as he passed and left him on the porch with his newspaper. He made himself a sandwich — through the window, he could see Annie spreading ashes around her pea plants against slugs — and ate it in the kitchen, feeding bits of pork to Louie, at his feet, and glancing over the week's mail. Three tradesmen's bills that he and Sarah would look at later, and in Tamsin's tiny, ornate handwriting from Ohio the news that winter was over at last and the twins were thriving and Eli had been taken on again at the sawmill and she was keeping chickens and selling the eggs.

He would write to his sister soon. When she made the sudden decision to marry Eli Pugh and travel with him to a town in Ohio, near Lake Erie, she and Charles had sworn to write monthly letters, whether there was news or not. Tam had kept her part of the bargain admirably. Her letters arrived mid-month, without fail: short, factual reports about weather, health, work, signed *Your devoted Tamsin*. Charles didn't know if his sister was happy, if she missed him and their father, what her boys were like. Was Eli, who had injured his leg a few years ago in some unspecified accident, able to earn enough to keep them? Was Tam raising chickens and selling eggs because they needed the income? Because she loved doing it? Because she had too much time on her hands and wanted an occupation? Charles had no idea. He had begun, years ago, by pouring his heart out to her when he wrote — they had once been so close, though she was older by eight years — but as time went by his letters to her became equally terse. He was teaching at the business college in Hartford. He was getting married and would live in New Haven, where he would take private students and do some work for Yale, first just copying, and then engrossing diplomas and documents. Charlie was born, a beautiful sturdy boy who looked like his wife's people. His wife and son died in a fire. He returned to Wethersfield and was teaching again up in Hartford. Their father seemed to be failing.

Tamsin expressed her dismay, satisfaction, sorrow, concern, horror, but went no further. Her letters never lost their curious flatness, as if she'd written them in her sleep. Did she still paint in watercolor? Was there a library near them? A school for the twins? Had she been to Lake Erie, which Charles knew was 240 miles across? And had she heard of Mr. Platt Rogers Spencer, the great writing master from Ashtabula, who had written books and started schools across the country, whose name was synonymous with the best penmanship?

After a while he no longer bothered to ask.

He and his father occasionally talked about making a trip out west to visit the Pughs. Six hundred miles from Wethersfield, Connecticut, to Geneva Township, in Ohio, near the city of Ashtabula. As the years went by, Charles began to see that such a trip was beyond his father. He thought of making the journey with his cousin Calvin, who would be a sprightly companion for sure, and who had been deeply attached to Tamsin when he was a boy. But he couldn't leave his father for such a period of time. And why couldn't she come east? Bring David and Maddox, whom none of them had ever seen. Visit her ailing father before it was too late. It was one of the small resentments of his life, and his letters to Ohio were no longer so regular.

He strolled over to the store. It was a gable-front building, gleaming white, with a Greek Revival facade. Matthew had had it painted only a month ago. The mustard-colored COOPER GENERAL STORE sign, its shiny black letters also freshly painted, hung just above the porch. The windows, Charles noticed, were sparkling clean.

His cousin Sarah Jessup, barely eighteen, was behind the counter in her long blue-checked apron, having a cheerful conversation with Mrs. Griswold about dried apples. She was a head shorter than anyone else in the family, and with her hair in braids, he thought, she looked about twelve. But she really did manage things admirably. He was teaching her to handle the books — it would be Sarah, they all knew, who would take over the store when his father was gone, rather than himself. He had no desire to be a storekeeper, and Sarah did. She also had a head for business and, she said, absolutely no intention of ever having a husband.

Charles raised a hand to her and went into the back room. Sarah's brother Cal, age fifteen, was there, reading a thick book. Two more were stacked by his side, as usual. "I don't like to be caught short," he always said. Charles had seen his cousin close the covers of one book and reach for the next as automatically, and as greedily, as if it was the other half of his sandwich.

Charles tipped the book up to get a look at the spine. "*Westward Ho!* What kind of book comes with its own exclamation point, Calvin?"

His cousin looked up. "It's an adventure yarn, which means please don't ask me to put it down and talk to you."

"A fine welcome home!"

The boy grinned. "You're the one who first told me that such things as libraries and bookstores existed! So don't complain if now I would rather read than chat with you."

"I will deal with you later, you young puppy."

Cal made a barking noise, but absently, as he dived back into his book.

The store was busy, and he should probably help Sarah out, or stop in to see his aunt Lottie. The Jessups lived in the house behind the Coopers, built not long after theirs — the two barns were back to back, and the Jessups' cornfield met theirs on one side. In between was a well-worn path from one house to the other and, beyond the house, the path straight down to the river. Lottie — "the lone lucid Legenhausen," Matthew called her — had lived with them until she married Edward Jessup, whose family owned one of the prosperous seed farms in the western part of the town, and moved with him to the house on Marsh Lane. The families remained tied to each other in a dozen ways — the children had always treated both houses as their own, and the two households ate Sunday dinner together nearly every week. As Magda became more and more irrational and difficult, Lottie had had to mother not only her own two but Charles and Tamsin as well, and Magda had resented her for it. When Magda left, her sister had been cut off — dropped like a pruned branch, Lottie said. Still, she liked to get news of her sisters in Pennsylvania.

But Charles was restless, and he was still agitated about his portable desk. He was also concerned about his father, who napped, it seemed, as often as Louie the cat. And if Sarah needed help she should give Calvin a nudge. They all indulged Calvin, who was smart, sweet-tempered, and — as his uncle Matthew often observed — the handsomest lad in Hartford County. Cal's mother, Charles's aunt Lottie, considered the boy idle. All he wanted to do was read. They were a reading family, but Calvin carried it too far. She had urged Charles to try to get him interested in penmanship, perhaps in becoming a teacher. When Charles broached the idea, Cal's reply had been, "With all respect, Cousin Charles, I want to be the kind of writer who needs only to write rapidly and legibly. I want enough penmanship to write books with, and that's all." He had revealed to Charles, under a vow of secrecy, the fact that he was working on a story about a man, half Algonquian Indian and half Yankee patriot, who becomes a hero of the Revolution Wars, fighting alongside General Washington, and then, when he has returned home to Wethersfield in triumph, albeit minus one arm, marries the girl who stood nobly by him when, in his childhood, he was wrongly accused of stealing a horse from her father's stable and banished from the town.

The idea came to Charles that, after his two-hour train journey, he needed to take a walk, and the walk would take him down Coleman Street, where one S. Chillick lived. He hadn't forgotten the man on the Green, and his letter to his brother. It would divert his mind, which was troubled on so many fronts.

Wethersfield was dusty and quiet in the May sunshine. Charles strolled down the length of High Street, past the Town Hall, and the square brick Academy where Tamsin, then Charles, then Sarah, and now Calvin went to school. He passed the house where, on the back porch during a rambunctious game of blind man's bluff, he had first kissed a girl — Bella Harrison, now married to a soap manufacturer and living in Glastonbury. He walked down the lane to Broad Street, past the offices of his uncle's seed company and, further down, those of his rival, Mr. Comstock, and across the long Green, where he raised his hat to Mrs. Levi Rice, who was walking her dog.

He only vaguely knew Coleman Street, but he found it without difficulty, just past the very end of the Green. It bordered the onion fields on the south side of the town. There weren't more than four or five houses on the street, and it petered out at the end into a dirt trail that led to a fence and a field where cows were grazing. The street was a pocket of silence, smelling of manure and dirt. The last house, at the end, fronted a vacant lot where a hole had been dug for a new foundation, with a pile of bricks dumped beside it. The little street seemed to be part of the building boom all over New England that Bernard liked to talk about — by next summer the fence and the field would have given way to a road lined with houses. Charles strolled over to the bricks: they were stamped with the simple E-I insignia, Emily's initials — all straight lines, easy to mold, one of Bernard's innovations.

Charles remembered when his parents built their house, how excited he had been as a boy — he was nine — watching it go up. They had lived upstairs from the store for as long as he could remember, and it seemed both miraculous and reassuringly normal to move into a real house, with porches front and back, and a barn where even as a boy he had a plan to set up a woodshop, and a creek out beyond the garden that curved its way down to the river, and two apple trees left over from the orchard that used to be there, a rope swing hanging from one of them, and his own room on the second floor where he could keep his treasures. The new house was full of places where he could go to escape the strife of his parents' marriage. And how right Matthew was: time had seemed to stretch forever when he was down at the river fishing for alewives, or climbing the apple tree, or playing with his wooden soldiers — he had exactly six, but along with some pinecones and a buttonhook, they were sufficient to recreate the battle of New Orleans (the buttonhook was General Jackson) on the floor of his bedroom.

A man came out of the front door of the last house. He bowed and said, "Good day." Charles, without thinking, asked, "Could you be Samuel Chillick?"

"I could indeed. Why do you ask?"

He wasn't sure what to say, so decided to tell the simple truth. "I was curious about Coleman Street. I've lived in Wethersfield nearly all my life, but I scarcely knew where it was — I didn't know it was so close to the Green. The street was brought to my attention lately, in New Haven. I'm a penman. Charles Cooper. While I was there, I wrote a letter for a man addressed to someone named Chillick on Coleman Street. For some reason, it stayed in my mind."

"And I looked, somehow, like a Chillick to you?"

The man seemed as different from his brother as it was possible to be. His beard was just as black, he was his brother's height, and there was a similarity around the nose and mouth. But Samuel Chillick was well-dressed and barbered, even elegant, with a pair of steel spectacles perched on his nose. His teeth, unlike his brother's, were white and even. He wore a camel sack coat and neat gray gloves.

"A shot in the dark," Charles said. "Wouldn't it be odd, I thought, if this was that very man to whom I just addressed a letter?"

"Odd indeed," Chillick said.

"Forgive me. Sometimes I speak without thinking. This whole conversation is presumptuous, and you are on your way out, and I am much too inquisitive."

Chillick laughed. "Not at all. I've not received the letter yet, but I'll be stopping at the post office later. Now I have something to look forward to."

"I'll spoil the surprise by telling you it will be a letter from your brother."

Chillick stopped, frozen. "My brother Roland?"

"He closed the letter only with *your dutiful brother*."

"He is in New Haven?"

"He was there a few days ago." What was the wording? *I'll be on the road soon.* Something about the road he would not be taking. "He is on his way home, as I recall."

Chillick looked blankly in the direction of the pile of bricks and mounds of dirt. The silence stretched out, while Charles searched for something to break it. "What a coincidence it is," he said finally, "that we're all from the small town of Wethersfield." He remembered his lie to Chillick's brother — that he was only visiting there. An instinctive distrust.

Chillick looked at him, and blinked. "My brother lives elsewhere most of the time. Though he does sometimes stay with me here for short periods." He spoke hesitantly, as if each word was standing in for some other word. Then he seemed to gather himself together. "Well, I must be going." He raised his hat. "It was a pleasure to talk to you, Mr. Cooper. Are you one of the Coopers from the general store in town?"

"The store is my father's."

"A very agreeable man, your father. I always enjoy talking to him."

51

Charles made his way back to High Street, trying to reconcile the elegant Samuel with the rough Roland. He thought about the awful stink of the man, of dirt and neglect and — how well he could remember it — burning. Burned flesh.

It was the same smell that had greeted him when, on his way home that June night, he sensed that there was something wrong and began to run.

I was not there, I was not there. For weeks afterward, as he lay staring at the ceiling in the spare bedroom at the Gaudets', it was almost all he could say to himself. And others said it, too — Philip, of course, but even Aunt Lottie, kindly, weeping and clutching his hand: *So terrible that you were not there, Charles.* His mother had not come to New Haven but had written to him with eloquent sympathy, then added her own harsh coda: *If only you had been home, caring for your poor wife and child.*

Emily never said the words, which would have implied blame — and she refused to blame Charles for an accident, she declared that over and over — but of course it was what she was thinking. Bernard had his own collection of regrets. If only the New Haven fire department had a modern steam-powered engine, like Hartford's, that could spray water from fifty feet away. If only Charles and Sophie had had a servant who lived in. And his favorite: If only the house had not been made of wood. Wooden houses were artifacts of a less enlightened time, Bernard said. Every structure should be built of fire-resistant brick — like his own house a few blocks away. But even he had said, not with blame but shaking his head with regret, *If you had been there. If only you had come home earlier....*

If, if, if. If the world was a different place, if he could turn back the clock, if he had been a completely different person....

And as time went by, he turned the idea over in his mind: *If I had been home that night, what would have changed?*

He had gone over it a hundred times, and he could see how it had happened as if he'd been standing there watching through a window: Sophie in her nightdress curled up on their bed — Charlie at her breast — the candle stand, with a taper burning, beside them

— Sophie dozing off, as she so often did when she was nursing the baby — Charlie flailing his fat little arms — the candle knocked off the stand — and the two immediately on fire.

If he had been home, he would most likely have been downstairs in his study, reading or working. The fire would move quickly, hungry for the quilt, the feather bed, the baby's gown, Sophie's loose hair. The fire would not wait for him to hear cries, to smell smoke, to emerge, puzzled, from his study, to call "Sophie?" To run up the stairs. And then what? Try to smother the flames. Try to save them. Fail, most likely.

That would be the picture that he carried with him — the flames, his failure. And they would be just as dead.

"Drinking whiskey at the Eagle Tavern!" Philip never tired of the words. He had flung them at Charles, screamed them at his parents — he would accuse Charles to whoever happened to be within earshot. "He was out with his friends at a beer hall and didn't get home 'til midnight."

This was partly true, and partly not. He had told Sophie he might be late, would probably eat something at the tavern. He had drunk a mug of ale and a draft of mineral water. And he was not with friends, strictly speaking. He was meeting with a couple of young businessmen — Ives and Blanchard — who wished to spread the art of penmanship, perhaps start a business school in New Haven, with Charles as the head of it, that would emphasize the teaching of a good script, like Mr. Spencer's chain of schools. They were convivial fellows, and they liked to talk. Blanchard had a hundred stories, Ives had a thousand jokes. The meeting lasted until well past suppertime. They ordered sausages and potatoes. It was after eleven when Charles got home, and the back of his house was a smoking wreck, those on either side of it were badly charred, and Sophie and Charlie were gone.

Emily had collapsed and been taken home, but Bernard and Philip were there, surrounded by a crowd. Bernard was calm, talking to a policeman. When he saw Charles running up the street, he went to meet him, enfolded him in an embrace, told him what had happened. Philip had fallen to his knees with his arms crossed over his chest, keening wildly. Charles heard the sound before he knew what it was, and as he and Bernard approached, Philip got to his feet, staggering, and embraced Charles like a brother, sobbing on his shoulder. It was only later, when he discovered that Charles had been at a tavern, that he turned on him. The fact that Charles, broken with grief, had been taken in by his parents, put to bed and cared for at their house, enraged him, and Philip had to be kept forcibly from bursting in and attacking his brother-in-law. Weeks afterward, he had assailed Charles on the street, and had to be subdued by passers-by.

Charles admitted to himself — though to no one else — that he was afraid of Philip — of his rage, his religious furies, his adoration of his sister, his feeling that the whole family had been wronged because Charles had been in a tavern when the fire started. Finally, his parents had told Philip he would not be welcome at home until his behavior ceased. It did, and he even offered a cold, obviously coerced apology. But whenever Charles was in New Haven, the knowledge that he and his brother-in-law were in the same city made him uneasy.

Philip, like his fellow members of the Temperance Society, was indignant that a place like Guthrie's could even exist. It had been a favorite topic since long before Charles's sin. The Connecticut legislature in its wisdom passed a prohibition law, Philip would say, tight-lipped. That had been a banner day for the state and for the city. And yet... Here he would hold up his hand so he could tick off the affronts on his fingers: New Haven still had its share of licensed taverns and alehouses, a brewery was operating openly on the river in Fair Haven, tosspots congregated at night in the darker corners of the Green passing bottles back and forth, the police had been corrupted, most of them drunkards themselves. And the populace did not care.

Philip's blazing religious zeal went far beyond his parents' comfortable Quakerism, and this had been true even when Philip was still a schoolboy. When Charles was first courting Sophie, he had made an effort to befriend her young brother. Charles taught Philip the rudiments of chess and took him fishing in the bend of the Mill River at the base of East Rock. Philip was a serious boy. He talked about his own studies — he attended a private academy in New Haven — but he also liked to hear about what Charles had studied in business college, and thought he might like to learn about business law and become a teacher if he did not become a lawyer. "I like rules," he used to say. "I like for things to be *right!*"

His liking for rules and rightness took on a new meaning when he came under the influence of an evangelical minister from England, the Reverend Lawrence Dudson, who gave a series of feverish lectures at the Gaudets' church — then the Congregational one on the Green — describing in lurid detail his four years as a missionary in China. Dudson had a long, jagged scar on one cheek from an attack by a heathen in Ningbo who was not receptive to the gospel of Christianity. Philip, at thirteen, was impressed by the scar and by Dudson's refusal to be turned from his duty by trivialities. (He had also contracted dysentery and nearly died of it.)

After hearing the lectures, Philip had a private meeting with Dudson, who was intrigued by the boy's fervor, and the two began a correspondence. Dudson returned to China, heading a missionary expedition to Nanking, and when one of his letters made its eventual way to New Haven, Philip would be fired up for weeks. He joined the China Missionary Society, the Temperance Society, and the Morality Crusade, and he insisted on leading the family in evening prayers, standing before them in the drawing room, eyes squeezed shut, wearing short trousers, a white neck cloth, and a fusty overlarge black jacket he had found somewhere. He tried to keep his adolescent voice from straying into falsetto as he prayed for wisdom, for heavenly guidance, for the conversion of the heathen millions, and — without much hope — for the souls of his family. Charles had learned not to catch Sophie's eye.

Philip had always been earnest and rather prissy — though with a sardonic edge that Charles had appreciated — but as grew up he became a small-minded, fanatical, mean, and completely ridiculous young man, just as earnest, twice as prissy, and possessed of a core of violence and anger. Philip, Charles always thought, should have been a meager, prim-faced, thin-lipped, ascetic-looking beanpole, but in fact he was ruddy and handsome like Bernard, with the same thatch of hair and prominent blue eyes with pouches beneath them, and a fondness for Hester's cooking and his father's cellar. His tirades about public drunkenness and the disregard of the Prohibition laws became especially furious when he'd had a glass or two of claret. He had had quite a bit of it the night he had assaulted Charles.

Sometimes Charles almost wished Philip would come at him again. Philip outweighed him and could probably outbox him, but it would have given him some satisfaction, he thought, to do his best against his brother-in-law. If nothing else, he could say what he longed to say: *What kind of god would burn your sister in a fire with her baby at her breast? What kind of god do you worship?*

If he could accompany that with a few hard jabs before Philip made hash of him, so much the better.

Charles left his hat and frock coat back at the house and joined Sarah and Cal in the store, not helping customers — he wanted the two of them to pick up the knack of that — but checking the stock, putting things in order, folding the yard goods and untangling the bootlaces. He made a trip to the storeroom — the Cooper General Store provided onions and potatoes and a few other things for the state prison in Wethersfield, and there was a stack of cartons and baskets for the wardens to pick up. Charles checked it against the weekly list — everything was perfect, Sarah was a marvel — and then he unpacked a carton of quinine powder and Hooper's Pills. He had always taken pride in the neatness of the store, starting when he was a small boy. He would take refuge there even after it was closed, slipping in silently to straighten the shelves and sweep the floors by candlelight, the sound of his parents' squabbling reaching him only faintly through the floorboards.

Toward evening, trade slackened, and he and Sarah sat down to go over the books and look at the bills. "I'm glad you're back, Charles," she said. "It's worrisome to think of you with those people in Pennsylvania." She barely remembered her aunt Magda, who had moved away for good when Sarah was six, and she said *Pennsylvania* as if she meant the planet Mars. "You know my mother and father think you're daft to travel down there so often."

"Twice a year, Sarah. It won't kill me."

"Father likes to enumerate all the ways there are to get money from Connecticut to Pennsylvania. He says, if Uncle Matthew insists on mistrusting the post office, there are overland mail couriers, who travel by stagecoach. There are also ways to employ the railroad to deliver money reliably from state to state."

"Your father is not the son of Matthew Cooper. He would as soon use a carrier pigeon as a courier person."

Sarah laughed out loud. "You are his carrier pigeon."

Charles shrugged. "The old man has his quirks and peculiarities."

"But we do love him, all of us, exactly the way he is."

"How did he do while I was away?"

"He is tired, Charles. Cal says it's as if Uncle Matthew has used up all his pepper." She brightened. "But not his salt. He still makes us laugh. He saw something in the newspaper about the city of Hartford hiring street sweepers, and he said they won't need them as long as there are fashionable women with petticoats. They sweep the streets for free every time they take a walk." She smiled. "I told him he should be glad of such extreme fashions. It takes three times as much yard goods to make a dress."

"You have not succumbed to the fashion, Sarah."

"Can you see me in petticoats, Charles? A hoop? I would look like a tea cozy." She smoothed her calico work dress over her knees. "New Haven, I suppose, is full of ladies dressed in the latest fashions."

He thought of Lily Prescott, and how her hoop had lifted to reveal her ankles. "I don't take note of such things."

Sarah snorted. "And I am Queen Victoria's footman."

❧❧

A letter arrived from Emily:

Darling Charles,

Of course you know by now that your little wooden desk is here. Hester found it when she went up to change your linens. She brought it down. I had never really looked at it before, and I was delighted by it. What a clever design. I wish I had a use for such a thing so I could commission you to make me one!

The terrible murder here has preoccupied us all. Perhaps you have heard of it? It might even be in the Wethersfield newspaper. The young woman is an acquaintance of ours, or at least her father is. Mr. Jonathan Trout, Bernard's partner in the ice-cutting firm in Hamden, out on the Cheshire Road. We have met Letitia many times, such a lively girl—such a death. The Trouts have no other daughter, so this is especially grievous. My heart goes out to them particularly because of the circumstances as the police have deduced them. It happened on that especially cold night last week. Letitia was in their back parlor. Her parents were out, and the housemaid had gone to bed early with a toothache. No one knows why he chose that house, or why she would let him in—for there was no sign that he forced his way. Letitia must have pulled a poker from the fire to fend him off with, and he must have wrested it from her by its red-hot end and then used it as a bludgeon. There was a struggle to the death, from all accounts, and the beating killed her. She was also robbed. He left behind some of his skin on the hot poker.

I cannot stop thinking of this scene, as you can imagine. The burial is tomorrow.

We will keep the desk safe until your return, and I hope that because it is here you will come and see us sooner than you might have planned to.

Devotedly,
Emily Gaudet

❧

"Do you know a man named Chillick, Father?" Charles asked when they were at supper. "Samuel Chillick, who lives out past the Green, on Coleman Street?"

Matthew was eating almost nothing, Charles noticed, but he wiped his mouth with his napkin as if he were having a hearty meal. "I do indeed. Samuel Chillick is a professor of some sort of science at Trinity College in Hartford, with a particular interest in weather forecasting and in clouds. He keeps instruments at his house for recording rainfall and calculating humidity and such things."

Charles stared at his father. "How do you know this?"

Matthew's eyes twinkled. "Ha ha, Charles. You think I'm just a slow old fellow who stagnates behind the counter of the store and naps on the porch. Who has a brain that's about as active as that hunk of potato on your fork. But!" He raised his forefinger in the air, then tapped his temple with it. "I am a recording machine like those I read about that they are making in France. Or trying to make. They have found a way to engrave sounds on a metal plate in the form of a groove that can then be made to reproduce them. Something about vibrations. I don't pretend to understand it."

"And what does this have to do with your brain, Father?"

"Ah — absolutely nothing. I was just employing a metaphor and passing on a bit of science for your edification."

"But Mr. Chillick?"

"He travels in clouds and rainfall gauges, not in sounds and vibration. At least so far as I know."

"And you were going to tell me how you came by all this information."

"By listening! And if what I hear is intriguing, I remember it. First of all, he lives in Wethersfield, and I like to think I know everyone in Wethersfield. Secondly, the man goes to my church. But I overheard him talking about the clouds when he was in the store one day."

"And what did he come in to buy?"

"Do not test me. I told you, I remember what is interesting. Whether Professor Chillick came in to buy a chamber pot or a pound of lard does not matter to me in the least." He glared at his son. "It was a quiet afternoon, and he was a compelling speaker, even surrounded by pickle barrels and dress fabrics. He was talking with a fellow professor — and please do not ask me how I know he was a fellow professor. Take my word for it."

"I do," Charles said meekly.

"Chillick was talking about the need for a cloud atlas, a book that would classify the different kinds of clouds by their shapes. The idea, it seems, is to gather pictures of them, and descriptions, and put them into a book so that anyone can look at it and identify the clouds they see. You know how some clouds have a flat bottom, as flat as the bottom of a teakettle? There is a reason for that, and there is even a name for them. *Cumulate* or some such thing. Do you know, Charles — it occurred to me that there is a name for just about anything you can imagine. Stop to think about it. That is astonishing, is it not?"

"Do you know Samuel Chillick's brother, Father? His name is Roland."

Matthew regarded him disapprovingly. "Is this a change of subject, or are you too marveling at the fact that everything has a name, even Professor Chillick's brother?"

Charles smiled. "I think it's a change of subject."

Matthew reached across the table and patted his arm. "You are a good son, Charles. *Du kannst mir sehr gefallen.* But sometimes I sorely miss my daughter. Tamsin always shared my fascination with the eccentric and the abstruse."

"I'm sorry if I disappoint you, Father."

"Never, my boy. I am just rattling on." He cut into his meat, but then put down his fork as if the effort was too much. As far as Charles could calculate, he had eaten about four bites of food. "And, speaking of my Tamsin, she is yet another reason for me to know who Sam Chillick is."

"Tam?"

"Sam was sweet on her when they were — oh, my goodness, let me think." He started to count on his fingers but gave up. "I don't know. Long ago. Before your mother departed the scene and before Eli Pugh entered it."

"I have no memory of him."

"You were absorbed in fishing in the cove with the Tyler boys. I don't think we had even moved to this house yet. Sam Chillick used to walk her home from ice-skating. You don't remember that? I suppose you were too young."

"I remember that Tam was quite a skater."

"Sam, as I recall, was not. In general, I have a vague idea that our lively Tamsin found him a bit stiff and dreary. He was no Eli Pugh." Matthew shook his head. "Just think. If she had favored him, she'd be living here in town, raising a bunch of Chillicks and being the joy of her father's old age. Instead, you have that unenviable job, Charles." He smiled at his son. "But why are we talking about this Roland?"

"I'm wondering if he has committed a murder."

"You're still teasing me."

"It does sound absurd when I say it aloud. But I'm quite serious."

Matthew looked up from his plate. "The funny thing is that I saw Sam Chillick in church Sunday morning. I went with Lottie and Edward. You were still asleep."

"So I do disappoint you!"

"I long ago accepted the fact that my son will not accompany me to church. And because I know Philip Gaudet would therefore conclude that you are to be damned when you die, I refuse to let it disturb me."

"And why was it a funny thing? Seeing Mr. Chillick Sunday morning?"

"It was the way he looked. Usually he is dapper, polite, friendly, smiling. But on Sunday —" Matthew paused. "On Sunday morning, I would have to say that Sam Chillick was not himself. He hurried out of the service without a word to anyone. Is it too melodramatic to say he looked like a broken man?"

Chapter Six

20 May, Tuesday. We have given up on *Westward Ho!* It was even more tedious, Elena said, than *Bleak House*, & this time I concurred, though I pretended I didn't. Sometimes it pleases me to argue with her because it's more interesting than agreeing.

I went with her to the library & we brought home a book of new stories by Mr. Melville, who has written mostly adventure tales set at sea. This one, though, is called *Piazza Tales*. The title appealed to us both. But none of the tales have turned out to be about piazzas, not as we know them — the immense Piazza Navona with its obelisk & fountain, or even small & insignificant piazzas like the one near Villa Fraguglia, where one can sit on a stone bench & watch the parade of people. In fact, the story called "The Piazza" is set entirely in New England, & is about as un-Italian as one could imagine. And it made no sense to us.

We got all the way through only one story in the book, set no more than any of the others in an Italian city, but in New York, & about a young man named Bartleby who is a scrivener! That is why I was drawn to it, that & its comparative shortness. And a perplexing tale it is, unlike anything I have ever read and, despite its lack of anything resembling a love story, Elena & I are both entirely compelled by it.

I wrote a letter to "my" scrivener, Mr. Cooper, informing him that if he did come to New Haven again, & if he did want a student, I would be glad to learn what he calls ornamental penmanship. I am strangely fascinated with it. I told him I have practiced on my own, using Prudence Anne's certificate as my model, but have produced only lumpish & ill-proportioned scrawls. I threw myself on his mercy! Help me, I begged. I wish to become a scrivener — a word I had not heard until I read the story of Bartleby. But of course a mere scrivener is not it. An exalted scrivener is what I mean, I told him, a scrivener fit for writing in the book of heaven in letters of gold!

But I would be happy with a proper steel pen, some good paper, & the knack of it.

In the newspaper, a piece about our local murder, which is particularly horrible. A young woman living just north of here, out near the gun factory, was bludgeoned to death with a poker & robbed of some of her jewelry. She was the daughter of a man named Trout who owns an ice-cutting company, & the reason I remember this is that the name is uncommon but also that, when I was perhaps fifteen, I drove out there with Papa, who was commissioned to paint a picture of the main pond — a very large oil painting, as I recall, of the pond in winter, white with ice, & surrounded by tall pine trees, with the Trouts' rather ordinary little house in the background. I remember Mr. Trout was pleased with it. And now his daughter is murdered. The case is unsolved, & being investigated by a private detective.

The other news — it was not in the newspaper — is that Aunt Julia has sent Prudence a carriage! I've taken Prudence out twice in her new chariot, revealing myself to the world as a wanton woman — if the world is paying any attention. Dora would wheel her out every afternoon if I let her, so she can gossip with the other baby-wheeling servants on the Green. The carriage is quite beautiful, with a fringed parasol, & was delivered to my door last week with a note. Sent to ease her guilt, I am sure, but perhaps it means Uncle Henry is softening? I would so like to take Prudence to see them all. I cannot bear to think of her adrift in the world, without a father, without a friend or a relation.

And so I do not think of it! Think about something else! But what? What? Ah — I have a new dress. I know I must be watchful of the money I have, but I felt the need of a summer morning dress that was light & cool, & so I had Beatrice make one made up for me. She is still there, on that nameless lane off Academy Street, with her French pattern books & her silks. She is older, her hair is grayer, & her fingertips are shiny & red, something I never noticed when I was younger. She now wears spectacles — or maybe she always did. She has made me a dress of lilac lawn, with a lace collar & pagoda sleeves bordered in pale greens & grays. Her stitches are as tiny & perfect as ever. The lace under-sleeves fasten with buttons, so I can remove them when I am at home — my own innovation. If it is cool, my purple India shawl will do very well with it.

Elena, of course, disapproved. She cannot know how much money Father gave me. She cannot know that he said: "Enough to keep you but not enough to indulge your foolishness." She cannot know that I said, "I am not foolish, Papa!" & then seen the look on his face.

But she knows that it is not much. She has a way of ferreting these things out, probably adding the housekeeping costs to the price of the lending library & the muslin for Prue's diapers, subtracting a percentage she works out in her head based on the salary she received from one of her Roman *signoras*, & dividing the remainder by some number that was whispered to her by the priest at St. Mary's in the confessional. She reached deep into her store of English adjectives — her command of our language is, unlike her brother's, formidable — to call me not only extravagant but profligate, reckless, & foolhardy. I would like to call her tedious, but I am too polite.

What is never spoken between us is the word *mourning*, but I know she thinks I should wear black for Tomasso. Every garment I wear is an affront to Elena & her family. I own nothing black, I don't even wear a black ribbon on my hat, or an armband, or a black sash. I wish Tomasso hadn't been killed, but I will not wear mourning as if he had been a husband, or even a proper lover. How I wish I were a widow! With a sad but eminently respectable story. But I am not.

The lacy lilac dress is an investment. It makes me look young & pretty. It's the dress of someone without a care in the world, & I will wear it if James ever calls on me, or for a penmanship lesson if Mr.

Cooper answers my letter & returns to New Haven to give me one. He may never do this — I think I shocked the poor man to the bottoms of his stodgy brown boots! I must be less candid. This is New Haven, Connecticut, Lily!

I wish I were in Rome, Italy. I picture Papa smoking his cigar after dinner, walking up & down the pebble paths in the garden, Mortimer limping behind him, passing by the various scenes of my debauch. Or riding through the dark & squalid streets in his much too roomy carriage — driven by someone else now, of course — wishing that his daughter, whom he has so acutely insulted, would write to him to say she forgives him & would like to see him, would like to introduce him to Prudence, that small Roman souvenir — the only grandchild he will ever have, most likely.

This is a fantasy. My father is deep into his latest painting — of some palazzo of some count on some Roman hill — & no doubt deep into his latest lady friend as well. There is a new one, I am sure. Mrs. This, a wealthy English widow, or Madame That, from Paris. Or one of Elena's Signora Somebodies, who did not ruin her breasts nursing her babies.

Does he think about me? About my baby? Does he wonder if she is a girl or a boy or twins or triplets? If she is healthy or six-toed or two-headed? Does he wish every day for a letter from me?

Strange to say — though he is my father, though I am his only child, though for all those years I was growing up motherless we loved each other deeply & were, you might say, best friends — strange to say, I have no idea.

Chapter Seven

In the railway carriage en route to New Haven, Charles read again his letter from Lily Prescott:

My dear Mr. Cooper, Scrivener,

This is a word I have lately learned, having read a story called "Bartleby the Scrivener." Do you know this tale? It is quite marvelous, about the kind of scrivener, or penman, who works in a law office as a copyist. His name is Bartleby — that is all, just Bartleby — and — well, I will not tell you more. I suggest you get hold of a copy immediately! It is very comical. Elena and I were both very taken with it and, in fact, read it aloud twice, once by her and once by me. To try to work out what it meant.

But that is not what I mean this letter to be about! I have been practicing my penmanship with a good deal of diligence. I am fascinated with it, and especially with what you call the ornamental kind of penmanship. (You see that I try to write those words with the proper flourishes, and fail miserably!) I attempt to match your style of writing on Prudence Anne's certificate of birth, but have produced only the most badly proportioned scribbles — something like a nest of wiggling worms one might find under a rock in the garden.

I do wish you could teach me and help me improve. And in consequence this letter is to say that if you do find yourself in New Haven again, and if you do intend to give lessons here, and if you can find any mercy in your heart for a humble penwoman-to-be, I hope you will send me a note or come by to see me. I wish to be a scrivener — a word I had not heard until I read the story of Bartleby. But of course a mere scrivener is not it. An exalted scrivener is what I mean, a scrivener fit for writing in the book of heaven in letters of gold!

With best wishes to you and to your family in Wethersfield, I am, faithfully,

Lily Prescott

❧

Charles was reunited with his desk, and then he had tea and a sandwich with Emily. Emily was full of the funeral of Letitia Trout. It had been very sad. Mrs. Trout had completely broken down, and who could blame her? Emily had gone the next day out to Hamden to sit with her, and the two women had shed many a tear.

She and Charles finished the first pot of tea, and Emily made another, just as Bernard came in from the brickyard and sat down with them. He was full of the new kind of molding machine he was trying out. Bernard was always keen on new contrivances that might speed up production. It was designed to not only produce more bricks in a shorter time but to minimize warping and reduce manpower.

Emily set a sandwich in front of him. He took a bite and talked around it. "It's a gamble," he said, "but one that I think will pay off in the long run. You should come out with me, Charles, and take a look at it. Your mechanical side would, I think, be impressed with what it can do."

Emily asked, "If you reduce manpower, Bernard, will not a number of your men be out of work?"

Bernard waved a hand. "There's always work. If they don't do this, they will do that, and it they don't do it for me, they'll do it for someone else."

"If the aim always is to reduce manpower, won't there come a day when that will no longer be true?"

Bernard frowned. "You know nothing about it, Emily. That Utopian day will never come." He took another bite of sandwich and washed it down with tea. "An able-bodied man will always work, and there's an end of it."

"This murder," Charles said, when he could. "Do you know who is investigating it?"

"A man named Harold Milgrim," Emily said. "He is a private detective the Trouts have personally engaged. I have not met him, he was not at the funeral, but Hannah Trout told me all about him. The Milgrims are an old New Haven family — New Haven and Hartford. His mother was a Hopkins, and he is related to the Footes as well. He is renowned for solving difficult cases, and has worked in London with Scotland Yard."

"Is this a difficult case?"

"Mr. Milgrim says it is not. He is well advanced in solving it, or so he told the Trouts."

"Really."

"I hope that is true," Bernard said, shaking his head. "When I was a boy growing up, such things didn't happen. Now the newspaper is full of them. We live in a violent age."

"Do you know where I could find Mr. Milgrim?" Charles asked. "There is something odd that I would like to make him aware of."

Bernard looked at him, startled. "About the murder?"

"Possibly. I don't know." Charles felt foolish. What did he have to say, really? There was a man who had been burned, who smelled of charred flesh, who dictated a letter that could mean nothing. But it was on the right day. "It's probably not important. And you say the case is practically solved. But nonetheless I would like to talk to this detective."

"Write a note, and I will see that Trout gets it, and he can pass it on to Mr. Milgrim. I will be going back to my office after lunch, and his house is on my way."

"Will you mind if I stay with you a day or two, then?" Charles asked. "In case I can speak to this Milgrim fellow? And I have a few other errands here in town, some professional business to take care of — "

Emily held up a hand to shush him. "Charles! You can stay for a month if you like! You are not only no trouble, but you are as dear to us —" He knew what she would say, and that her eyes would glisten with tears as she said it. "As a son. And don't ever forget it."

❧

"All written forms come from nature," he said. "From the landscape we see every day. So it is easy for us to learn them. They come naturally to us because they reflect our world."

He had carried his desk with him to York Street, chancing a mid-afternoon call. The house was near the corner of George, just a block or two from the buildings of Yale — a tall, narrow townhouse, black-shuttered and black-doored, with a handsome fish-shaped bronze knocker.

Lily Prescott was at home. There was no evidence of her child, which was a relief to him. Had he been required to dandle someone else's infant on his knee, he would not have done it easily, and he was glad that the proof of Miss Prescott's Italian indiscretion — whatever it had been; he imagined some perfidious nobleman — was not present as a reminder.

The parlor where she received him was dark, the walls covered with oil paintings, the curtains closed against the light. Charles could see, even in the dimness, that the carpet wanted cleaning, a layer of dust coated the dark wood of the mantel, there were ashes in the grate. Miss Prescott suggested that they go upstairs to the drawing room, which was brighter, and where they sat at what she said was her work table. On it was a bottle of India ink, and Charles pulled out a steel pen and a lined practice sheet.

"Ovals, arches, branches," he went on, hoping desperately not to sound pompous but not sure he was succeeding. The little lectures he gave to his students sounded different in the Prescott drawing room, where the walls were covered with large oil paintings and Lily Prescott's soft white hand was mere inches away from his on the tabletop. He felt himself becoming aroused, and he pulled his chair closer to the table. "Nature herself," he said, "is full of flourishes. The waves in the ocean, the clouds trailing across the sky, the way the branches intertwine in the trees and form Vs and Ws and the letter T...." He dipped the pen and demonstrated, making first a W and then a T. "Here. Try it."

Reluctantly, she took the pen, leaned over, and wrote a capital W.

"You see?" Charles was delighted. It was quite a respectable capital W. "With the broad nib, all is changed, all is suddenly ordinary no longer. Not mere letters but something finer."

"Write my name," she said. "Lily Prescott. Show me how you would write it."

Charles flushed. Back in Wethersfield, there was a scrap of paper in his bedroom on which, one hot night, he had written her name, not once but over and over, scarcely aware of what he was doing. He had liked especially making the capital L and then the smaller one, and the capital P, which he embellished to match the extravagance of the *L*. And all the time he was writing he was imagining her hair, her tiny waist, the swaying of her skirts.

"You have an excellent name for calligraphic writing," he told her as he wrote.

"Calligraphic? Is that what it's called?"

"Sometimes. The word *calligraphy* comes from the Greek, and means beautiful writing."

"And why is my name so excellent? It seems quite plain and unromantic to me."

"Not at all! It's graceful and balanced, and the capital L is one of the loveliest of the letter forms."

"Again," she said. "I want to see how you do it."

He wrote it again, slowly, and then once more, flourishing it more elaborately, and then in a perfect copperplate, and then in the German style, and then in a more utilitarian business hand, but one that was still ornamented, still elegant — the hand he advocated for his students.

"You are astonishing, Mr. Cooper! It does turn my familiar old name into something that resembles fine art."

Her way of expressing enthusiasm was so extreme that he felt he should distrust it. "You really do like it, Miss Prescott? You are quite sincere?"

"My goodness — *yes!*" Her eyes gleamed with excitement. "I'll tell you the truth, Mr. Cooper. I like this very much for its own sake. But there may come a time when I will have to earn my bread — mine and Prudence Anne's. And I have often thought of becoming a teacher. But not a governess! Not living in someone else's home and looking after the same child year after year. No, if I became a teacher, it would be in a school. With a variety of students and a new challenge every day. To teach in a business college would suit me nicely!"

"You — *you* may have to go out to work, to support yourself?"

The idea was appalling. In spite of her impetuousness, she was so much a lady, so clearly someone who should wear lace and summon the servant when she wanted a cup of tea. He was distressed to think she might have to earn her keep — work in a millinery shop or take in sewing. And yet, too, there was her touch of what she had called Bohemianism.

"I told you what my situation is with my father."

"Well." What should he say? She told him too much. He didn't know what to do with it.

He had figured out what it was about Lily Prescott that reminded him of Sophie. It had nothing to do with how she looked — but about how he felt. That stirring inside him, that longing. It was what he used to feel when he got into bed with his wife, when she was naked with him under the sheets in their dim-lit room.

He had the sudden whimsical idea that he would ask Lily Prescott, then and there, in her drawing room, on a warm afternoon in late May, if he could become her rescuer. If she would run away with him. He would save her from penury, from her father's hostility, from the lonely life of an unmarried mother. He would replace the anxiety in her strange green eyes with — what? Love for himself? Probably not. She was so far above him, too beautiful for him to aspire to. But friendship and gratitude, perhaps, could turn into a form of love.

These thoughts were not whimsical — they were lunatic. After an uncomfortable silence, he said, "That is a very practical thought, Miss Prescott, and a wise one, too, I suspect. There are, at present, few ladies teaching in business colleges, but no doubt the demand will increase."

This did not, in fact, seem to him to be true. He had heard there was a lady teacher, and even a few lady pupils, at Mr. Spencer's business school in Washington, D.C., but the only woman on the faculty at the Standish College of Business in Hartford was sad little Mrs. Barwood, a widow and the sister of the founder, who taught not Penmanship but Commercial Composition, with an emphasis on grammatical skills and spelling. The only other female teachers he had ever heard of were schoolmistresses who taught children reading, writing, and arithmetic — and the writing they taught was of a low order. He remembered Miss Farebrother, his teacher at the Academy in Wethersfield, whose chief delight was in comparing him unfavorably with Tamsin, who had passed through her classroom half a decade earlier. He could not recall much emphasis on beautiful penmanship. He had learned those skills exclusively from male teachers.

"I could get you a practice book, if you like."

"The workbook you mentioned? With forms that can be traced?"

"Exactly. It would be a start. A workbook and a broad-edged pen."

He could bring them the next day. For the moment, he left her with one of his own pens — a good one, that had come from England — along with paper and an alphabet he wrote out for her, in both capitals and small letters.

"Do practice your letters. But I warn you that the joining of the letters is nearly as important as the forms themselves. Everything must be flowing and smooth, one letter leading to the next the way a vine produces one leaf, then another — all a harmonious whole."

"You should be a poet," she said.

He laughed. "Sometime I'll explain to you how to use an oblique penholder. Then you'll really hear me spout poetry."

"Oblique penholder!" she cried. "The very words are like a sonnet by Mrs. Browning!"

When he left, she gave him her hand, and he took it, not sure if he should bestow a kiss. He considered it for a second, but finally did not.

❧

He was exactly on time for his appointment with Harold Milgrim, whom he had arranged, through Mr. Trout, to meet at eleven the next morning. Milgrim's office was on the third floor of a fine new building on Park Street. On the door, HAROLD H. MILGRIM, ESQ. was printed in ornate gold letters, with no clue as to what role Harold Milgrim played in the world or what meaning "esquire" had when attached to his name.

Inside, a pretty young woman in a high-collared dress greeted him cheerfully. "You are Mr. Charles Cooper? Mr. Milgrim is late," she said, smiling as if this were good news. She was perched on a stool behind a wooden desk. "Please take a seat, take a magazine. I can't think that he will be very long."

After a quarter of an hour, Charles put down *Harper's Monthly*, in which, remembering Miss Prescott and her father, he was reading an article about dress reform, and took out his watch. The young woman was writing what looked like a letter. Charles wondered who she was. Milgrim's sister? His wife? Did she work for him as a kind of secretary? How very odd.

"Is he always late?" he asked the woman at the desk.

She glanced up at him with a reassuring smile. "Well, yes, he is," she said. "But he can't possibly be much longer."

But he was. It was nearly 11:30 when Charles heard whistling in the hall — something vaguely operatic, he thought, though he didn't know what — and a tall, sandy-haired man, long-chinned and clean-shaven, came through the door. Even from across the room, Charles could see that his eyes were an unusual light, brilliant blue. He broke off his whistle when he saw Charles. "Mr. Cooper? What a

73

relief that you didn't give up on me and simply leave! Or maybe you were late, too? Tell me you have not been sitting in that uncomfortable chair watching Miss Mullen write to her beau for an entire half hour. Or was she reading a novel?"

"Oh, Mr. Milgrim. Do give it a rest! Mr. Cooper has languished there, alternately reading a magazine and checking his pocket watch, for at least a half hour. While I worked diligently at your correspondence. Is that not so, Mr. Cooper?"

"Don't let her force you into a lie. Harold Milgrim," he said. "I'm happy to make your acquaintance." He stuck his gloves, which were a peculiar shade of reddish tan, into a side pocket, and shook Charles's hand firmly. He not only employed a young woman as, it seemed, his secretary, he also wore a soft hat and striped trousers. "Is it noon yet?" he asked. "No, not quite. Then I shan't offer you a sherry. I always wait until at least the stroke of noon. And the stroke of six — P.M., of course — for whiskey. One must have standards, and keep to them. Remember that, Miss Mullen!"

"Oh, do stop, Mr. Milgrim! Here is a message for you from George."

"Ah — the good George. At last! One of my assistants," he explained to Charles. He took the folded paper Miss Mullen handed him, opened it and read it swiftly, looking pleased. "You can tell him yes, that will be perfect, Miss Mullen. And tell him I said that he has been abominably clever."

"Abominably? I will make a note of that."

Milgrim opened the door of the inner office. "Come in, Mr. Cooper. I've been most curious to meet you since I got your note to Mr. Trout yesterday. I do feel as if I have this case in the bag, but it never hurts to accumulate information."

He closed the door and sat down behind a desk, motioning Charles to a seat in front of it. Against the wall on either side of the desk was a glass-fronted bookcase. On top of one was a bust of Aristotle with sightless eyes, on the other a large, moldy-looking stuffed owl. Milgrim's chair was a Windsor-style that had been converted into a seat that swiveled. The detective saw him noticing it. "Do you like this chair? It's a wonder! Do you know that it was invented by Thomas Jefferson? He was also the inventor of the dumbwaiter. What a mind the man had! And at his house at Monticello he devised a most ingenious arrangement. His bed was built into the opening between two rooms. Can you picture it? Like the waist of an hourglass. On one side, his dressing room, with wardrobe, washbasin, et cetera. On the other, his office. So that when he awoke, depending on his mood, or perhaps what hour it was, he could either perform his various Jeffersonian ablutions and dress and greet the world, or he could go to his desk in his nightshirt and read, write, do whatever statesmen and presidents do when they are at work. Of course, how he handled all this if he was not sleeping alone is something that is not dealt with in the history books."

While he talked, Milgrim took from a cupboard behind his desk a crystal decanter and two short-stemmed glasses. "We may as well be ready," he said. "I'm sure we will not be finished with our business by noon. And sometimes Miss Mullen will bring in a plate of very cunning little cookies that she makes herself, with lavender in them. Fancy that! I'll wager not even Thomas Jefferson had a young lady in his life who made him cookies flavored with lavender. They are really very good. She could always go into the confectionery business if I decide to dismiss her!" He grinned. "But you know, she's just too damned pretty to fire, even if — and this is the truth — she does almost no work. She writes long, misspelled letters, full of inkblots, to a fellow with the improbable name of Archibald March — and yes, she calls him Archie — who is spending the summer in North Carolina. Now who would desert a pretty girl like Miss Mullen to visit a place like North Carolina? Not someone she should be taking seriously as a suitor, I tell her. But she pays me no mind. Ladies in general pay me no mind! I can't think why. And I believe there is a strong possibility that she has invented Archie March out of whole cloth, right down to his ginger moustache and his liking for collie dogs. It is just the kind of thing she might do, for her own amusement."

As he talked, he arranged the decanter and the glasses, found a pair of spectacles in a drawer, cleaned them with a bright red pocket handkerchief and adjusted them on his nose, uncapped his inkwell, and rummaged through a drawer until he found the pen he was seeking. When all was arranged, he pulled a business card from his waistcoat pocket and handed it to Charles. It said:

HAROLD HOPKINS MILGRIM, ESQ.
INQUIRIES OF ALL KINDS
268 PARK STREET (nr. Elm)
NEW HAVEN, CONNECTICUT

"Thank you," Charles said. "All kinds, eh? That about covers it."

"I like to remain flexible! How true it is that a foolish consistency is et cetera et cetera, as Mr. Emerson has informed us. I hope I am never accused of it." Milgrim hit the desk briskly with the flat of both hands and said, "Well! Mr. Cooper! First I will tell you that I am assisting in this investigation at the request of Mr. Jonathan Trout, the father of the murdered young woman. The New Haven police are officially in charge, but as is so often the case with the New Haven police, who are few and stupid, the investigation is going forward at the pace of — no, not a snail. At the pace of a pebble. The stalwart police of our city took care to trample the murder scene, to tidy it mercilessly, and to prematurely clean up the poker that appears to be the murder weapon and hustle it away to headquarters wrapped in burlap. And needless to say they have not heard even rumors of the very interesting science of fingerprinting, which is beginning to be practiced in London and on the continent. I have some knowledge of it from my work with Scotland Yard. In five years, it will be standard practice in all enlightened police departments. New Haven will probably not be among them." He took a deep breath. "Accordingly, Mr. Trout, who is the friend of my uncle Ralph Milgrim, and who had heard about my capabilities, such as they are, and who has no illusions about the competence of the local police, hired me on. Now. Mr. Cooper. You have heard of Monsieur C. Auguste Dupin?"

Charles was startled. "No! What has he to do with the case?"

"Ha! Directly, nothing. Indirectly, it remains to be seen. He is a fictional character, a creation of our American author Edgar Allan

Poe, whose tales of crimes and their ingenious solutions by Monsieur Dupin are famous in Europe but little known in his homeland, which, I fear, knows Mr. Poe only for his lurid and ridiculous poem 'The Raven.'"

"Nevermore," said Charles.

"Every true American knows that the word *nevermore* is the trademark croak of a large black bird. But ask them about Monsieur Dupin, and they will look at you blankly."

"As, in fact, I just looked at you."

"I recommend the stories to you, Mr. Cooper. They are quite marvelous! And Monsieur Dupin, you should know, though merely a figment of a writer's imagination, is one of my inspirations. He solves crimes as if they are puzzles, and he does so by means of ratiocination."

"Rational thinking?"

"Exactly! Not to belabor the point, but let me say that a talent for rational thinking, as you put it so perfectly, is what the police force in our otherwise delightful city is most conspicuously lacking in the ability to exercise. I, however, possess that ability, at least in some degree. It may be the only talent I do possess. I play the fiddle — but just well enough to know that I do not play it well at all. In my college days, I was a gifted coxswain. I am fairly tall, as you see, but slight. I was especially so in those days — as thin as a pin, my mother used to say. I was president of the boat club during my final year. One of my deepest regrets is that I was at Yale a decade too early to participate in the annual boat race with Harvard. In my day we just rowed, whenever we got the chance, and against whoever would have us. And usually beat them handily, too!"

Milgrim looked vacantly across the room, as if imagining himself sitting with his megaphone, wearing a Yale cap, in the stern of a racing boat. Then he smiled, as if the race had ended and the Yale squad were waving their oars in the air in victory. "But you did not come here to hear me talk about my college athletic career," he said. "Or so I assume! Wouldn't it be wonderful if I were wrong and we could sit here talking about the day our varsity out-rowed, out-maneuvered, and thoroughly out-performed Princeton's weak excuse for a crew and took home the Stethers Cup in 1845? But — in short, Mr. Cooper — if you have no questions, pray tell me why you did wish to see me, and what you know about this dreadful business out in Hamden."

"I may have spoken to the man who committed the murder, the day after it happened."

Milgrim's attention was suddenly focused. His eyes narrowed and lost their genial twinkle. "Well," he said. "That is news indeed. Tell me more."

"I am a professional penman," Charles said. "I teach at a business college in Hartford, and I have done work for Yale, and for the state of Connecticut, engrossing official documents and the like. I used to live in New Haven and I know it well — it's a second home. I was passing through here last week, as I often do. Stopping with friends."

Milgrim was taking notes, writing in what seemed to be a curious kind of shorthand, and seldom turning his gaze away from Charles. He looked down only to dip his pen.

"Sometimes, when I'm here," Charles continued, "I set up my desk on the Green so people can avail themselves of my services. Letters or other documents. Ornamental birth certificates, baptismal certificates, deeds. Occasionally someone brings the family Bible to have me inscribe a death in it, or a marriage. Last Thursday — that would be the eighth of May — I wrote a letter for a man that struck me as odd at the time. It strikes me as even odder now."

"Yes," Milgrim said, scribbling. "Odd. How?"

Charles told him about the letter, the man's rudeness, his burned hand. The scene came back to him, and the fellow's face. He was sure that, if he had any talent for representation, for pictorial art rather than simply the art of decorative lettering and engrossing, he could draw a picture of it, it was so clear in his mind. But likenesses, especially, had always been beyond his powers. He described as best he could the black beard, the broken teeth, and the general raggedness and filth of the man's clothes. "I could tell that, despite his appearance, he was not an uneducated man," Charles said. "But one of his hands seemed to be badly burned, which was I think why he could not write the letter himself."

"Ah. Hand. Badly burned." Milgrim took a new sheet of paper and continued to make what looked like the random marks an actor might make onstage to mime the act of writing.

"And another thing," Charles said, and stopped.

Milgrim raised his eyebrows, waiting. Finally he said, "This is what you came to tell me. The crux of it."

Charles nodded.

"Something about this is difficult for you, Mr. Cooper. Take your time."

Milgrim kept his spectacled gaze fixed firmly on Charles's face. The room was quiet. From Miss Mullen's office there was complete silence. The two windows behind Milgrim's desk were open. The noonday sun poured in, but the noises of the street were muted on the third floor. Charles looked at Milgrim's page of scrawled marks; despite the haste with which he had written them, they were orderly and even, with a pleasing symmetry, like writing in Greek or Persian.

"There was an unpleasant smell about him," Charles said. "The smell of burned flesh. Faint but quite unmistakable."

If Milgrim was surprised, he did not show it. He merely asked, "And how, Mr. Cooper, do you know what burned human flesh might smell like?"

Again, Charles didn't answer right away. He could not be sure that he wouldn't succumb to tears, which had always come to him with shameful ease. He did not wish this to happen in Harold Milgrim's office. "My wife was killed in a fire. Burned to death. And my baby son. Four years ago in this city," he said, his voice breaking only at the end.

Milgrim threw down his pen and sat back in his chair. "I remember that fire," he said. "At night, was it not? Somewhere off State Street? Wall Street? Yes." He folded his arms. "Your wife," he said. "Your baby son." He was silent for a long moment, and then he said, "What agony it must have been for you to encounter that smell again. I imagine it is not easily forgotten." He frowned down at his desktop. "I am so very sorry."

Charles was the first to speak. "The man on the Green, the man with the — unfortunate odor — he dictated a letter to his brother, who lives in Wethersfield and who, I have since discovered, is a highly respectable gentleman. A deacon at the Episcopal church. A professor at Trinity College, and a scientist interested in meteorology and cloud formations."

"Cloud formations!" Milgrim looked up and smiled. "*Do you see yonder cloud that's almost in shape like a camel?*" He lowered his voice, ceased to smile. "*By th' Mass, and 'tis like a camel, indeed.*" Milgrim returned to his original voice. "*Or like a whale.*"

Charles chimed in at last. "*Aye, very like a whale.*"

Milgrim clapped his hands. "Oh, excellent, Mr. Cooper! We are Hamlet and Polonius to the teeth!" He took up his pen again. "But Professor Chillick's clouds are, I suspect, less comical and more scientific."

"He is working on a cloud atlas, I understand. A sort of encyclopedia of cloud types. I know nothing more about it, but I have met the man, and he seems personable and intelligent. Nothing like his brother."

"His brother lives in Wethersfield, too?"

"I think not. Chillick put it strangely when I asked him. He said: *My brother lives elsewhere most of the time*. Perhaps he too is an itinerant something-or-other. Not a penman, but — perhaps a day laborer? A dock worker?"

"Yes. That is most interesting. And this letter said what?"

"It announced that he was on his way home, and that he had accomplished some task. I had forgotten the exact wording, but this brought it back."

Charles took from his pocketbook the blotter that had been tucked into his portable desk, and handed it over to Milgrim. "You will need to use a mirror to read it," he said. "And the lines do cross each other. But it was a fairly clean blotter when I used it, and by chance I haven't had occasion to use it since."

The detective sat forward again and stared at the blotter. "I can't make it out. And I am not so vain — yet — that I keep a mirror in my office," he said. "Wait! The washroom! Come. It's right down the hall."

He led the way back into the reception room. "Just off to the washroom for a moment," he said as they passed Miss Mullen. "Any of those cookies about today, Miss M.? If you came up with a few, I might think twice about letting you go."

"What nonsense, Mr. Milgrim!" Her voice floated out behind them.

The washroom was at the end of the corridor, and the two of them had to squeeze into it. "The joy of a brand-new building, Mr. Cooper," Milgrim said. "All the modern conveniences."

Not much light came through the window. Milgrim held the blotter up to the tin mirror over the basin. "This is difficult. It's very — why, what handwriting this is, Mr. Cooper! You are a penman indeed! Well. Let us see what we have here. *You have your wits.* And this. *Your beautiful brother.*"

"*Your wish,*" Charles said. "And *dutiful.* And see there — this is quite clear — *settle up as discussed. We will settle up as discussed,* is what it said."

Milgrim held the blotter, turning it one way, then another. "Yes," he said. "Yes, I see. I see it all. Dutiful brother. And here? *The object* — what is this?"

"As I recall, it said, *The object is in my pocket.*"

"Good God." Milgrim turned and slumped against the wall opposite Charles, who stood backed up against the water closet. "The ring."

"What ring?"

"The ring that was stolen. It seems that — oh, this is very bad. This is monstrous."

"If you would explain...."

He held up the blotter. "Has anyone seen this but you? We will keep it to ourselves for now, Cooper, if you don't mind. I don't want the police to add it to the mess of nonsense they call clues. This could hang the poor bastard."

"Which poor bastard?"

"Both of them. Your personable and respectable professor friend who is compiling an atlas of clouds, and his foul-smelling brother." Milgrim stood frowning in the tiny space, with its faint odors of urine and ammonia. "We need to find out the truth of it," he said, then, realizing that the washroom was a ridiculous place to be, he led the way back down the hall. Miss Mullen held out a plate of cookies as they passed her desk, but Milgrim hardly noticed her.

"Mr. Milgrim! Cookies!"

"Ah. Hand them to Mr. Cooper, if you please. And thank you, Miss Mullen. Thank you a thousand times. You are too good."

She stared at him.

Charles followed Milgrim into his office and shut the door behind them. Milgrim flung himself into his swivel chair and regarded the blotter in his hands as if it were the picture of a scene of horror. Then he looked up at Charles, shaking his head slowly from side to side. "Sherry," he said. "It's the only recourse we have at the moment."

They drank a good deal of it, and each smoked one of Milgrim's Cuban cigars, while he told Charles what Mr. Trout had told him: that Professor Samuel Chillick had been engaged to marry Trout's daughter, Letitia, and had given her a ring — gold filigree, set with three rubies — that had belonged to his mother.

"Miss Trout wrote to him — this is nearly a year ago now — to break off the engagement. He in turn wrote to her requesting that she return the ring. She did not reply. She had not replied, in fact, to a series of notes he sent her — four in total, it is thought." Milgrim paused. "This has been a great embarrassment to her parents. However, the motives of a dead woman are not pertinent to the story. Or probably are not. Meanwhile, because the ring was taken from Miss Trout's finger, presumably by her killer, Mr. Samuel Chillick is the chief suspect, and the logical one."

Charles said, "No matter what that letter said, and what it implied, I do not believe he killed her."

"Because?"

"You get a feeling about people. My father knows him, and has nothing but respect and admiration. I only spoke to the man for a minute or two, but his whole manner, everything he said — it was all about innocence, Mr. Milgrim. Unless I heard him confess it himself, I would not believe him guilty."

"Well, perhaps he isn't. The police in New Haven are convinced the crime was committed by a passing tramp. They view it as a robbery gone wrong, and a tramp was seen in the neighborhood not a week before the crime. For Inspector Durward, the easy explanation is the best. It's the tramp what done it."

"It's the brother what done it," Charles said. "We don't know why. But after all, the ring was his mother's, too. But he did not do it at Samuel Chillick's behest."

Milgrim raised his index finger. "Ah, but consider this, Mr. Cooper. Samuel Chillick has been questioned by two policemen from Hartford, who were sent to Wethersfield to assist the investigation, as the phrase goes. In this case, the phrase means very little. But they did discover that Professor Chillick has no alibi for the night in question. The murder took place at eight o'clock or thereabouts on May seventh, a Wednesday. Chillick's story is that he had taken the train to Boston two days before, on the fifth of May, to stay with a friend of his, Mr. Edward Davenport, who is quite well-known in naturalist circles. Birds, mostly. He has traveled the world collecting specimens for, among other places, our own Yale College. While he was in Boston, Chillick went to a meeting of the Meteorological Society at the Athenaeum, took dinner with a colleague at his club, and spent the crucial Wednesday with Davenport, who was embarking for England, and thence on a sailing cruise along the coast of Wales. He intends to catalog the seabirds there, observe their nesting habits, and steal their eggs, which is what these naturalist fellows do without a qualm. Chillick saw him off on the *Delta* on Thursday evening, and then took a late coach home. By the time he was back in Connecticut, poor Letitia Trout had been dead for at least four hours. Convenient, eh?"

"But of course if he got his brother to do the deed, it matters not whether he was in Boston or in Africa when it happened."

"Nonetheless, the alibi, for whatever it's worth, must be proved. I have sent a letter to the master of the docks in Liverpool, where the *Delta* is heading. Mr. Davenport will be asked to confirm the presence of the friend, and the ship's captain will be asked if he can corroborate it."

"This will take time."

Milgrim sighed. "We will be, at best, well into June, I fear."

"I am imagining Mr. Chillick living in hell until his name is cleared. My father saw him in church. He says he looked like — I quote — a broken man."

"The kindest explanation of that is because, now that he has been questioned, he can see his brother's letter in a new light — one that seems to incriminate him. And the letter had a witness! On the other hand, if he did engage his brother — who is still at large — to commit a heinous crime for him, his distress could also be due to the fact that, alibi or no alibi, he is about to be discovered."

Charles threw up his hands. "I'll say it again. Samuel Chillick would not do such a thing."

"A feeling about people is one thing, Mr. Cooper. Ratiocination is another." Milgrim drained his sherry and poured himself another. He held the decanter over Charles's glass and raised his eyebrows. Charles nodded. Milgrim said, "I'll tell you what. Let us finish our sherry. And then, in the absence of George, will you act as my assistant? I would be so pleased! Let us climb aboard the afternoon train and have a pleasant journey up to Wethersfield and talk to Samuel Chillick ourselves. One can learn a good deal simply by observing."

Chapter Eight

27 May, Tuesday. At breakfast a note from Mr. Cooper to say he has been called suddenly away & will not be able to bring the workbook for a day or two. I am amused to see that this has disappointed me! The fabric of my life is very skimpy.

I divert myself by practicing the writing of Prudence's name, using Mr. Cooper's steel pen — no, it does not scratch the paper if it is held absolutely correctly — & also his script as a model. I have copied out the alphabet he wrote for me, a laborious task that took me all one long afternoon. The capital letters are immensely difficult. I like best the most elaborate ones, the ones that are nearly impossible. The *S* with all its complex looping! And the *E*. I do not at all like the *Q* as he wrote it, & am staying with the *Q* I have always penned: a circle with a curly tail at the bottom. Much more artistic.

Elena looked over my shoulder. I like to think I am doing well, but she said, in her schoolmistressy way, "Some letters are too big, some too small. Some few, however, are *molto bello.*" To say that she does not know her place is a woeful understatement!

About Mr. Cooper she is disapproving but also curious. Unlikely though she must know it to be, she is deathly afraid I will find someone to marry. And then what will become of her, when I no longer require a companion? The prospect of seeing Elena off on the next boat, waving my handkerchief as it moves out to sea, is thrilling to think about. *Arrividerci, Elena! Buon viaggio!*

In the real world of York Street, New Haven, Connecticut, however, Elena & I live in an uneasy peace. Sometimes she bores & annoys me to death, but there are other times when I almost like her. She is intelligent. Her command of English is impressive — she not only speaks it but reads it & even writes it — talents she has picked up entirely from a life of being a servant in English & American homes — since she was nine, she told me. Her fluency with the language has taken her far. Her mother knows only the English that a cook needs to know. I remember how Angelina used to say *rare roast beef* or *fresh bread*, rolling the *r*'s so thoroughly that the words seemed to stand for exotic dishes instead of the dull staples of our American diet. Her brother could hardly write more than his name, & his English vocabulary was limited to *dolce far niente*.

"Limited" is perhaps the wrong word. Tomasso could say *You are my window pane, you are my rutabaga pie*, it hardly mattered. Women would fall at his feet. Some women.

I confess only in these pages that I'm deeply hurt at the failure of my father to write to me. It has been six months since we parted in Rome, since he stood in silence by the carriage while our traveling cases were stowed. As always, he kept his eyes averted from my expanding middle. And when I embraced him, he unbent only slightly — I believe, though I am not sure, that he planted a tiny, grudging kiss somewhere in the vicinity of my ear — but he said nothing. As we drove away, I looked back. He stood tall & stern in the drive. He raised his hand, once, & that was the last I saw of him.

And Aunt Julia. I had another note from her, in which she says *Flossie often speaks of you*. Little Flossie, who is now fifteen years old, & whom I have not seen since she was in pinafores! We were not quite five years apart, Flossie & I, & we were friends. I wonder what Aunt Julia has told her about me, if Flossie even knows I am back on York Street. If Uncle Henry calls me what Father called me. *She often speaks of me*. Was that meant to be a comfort? What is the opposite of comfort? A crown of thorns? Yes. That describes it precisely, including the headache I get when I think about it.

But oh, I miss them. How is Uncle's gout, I wonder. What does Flossie look like at fifteen, nearly a young lady? I remember her as a slight, flat-bosomed tomboy. Aunt Julia used to serve the most delectable Darjeeling in her old Blue Willow pot, with the picture on the side of the eloping lovers who turn into beautiful birds. I would love to be there now, watching her pour the tea into her pretty Chinese cups.

No: what I would love is to be a bird, & just fly away.

There are open-minded people in this world who would not condemn me. True Bohemians, Papa! Who are not bound by convention, who examine what society thinks is proper & are able to dismiss it if it is unreasonable or cruel. The punishment should be appropriate to the crime! And was my crime so disgraceful? To give myself to a beautiful young man on a hot Roman night? Or two.

As a result of which indiscretions I have my lovely baby.

She sleeps in her cradle next to my chair. The windows look out on our back garden, such as it is. I remember it as damp and green and flourishing, & now it is a weedy, overgrown wilderness. But even in its disheveled state, it is beautiful — what garden is not? — & quiet, & far from the dust & grime & the stench of the horses that pass on York Street. The roses are in full, lush blossom, & fragrant — no amount of neglect can hold them back. Those blue flowers whose name I cannot remember but which I loved as a child are bright against the box hedge. Also the pale purple clematis. There used to be glorious white peonies, & I remember how they began with tiny, unpromising dark red shoots, appearing out of nowhere, but there has been no sign of them. The formal herb garden, with its brick border & a cracked marble Pan, keeps a few of its plants — the rosemary is nothing but a half-dead twig, killed by the winter, but there is marjoram, which with one crushed leaf brings all of Italy back to me, & dill, & parsley, & mint, & a few other things Elena & Dora have planted or coaxed back to health. Elena also has planted garlic, which she says will grow from bulbs like onions. It is much stronger than onions, & has a definite stink. As a child I hated it, but I have grown used to its pungency. It stays on the breath, but chewing a few leaves of mint removes it. All Italians know this. It is something Angelina taught me.

My father sent instructions for planting this herb garden when we first lived in Rome, when I was small, hoping to entice my mother here. If she had given in, had overcome her terror of the ocean & let him bring her to America, how different might all our lives be.

Two days ago I fell asleep in the garden, just for a moment, on the bench in the sun, & dreamed that I was back with Papa at the Villa Fraguglia. Someone was jabbering at me in rapid Italian. I knew it was urgent, but I couldn't understand a word. I woke feeling, at first, relief that everything was as it should be, Prudence asleep at my feet on a blanket, the sun warm & the garden fragrant, but then, quickly, what came to me was regret that it had been a dream, that I was sitting not in our garden in Rome, with its stone paths, its statues of Persephone & Flora, the espaliered plum trees against the old brick walls, the bed of deep blue irises that I loved so much, & the grove of olive trees that bordered the stables — not there, but in our overgrown back plot on York Street in New Haven with its bedraggled hedge & fractured Pan.

It is another warm spring day, pushing toward summer. There is a small breeze coming through the window. This is not a time of year to be alone.

So many things not to think about.

I dip my pen & write *Prudence Anne Prescott*, endeavoring to keep proportion in mind, to keep the whole of it graceful & balanced, like a formation of birds swooping across the sky.

Chapter Nine

"Miss Mullen is an orphan, one of the protégés of my aunt Martha Milgrim, who does Good Works, and please use capital letters for the G and the W if you are taking notes."

The two men were in the railway carriage, sharing a lunch of chicken sandwiches and squares of Cheddar cheese that Miss Mullen had somehow found for them, and a few of the lavender cookies, which Milgrim had tucked into his pocket. They had passed through Meriden and Glastonbury, and were nearing the Wethersfield depot, and they had already covered several subjects, including Mr. Milgrim's athletic career, which involved not only rowing, and the crucial race against Princeton, but the game of baseball, and an equally crucial game against the Harvard nine. He compared the merits of the Massachusetts rules of the game with the Knickerbocker rules, which he preferred, drawing diagrams with a pencil on a scrap of paper. They had also talked about Charles's duties at the college, including the course he had developed in business mathematics, and Milgrim was so engrossed by the subject that it took them from Middlefield to Cromwell. What he liked about mathematics, he said, was its lack of ambiguity. "What else is there," he asked, "that always has one definite answer to every problem that's put to it?"

"My father," Charles observed. "The difference is that in mathematics the answer can be proved."

"And my aunt Martha, too, come to think of it. I suppose everyone has a mathematical relative." He finished his sandwich and wiped his fingers discreetly on his pant leg. "But tell me — have you read Euler's *Elements of Algebra?*"

Charles had not.

"Nor have I! But it sat in my bookcase for many years, the gift of a well-meaning tutor of my youth. In fact, it sits there still! Too many abstract notions and not enough sums and fractions. Theoretical mathematics can be dangerous. Ratiocination taken to its absurd extreme. You may recall the death of Archimedes, who was so engrossed in pondering the mysteries of geometry that he didn't notice a Roman invader, who speared him to death because he assumed the poor fellow was being rude and arrogant. No, my interest in mathematics is purely practical, Mr. Cooper, as I suspect is yours."

"Entirely," said Charles, and hence to a discussion of Mr. Milgrim's own office, which he ran, he said, according to the Aristotelian-Dupinian principles ("I do not think Poeian can be a word") of logic and organization, not for profit. Though profit was not scorned should it come his way.

Charles said, "It is unusual to have a female secretary."

"I suppose it is. But she does brighten up the office! One effect of the position is that Miss Mullen is unable to wear twelve ridiculous petticoats and a hoop. They would prevent her from sitting behind the desk."

"Does that distress her, do you think? Not to wear what is fashionable." Or to be considered so poor, he thought to himself, that she could not dress well. To dress like a housemaid. Though Miss Mullen looked nothing like a housemaid.

Milgrim laughed. "Miss Maud Mullen? Heavens, no. Perhaps, in fact, she wears the full complement of petticoats when she is out in the world with her Archibald. But I think her sober dress in the office is quite agreeable to her. So long as they are not wedded to a voluminosity of skirts, I am convinced that employing women as secretaries is intensely logical. Women are born to nurture, to take care of things, to spread an atmosphere of sweetness and light. I think no one can dispute that — and where are those qualities more welcome than in an office like mine? But women are also, as any rational man cannot help but be aware, highly intelligent beings whose brilliance is usually squandered on tending to the needs of home and children. I know not what to make of the letters to Mr. Archibald March, but at the moment, at least, Miss Mullen claims to have no desire for a husband or a batch of babies."

"Nor does my cousin Sarah," Charles said, "who manages my father's general store in Wethersfield. She is a model of efficiency and organization and, I believe, one of the most contented young ladies I know. But there are no Archibalds in her life."

"Good for Cousin Sarah! So many wives and mothers in this world, but so few contented and efficient managers of general stores. Her intelligence would be wasted if she did not work in some capacity. As is true of Miss Mullen. She is much too intelligent and too impatient to be a laundry woman or a seamstress. So sitting at a desk in my outer office and being paid — not lavishly, mind you, but decently — to take care of the books, such as they are, and to write my letters, as well as her own, and to generally look after the office as if it were her home and after me as if I were her — well, family, since most of hers is back in Ireland — this is all most agreeable to her, Mr. Cooper. And to me! We get along capitally. And she packs an excellent lunch, a competence that a male secretary would probably not include among his talents." He popped a hunk of cheese into his mouth. "Of course, Miss Mullen has not had the advantages of attending a business college. Ladies do not do such things, is that right?"

"If they do, I'm not aware of it. There are no female students at the school where I teach. I have had a few private female penmanship students — " Here Charles thought of Lily Prescott and smiled to himself, then added, to account for the smile, "Once, for example, I spent a week at a seminary for young ladies in Amherst, attempting to improve the handwriting of a dozen or so of them."

Milgrim raised an eyebrow. "That must have been a piquant entertainment!"

"Some of my students were charming girls. And I was well paid."

"Ha! They could have had my services for nothing!"

There were two bits of cheese left. Milgrim offered them to Charles, who took one. Milgrim ate the other, then said thoughtfully, "My Miss Mullen would do well to improve her penmanship. It ranges between the purely serviceable — the plodding hand of some earnest young clerk in a steamship office — and the flowery. She has a habit of adding tails to her letters, and not always appropriately. Her small *q* looks like a squirrel nibbling a nut, and her *h* is like a cat in heat!" He chuckled. "Aunt Martha saw to it that Miss Mullen had lessons in drawing and watercolor painting. She did not take to it, though her efforts were fairly accomplished. I think her tails — and the occasional startling flag flying as well — are the expressions of an artistic ability that, for reasons of her own, my secretary does not wish to encourage in herself." He glanced out the window. "What is that building? It looks like a prison!"

"It is a prison indeed, Mr. Milgrim. The Connecticut State Prison is one of the wonders of Wethersfield. It means that we are nearly at the depot."

"Well! How very educational. And what a pleasant journey this has been, despite the usual smuts and cinders." Milgrim searched his left-hand pocket for his gloves, found them in his right-hand pocket along with the cookies, took out a cookie for himself and handed one to Charles, and set his hat upon his head. "And now for Chillick."

It wasn't far, so they walked down Watering Lane to Broad Street and Coleman, but the afternoon was warm. Charles would have liked to unpin his cravat and stuff it in his pocket, remove his coat and sling it over his shoulder. He thought about the article on dress reform he had been reading in *Harper's*. Women in trousers, women without corsets. That was something he would like to see.

Coleman Street was as quiet as ever. Some progress had been made on the brick foundation of the new house, but the only other change since Charles's last visit was the profusion of roses in bloom all along the street. There was even a bush, boldly pink, clambering over the fence in front of Chillick's otherwise austere white house.

The servant who answered the door — an elderly woman with a white cap on her silver hair — said that Professor Chillick was in his laboratory, but she would let him know they were there. She showed them into a very plain parlor. There was no carpet, and everything but the floor was painted white. The tabletops were bare, as was the mantelpiece save for a clock, and there were no pictures on the walls. There was no evidence of wife or children, just neatness and order, an almost Spartan simplicity. It looked like a place where no one lived. Charles found nothing else to look at while they waited except the clock, which appeared to be made of rosewood. The top rounded up to a point, like a Gothic window, and painted on the front of the glass door was a pair of monarch butterflies and, in very fine gilt script, the words *Atkins, Whiting & Co. Bristol Connecticut.* The tick was very slow, as if the clock was about to wind down, or die entirely, and the time was off by at least an hour.

As Harold's assistant, whatever that meant, should he be looking for clues? What was the significance of the clock that told the wrong time? And the butterflies?

The door opened and Chillick came in, tieless and in his shirt-sleeves. His spectacles were pushed up on his forehead. "Forgive me, gentlemen. I hope you didn't wait long. How may I help you?"

Charles made the introductions, Chillick indicated a plain but very serviceable couple of chairs that flanked the hearth. When they were seated, Milgrim said, "Cooper, perhaps you could begin."

"We have met, of course, Mr. Chillick," Charles said, slightly startled. Milgrim could have warned him that the opening lines would be his. Instead of talking about mathematics and Miss Mullen in the railway carriage, they should have been planning their strategy. "When I walked by your house and we talked about your brother's letter. And what a coincidence it was."

Chillick said nothing, just bowed. His manner was not friendly.

"Mr. Milgrim is assisting the police with their investigation of the murder down near New Haven," Charles went on.

"*Supplementing* might be a better word," Milgrim put in. "*Supplementing* the police inquiry. At the request of Mr. Jonathan Trout, the father of the victim. And Mr. Cooper is assisting me."

He stopped, so Charles continued. "We are curious about the letter you received last week from your brother."

"Are you." Chillick sat up straighter and folded his arms across his chest. "Well, there's another strange coincidence, Mr. Cooper. Last week you strolled down the street where I live to chat about this and that, and today you are here investigating a murder."

"By a somewhat circuitous route, I am here in fact because of that letter." Charles waited for a comment, but there was none. The slow ticking of the clock was audible. He said, "I understand that the police have spoken to you." Silence.

"Because of your connection to the Trout family," Milgrim put in. Silence.

"I wondered if your brother has returned here, as he wrote in his letter to you that he would," said Charles. "Because you are connected to the Trouts — well, so is he."

Chillick glared past them both at a beam of sunlight on the floor, but he didn't speak.

Harold sighed, stood up, and walked to the fireplace. He studied the lettering on the clock for a moment, then turned to face Chillick. "A woman was murdered, Mr. Chillick. You are a suspect because you were once attached to her and she had in her possession a ring that you valued, which was stolen by her murderer. That is all that was taken. A ring that was apparently in dispute between you."

"I did not murder Miss Trout." Chillick spoke through clenched teeth.

"I think you are telling me the truth. Hence my questions about your brother, who was in New Haven when the murder took place."

Chillick stood up then. "I do not wish to discuss my brother. And I would like you to leave now, sir. Both of you."

Harold pulled out one of his business cards and offered it. "Perhaps we will talk at another time."

Chillick ignored the card. "I think it's likely that that will never happen."

"Nevermore, Mr. Chillick?" Harold paused at the door and set his card down on one of the bare tabletops. "I hope that is not true."

Chapter Ten

1 June, Sunday. **Now that I have voiced it — to Mr. Cooper last week — the idea has begun to haunt me, that Papa may completely abandon me, that I may use up all the money & have to find a way to earn my own keep.

Surely he would not let this happen! But nothing is sure in this world. And there is no sign that he will relent. He knows how long what he gave me will last. It is impossible for me not to await the mail every morning with eagerness. Surely Papa will write today! And then when he doesn't, I wait for tomorrow: Surely tomorrow!

I have been here seven months. I have nothing of my own, only what Papa has settled on me. When it is gone, we will starve. Or rather, we will starve unless I do one of the two things that are all I can think of in the middle of the night when I am awake with Prudence. Sometimes I talk to myself, going over additions & subtractions, taking myself down blind alleys of hope & struggling up huge mountains of dejection. The oil lamp throws its flickering circle of light around us for a few feet, & beyond that is darkness. It's into the darkness that I stare — thinking, thinking.

Two things. One, I can throw myself on the mercy of my uncle Henry — weep, beg, hope that the coos & smiles of my Prudence will melt his heart.

Two, I can find a husband, a man who will clasp my tainted self to his bosom & save me.

There is one, and there is two. I search my brain for a third, but nothing comes.

❧❧

Mr. Cooper had been called back to Wethersfield, which gave him the opportunity to bring me what he says is a superior workbook. He said he could have purchased one for me at a stationery store, but he had a supply of these in his study at home: *The Compendium of Penmanship*, written by one of his old teachers.

He remained in New Haven for nearly this entire week, & was free on three successive afternoons, & so I had three lessons — at my house, *tête à tête*. When he called on the first day — and, luckily, I had put on my beautiful new morning dress — he commented that he was surprised to find me at home, which made me laugh. Where would I be? Out paying calls on my social circle? Showing off the baby to my lady friends? I wonder if Mr. Cooper can have any idea of what kind of life is led by someone like me.

But perhaps he was just being polite.

He brought the workbook, which I insisted on paying him for. He didn't want to take anything for that or for the lessons, but — Elena would have been horrified, but Elena was not present — I insisted. It was an awkward moment for both of us when I gave him the money, but we forgot it soon enough, & he became deeply absorbed in teaching me, & I in learning.

The workbook is indeed quite a nice one, with stiff covers & plenty of smooth, lined practice paper. The diagrams in it are daunting — all Basic Principles & Seven Steps & Essential Postures — but Mr. Cooper made everything much simpler. He is a gifted teacher, kind & patient, a bit pompous, but so passionate about what he does, it is infectious. He makes everything clear, like how to contrast a slender upstroke with a shaded downward one, & how to rise out of a stroke at the end of a word, tapering the tail of the letter in a graceful twist.

"It's like a melody drifting to silence at the end of a piece," I said.

The comparison pleased him. He often looks at me in delight, as if I'm some new & exotic writing implement. "It is very much like music in many ways," he said. "There's a rhythm to the writing, & if the rhythm isn't right, everything else is off."

I immediately saw what he meant. It's all in how the arm is held, & the range of movement it is allowed, & the transfer of motion from the arm to the wrist to the hand — a process that is much simpler than it appears in diagrams, but still must be mastered. I copied the movements of Mr. Cooper's arm as best I could, but for the most part he let me go my own way, just putting in a word here & there, pointing out a lapse, praising when the lettering looks right. Too much praise, I think.

When I told him he should write his own manual, he confessed, with a blush, that he was working on an instruction manual for a script based on the Italian model — which of course, immediately got my attention. I told him the only Italian writing I knew was the letters chiseled into the stone of ancient buildings by the Romans.

"Do you mean to give your students a mallet & a chisel along with the workbook?"

"And a block of stone, too," he said. "I could have quite a sideline in the quarry business."

But what he means is a way of lettering that was popular in Italy in the sixteenth century among the Italian writing masters. He is devising a way to make it with what he called *curve patterns* & *angle patterns*, & — well, I don't know what else, but it's delightful to see his excitement.

I encouraged him to remove his coat & work in his waistcoat, which is made of a very nice figured material. His cravat is neatly tied, & his shirt cuffs are clean & starched. His portable desk is neatly compartmented, with an ingenious pair of handles & a special compartment for his ink bottle. It is soothing to look at him.

We sat across from each other at the table in the drawing room, where as a small child I did my lessons with Mademoiselle Lefèvre, & where my father & I would play card games — Snap, or Trade & Barter — in the evenings after supper, & read together, & make magical folded paper animals. In ten seconds he could make an elephant from a page ripped out of the newspaper!

Over Mr. Cooper's head is the painting of Lake Como, the view from Papa's villa, complete with the garish crimson sunset that seems exaggerated but is actually quite true to life. On the mantel are three framed pen-and-ink sketches, each propped on its own little wooden easel, of our house in Rome — in one of them you can just see Mortimer, lying under a tree, with his head on his paws. Mr. Cooper did not comment on them, but he studied them at length, especially the sketches, before we began work, & I felt a rush of pride. In spite of everything, I am not no one. I am not insignificant. My father is Orlando Prescott!

Papa is everywhere in that room. But I was not unhappy to be there with my scrivener, whose presence gave it an entirely new feeling. I was a schoolgirl again, for an hour or two, laboring over my lesson! The room was wonderfully peaceful while we worked. I thought it best to keep Prudence in the background. She takes a long nap in the afternoon, after spending most of the morning with me, being fed, & cooing, & playing. (What on earth do we do together that I call "play"? Whatever it is, we are both absorbed by it!) I often put her to sleep down in the kitchen. The stove makes it beastly hot & stuffy at this time of year, & Dora will not open the windows onto the street because of the grime & the smells, but she & Prudence do not seem to mind. I had the rocking cradle brought down so the baby can be tended when I am occupied. Dora also likes to carry her around in a kind of flannel sling she has devised, which supports the baby's wobbly little head & leaves Dora's arms free. When I came into the kitchen the other afternoon, they were at the window, & Dora was saying, "Those are people's feet walking by, Miss Prudence. And that is a carriage with four horses. And that is a very fine dog!"

Dora has lately become thin-lipped & surly with me, which is most unlike her & as if she's been infected with Elena's disapproval. (I suppose there is a stigma in this puritanical city against working for an unmarried mother.) But with the baby she is all smiles. She takes her out almost daily, just for half an hour — I really cannot spare Dora for longer than that. Prudence seems to like Dora, who has no inhibitions about producing ridiculous noises for Prudence to laugh at — a dear little chuckle that bubbles out of her so that the rest of us laugh too. It is irresistible! Dora also makes sugar-teats for her, & another kind that mixes sugar with a great lump of fat, which would not be something I would like to suck on, but which quiets Prudence very well. I knew nothing about babies when I stepped off the train from New York last November. All I knew was that I had one in my belly, kicking mightily, & that I intended to love it & mother it with all my heart. Beyond that I scarcely thought. But Dora & Elena have shown me the tricks of mothering — both of them spinsters but with more experience of life than I ever had! I do not follow every bit of their advice, that is for sure, but I cannot deny they have been a help.

Elena was home on the afternoon of my first penmanship lesson, but she remained in her room, sewing or reading her Bible or whatever she does. She was out for the other two — where, I know not, & do not ask her about. She is as enigmatic as ever. Is she miserable here away from her homeland, or happy in this new life? I don't know that, either. We continue to read aloud in the evenings, at Elena's insistence — partly, I think, so that we do not have to talk. Reading is certainly preferable, but I am being driven slowly mad by our start-and-stop approach. It is rare that Elena will agree to finish a book. So many of them disappoint her, just as people in real life might. We have abandoned many good books from the library, & have now taken up the novels of Miss Austen, from my own bookshelves — all of which I have read, but they do bear re-reading, & each, reliably, is about romance! They are also very witty. Even Elena sometimes gets the humor.

I have been glad, each day, to be alone with Mr. Cooper in that peaceful back room. Here is something I know: during my lessons, while I am bent over the letters, trying to make my swirls & curls correspond to the swirls & curls in the *Compendium* — & not succeeding very well — Mr. Cooper is staring at me across the table.

Strange how you can feel another's gaze on you, as if it were some-thing tangible — a scent, or a cool breeze. He stares at me steadily, & when I raise my eyes, he drops his — but not before I see the look in them.

I'm getting to like those gentle grayish eyes of his. And his small, rather wide nose & neat hands & plain brown whiskers, too. He is a bit rodentlike. But such a nice little rodent, like a pet mouse you can carry in your pocket, or the squirrels that scurry about digging up acorns in our back garden.

This image comes into my head because I cannot help myself, & then I think how unkind it is. But I don't mean it unkindly! I really do like Mr. Cooper very much, & I try to coax out a smile as often as I can because it improves his looks so much & because there is such a sweetness to it.

When he came to the door for my third lesson — it was a fine afternoon, cool & bright — I suggested we walk down to the Green before we began. Elena, whose disapproval of such a scheme would have seeped through the house like a miasma, was of course merci-fully absent. I ran down to the kitchen to tell Dora, kissed my baby, found my parasol, & we set off.

I took his arm. We had become quite easy together, & I was sorry that that afternoon would be our last for some while. He was returning to Wethersfield where, he said, his father was not well & needed him. As we walked, he told me about his father, who has lately become weak & aged beyond his years & is now scarcely eating anything, & about the cousins who keep his father's store when the old man is ailing. The Coopers are an old Wethersfield family, & it was his grandfather who began keeping the general store there. They have always been traders & merchants, he said.

"Until you," I said. "A writing master!" I wondered how he & his profession fit into his family, & if they were perhaps shrewd in the ways of storekeeping but otherwise simple, uneducated people — but he said his cousin aspires to be a great writer & has to be dragged away from his reading almost by force to sweep the floor or mea-sure out a pound of coffee. His family, as he describes them, sound delightful, & he & his father seem to be, above all else, the best of friends — as Papa & I once were. This we do not talk of, however.

Mr. Cooper also told me — just in passing, in response to a comment I made — that he had been married & his wife had died four years ago. This was a surprise to me! He never seemed to me like someone who had been married — & then, as soon as he said it, he did. There is something very comfortable & husbandly about him.

The topic of his wife seemed so painful that I asked no questions, only said I was sorry. It is a good quality in him, that after four years there is still a scar — though not such a deep one, I well know, that he cannot appreciate my *beaux yeux*. The thought entered my mind that a writing master's salary, whatever it might be, is apparently adequate for the support of a wife.

As we were walking near "our" bench, he asked me if I remembered the fierce man with the black beard. I said that I did indeed — a filthy brute.

"When he walked by you on the path," Mr. Cooper said, "I remember that he nearly bumped into you. What was your impression of the fellow?"

All I could say was that he looked as if he had come straight from a coal mine. Also that he had the mad, fevered eyes of a maniac. Also that he stared with the utmost insolence at my bosom, though this I did not tell Mr. Cooper.

"He spoke to you. Do you recall what he said?"

I did not, though I was sure it was something offensive, & I asked him why he wished to know.

"A man of that description is suspected of a crime," he said. Then, I suppose assuming I would be terrified at the idea, he added, "But it is nothing. Please do not worry about him. The world is full of suspicious characters."

"That is not very comforting! Certainly a world full of suspicious characters I'm not aware of is more worrisome than one of them who happened to pass me on the Green three weeks ago!"

Then something happened. Mr. Cooper's laugh broke off, & I could feel his arm tense where I held it. He let out a soft "Damnation!" for which he immediately apologized.

"What is it?" I had seen nothing, just the usual passers-by, none of whom looked like anything but ordinary Connecticut citizens. "Did you spot one of our suspicious characters?"

He did not respond to my joke. "I saw someone I would rather not have seen," was all he said, but he turned abruptly, & we made our way back to York Street in a tense silence.

We walked so rapidly that I was quite tired when we arrived. Dora brought tea, & Mr. Cooper became calm again, but not cheerful. Something was bothering him. We drank our tea, settled down to work, & improved my penmanship for more than an hour, until my hand was cramped & sore. Mr. Cooper, so kind & attentive in most ways, is oblivious to the pain fine writing can inflict, I suppose because he no longer feels it — or is too dedicated to his art to care.

So I was glad when he interrupted the lesson & said, "Ah — while I think of it, & before I forget again —" He pulled a business card from his waistcoat pocket. "Forgive me," he said, laying it on the table. "I do not mean to dwell on unpleasant subjects. It's about that man we were speaking of. I was distracted from what I meant to say. I have promised a friend — if you think of anything else that might be important — or perhaps, if your companion noticed anything? Would you send a message to this fellow? His name is Harold Milgrim, & he is a detective with an interest in the case I mentioned."

I thought all of this extremely mysterious & intriguing, & would have liked to ask him more, but it was clear from his manner that it was not a subject he wished pursued. I promised, took the card, & tucked it into my workbook. And then — tired of ink & paper, & wishing to make him smile — I laid down my pen & said, "I had an odd thought. As I labor here, it strikes me that it doesn't matter what one writes. Words can be made to look beautiful, graceful, elegant, even if what they say is cruel, or spiteful, or even malevolent."

He did not disappoint me. His smile begins slowly, then widens until eventually he shows his teeth which are not large & rodentlike at all, but markedly small & a little crooked, like a child's teeth. "It is not the fault of the letters, Miss Prescott."

"Of course not! Any more than a bejeweled dagger would be at fault if it were plunged into someone's heart. Or a large & ancient oak tree that fell & crushed everyone under it."

That made him laugh. "You have as clever a way with words & images as you do with these letters."

"Do I really have a way with letters, Mr. Cooper?" I made the question playful. "Or are you flattering me because we have become friends?"

He blushed — some color in his face is very becoming — & then he said two interesting things. The first was, "I am delighted to hear you say that we are friends, Miss Prescott, for I hoped that we were."

This was an emotional speech, & it took him a few seconds to recover from it, during which I considered touching his hand, which rested on the table, but thought better of it & instead just looked at him in what I hope was a winsome way. I do not have complete control over my winsomeness, though I know it is there.

Then he said the second interesting thing: "I have indeed been encouraging you. As a teacher, I am convinced that students thrive on praise more than on criticism. It is true, though, that you have a natural ability. But beyond that, there is something about your efforts that I do not often see."

"Really!" I picked up the paper I had been writing on & turned it so we could both look at it. We leaned our heads somewhat closer together across the table. "And what on earth is that, besides the uphill path that I now can see I seem to insist on taking no matter how many ruled lines I try to follow."

"That is not important. It's something many beginners do, & you will rise out of it with practice. And perhaps we'll adjust the angle of your paper on the table — the problem can sometimes be solved as simply as that. But what I want to say is that you have what I can only call your own style. I have seldom had a student whose work I could describe this way. Your lettering is very beautiful — perhaps not as straight & regular across the page as it will be when you have worked at it more. Consistency is also something that comes with practice. But it is pleasing to look at, & it is also — I can only say *original*. Look — here — the way your small letters connect, with a sort of spike, & the way they end, not precisely with a flourish, as you have practiced, but almost with an angle, which then tapers off. Do you see?"

"I do," I said. "How strange. I have no consciousness of doing that. Oh dear — it does not seem to flow along smoothly like a stream, or a vine."

"It is your natural hand, & it has its own rhythm." He beamed at me. "And then look at this. The simplicity of this *S* in the midst of its frills & furls. I almost want to say the *strength* of your *S*. Or of this capital *K*, or the *M*. What I describe is especially striking in the *M*."

I studied it for a moment, trying to see what he saw. "It looks rather belligerent, maybe."

"There are better words. But — yes, there's something. These letters assert themselves. But what I mean to say is that they are really quite magnificent!"

It crossed my mind that he was condescending to me, either as a woman deficient in the masculine arts, or as someone he admired & wished to please. "Magnificent seems a grand word for my little scratches."

"And yet magnificence is part of your style. You have your own fashion. You write like no one else!"

He seemed sincere, & he also seemed to assume I would be happy to hear this, but in truth — all I wanted was to write like everyone else so that, should I need to teach penmanship, I could do it. I hesitated, but I decided it was best, up to a point, to be honest with him. "Does that mean I will never be able to be a teacher?"

We looked at each other across the table, & his face became serious. I sensed — as I had sensed his eyes on me when my head was down — that he wanted to touch my hand a minute before I had wanted to touch his. But he did not. He said, "No, Miss Prescott. I believe you would be an excellent teacher. But I cannot conceive that the day will ever come when you will need to earn your living as a teacher of penmanship."

We continued looking at each other for a second or two longer than was strictly respectable, but it went no further than that.

Or not much. When it was time for him to leave, he said that he would be sorry to bring our series of lessons to an end. "You are progressing so rapidly, however…"

"In my own eccentric way."

He smiled into my eyes. "Yours is a pleasing eccentricity, Miss Prescott. And you write so well that soon you will require no more instruction."

"Ah, but if I want it…?"

He blushed again. I could not resist flirting with him. It is not as it was with Tomasso in Rome, but Charles Cooper is an agreeable man, & grows more so the better one gets to know him.

"I expect to be in New Haven again in a month or so," he said — a neutral-seeming statement that, I knew full well, meant that he would find an occasion to be in town, & would call on me when he was.

"Then I shall work at my pen exercises in happy anticipation."

We looked at each other again in that way before I gave him his hat & his gloves. Before he left, he returned to what we had talked about earlier. "You know — your observation is very true, Miss Prescott, that it doesn't matter what the letters spell out," he said, buttoning a glove. "Just as beautiful letters could speak of something cruel, so could inferior penmanship say something beautiful."

"So that if a man had a letter from a lady who had only the most basic command of her letters, he would still be glad to receive it if she wrote: *I love you passionately, and every day without you is an agony to me.*"

His laughed, but sobered immediately, left off his glove-buttoning, & said, earnestly, looking into my eyes, "And if she wrote those words in a lovely & distinctive hand, he would be in heaven," which I thought was a very agreeable thing for him to say — especially so because he then bowed over my hand & kissed it.

Chapter Eleven

Charles walked for an hour around the city. He was overwhelmed by the time he had spent with Lily Prescott. The walk, the tea, the lesson in the drawing room in a house where there seemed to be no one else present. Their conversation at the door.

What had it meant? Her soft words to him. Their quick intimacy. Her frankness, that spoke of an intimacy that he had never experienced with any woman but his wife. Until they were all but engaged, Sophie had never looked at him the way Lily Prescott did.

He saw Lily in his mind in a series of vignettes. Her hand raised to tuck in a stray lock of hair, so that her full sleeve fell back and he could see her soft arm. Her puckish smile when she asked, "Are you flattering me because we have become friends?" Her hand pressed to her bosom in a moment of strong emotion, or in an appreciation of his humor — he could not remember why she had done it, but her hand had rested there, her fingers splayed between her breasts, and his eyes had strayed to it hungrily.

But the memory of her soft hand under his lips was the most vivid, the most debilitating to him. It had very nearly erased the shock of suddenly catching sight of Philip Gaudet marching plump and scowling across Temple Street from Center Church, with his head down and his hands in his pockets. Why had he looked up when his path crossed theirs? It was as if he had a bloodhound residing in some small corner of his under-furnished brain that alerted him. *There he is! Your enemy!* "Arf arf," as Calvin would say.

The look on Philip's face had been first surprise, then a sort of "I knew it!" expression, followed swiftly by something Charles could only describe as quiet triumph. And yet Philip didn't slacken his pace. He spoke not a word, gave not a sign that he had seen or recognized Charles, merely charged on down the path toward Elm Street, leaving Charles as limp as glove leather.

Try to forget it, he told himself. He is nothing to you. He wishes to see you as little as you wish to see him. Or nearly.

Charles had walked in a circle from York Street over to the old canal and west on Broadway as far as he could go, then back down Howe Street to Elm again, and ended up not far from the building on Park Street where Harold Milgrim had his office.

Charles wished he could uncover something that would exonerate Samuel Chillick, and he knew that Milgrim wished it as much as he did. He had been gratified by Milgrim's last comment on the subject, as they parted on the railway platform in Wethersfield — Milgrim to return directly to New Haven, Charles to spend the evening with his father. "I'm glad we had our unpleasant interview with Mr. Chillick," Milgrim said. "Difficult, aloof, and downright offensive though the man was, I do not think he is capable of beating to death a young woman he was once engaged to, just to retrieve a ring, whether it was his mother's or not. In other words, I agree with you, Cooper, and I respect your initial impression of him, for it was mine as well. Nothing is so worthy of respect as an opinion that matches one's own, and ratiocination be damned!" He spoke above the noise as the train thundered in, scattering soot, the whistle screaming. They shook hands, and Milgrim added as he stepped up to the carriage, "Be vigilant, Cooper. Keep an eye on our fellow when you can. And let us stay in touch. I do think of you as my assistant, you know."

What neither of them had voiced was the fear that, if the police wanted to make an arrest, they would seize on Samuel Chillick because of what they considered his powerful motive. His alibi, when it arrived, would be helpful but was no guarantee of justice. His motive remained intact, and if some brutal third party had done the killing at his behest, Chillick was no less worthy of hanging.

108

The letter that seemed to point to that possibility was known to no one but Charles, Milgrim, Chillick himself — and his mysterious brother, of course.

Charles turned onto Park Street and pulled out his watch — it was close to five o'clock, and the Gaudets would be expecting him for tea. But, in his capacity as unofficial assistant, he decided to stop at Milgrim's office, report what Miss Prescott had said, and see if there was any news.

He found Miss Mullen behind her desk, copying out a list of numbers from scraps of paper. Her employer, she said, had left for the day. "He was due at one of his innumerable events. I can't keep track of them all, and fortunately I am not hired to do so. Perhaps a ball? Though he left rather early for that."

Charles was taken aback. "A ball?"

"Or a dinner party or a musical evening or what-have-you."

Miss Mullen had put up her rather unruly hair in plaits wound around her head — an old-fashioned hairdo that went with her modest skirts, which were tucked around the stool she sat on like a tablecloth around a tea table. He saw her suddenly as a country girl in Ireland, and found that he was intensely curious: when had she come here, and how was she orphaned, and what were the circumstances under which she became one of Mrs. Milgrim's charitable projects? He sneaked a peek at her handwriting — it was not so very terrible, and he saw neither tails nor blots.

"There are sides of your employer I have not seen," he said.

"Yes, he seems such a sporty chap, like someone who has just come in from a day in the country and wants nothing more from his evenings than pipe and slippers before the fire. But he leads a very fancy life. It's in the Milgrim blood!"

"What kind of blood is that?"

"Very, very blue, Mr. Cooper. The Milgrims! Why, New Haven, Connecticut, would probably not exist without the Milgrims!" Her eyes crinkled up when she smiled. "Or so they would have you think. The truth is that Mr. Harold Milgrim can afford to be so low — with his soft hats and his lack of a proper waistcoat — because he is so very high."

"I see. Or rather I will, once I have thought it over. I will have to work a bit to imagine him wearing a tailcoat and a starched shirt-front on a regular basis."

"Turtle soup and champagne," Miss Mullen said. "He is a unique character and does bear a bit of thinking about. But at any rate, he is not here. May I help you, Mr. Cooper?"

"Not really. I'm leaving for Wethersfield on the morning train, and perhaps you could just tell him that I have passed along his card to a woman who had a glimpse of the fellow he and I were concerned about."

"The black-bearded poker-wielder?"

Charles was startled once again. "He has told you about the case?"

"Of course. He claims he gets his best ideas when we chew them over at lunch along with our fish paste sandwiches. Mr. Milgrim's aunt Martha often sends them over to us when we are working too hard to stop. Who is this woman?"

"A sort of — a sort of friend of mine," Charles said, stumbling. How tame and inadequate the word seemed, compared to the strange power it had had when it was uttered in the entrance hall on York Street. "Miss Lillian Prescott. I don't think she has anything important to add — she merely told me that the man looked mad. As indeed he did."

"Mr. Milgrim should probably talk to her. Sometimes people notice things they are not aware of noticing until he reminds them. He is quite clever that way."

"She lives on York Street."

"Is she the daughter of the painter? Orlando Prescott?"

"Why, yes, I believe so." The heartless father. He had not known his name was Orlando — it was as if he had been marked out for Bohemianism the day he was born.

"His paintings are all over New Haven — as pervasive in this city as elm trees! Even Aunt Martha Milgrim has one, a painting of her house with a beautifully gaudy sunset behind it."

"I believe he specializes in sunsets." He had seen a painting in the drawing room on York Street that boasted an impressive one, and another in the hall, smaller but even rosier. "Mr. Milgrim may be hearing from Miss Prescott. She has a companion, an Italian woman who was also present that day, and who should perhaps be questioned."

"I have no doubt of it. I will communicate all this to Mr. Milgrim. He will be delighted to hear it!" She narrowed her eyes at him. "I cannot help but notice, Mr. Cooper, what a very nice waistcoat you are wearing. I do like that fabric!"

When he was leaving, she reached across the desk and held out her hand, to give his a hearty shake. "Have a pleasant trip to Wethersfield. I hope you will find your father improved in health. And I hope we will see you when next you are in town."

He pondered Miss Mullen as he walked back to Bradley Street. It astonished him that she knew his father was ill. Did Milgrim tell her everything? And how did she know Miss Prescott's father was a painter? He felt, as he left her, that life — his life, Miss Prescott's life, the lives of the Milgrim family of New Haven and of Miss Mullen herself — was like nothing so much as a large and complicated tapestry, like the German hunting scene hanging in the parlor at his aunt Mina's in Manheim. And he himself was but a tiny figure in it, perhaps a rabbit, hunched in a corner, looking out at the pattern in wonder.

When Charles arrived at Bradley Street, he went first to his room above the stable, where he washed his face and combed his hair. He looked at his face in the mirror above the washbasin — gray eyes, short nose, brown whiskers, and hair that was beginning to thin exactly as his father's had. He knew that, after so many hours in the company of Lily Prescott, he was changed utterly, but it was the same old face. The same old Charles. He smiled at his image. Could a woman like Miss Prescott love such a face? It wasn't much, he was aware. *You are an unremarkable fellow*, he had often said to it. But he knew himself to be good-hearted, and intelligent, and not without a certain likability. Sophie Gaudet, after all, had loved him.

And so he was thinking, appropriately, of her when he went down to the drawing room, where Emily and Bernard were sitting at the tea table.

Instantly, he knew there was something wrong. He dreaded bad news. Bad news, he thought, had washed over him in great waves for much of his life.

"What is it?" he asked in the doorway.

Bernard said, "Come in and sit down, Charles." The words were utterly without cordiality. Charles's heart sank.

"Philip has been here," Bernard said. *Thank goodness I went for a walk,* was Charles's first thought. Bernard went on: Philip had seen Charles downtown with a woman — a very gay young woman, Philip had said, a woman he had described as a Jezebel, hanging on Charles's arm and smiling freely into his face as though they were betrothed. The height of fashion, he said. And with a purple parasol. They had seemed very intimate.

In the silence when he was finished, Emily raised her head and looked at Charles pleadingly. "What is the meaning of it? Who is this woman? Please tell us what this is about."

Explain it away, her face said. Tell us with a laugh that the woman is your cousin — some Legenhausen *fraulein* from darkest Pennsylvania, which would account for everything!

Charles looked stubbornly away from them both, at the blue toile wallpaper, which showed two scenes, endlessly repeated: a pipe-playing shepherd and a dancing shepherdess. He considered saying nothing at all. He had read the Bartleby story when he was in Wethersfield — Calvin read all the new books, it was what he spent his pocket money on — and the words went through his head: *I prefer not to.* Had he ever uttered anything so rude in his life? The temptation was great.

But he could not be rude to the Gaudets. He said, stiffly, "She is a student of penmanship. It was a fine afternoon. Before the lesson began, we took a walk. What business this is of Philip's is a mystery to me."

Bernard said gently, "The boy was thinking of your vow, Charles."

"My vow!" He tore his gaze away from the wallpaper and looked at Bernard. He knew there were tears in his eyes, but they were tears of rage. "I made a vow — to myself, as I recall, not to your son — never to marry again or have a child. I did not vow never to walk on the Green with a woman! I did not vow never to act as a writing master to a woman! I did not vow to never do anything that might upset Philip Gaudet!"

Emily laid her hand on his arm. He was tempted to throw it off, to get up and take himself down to the station and sit there until the next train roared into New Haven. He was rigid with anger, his head a jumble of thoughts. A purple dress and a purple parasol! A Jezebel! He recalled the smirking expression on Philip's face, as if to say: *I've caught you now, you scoundrel!*

"Charles," Emily said. "We all know how excitable Philip is. Can you assure us that this woman is merely a student? A pleasant young person you have struck up a kind of camaraderie with? She is nothing more to you than that?"

In that moment, he knew that he was in love with Lily Prescott and that he had to ask her to be his wife. Despite her situation. Despite his in-laws. Despite his having known her for only a month. Despite everything. His vow, made four years ago in the extremity of his grief, was preposterous, and it was wrong of them to hold him to it. He had been twenty-four years old!

Sitting there at the tea table, with Emily's hand — mourning ring and all — resting on his arm, he was stunned by the power of his feeling. *I love you passionately, and every day without you is an agony to me.* It overcame all his other emotions — filial duty, remorse, love for his dead wife.

He said, "No, I'm afraid I cannot assure you of that. She has become much more to me than a mere student. And you may tell Philip she is no Jezebel! She is worth twenty of him."

There was a stunned silence in the room. Emily removed her hand.

Charles stood up. "I'll be on my way. Thank you, as always, for your hospitality. I assume you will be glad to see the last of me."

No one said anything. He went up to his room, retrieved his bag and his portable desk, and carried them down. Joshua was in the yard. Charles gave him a quarter tip and sent him out to hire a gig to take him to the train station. No doubt his face was thunderous. Joshua asked no questions, and if Bernard and Emily didn't like it, that was too bad.

Chapter Twelve

2 June, Monday. I asked Elena about the man we saw on the Green the day we met Mr. Cooper. She has been preoccupied & withdrawn lately, lost in her own concerns, whatever they may be, but to this she responded with a vigorous shudder.

"Really a dreadful person," she said, rolling her *r*'s even more than usual.

"Dreadful indeed. That is really all I can recall about him, just a general impression of very extreme dreadfulness."

"He was vile," Elena said, looking down into her soup.

"Do you remember what he said when he walked past us? I know he spoke, but I didn't really hear the words."

"I cannot repeat them." Elena raised her napkin to where her moustache would have been if she had not bleached it away.

"You must tell me, Elena. The man is suspected of committing a very serious crime, & my scrivener, Mr. Cooper, is trying to help the police investigate it."

This was a long stretch of the truth, but it got Elena's attention. "What crime?"

"I do not know."

She looked at me in puzzlement. "How can it help for me to repeat his words?"

"That I do not know, either. But the police want to learn as much about him as they can."

"They are not words I like to say."

She could be so wearisome, & I was about to tell her that when she burst out, "*Putana!* It is what he called us."

"What?" I was both amused & disturbed. "That filthy, frightful person spoke Italian?"

Elena hissed at me, "Of course he did not speak Italian! He said it in English."

"Tell me what he said, Elena. In English, please. It is not so serious. Just a deranged man on the street. It has nothing to do with us."

"He said: *It's whores like this that are the root of all evil.*"

"No."

"*Si.*" Elena crossed herself. "Exactly that."

For a moment I entertained the thought that the man had been some sort of emissary from Papa. But that was ridiculous. The man was a boor, a maniac. I remembered how he had tried to brush against us. And that he stank.

"I didn't hear him say that. I just heard a mutter that I couldn't make out."

"All I can tell you is this is what he said."

"He was a madman." I leaned across the table & squeezed her arm. "Elena, I hope it hasn't been bothering you all these weeks."

She put down her napkin, gripped my hand, & let out a little sob. "I felt the *mal occhio,*" she said.

But Elena is always feeling the *mal occhio.*

I thought perhaps we should talk to Mr. Cooper's detective friend. It would be a diversion. I had looked at his card. *Inquiries of all kinds.* What kind of man would have such a card?

We each had a glass of wine with supper, & afterwards Elena read aloud several chapters of *Sense and Sensibility.* I corrected her pronunciation from time to time, especially of names — she finds *Willoughby* & *Jennings* especially difficult. Elena's fluency is far ahead of her pronunciation, which is adequate to most occasions but warps badly when she is really absorbed. She has asked me to correct her, but of late, whenever I do, she seems testy. I do it anyway.

For the most part, though, I was only half-listening to the troubles of Elinor & Marianne Dashwood. I was thinking. I find that things go best for me if I imagine them thoroughly beforehand. It was my rashness, my lack of *prudence*, that led me into the fiasco with Tomasso, & so now I devote much of my time to planning. I make preparations for events that may or may not take place. Most, in fact, do not — the letter to my father, for one, remains in my head. Lately I have been working out the details of a visit to my aunt. I would hire a carriage — she is too far out in Westville for me to walk alone — & I would not take Elena with me. I haven't decided whether to take Prudence or not. I would wear my most sober dress — not the lilac, maybe my dark blue silk—and my ugliest, oldest bonnet. I would arrive somewhere between three & four on, say, a Thursday afternoon, when I know she is most likely to be alone, sitting over her embroidery. The maid would show me into the drawing room, & — well, beyond that my imagination won't take me with any certainty. Would she refuse to see me? Take one look at me & faint away? Clasp me in her arms & call me her prodigal niece? Lecture me about my sins & then throw me out?

Would such a venture be prudent or reckless? For the moment I give up on it. But I have a great need for something to happen!

By the time Elena began to yawn & look for her bookmark, I resolved that I would send Dora to Mr. Milgrim's office with a request that he call on us. It was not much, but it was something.

And yet—I continued my thoughts as I lay in bed later waiting for sleep — my impulsiveness in Rome was not entirely a disaster. I had begun to flower — I could feel myself opening, like a blossom, like the lush & beautiful roses in our garden. Such happiness. Are we not meant for it? And if it was blighted — well, that does not undo what I once felt, & no one can convince me that those feeling are wrong!

Life cannot be planned in every detail. One has to leave room for the hazards of *la fortuna*.

Chapter Thirteen

"Time has slowed, Charles. It is no longer speeding along like a railroad car," Matthew said. "In that way, at least, an old man can become a boy again."

"You are not an old man."

"Then why do I feel so much like one?"

"Will you eat something, Father?"

"I'm not quite ready, Charles. Maybe later in the afternoon."

Charles took his father's hand. He had returned to Wethersfield to find his father not well at all. He was lying flat on his back in his old metal bed in the back parlor and, except for the V his feet made sticking up at the bottom, he was scarcely a bump in the smooth counterpane. He is fading away, Charles thought. Is it possible to just get smaller and smaller until you are not there at all?

Matthew asked him, as usual, about the Gaudets. Charles didn't tell him about the rift. He talked instead about Bernard's brick-molding contraption. "It's another miracle machine. It saves time, it saves money, it spits out perfect bricks with the speed of a wagon going downhill."

Matthew smiled. "And does it brew a pot of coffee and make doughnuts too?"

"When you're feeling better, perhaps we could take a trip down to New Haven together. Bernard would love to show it to you."

"You know that will not happen, son."

For more than one reason, Charles thought.

Sarah came to the door. "Dr. Pettengill is here, Charles."

Charles relinquished his father's hand. "I will just walk down to the store, Father, and see how things are going."

Pettengill with his pot of leeches. He regretted that his father insisted on calling old Dr. Pettengill, whose ideas about medicine had been formed when the century was new. Charles had always been sickened by the sight of leeches slowly engorging, but Pettengill seemed to love them the way another man might be fond of his horse or his dog — Charles wondered if they had names. He remembered vividly a scene from his childhood when the doctor came with his jar of the creatures to bleed his father for a painful sprained ankle. His favorite leech — a shiny brown thing more than half a foot long — would not fasten on. Pettengill had pricked his own finger with a needle and smeared the blood on Matthew's leg as bait, at which the leech made haste to bite and begin its filthy operation. Charles had fled from the room, gagging. But Matthew swore by the practice. Charles had given up arguing. Sarah would sit with his father while the leeches were at work.

After the last leech was dislodged and taken away in Dr. Pettengill's jar, Charles went in to see Matthew. Louie had leapt back on the bed and was curled up at the foot. Matthew lay with his eyes closed, his chest barely moving. When he lay still, his breathing was so quiet he seemed dead, but as soon as he exerted himself he would gasp and become red in the face. "Not enough blood is being pumped through his body," was the way Dr. Pettengill put it — the blood-letting was meant to ease the congestion.

It seemed to make sense, but after the treatment, the patient was weaker than ever, too exhausted to talk. Charles sat in the chair beside the bed, with just one candle, and watched his father's still face. He knew he resembled Matthew, just as Tamsin did Magda. "The women got all the looks in this family," Matthew used to say, and everyone knew it was true. Charles had his father's small frame and neat features and receding hairline, and he knew they both had a habit of poking their heads forward to make a point or express puzzlement—a habit he had tried without success to break himself of.

And their voices, people often said, were identical — clear and carrying, and often with an ironic edge. Both light baritones, they had sung together in the church choir until Charles stopped attending.

When Matthew didn't speak for a quarter of an hour, Charles said softly, "Father?"

Matthew opened his eyes. "Yes," he said, and sighed. "Those nasty critters did me good, I think." He reached out for Charles's hand. At first Charles had felt awkward sitting with his father's hand in his. But he was getting used to it, and it expressed, he thought, much that they did not say. "Is Tamsin here?"

"Not yet. I've written."

Matthew nodded. "Stay with me."

"I will. And I wondered, Father — I thought I should ask. Do you want me to write to Mother?"

Matthew's eyes had been about to close again, but at Charles's words he started up, and hoisted himself on one elbow. "No! I do not wish you to write to your mother! You must promise me that you will not!" His breathing became labored. "All I want is peace, Charles, and where your mother is there is no peace."

Charles calmed him, promised not to write, and sat at Matthew's bedside until he slept. They all thought it was best that he have someone with him at all times, and a cot was brought in. Calvin had been staying with him during the night, but now that Charles was home, he took over. Louie went back and forth from cot to bed, and often slept draped over Charles's feet. One cool morning he awoke to find the cat tucked under the covers with him, snuggled into his armpit.

He had written to Tamsin:

You should come if you can, and bring the boys. Father is fading. I do not know what ails him, and he is not in pain, but his breathing is not good, any exertion exhausts him, and he has become as thin and frail as an autumn leaf. He wants to see you, Tammy. And so do we all.

The one time his sister and her husband came east to visit was soon after the railroad opened. Charles had not yet married Sophie, Tamsin's twins were not born, and Matthew had been a vigorous man of barely fifty. Tamsin had been less high-spirited than before her marriage, Charles remembered — quiet and agreeable, content with long silences, more eager to help Annie in the kitchen than to sit down with Charles and talk as they used to. Eli hadn't had much to say, either, but was pleasant enough — he had made himself useful around the place, swaggering in a buckskin vest, and tended to drink too much whisky after supper and go up to bed early.

Tamsin's letters had always come regularly, and — partly because they were so terse, so unlike her — Charles had a great need to see her. She had cared for him when he was small, in the days when the feud between their parents had raged like a small guerilla war, with battles breaking out in odd places and at odd times — Charles had more than once been wakened in the middle of the night by their voices. Magda was inclined to furious bursts of anger that could be triggered by something as small as an ant in the sugar, or an expression on Tamsin's face. In one of her malignant fits, she had once thrown a pot at the girl, and it struck her high on the cheekbone, blacking her eye. As Charles grew out of babyhood he too was subject to his mother's temper, and, increasingly, anything any of them did could drive her to harsh words and small bursts of violence.

After she threw nearly every dish in the dining room cupboard at the chimneypiece, she was taken — by Dr. Pettengill, in fact — to the Lunatic Asylum in Middletown, where she spent many months. At first she was strapped down. Tamsin, who was allowed to go with Matthew to visit her, described this to Charles with horror — the straps were filthy, she said, with blood on them, and the buckles rusted, and Mother had spoken to them only in German.

Hers was a classic case of hysteria, her doctor said. But she improved in Middletown. She became quiet and seemed contented, and when she came home she was cheerful, and baked *kuchen*, and told them funny stories about her fellow inmates. Her mood lasted for a few months before it began to erode again under the pressure of whatever it was in her brain that drove her. She was taken to the asylum at intervals throughout Charles's boyhood, and usually went quite willingly, sitting up in Dr. Pettengill's buggy as if she were going to pay a call. There was a doctor there named Jones, who could calm her simply by talking to her. He was very good-looking, Tamsin said, and spoke excellent German. He had been in medical school in Vienna.

"It's a holiday for her," Matthew once said, with bitterness. But Charles knew that his father, like all of them, relished the serenity of the house without Magda in it.

It was Dr. Jones who, after three or four years, met with Matthew and Magda and suggested that they live separately for a time. Magda arranged to move to Pennsylvania and stay with her sister Mina and her husband, Uncle Stanislaus Gruenewalder. Charles had never seen this aunt, but thought kindly of her because she sent him a marzipan pig every Christmas.

They came in a coach to pick her up on a cold day in early winter, soon after Charles's fourteenth birthday. Aunt Mina barely acknowledged Charles and Tamsin, and would not speak to Matthew at all. Aunt Lottie Jessup was there to see her sister off, but Mina paid little attention to her. Charles remembered the long letters his mother had written in the midst of her rages, sitting at her desk in the parlor with her back to the room, still but somehow not calm, like a tinder box that needed only a small spark to ignite it. He always wondered what she had written about him, and about his father and sister and aunt. His mother's malevolence seemed strongest against those who loved her. He wondered too how she would fare in Pennsylvania, if she would feud with her family there as she did with everyone but the cat.

Like her sisters, Aunt Mina was a handsome woman, with heavy blonde hair and a high-bridged nose. The three of them looked remarkably alike — Lottie more delicate, Magda more conventionally pretty. Aunt Mina was wearing a traveling cloak trimmed with tatty fur, and her face was hard under her bonnet. Magda had put on a bonnet with a veil, and she stood in silence while Uncle Stanislaus supervised the strapping of her trunk to the roof and stowed the rest of her luggage. Then he shook hands with Matthew, looking glum. Perhaps the prospect of living in the same house with his troublesome sister-in-law was not quite to his liking. Magda said not a word of good-bye. Stanislaus helped her into the coach, the driver touched his hat brim and clattered off, and they were gone, leaving the Coopers and Aunt Lottie standing in a row by the front gate. It was like the silence the morning after a nor'easter.

Lottie muttered something to herself in German, hugged them all, and returned to her house around the corner. Tamsin and Charles wept, more out of bewilderment than grief, but Matthew's only comment before he went off to the store was, "I wish I minded this more than I do."

Within a week Annie — plump, affectionate, brisk, red-nosed, a distant cousin of the Jessups from New London — began coming in two or three times a week to help Tamsin. Then, just before Christmas, when Annie herself was having trouble at home, she came to stay. They gave her the little chamber under the stairs. She did the cleaning and washing and most of the cooking, and freed Tamsin to work in the store with her father.

Charles told himself he would remember only good things about his mother — her calm, happy days — and not dwell on the quarreling and the broken dishes and the bloody restraints. When things were tranquil, Magda had not been a bad mother. The Legenhausen women were famous for their baking, both in the old country and the new, and — except for the strange periods when her rage at the world was accompanied by a refusal to eat — she was happiest when she put on her apron, pushed up her sleeves, and turned out her specialties: *Bauernbrot*, and sweet buns rolled around a sugar filling, and a sweet, juicy apple strudel with raisins. On one memorable occasion, when Charles was turning ten, she baked him a *Geburtstagskuchen* with toasted meringue on top. (When he said *Geburtstagskuchen* to his father, Matthew responded, "God bless you!") Charles loved hearing German, a big, hospitable language that was somehow like his mother's *kuchen*, or her *stollen*. When he thought of her at her best, she was in the kitchen, sifting flour into the big brown bowl and singing *Blau, blau, blau sind alle meine Kleider, Blau, blau, blau ist alles, was ich hab.* Charles used to sing the old songs with her but softly, too shy of his German to let his voice be heard. He sang them now, sometimes, when he was alone, and they always carried with them the smell of sweets baking in the oven.

The birthday *kuchen* phenomenon had never been repeated: Charles's birthday fell in November, and the coming of cold weather always brought on Magda's worst fits. On his fourteenth birthday, in the midst of her packing, and the stony silence that surrounded it, no one had remembered to make a cake at all.

At first, Matthew himself rode Mavis, the big sorrel mare, down to Manheim and back to deliver the twice-a-year stipend he had agreed to pay his wife. These visits, no matter how brief and businesslike, never went well — there seemed no prospect that his wife would ever return to Wethersfield — and it always took him time to recover, an entire day when he sat with the cat on his lap looking gloomily at nothing. When Charles was eighteen and Tamsin had married Eli Pugh and gone to Ohio with him, he took over for his father, sometimes on horseback but usually going by stagecoach. He looked forward to it every time. Sometimes the visits were agreeable, sometimes not. The shorter the better, he had learned. He had also learned not to cross his mother, to say little and agree to much, but as years went by he would sometimes rebel, and a ruckus would inevitably break out before he left, usually over something so small that no one but Magda was ever sure exactly what it had been — but the consequences were dire. The food was always toothsome and plentiful, but the atmosphere was unendurable.

Matthew's condition was unchanged for a week. He ate almost nothing and slept nearly all the time, getting out of bed only when absolutely necessary. They took turns sitting with him — Aunt Lottie came almost every day. She brought him a mess of red cabbage stewed with vinegar and caraway, which he always had loved, but he ate only a little. Once or twice a day he sat propped up, and someone would try to spoon some broth into him, or tea. Charles picked a small handful of early raspberries and got his father to eat a few of them. Sarah had the idea of whipping cream into a froth with maple syrup and feeding him a few spoonfuls, which he ate eagerly. "That is what he was waiting for," she said happily. "I'll give him some more later. It will build him up in no time." But later he just turned his head away.

When Charles wasn't with his father or in the store, he sat on the folding chair on the porch, reading the books Calvin lent him. He had read some stories by Mr. Poe, including the ones about C. August Dupin — "The Purloined Letter" was especially interesting to him, the idea that the solution to a problem could be right before your nose. A brilliant concept, he thought, and wished he could talk it over with Milgrim. Then he began the first volume of a new Dickens novel, *Martin Chuzzlewit.* Calvin had chuckled steadily all the way through, and pressed it on him as the funniest book he had ever read, but it seemed to Charles that Mr. Dickens had lost all his geniality when he sent his hero to an America that he depicted as a land of boors and idiots.

Still, the book kept his mind from the thoughts of Lily Prescott that were tormenting him, and from his other cares — his father's increasing weakness, the store to be run, goods to be ordered, tradesmen dealt with, orders taken and filled. They ran out of the good China tea Matthew had always carried, and for a day or two no one had any idea how to get more — their usual supplier had died and his importing business was defunct — until Sarah remembered that she had seen a flier about a coffee and tea merchant in Hartford. She drove there herself in the wagon and sought him out. Sarah, it must be said, was in her element.

At night, before he dropped off to sleep on his cot, Charles had difficulty keeping Lily Prescott out of his head. He had been so positive, while he sat with the Gaudets and endured their disappointment in him, that even after such a brief acquaintance he loved her enough to marry her. *I love you passionately, and every day without you is an agony to me.* She had said the words jokingly, but the eagerness in her face — that must have meant something. Their intimacy had been great — it was not his imagination.

Now, back in the humdrum world of Wethersfield and the store and the sad reality of his father's drift toward death, he was not so sure. Marriage? Was he brave enough? He had a sense that any streak of Bohemianism he might have in him was about the size of a fingernail paring. He needed to think about it — what he really needed, he thought, was a solid week, alone, with no distractions, to ponder what it would mean to marry Lily Prescott. What he did know was that he wanted her, as a woman. Just to touch her, he thought to himself — just to place his hand on her breast. Just to put his lips on her bare shoulder. He had never experienced anything so powerful as that desire.

He didn't dream of her — or not that he was aware of — but he was dreaming often of Sophie. Not only the nightmare, though he woke from it, sobbing, once, and it stayed with him that whole day, like a reproach. On another night he woke up spent and gasping from a dream in which he had begged her to take him in her mouth, *please, please Sophie, do it because you love me,* and she had done it, just as she had in life, and she had not liked it any better in the dream. He lay awake with the thought nibbling at his mind — no matter what he did to kill it — that Lily would not shrink from it, she would like it, she would want it.

In the daylight, he was ashamed of his thoughts, and especially for having them in the room where his father slept. But not so ashamed that he didn't return willingly to the picture, night after night, of Lily in his bed. Twice he drafted letters to her, trying to express the idea that he missed her company. *Our lessons were a very great joy pleasure to me, I miss you them very much and am sorry they had to end so soon,* was the least stilted sentence he wrote, and it was sadly inadequate to his purpose, which was to convey his feeling for her without seeming pitiable. He wasted a good deal of paper and decided it would be best not to write at all but to wait for her to write to him, as she said she might. And then suddenly, one afternoon, he dashed off a note that said very little: he had enjoyed the lessons, hoped she had as well, trusted she was getting on with her penmanship, and hoped to see her soon but his father was declining. It was only a few sentences long, but every word gave him misgivings, and finally he stuck it into an envelope, sealed it, and posted it before he could tear the thing up.

He was also intermittently preoccupied, especially when he sat by his father's bed, with the question of his mother. In spite of everything, she was still Matthew's wife, and it felt wrong not to write and tell her he was dying. He considered doing so, despite his father's wishes, but he couldn't bring himself to not only disobey his father but disturb the peace of the sickroom — and disturbed it would be, whether she was distraught and grieving or cold and indifferent or angling for a bigger inheritance than what Matthew had left her. Charles recalled the last time he'd seen his mother, the way she had looked at him, almost with dislike, taking, without a thought, the side of his cousin against him, and it occurred to him that when his father was dead he might never have to see her again. The prospect was complicated.

Something else about his mother had begun to nag at him, and he kept trying to puzzle it out, but it would not come to him.

On Saturday afternoon, when he had been home a little more than a week, he fell into a doze as he was reading on the porch. Annie shook his shoulder. She had been sitting with Matthew. "Something is happening," she said. "He is agitated, and his breathing is different. I think you should come."

When they got to the doorway, Matthew had quieted and was lying back again on the pillow, his face calm and his eyes closed. "He is better, thank God," Annie said, but Charles sensed that the silence was of a kind he had never heard before, and when he approached the bed, he saw that his father was dead.

Annie and Aunt Lottie washed the body, wrapped it in a sheet, and laid it out on the bed where Matthew had died. Charles visited the coffin-maker. Annie sponged Charles's old black coat clean and replaced a button, and made armbands for him and Calvin, and trimmed a black bonnet for herself. At intervals throughout the day, Charles could hear her weeping.

They closed the store for two days, and on the second a crowd followed the coffin to the burial ground behind the Congregational Church just across High Street. It was lowered into a grave near those of Matthew's parents and his sister Kate, who had died in childbirth thirty years before, and her baby, Jeremiah, who had died with her. Her husband had married again and lived in Vermont. There was a place in the plot for Magda, who might or might not lie in it someday.

Everyone in Wethersfield patronized the Cooper General Store, everyone knew Matthew, and everyone was grieved at his death. Charles shook half a hundred hands and listened to half a hundred tearful appreciations of his father's goodness and honesty and humor.

He kept putting off writing to his mother. The proper thing to do, he knew, was to go to Manheim and tell her, and he kept making excuses to himself about why he couldn't. He did write to the Gaudets — this was painful enough — to tell them Matthew was gone. He wrote nothing else and he signed it, after some thought, *Respectfully, Charles Cooper.* They would want to know, and they might be glad that Charles had wanted to tell them.

He wrote again to Tamsin, wishing she were there and vaguely angry that she was not. In fact, in the days after Matthew's death and burial, what he felt more strongly than anything was a general-ized resentment at, it seemed, most of the world. At his mother for abandoning him. At Bernard and Emily for being cruel and unrea-sonable. At his father, of course, for leaving him not only bereft of his favorite companion, the father who was a continual delight to him, but in the position of being head of the family, a position he did not relish.

He was lonely, despondent, irritable. He had a hankering to play a game of chess, to take his mind off things, but Matthew was the only person he liked to play with — they were not great players, but they were evenly matched. The house was empty without his father, no matter how many people were in it. Neighbors kept stopping by. Aunt Lottie came over daily, exuding wordless sympathy and bringing food, until he finally told her it wasn't necessary, hurting her feelings. Back in his own bed, he was sleeping badly, expecting every night to be awakened by some need of his father's. He wanted nothing more than to fill his knapsack and spend a week alone tramping in the woods as he used to do when he was younger, camping out, fishing, thinking about the complications of his life. What he had to do instead was go through his father's belongings and give things away, go over the will with the lawyer, be a comfort to Sarah, who tended to break down in tears in the middle of measuring out a pound of lard. Decide whether to rebuild the ancient chicken coop in the back yard or tear the whole thing down, patch the hole in the barn roof — noisy jobs that he had put off while his father was lying sick in the back parlor.

Each day was an eternity — it was as Matthew said: time had slowed to a crawl, but not in a good way, not the way it did in the world of a child. He had never felt more adult, more called upon to make decisions and get things done. On one particularly hot afternoon he and Annie dismantled Matthew's bed and carried it upstairs, then cleaned the downstairs rooms, both of them dripping with sweat. On another day he stood behind the counter at the store to give Sarah some time away, and he snapped twice at Calvin for slacking off — the second time, he could see, offending his cousin deeply, but he didn't apologize. The post office was an adjunct to the general store, a shed with a counter and Zeke Robbins behind it smoking his pipe and trying to look busy, and Charles began to haunt it, waiting for word from Tamsin, or from Lily, or from Harold Milgrim with news of the Chillick case — that, at least, would distract him from his own troubles. But he said to himself that nothing, nothing would ever happen to him again. He was twenty-eight years old, and his life was over.

Toward the end of the week, he had a letter from Lily, which must have crossed his in the mail. At first he could only stare at the writing on the envelope, his heart pounding. He had wanted a letter so desperately that it was hard to take in the fact that he was actually holding it, that it was written in her own, unmistakable uphill-slanting hand. Zeke Robbins was watching him with interest, and Charles walked across the street and sat on the back porch, alone, before he tore it open:

Dear Mr. Cooper,

You left New Haven at just the wrong time. What good progress I was making with my letters — was I not? And now you see what is happening to my N's and my H's! And as for the consistency that you bewailed the lack of — well, the inconsistency of my consistency is more consistent than ever!

I do practice. And, not having much else to do, I practice a good deal. I bought a rather beautiful notebook at the stationery store and have begun keeping a journal, if for nothing else than to inscribe the humdrum details of my life in beautiful lettering. (This may be compared to using a Chinese vase to display a bouquet of pigweed and dandelions!) But just as my piano-playing has suffered without the guidance of Signora Boldoni (the martinet who taught me in Rome), my penmanship continues to be distinctly off-key no matter how much I work at it.

Your Mr. Milgrim called on us, to hear Elena's and my impressions of the rude man on the Green. How different the same event can be to two people who may witness it! Elena has the man wearing a black cap and black gloves. He had teeth missing, and he made a rude remark to us in a voice that was as clear (despite the teeth!) as a bell. He then walked off in the direction of Chapel Street. The man I saw was bare-headed and gloveless but had filthy hands and muttered something under his breath and went off to the north, toward Elm Street. Poor Mr. Milgrim probably found the two of us to be unreliable and useless witnesses. But he was very polite. He certainly seems quite intelligent enough to catch the fellow he's after, especially if you are helping him do it!

And now I look back and observe what a self-centered opening sentence that was. I do apologize, and sincerely hope this letter finds your father much improved in health and appetite. I hope too that you will soon find your way back to the Elm City and be my scrivener version of Signora Boldoni again!

With my very good wishes, your faithful
Lily Prescott

Charles put the letter down and looked out at Annie's sunflowers in the long back garden, the waist-high rows of corn, the barn roof against the blue sky, his aunt's house in the distance with its brick turret. What a beautiful world it was, in spite of his woes, and perhaps his life was not quite over.

Chapter Fourteen

14 June, Saturday. How to write about this? It is better not to, I know, & yet it is so alive in me, it has in a way taken over my life, & now I have been writing in this journal for so long that when something happens I must put it in.

Mr. Milgrim came to ask Elena & me questions about that man on the Green. Elena would not tell him what she had heard, about whores like us being the root of all evil. I had to say it, & Elena just nodded, shame-faced. He was gentle with her, & he asked her other questions that she answered, but all the time he was looking at me. And I was looking at him.

It was like seeing Tomasso in the stable yard.

Harold has now been here four times. He comes in the afternoon & stays until suppertime. And then twice has come back. We talk. We talk, & we become more & more free. It is hard not to be free with him! He is much like me, I think — he cares little for convention, a quality he was born with I am sure, & that I have acquired by necessity. I have never met anyone like him. Is this what is called love at first sight? I feel like a giddy schoolgirl. I have been overwhelmed before — with James, & then with Tomasso. But this is something else.

At first — after that moment when he walked into the parlor & it was like being hit with something — at first he seemed silly, he is what Aunt Julia would call a *rattle*. But soon —

I need to write — just writing, Mr. Cooper, dear Charles, nothing beautiful, no attempts at art, just my old *running hand*, as you would call it. Running uphill, of course. The writing is a help to me, no matter what I write or how tired I get. Harold. Harold. I want to see him on paper so I can study him. I want to understand who he is. The writing pins him down for me. So he won't fly away.

I know he likes the way I look because he has told me so, & not only once. But he didn't have to tell me. I see it. I like the way we talk to each other. He does not defer to me the way Mr. Cooper does. He talks to me as if we were both men, or both women! And he talks too much, he seems to know everything, & if he doesn't, then he pretends he does, he invents it, with that gleam in his eye. He makes me laugh, sometimes in spite of myself — but it's so good to laugh!

Then he looks at me & falls silent, & this is when I like him best. His eyes are as blue as the sky — eyes are often compared to the sky, but in this case with truth. I have never seen such a clear, bright blue, as if there's a light behind them. He is tall & slender, but solid, somehow. He is clean-shaven, & his features seem carved, the skin of his face tight to the bone. He wears his clothes with distinction, & they are like the clothes of no one else. The way he looks — the way all the pieces of him are assembled — is perfect. To me, at least.

He is also rich. I know who the Milgrims are. Father painted a picture of Harold's grandmother's house, I think, or his great-aunt's. And had some sort of flirtation, or worse, with — another aunt? Or a cousin? It was during one of the summers we spent in New Haven because father feared the *mal' aria* in Rome. I was preoccupied with my friends — this was at the height of my intimacy with Margaret Brock & Lizzie Dale & Sally Carlisle. We were still just girls, we still wore ringlets & pantalettes. We walked to and from Miss Derrin's Seminary together every day, pretending not to look at the rowdy boys from the grammar school playing ball on the Green. We were in & out of each other's houses all that summer, & Margaret & I pricked our fingers & swore we would be best friends forever, & then Sally & I did the same thing. Such foolishness! Such fun!

But behind everything, there was always Papa, more important than anyone, bigger than anyone. Orlando Prescott is a large figure in every way. Everyone noticed him as he strode through town, or rode in the brougham, with his fat brown beard, wearing his red bow ties & the beautiful waistcoats that he had made for him in Rome. I used to think: This is my Papa! I was so proud of him. And he of me when I sat at his side. You are my pet bird, he would say. My rusty robin. My golden daughter.

He painted at least a dozen local scenes every summer, for his gallery in New York — sunset views from the top of East Rock, & shoreline scenes from Branford & Milford — those were what he liked best — & he painted the three churches on the Green. Every artist who has ever set foot in New Haven for more than a day has painted the three churches on the Green. But he also had commissions for some of the grand houses in town.

I liked to go with him. Mr. Joseph Fellowes, Papa's assistant, would precede us in the buggy & set up the easel & arrange the palette & put out my father's rags & turpentine. There was a parasol that could be put up over the whole apparatus if the sun was too hot. Mr. Fellowes knew just what to do so that all Papa had to do was wield his brush!

Mr. Fellowes was a very mediocre artist who worshiped Papa & would have helped him for nothing, but in fact Papa paid him well & encouraged his wretched work. Even I, at thirteen, could see how bad it was. But Papa loved anyone who painted, who had the soul of an artist. Mr. Fellowes had the soul but lacked the talent, which my father thought was tragic, & so he was especially nice to him.

Papa liked to paint either early in the morning, when I did not usually accompany him, or toward evening, when I often did. We would bring a picnic supper, & I would sit on the grass with my book. Papa didn't like to pause for a formal meal, though when I wasn't with him, he sometimes did have dinner with various Fosters & Footes & Milgrims. There were always so many people at those houses, they always have immense families. I may even have seen Harold Milgrim, one of the young men who played tennis or made up boating parties or drove out in a wagonette, singing & making noise the way the puppies of the rich are allowed to do.

The Milgrims have long been in the shipping industry, as I recall — sea captains, and ship builders, and the West Indies trade, and other things I am not aware of but which make them a great deal of money. Some Milgrim or other has a large establishment at Long Wharf, which Papa was also commissioned to paint, with the harbor and a ship or two in the background. Papa has great respect for people who make money, & he used to like talking about the Milgrims & their vast web of relations. They were philanthropists, too, he said with approval, whose money paid for libraries & foundling homes & hospitals, & they also had an interest in a natural history museum that was planned at Yale.

I'm astonished at how much Papa told me remained stored away in my head & how much I can bring back, now that I have reason to.

Harold Hopkins Milgrim. I write his name in this notebook, over & over, with every frill & flourish I'm capable of. I wish I knew everything about him. And perhaps, as these days go by, I shall.

In my newly reformed scribble, I sent a letter to my scrivener. I thought it would be odd if I didn't tell him I had met Mr. Milgrim. Poor Charles — I am going to call him Charles now, to prove that I'm a hussy. His father is gravely ill, his woes are no doubt many, but I know that he thinks about me — I wonder how often, & what those thoughts are. Charles is true-hearted, that I also know. He reminds me of Mortimer, the old dog — a comparison that doesn't sound very nice, but I mean it in a complimentary way! I miss Mortimer so very much.

I don't yet know enough about Harold to compare him to anyone else, or to judge his capacity for devotion. In a way, I don't even care. The excitement is the way I feel. As if I were young & carefree & being chased down a path in a Roman garden.

We played piano-fiddle duets one evening — he brought over a volume of Busoni — & it made us both happy, though the music we produced kept reducing us to laughter. He is even more inept on the violin than I am at the spinet! Which is also sorely in want of tuning. But then so was his fiddle.

Yes, I think there is such a condition as love at first sight. That doesn't mean it will be a love for the ages, & I try not to give in to the temptation to believe it is. Or even to hope it. I tell myself that his function is to divert me from my troubles for as long as he wishes to.

Still, it's sometimes people of very rich & very secure families who are the least bound by convention. At least in Rome that's true.

Yesterday, Elena told me, was the feast of St. Anthony, her favorite among the saints. He is the patron saint of hopeless cases. She often prays to him, though she didn't tell me what are the hopeless cases that have troubled her. "Did he help?" I asked, & she said, very positively, "Oh yes!"

Would it not be delightful to believe such nonsense?

Chapter Fifteen

Charles was sitting on the front porch with the cat one evening after supper when a coach pulled up and Tamsin got out. The driver deposited two suitcases and a canvas carrier on the front walk. Charles leapt from his chair and lifted the two boys down from the step — David and Maddox, age six, who looked exactly alike — and clasped his sister in his arms.

"Tammy! I can't begin to tell you how glad I am that you're here."

"Then don't," she said, pulling away and holding up her hand. "I'm so tired, Charles, and the boys are half-dead. I don't mean to be discourteous — oh, it is so good to see you — how old you look! — but we have traveled all night. We need only to go to sleep."

"Wait — no." He picked up the two suitcases, hauled them up to the porch. The boys were trying to carry the canvas bag between them, but Charles took that too. "I have to tell you." He held the door open, and the boys filed in. "Tamsin — you have not had my letter yet. You could not. I have to tell you, Father is dead. We buried him on Tuesday."

She sat down suddenly on the top step. "Oh, Charles, I can't be without Father! I have left Eli, and my boys and I have come home to stay." She sat crying while the twins, broad-faced boys who looked remarkably like their blond Pennsylvania cousins, stood solemnly on the other side of the door.

Annie came out on the porch, and when Tamsin saw her she stood up and seemed to collapse into Annie's arms. Annie held her, looking at Charles over Tamsin's head with the tears leaking from her own eyes. Charles had the mad thought that only his father would be able to comfort them all — if only he were there, and Tamsin could weep on his shoulder!

After a minute, Tamsin gave a massive sigh, stood straight, smoothed her hair. "I am so sorry I didn't come a week ago. I would have liked to see him just once more." She wiped her eyes on her sleeve. "Tell me what he died of, Charles."

"He seemed to die of nothing. He wasted away. He was never in pain. He died easily." *Agitated*, Annie had said. *Struggling.* But Charles could no more think of this than he could think of Sophie and the baby in flames. And his sister did not need to hear it. "Dr. Pettengill thinks something was blocking the blood to his heart. He just got weaker and weaker until he was gone."

"Poor Father." Tamsin leaned against him, and he realized how thin she was. *Skinny as a bag of sticks,* his mother used to say. "I so looked forward to seeing him when I arrived. I imagined him with his arms outstretched. How his face would light up. I imagined —"

She was about to break down again, but Annie stepped in. "Look at those children. Dropping where they stand. You're David? Maddox? Then you're David. Do they want supper, Tamsin?"

"We had sandwiches on the road."

"Then come inside, young gentlemen, and wash your faces and we'll find you something to sleep in. Your uncle's old nightshirts have been waiting for an occasion like this."

Charles had nearly forgotten he was an uncle. It struck him suddenly that everything was changed. His father was gone, his sister was here, he was no longer Matthew's son but Tamsin's brother and the uncle of a pair of six-year-old boys.

"Come," he said to his sister. He put his arm around her narrow shoulders and led her inside. "We'll make a pot of tea in the kitchen and then you can be off to bed, too."

Annie went upstairs to prepare the bed in Matthew's old room for the boys. Tamsin's bedroom had long been used as Annie's sewing room, doubling as a study for Charles, but there was still a small bed that could be made up for her. Tamsin kissed the boys and they followed Annie — obviously exhausted, but still remarkably docile children, Charles thought.

Tamsin sat at the kitchen table, looking around as if she had never seen it before. "What has happened to mother's old breadboard? And those checkered curtains — oh, Charles, there is so much to say."

"Would you rather go to sleep now and talk in the morning?"

"No. I'm awake now. We all managed to sleep a little on the train, and I even dozed off in the coach from the station. We took the train to Hartford, and then I hired the stagecoach to bring us here."

"You should have written to tell me you were coming!"

"I left on an impulse."

"Just as you left ten summers ago."

He had forgotten her self-mocking laugh. "So I did. Perhaps ten years from now I shall do a third impulsive thing."

The kettle was hot, and he poured water into the pot with a handful of tea leaves. Strong tea was what she needed.

"Father's famous China tea," Tamsin said, inhaling it. "Have you sugar?"

He had forgotten she liked her tea sweet. He put the sugar bowl in front of her and watched her spoon it into her cup, saw how the sinews stood out on the backs of her hands. The boniness of her wrists. Her blonde hair was coarse and uncared for. Her face was all hollows and angles, her cheekbones sharp, her skin not good, and her eyes looked as if they had not closed in a week. In the dimming light, she looked forty.

"Tam. Are you all right?"

"No, I am not all right." Then she took a sip of her tea and sighed deeply. "But it's good to be here. Talk to me, Charles."

They talked until nearly midnight, first in the kitchen, then when Annie shooed them out, on the porch, and when the bats began to fly — Tamsin hated bats — Charles brought the lamp inside to the parlor. Late as it was, the smell of sugar and butter cooking together came from the kitchen: Annie was baking a coffee cake for breakfast.

139

Tamsin unlaced her boots and kicked them off — one landed upside down, exposing a sole with a hole in it — and stretched herself out on the old brocade settee, propped on a pillow she had embroidered ten years before. She held another to her chest as if it were her old doll.

In the light from the lamp on the wall, he could see how tired she was — a fatigue that perhaps had nothing to do with a train ride from Ashtabula to Hartford.

"You don't want to go to sleep, Tam?"

"Not yet." She suppressed a smile. "You remind me so much of father."

He ignored that. "What is this with you and Eli?"

Her face was suddenly completely without expression — her face like her letters, communicating nothing.

"Tam?"

"I cannot live with him any longer," she burst out. "I — He —" Her voice wavered, and she began to chew on her lower lip, struggling with what she wanted to say. Her teeth were still white and even — the famous Legenhausen teeth, all the women had them. "When he is drunk and they get in his way, he beats the boys, and — no, he doesn't beat me, but he —"

"What is it?"

She shook her head. "It's too hard. I just got here. I will tell you eventually."

Eli Pugh was a Welshman who had come from the coal mines in Cardiff to work at the charcoal kiln in Glastonbury. He was tall and black-haired and devilishly handsome, and he was a champion on the fiddle, not only the songs everyone knew but polkas and waltzes and even classical pieces he had picked up somewhere. If he heard something once, he could play it. He was fiddling at a dance where Tamsin stood watching him until he noticed her, set down his fiddle, and got someone to introduce them.

Matthew didn't like Eli's roughness and his volatile temper. "He is like your mother!" he had said once to Tamsin. "The same feeling comes over me when I watch Eli Pugh that I used to have with your mother, that a volcano was about to erupt."

Tamsin wouldn't speak to her father for a week after that. She would hear nothing against Eli, even when he decided, suddenly, that the smart thing for a collier to do was to settle in farm country and deal in horses. Tamsin thought it was a splendid plan. All he had to do was pick up his fiddle, or turn his deep-set brown eyes on her, and she was gone. Charles saw it happen. Tamsin was twenty-six and beginning to think she would never meet a man she liked, and so within six months she had headed west in a flimsy buckboard wagon with a man none of those left behind liked or trusted.

"I suspected something was wrong, Tam. You letters have been sparse, and silent."

That made her laugh. "You have always had a funny way with words, Charles. Of course they were silent. Letters by their nature are silent. They cannot help it."

"You know what I mean. Your letters said nothing!"

She put her head back against the arm of the settee, closed her eyes. "He had to read the letters before they were mailed. He had to approve. I didn't dare put a word wrong. He is a brute, Charles. You see how the boys look. They are near afraid to breathe. But it wasn't just that," she went on. "We have lived all these eight years and more in the house made of logs that Eli built when we first got to Ohio. It was supposed to be temporary shelter, and we were always going to go on to Ashtabula and open a livery stable, but we could never afford to do anything but try to survive. He did put a room on the back of the cabin, where the boys slept — so badly built the walls would shake in the wind, and the roof leaked. The truth is, Eli would rather drink and play his fiddle than work."

Maybe it was the flies that finally drove her away, she said. "Eli keeps four horses — he hires them out, but only when nothing better is to be had. They are ancient nags, Charles — they are the horses he could afford. The stable is neater and tighter than the cabin. But it was built very near it — Eli doesn't have the sense of a bag of oats! So imagine the flies. They would come in through the cracks — a plague of them, every summer. I'd put the boys to it. They would mix mud with water, or mash paper into a paste, or stuff the cracks with bits of old clothing — though mostly we wore our old clothing until it was rags. The flies would light everywhere, they spoiled the food, fly-specks all over everything. I would sweep up great heaps of them. And the heat in the summer — oh, Charles, do you know what it's like to make candles on a hot day in July?"

"You made your own candles?"

She just looked at him. "I made my own everything."

Charles thought of his father's store, with its neat rack of candles, and oil lamps hanging from hooks, shelves of overalls and calico and sturdy boots. It was good that Matthew hadn't known all this. Though if he had known, he would have sent Charles to bring her back. Charles knew that he was still angry with her for leaving them all, to move so far away — so easily, it seemed — so glad to go. They had missed her badly. How could she not have missed them? He had thought this a hundred times in the years since she left, and consolation for them all had been that she was, at least, happy there, she was with the man she loved, however much they might disapprove. And now she was revealing him as a man who had no sense, who cared nothing for her comfort, who drank too much. What a waste, he thought — his beautiful, gifted sister.

"But I had my hens," Tamsin said. A smile softened her face. Her beauty was still there, somewhere — hidden by trouble. "My girls. They were all red hens, and I named them Rosie and Scarlet and Cherry and Ruby. Beautiful plump birds, and they were good layers, all of them, except for once when Scarlet went broody, and — " She began to weep as she talked, but caught herself. "I know. It's silly to cry over my chickens. I gave them to Nancy, my neighbor, who drove us to the train in Ashtabula. Eli would have let them die. He wanted the egg money, I can tell you that! But the chickens could have been machines made of wood and metal for all he cared about them."

"But he didn't beat you," he said. "Does that mean he was good to you? Surely Eli loves you, Tam."

"Oh yes, he loves me." She suddenly began to laugh. "Yes, he loves me! He loves me so much he cannot keep his hands off me, his filthy hands. If I had one night's peace in eight years it's only because he passed out at somebody else's house and didn't make it home. He took his pleasure of me whenever he wanted — in the afternoon, even, when the boys were just outside playing in the yard, and I'd be kneading bread in the kitchen, or cleaning out the ashes from the grate — he would come up behind me — he would not let me say no, he would force himself on me, he — " She turned her head into the cushion and said in a muffled voice, "I never argued with him. Because of Mother and Father. Arguing to me is like poison, or like the flaring up of a disease that can kill you if you let it spread. So I said very little. I just — I grew to hate him." She wiped her eyes and sat up. "Forgive me. These are not things you want to know."

"It's all right, Tam."

"I have had three miscarriages," she said wearily. "And thank God for them. Imagine if we had had more children in that house. Imagine raising a daughter with such a brute of a man. In such a place." Her face crumpled up again. "The last one — last year — it went quite late, it was so small, but perfect — it was a girl. I would have named her Elizabeth. My little Betsy. And I was glad, Charles, when she was born dead. Glad!"

"Hush," was all he could say. "Hush, Tammy. You're home now. We'll take care of you."

❧

Charles had another sleepless night. His mind started with the chicken coop — if Tamsin was here to stay, he would fix it up for her and stock it with the prettiest hens in Hartford County — but soon drifted to Lily Prescott. She was like his evening prayer — the last thing he thought of before he went to sleep. *Your faithful Lily Prescott.* She had signed herself that way twice. What did it mean? Anything? Nothing? Everything? *I hope you will soon return to the Elm City.* A conventional sentiment, or an echo of what he had seen in her eyes when he left her last? He had read her letters so many times they were ragged, but he was no closer to extracting her real feelings from them than the day they'd arrived.

He wished he could tell Tamsin about her — what little there was to tell. *I am in love, desperately in love, with a woman I have known for six weeks. A woman with a baby whose father is a mystery. I think of her constantly.*

The old Tamsin would tell him to follow his heart. The heart has needs that do not have to be justified, that no one else has to understand. Take the next train to New Haven and tell her how you feel!

And the Tamsin of today would tell him to forget Lily Prescott and put such nonsense out of his head.

He would tell his sister exactly nothing.

Toward morning he slept, and when he awoke he knew he had dreamt of Lily — at last — but the details eluded him. He lay there in frustration, trying to catch hold of the tail of the dream and bring it back. Something about a bracelet? Was she peeling a piece of fruit? Was there a silver knife?

He gave up and got out of bed, feeling tired and out of sorts. A good day to knock apart the old chicken coop and put it together again. What else did his life hold but such mundane chores?

It was late. The twins were already outside, and Tamsin sat at the kitchen table talking to Annie. She looked better after she had slept, and bathed, and washed her hair, and braided it into two plaits. In an old calico dress she had worn when she was twenty, she was almost like herself again, except that the dress hung on her.

"If you give me a needle and thread, I'll take it in," she was saying to Annie, and Annie said, "Let us help you fill it out instead. We'll have you plump as a pumpkin in no time."

Annie had made a blueberry cake, and almost half of it had already been eaten. Tamsin cut a piece for her brother. "Mother's *blaubeere kuchen* recipe, Charles. Oh Lord. How is she? We didn't get to that last night. It's hard for me not to think of her as dead. But she is not dead. Do you still go to see her?"

Charles poured himself coffee from the pot on the stove and sat down. Annie did her best, but the *kuchen* was nowhere near as light as Magda's. "I was there in May. She is very much alive and kicking. Mostly kicking."

"I wonder how she took the news of Father."

Charles had not yet written to her. Tamsin made him get out paper and pen and ink and do it at once, in the middle of his coffee and cake. "It is unfair not to tell her."

"I thought the lawyer could do it," he said, ashamed of himself, trying to keep crumbs off his paper. "I know that was wrong. It's just that I've seen her too recently. The experience has not entirely worn off."

"She is unchanged."

"No, she is very much changed, I think. She is better away from Father, away from us all. But she is still Mother. She is difficult and unpleasant and says whatever comes into her mind, no matter how cruel. She seems not to care a fig for any of us."

"Oh — *that*. Our mother hates us?" Her smile was rueful. "I got used to that long ago."

"She was a mother like no one else's."

"That she was. Do you remember the look she would get in her eyes, Charles? *The convulsive stare*, her doctor called it. What was his name? Dr. Jones. It was the look of someone about to go on a murderous rampage! And she nearly did, once or twice."

Tamsin looked more like their mother than ever. Looking at her, Charles saw his mother's face, and could almost see the look in her eyes that his sister was talking about. "Yes," he said, and something clicked in his brain. "I remember. I used to hide when I saw it coming."

"And yet now, after living with Eli for all these years, I wonder about her madness. They called her hysterical, and hysteria can mean anything, as long as it's applied to a female. If I were a doctor, I'd prescribe extra help in the house. Mother was overworked, if you ask me. She was exhausted, and irritable, and she needed a rest. The asylum gave her one! That's all her famous cure was about. A little time to herself."

"If it were that simple."

"You have never kept house. Especially when pregnant. I remember well when we moved into the new house, Mother standing in the doorway as the furniture was carried in. She was happy about the house, of course she was, but she wept a little, too. You may not remember this, you were probably out in the barn with the horses, or up in your new bedroom with your toys, but she almost got into one of her states that day."

"Because —?"

"It is twice as big, she said. What will *Frühlingsputz* be like?"

"I do not know *Frühlingsputz*."

"Spring cleaning."

An image came to him of a furious Magda, her skirts tied up, a rag around her hair, down on her knees, scrubbing and scouring and muttering to herself in a mixture of German and English. "How could I forget?"

"Dirt made her almost as angry as we did." Tamsin smiled. "Before the summer is over, I'm going to take David and Maddox and visit her."

Charles raised his eyebrows. "Don't say I didn't warn you."

"There is much I would like to talk about with my mother." Tamsin took another piece of *kuchen*. "This is not bad. Just not very German."

"Our Annie is pure New England."

"A people not renowned for their cooking. And I can say that because I'm one of them." She brushed the crumbs from the front of her dress and said, "You probably don't know that Mother lost babies, too. Two, I think, in those eight years between you and me."

"I did not know. Father never told me."

"That is so like Father. *Can we talk about something less unpleasant, please?*"

"Tam — he has been dead less than a week. Don't speak ill of him."

"Oh Lord, Charles, you know I loved him. I went to his grave this morning, across the way — seeing his name there, chiseled into the stone, was —"

"I know. It's hard to believe he is gone."

146

"He was the dearest man on earth. He saw his duty very seriously, to make up to us for all that Mother was not."

"He did that."

"He did. But — you know, Charles, I have tried very hard over the years to understand our mother. Perhaps Father was not perfect. And temperamentally he and Mother were not a good match. She was all Teutonic *weltschmerz*, he was all Yankee optimism. Though they were very passionate together when they were younger. When I was a little girl, before you were born."

"How could you know something like that?"

"You just do. I would see them together. Mother used to try to teach Father German — naughty words, I think."

"Like what?"

She laughed. "Like none of your business, Charles!"

"I wish I had known about the lost babies."

"They helped her to her madness, I think — and that's something I can understand."

Charles frowned. "No. No matter what your sorrows were, you were never like Mother. I refuse to believe it."

"My madness was different. I turned it inward. Our place in Geneva Township was no more than a mile from the Grand River, and more than once I was tempted. But there were always my boys. They were what saved me. Twins! I nearly died when they were born. There was blood from the cabin to the creek, it seemed!"

"Damn it, Tamsin! You told us none of this!"

"I would have. You can't think how badly I wanted saving! But I could not. And Charles — I know almost nothing about what happened to you. Your wife, your baby son."

"I suppose we'll get to that."

She shook her head sadly. "As a family, we have not been fortunate in our marriages, have we?"

The arrival of his sister did not prevent Charles from listening desperately every day for the whistle of the train that brought the post, then hanging around in front of the post office while Zeke, with infuriating slowness, opened the pouch and sorted the mail.

Tamsin had been home a week before anything arrived for him. He walked over to the post office on a hot afternoon. As always, he imagined a letter from her, saw the creamy paper she used and his name in her handwriting. He had answered Lily's last letter with the news about his father's death, and a hope that he would see her before much longer. He had heard nothing from her, and there was nothing from her in that day's post, but there was the letter he had been awaiting from Harold Milgrim.

He sat down on the steps of the store to read it. Word had come at last from England: Samuel Chillick's friend Edward Davenport, before he set off on his Welsh expedition, had vouched for Chillick's alibi. He had been with him on the evening in question until quite late. The *Delta* had been set to sail on the morning tide, and the passengers had embarked the evening before. Chillick had come aboard, drunk whiskey in his friend's cabin, and dined with the captain. The captain added a note, saying he had welcomed Mr. Chillick aboard at approximately six o'clock on Wednesday evening, May seventh, and had seen him and the other guests off the vessel sometime before nine, which is when all guests were required to return to shore. Milgrim wrote:

I think it would be useful if you informed Mr. Chillick of this development. I would come up to Wethersfield myself to do so, but I am very much occupied here. And I would call on our Hartford colleagues to do it, but I fear they would have the same reaction as Inspector Durward here in New Haven — to wit, a complete lack of interest. And, as we know, it does mean very little. But as we also know — and it should serve as the motto of our investigation: one can learn a good deal simply by observing! As you tell Mr. Chillick about it, observe his reaction. Perhaps he will at least be polite this time.

He added a few lines at the end:

*The summer frivolities of New Haven have me in their clutches —
there is a great deal of shoreline to be explored in boats, a surfeit of base-
balls to be thrown and caught, pretty girls to be entertained. But this does
not mean my staff and I are not hard at work. The thing is to find Roland
Chillick. That aspect of the case is stalled, but perhaps the professor will
bang it into motion again! I look forward to hearing from you on that
subject, or any other that strikes your fancy. Drop us a line! Miss Mullen
is mad to know how you are faring, and when you will return. As am I!*

Charles smiled as he read it. The summer frivolities of New
Haven indeed. Dinners and boating parties and cucumber sandwiches with the idle rich.

He went into the store, where Sarah was having an earnest discussion with young Mrs. Henry Harris, newly married and unsure
about the merits of calico and chintz for a pieced quilt. Calvin was
selling someone an axe handle, but his book was stuck in his back
pocket. Charles unpacked a shipment of saw blades, hauled some
trash outside for burning, and noted that a windowpane was cracked
in the storeroom window.

Back at the house, he looked at the chicken coop and checked
through the lumber in his workshop — he had enough scrap wood
but he needed ten-penny nails. He played triple-catch with his
nephews. He was trying hard to be friendly with the boys but not
to overpower them. He could see that they were a little afraid of
him — the legacy of a brutal father. He told them yes, he would
hang a second swing from the other apple tree — another day. Yes,
they could help him build the coop if they went down to the store
and got a hundred ten-penny nails, and if they asked politely Sarah
would also give them each a handful of peppermints. They should
tell her he said so.

All the time he was thinking about Samuel Chillick and what
he would say to him, and later in the morning, he walked over to
Coleman Street. He left Tamsin sitting on the back porch with

Aunt Lottie and a bamboo fan, a pitcher of lemonade on the table between them along with Lottie's big straw hat. David and Maddox had taken over the apple trees, one climbing while the other took a turn on the swing.

"They're settling in," Charles said. "They seem to be having a fine time."

"We had no small trees like that for them to play in," Tamsin said, watching them anxiously.

"They will be fine. We climbed those trees ourselves, Tam!" Charles squeezed his sister's shoulder. Skin and bone. "If I squint and divide the twins in half, it's myself I see out there," he said. "Climbing up high enough to spy on the store. I liked to watch secretly who went in and who went out. It seems like yesterday." He laughed. "That's what Father was always saying. How time does zip along!"

"Your voice is so like his it. It's uncanny."

"So I have been told since I was fourteen."

Lottie sighed. "Such a dear and funny fellow. Did I tell you what Calvin told me the other day? He wants to find a wife someday who is just like Uncle Matthew. And why? Because you never knew what he was going to say."

"That is true of Calvin himself," Charles said.

"I wonder if that's such a good quality in a spouse," said Lottie. "I almost always know what Edward is going to say, and I find it very reassuring."

Charles went the back way, where it was cooler, down Marsh Lane to Broad Street and across the Green. A strong smell of onions wafted over from the acres of them to the south. On Coleman Street, it was as quiet as ever — not a brick had been moved on the construction site, and even the cows were absent from the field at the end of the road.

Samuel Chillick answered the door himself and led Charles into the cool of his white parlor. The room was as bare and white as it had been last time he saw it, but the mantel clock, Charles was glad to see, had been wound and told the time correctly. Chillick was again in his shirtsleeves, as if he had just come from his laboratory. Charles liked the fact that he had not felt compelled to put on his coat and tie before he answered the door. Lately, any attempt at comfortable clothing struck a chord in him — maybe he should become a member of Miss Bloomer's Rational Dress Society.

They sat on the two chairs by the hearth. Chillick immediately said. "I behaved abominably to you, sir, the last time you were here, and I'm deeply sorry."

"It's nothing! Of course you were distraught."

"I was, but I also must confess I was put off by your friend Mr. Milgrim."

"Milgrim?"

"He seemed — I don't know how to say it. It was as if everything was a joke to him." Chillick grimaced. "Forgive me — I am too frank sometimes. I suppose it is just his manner. But I did not mean to be rude to you, Mr. Cooper."

"We came on a painful errand. It was perhaps natural."

Charles didn't know what else to say. As he remembered, their errand had been nothing in particular — a dirty train ride merely to speak to Chillick about his brother and the murder and then see how he reacted. *One can learn a good deal simply by observing*, as Milgrim liked to say, and it was no doubt true but also maybe somewhat cold.

"You are most kind," Chillick said. "But I should not have seen the two of you as a package, and I apologize."

"Well, only half the package is here today, and my message may be somewhat more agreeable. Your friend Mr. Edward Davenport has confirmed your alibi."

Chillick's smile was restrained. "Since that is certainly not a surprise to me, I'm only glad to know that he survived the voyage and arrived at his destination intact."

They talked about the sinking of the steamship *Pacific* in January, out of Liverpool. Everyone lost. Charles thought again of Lily — it didn't take much to bring her from the back of his mind, where she was always hovering, to the front. She had crossed the ocean in November.

151

"An acquaintance of mine was on board the *Pacific*," Chillick said. "An eminent astronomer from Boston."

"I'm sorry to hear that. Winter is not a good time for an ocean voyage. I believe it is quite a bit safer in the summer."

"I have twice been invited to give talks in London," Chillick said, "and I confess, to my shame, that I have refused both times. I'm familiar enough with the tricks of weather to know that no time of year is really safe. I have a great dread of the ocean — that limitless plain of water. I don't know where that comes from, but it is powerful. Maybe my fear of the deep is some sort of offshoot of my fascination with the skies. You've heard of these men who go up in gliders? In France, they have done it, I know. I would go up in a winged flying machine in a moment!" He brightened. "I wonder, Mr. Cooper, if you would like to see my little laboratory."

Charles said that of course he would, and Chillick led him through the back of the house to the yard, where a path across a sparse lawn led to a white-painted shed. "Laboratory is a bit grandiose — that's what my housekeeper likes to call it. I call it my weather room. I come out here twice a day to take readings." He smiled. "In truth, if I can, I come out here much more often than twice a day. The idea is to add up all the readings and get the mean."

The shed was dim, but Chillick threw open a pair of shutters on one side and the light poured in. It was as white and spare and orderly as his house. On a shelf was a dog-eared notebook, an inkwell, a selection of pencils and steel pens. Various instruments lined the walls, along with a faded portrait of a man in a wig.

"This is where I sit and smoke and make notes for my cloud atlas — my pet project, on which I am making precious little progress. I do better with my obsessional observations." Chillick pointed. "Hygrometer, barometer, thermometer — there's another thermometer outside on the north wall, where it is said the most accurate readings are to be found. I also have a thermometer that records both the daily maximum and the minimum — it's called a Six, not for any numerical reason but because it was invented by a man named James Six. He is the elaborately bewigged gentleman on the wall — a gift from my students, a bit the worse for wear, poor chap, after a few winters out here in the shed."

"Your barometer is very handsome."

"I have a weakness for fancy barometers. I am normally a very plain man, but — well, you see. Who could resist such a thing? Mahogany, with an ebony inlay, and I went all the way to Philadelphia to get it! But I also have a Cape Cod glass — a water barometer — this teapot thing on the wall. The water rises up the spout as the atmospheric pressure changes. It doesn't work very well, but it too was a gift from my students a few years ago, so I'm fond of it. And I have a liking for any kind of a machine, no matter how primitive."

Outside, he showed Charles a lead pipe fitted into a box on the side of the shed. "A rain gauge," he said. "Worse than primitive. They were probably using them in the Stone Age, made of clay. But it does the job."

"Do you have a snow gauge as well?"

"Ha! I go out and stick a yardstick into the snow. You see — it is not so difficult to be a meteorologist. And that is a wind sock — there, on the roof. A bandana on a pivot. Wind direction can tell you a great deal about whether the air will be cooler or warmer, and the sock tells me something about speed, too, as does the smoke from Mrs. Warner's chimney — just there. Mrs. Warner is my chief assistant, though she doesn't know it."

"So tell me what celestial phenomena are occurring right now."

"We are experiencing a light breeze, almost none — probably not even five miles an hour, from the southwest. The temperature, as you can see, is eighty-four degrees Fahrenheit — this morning at dawn it was sixty-two. The humidity — oh dear, what an unpleasant day it is — the humidity is in the middle seventies. And — look at the clouds. Not a speck of rain in sight. You probably don't need a meteorologist to tell you it's a typical Connecticut summer day."

"Meaning that it's too damned warm and humid by half!"

They sat down on the back steps. Chillick took out a short-stemmed pipe. "It's certainly too hot to smoke a pipe," he said.

"But I do it anyway. I'm as much a slave to my pipe as I am to my Philadelphia barometer."

"What drew you to it? Weather and clouds and the need to measure and record them."

"I remember, when I was a boy, watching a storm approach one day." Chillick lit his pipe and sucked on it until he got it going, then leaned back on his elbows. "A great fleet of black clouds was rolling in from the east, moving fast. I sat on the porch and watched it, mesmerized. It was like watching the approach of some wild creature. Finally the cloud mass reached Wethersfield, with fearsome winds and huge gusts of rain, and then hailstones. Terrifying!" He looked over at Charles. "I was at just the right age that it captured my imagination. I became curious about the weather — this thing we live with every day. I began by measuring rainfall. Then I put up a wind sock — one of my mother's old stockings. Then I enlisted the family barometer — one of those devices where a miniature woman comes out of her house if it's going to be fair and hustles back inside if rain is coming. I started keeping a notebook full of readings, and I learned a little about clouds. I was famous at school for being able to predict the weather. It was my only claim to fame — I couldn't kick a football to save my life."

"Besides the stuff of daydreaming, I must admit I have no idea what a cloud really is."

"It's nothing but a very unromantic cluster of water droplets and ice crystals. Their proportions are endlessly changing as they're blown about by the winds, which is what makes them so fascinating to watch."

"A blue sky is so much more interesting with a cloud or two in it."

"That could pass for a philosophy of life."

They sat for a minute contemplating the wind sock, which was almost immobile against the endless blue sky. Then Charles said, "I can only put it off for so long. It's really your brother that I am here to talk to you about. And I am aware that what I have to say may offend you deeply."

"Try me."

"I will tell you first about my mother."

"Your mother?"

"Yes. I fear that is where I must begin." He was reluctant to talk about his family troubles with a relative stranger, but what he wanted to say to Chillick would be deeply insulting if it were not true, and the thought had come to him that setting the scene with his own experience might smooth the way. He said, "My mother and my father separated when I was fourteen years old."

"That must have been difficult for you."

"It is not pleasant to have to say this, but no, in fact, it made my life easier. All our lives, probably including my mother's. She and my father were continually at odds — this, I know, is not so unusual. But my mother had periods of what I can only call insanity. Madness. She became violent and uncontrolled, feverish, she didn't sleep, she would not eat, and she seemed to take a dislike to everyone in the family. In time, she began to live for brief periods — well, some not so brief — at the asylum in Middletown."

Chillick breathed out a stream of smoke and said, "I see," and Charles knew he had guessed right. "I've been thinking about her lately," he continued, "and I've been thinking about your brother as well. *The road I will not take.* I remembered the curious words that he dictated to me, and it is perhaps far-fetched but I began to wonder if perhaps he meant the road to Wethersfield from New Haven that runs straight through Middletown and passes by the asylum. Which is perhaps where your brother has been kept on and off over the years. If it was what you meant when you said he sometimes lives elsewhere. And which he may have fled from when I saw him in New Haven. And that perhaps your brother is not, in fact, entirely stable, and not always responsible for his actions." He remembered that it was these words that had angered Chillick last time, and he added, quietly, "The look on his face was the look on my mother's face at her worst moments. In her eyes. A look of mania. Unmistakable to someone who grew up with it."

"Yes."

Chillick rubbed his hand through his hair, his face not indignant but tense with thought. Charles waited. The wind sock fluttered, subsided, fluttered again. The hint of a breeze did nothing to cool him off. His mind wandered to Tamsin — he should have brought her along. It was Tamsin who was thoroughly familiar with the asylum and its workings, and maybe Chillick could have talked more easily to her.

Chillick looked over at him, finally, and said, "And what was the fate of your mother?"

"My mother's last stay at the asylum was nearly two years. Then they decided she was well enough to be released. Not to go home, but to go to her sister in Pennsylvania. It was out of the question for her to live with my father — with us. That was in 1842. I was fourteen. She lives with her sister still. I see her sometimes." He wasn't sure how much to tell — it all sounded misleadingly ordinary and straightforward — but he decided to stop there. "And that is what I came here today to say to you."

"It's a sad story. But with a happier ending, perhaps, than the story of my brother."

"We don't yet know how your brother's story ends."

"It's been a long time since I hoped for any good news of Roland. My brother was first committed to the asylum when he was eighteen. That is nearly seven years ago. He is ten years younger than I am. My father and I visited half a dozen institutions in Connecticut and Massachusetts, looking for a place that would treat Roland as a human being rather than as a troublesome wild creature, a mad dog, who could not be shot and so needed simply to be subdued. Some of the places we saw were barbaric. Middletown was not perfect, but it was by far the best we found that was close enough to allow us to visit him."

"My father did the same," Charles said.

"Did he?" Chillick looked at him with interest. "I would like to talk to your father sometime. Nothing is more difficult and more wrenching than having to commit someone you love to such a place, however enlightened it is."

"He died a week ago."

Chillick started. "Old Mr. Cooper, at the general store? I didn't know. I've been in Hartford — I have a room at the college and sometimes stay there. And when I'm here I'm preoccupied with my devices and machines to the point of — well, I was going to say madness but that is not quite what I mean." He managed a smile. "I am sorry about your father. What a good fellow he was."

"He was. And he did his best to be good to my mother, as I'm sure you and your family did your brother."

"Nothing worked with Roland. He had care and affection in abundance but they went only so far. In fact, they went hardly anywhere."

"And like my mother, he was at the asylum only from time to time?"

"He stayed for longer and longer intervals. We took him there after my mother died, three years ago, for what we all knew would be a permanent stay. Roland was deeply affected by my mother's death. He and my father were increasingly at odds — Father had little patience with him. Father now lives in New York with my sister. He never sees Roland. He says his heart has been broken by him too many times. I have sole charge of my brother. And yes —" Chillick's face was grim. "Your assumption is correct. He has been missing from the asylum for more than a month. His doctor — Robert Brown, his name is — he wrote to tell me early in May that Roland was missing. He expects him to make his way here eventually — he says Roland talked about me incessantly in the days before he disappeared — raved, is what he said. What my brother raved about I do not know. Perhaps he was angry with me. I admit I hadn't been to see him since the middle of March."

"And he hasn't shown up here."

"No. I cannot help but fear that he is dead."

"I hope that is not the case. We don't know yet what —"

"And I also fear that he will be done an injustice." He looked at Charles with anger not entirely masked by politeness. "I know that you and Mr. Milgrim think he killed Letitia Trout, Mr. Cooper, and I am equally sure that he did not. You have to remember that Roland is my brother. I am fond of him, and I know him as he really is — as he was."

"Mr. Chillick — "

"Roland is unbalanced — I do not argue with that. He has been called a lunatic, whatever the definition of the term may be — but he is not an evil man. There is so much good in him! He was always complicated. He would throw rocks at birds and then cry if he hit one. He is divided against himself — well, I suppose we all are, but Roland has no control over it, or so it seems. Good and bad, black and white, storm clouds and blue sky — they were all there, and you never knew what would emerge at any given moment."

"A bit like my mother."

"Yes — and try to imagine your mother killing someone! You know she could not do it!"

Charles remembered her throwing the pot at Tamsin, and the time — he was perhaps eight years old — she had flung herself on Father with her hands around his neck, then broken down in sobs. A feather of sadness touched him. He had a sudden memory of his mother, sitting in her chair on the left side of the hearth, with their old tabby cat, Barney, on her lap, and felt a rush of affection for her. Fierce though his mother could be, impossible though life with her was at times, he knew Roland Chillick was in another category entirely. His mother always had a roof of sanity over her head — Roland seemed to be naked to the elements.

"No," he said. "I admit that I cannot imagine my mother killing anyone."

"You must believe me — nor could Roland. And certainly he could not murder Letitia Trout. It's horrible to think she is dead," Chillick said, looking away. "She was such a pretty little thing. Lively. I tend to be rather serious. Perhaps even dour. She once said that, if I was a loaf of wholemeal bread, she was a cupcake." He gave a harsh laugh. "And so she was. A sweet little cupcake of a girl."

"If she had given you back your mother's ring, she might be alive," Charles said, and then wished he hadn't.

But Chillick didn't take offense. "If it was my brother who killed her, I suppose she would. I will never know why she did not. Except that she loved that ring. It suited her — a dainty little gold ring, with a row of three rubies. It was not particularly valuable, but it was a ring my mother had worn a good deal. Against all the rules of propriety, Letitia chose not to return it. Was she just greedy? Stubborn? Angry, perhaps, at something I had done? I will never know."

Charles thought of something. "Did your brother know Miss Trout?"

Chillick frowned. "Roland met Letitia once, when he was home here for the day, visiting. I had told her about him — the good parts and the bad — and I wanted her to meet him. He was very taken with her, and she was kind to him."

That's why she let him in, Charles thought. *She was kind to him one last time.*

"He could not have killed her," Chillick said, as if he had read Charles's mind.

"Unless he is madder than you think."

"He is not!" In his anger, Chillick resembled — fleetingly — his unfortunate brother. But he calmed instantly. "No — you're right. I have no way of knowing what his state of mind was."

"His doctor —?"

Chillick waved a hand. "He said Roland had been agitated. Roland was always agitated." He pushed his spectacles up on his head and rubbed his eyes. "What a mess. I've been hoping all this would somehow go away, but — tell me again what he looked like when you saw him."

"He was — I suppose the word is irascible. And he was very dirty, in rags. His clothes were what a workman might wear. I noticed because he spoke well, and seemed, somehow, to be a gentleman." This was a slight exaggeration, Charles thought, remembering the man's rudeness to Lily and Elena.

"He was certainly raised as a gentleman. He was meant to follow my father and me to Yale. Though by the time he was in his teens we had pretty much given up that idea." He ran his hand through his hair — a nervous habit. "It is not an easy thing to talk about."

"No, it is not."

Chillick stood up and knocked out his pipe, then stood peering up at the blue sky. He was a nice-looking man — Charles had a brief moment of envying his head of thick, dark curls — and was certainly intelligent and capable. Charles wondered about his life. It seemed a lonely one, focused entirely on work, and there was a melancholy about him that didn't seem explained simply by his having a brother in an asylum. The spare neatness with which he surrounded himself seemed sad, and the empty silence of the house — today not even a servant in evidence. *One can learn a good deal simply by observing.* Except here, perhaps, where life had been carefully arranged so that there was nothing to observe except rainfall and humidity.

"Mr. Cooper." Chillick looked down at Charles, his face calm and resolute — as if his examination of the sky had told him something. He almost smiled. "I have an idea. It is an imposition, and I'm reluctant to ask, but I wonder if you would consent to go down to Middletown with me to talk to Roland's doctor. I've been dithering too long, absorbed in my own work, and, frankly, neglecting my duty. That has been very wrong of me."

"I'm not sure what you could have done."

"I should have made inquiries, at least, instead of simply hoping that Roland would turn up and explain himself. I want at least to go and talk to his doctors, the people who saw him last, and I admit that I'm dreading it. I would appreciate your company enormously. You have some experience of this, and also you have seen my brother more recently than I have. Perhaps that would be helpful."

"I would be glad to go with you." Charles thought for a moment, then said, "Would you consider having my sister accompany us? You remember Tamsin — I think you were acquainted long ago."

Now Chillick did smile. "Not a girl easily forgotten. I thought I caught sight of her at services on Sunday. I've been wanting to ask you about her."

"She lives in Ohio, but is here on a visit with her sons. She has six-year-old twins."

"Twins. Little Tammy Cooper. I'm glad she is well. I would be very happy to see her."

"It was Tamsin who always went with my father to the asylum — she insisted on seeing Mother. My mother could be cruel to her, but Tamsin has always been able to forgive her. Better than I have, or my father. It's more than forgiveness — she seems to understand my mother's madness. And she is familiar with the place."

"If she would agree to go with us, nothing could please me more."

"Tomorrow morning, perhaps? I can drive our carriage. It may be a tight fit, but we will manage."

"Yes — tomorrow. I now feel, suddenly, that there is no time to be lost."

Chapter Sixteen

20 June, Friday. On Tuesday I hired a carriage to take Prudence & me out to Aunt Julia's in Westville.

I dressed Prudence in her sweetest white gown, & the embroidered cap Elena made for her — much more intricate & beautiful than anything I could have done. Prudence can sit quite well now when she is propped, & can hold her head up. I fixed a nest of pillows for her on the seat beside me, & she seemed to like the wind in her face. She slept a little, & when she woke her toothless smile appeared as soon as she saw me, as if nothing could make her happier than waking up to find herself the beautiful Miss Prudence Prescott out on an excursion with her mother.

The idea seemed a hopeful one. If Aunt Julia could but see my lovely baby, I thought, all would be well. Uncle Henry could be dealt with — perhaps — if my aunt was on the side of Prudence. I relied on her kind heart, her love for me — I know she must want to know my child, to embrace her as a Prescott. Who can resist a baby, no matter how disreputable her origins? I often think of what life will be like for Prudence as she gets older, with no family to turn to, none of the cousins & uncles & aunts, the visiting back & forth, the marriages & new babies & playmates that give a life its *thickness.* Her life is as thin as this paper — no father, a grandfather who refuses to admit she exists, a mother beyond the pale. Why must these things, none of them her fault, cut her off from the world & doom her to an unnatural isolation — as if I had, after all, decided to leave her in a Roman convent?

My heart was in my throat as the carriage approached the old gabled house. I knew it so well. The wide porch & the black shutters. The half-circle of the drive. The huge red barn behind. I had not seen the place in more than two years. I bade the carriage driver stop in the street in front.

The house glowed in the sun. The yellow clapboards looked freshly painted, & the barn, too. A clump of black-eyed Susans was in full bloom on either side of the front steps, & flowering vines I don't know the name of twined around the pillars of the porch. The curtains in the front windows, both upstairs & down, were drawn against the glare of late morning. Everything was very well kept, the grass like a carpet of moss, & not a leaf or a speck of dirt on the walk. I thought of my own house, which seems to suck in the dust & dirt of the street hungrily. Dora cannot keep up with it. I know she is overworked, & am always fearful she will not return one of these Sundays. A friend of hers comes in once a week, for a dollar every time, to help with the laundry — there are so many diapers, & in hot weather we have a constant need for fresh clothing — but I can afford no other help.

I worry always about money. I wake up to it & go to sleep to it. I have never kept a house before — maybe everyone is plagued with these cares? They parade before my eyes when I'm trying to go to sleep: the ice man, the trash man, the laundress, the boy who brings the wood, all of them with their hands out. The list is endless, & I fear adding to it. And yet I know that, with only one servant — or one & a quarter, if you count Elena — we have become rather slatternly. And how I hate these petty demands on my time & attention! Will Harold notice the grime on the mantel, the dust kittens under the couch?

And so I gazed up at Aunt Julia's pristine house not only with sadness & nostalgia — though I had those in full measure — but with what is not pretty but I know is there: envy.

Not that I would ever want to be married to a stick like Uncle Henry Tuttle, no matter how prosperous a manufacturer of augers, bits, & gimlets he was!

I sat in the carriage, watching, for nearly half an hour, Prudence on my lap. Not a human creature appeared, just a tiger cat I'd never seen before who came around the side of the house & stretched out on the porch to sleep in the shade. I thought if I waited long enough something would happen. Someone would appear, even a housemaid. Or Flossie — *Flossie often speaks of you* — would come running out. How could any house be so silent on a Tuesday morning? I wished I had the simple courage to go & knock at the front door. I tried to summon it up, but could not. A picture kept intruding, of my aunt at the window, peering at me through a slit in the curtains, & Uncle Henry at her side forbidding her to come out to greet me.

I have had three notes from her, & the delivery of the carriage. I wrote to thank her, a letter that I intended to be brief & cordial, but I fear it leapt out of my control. I have had no reply. And yet Aunt Julia was like a mother to me — she & I both felt that.

I sat there in the silence of a summer morning, feeling completely alone, & suddenly, from the bottom of my heart, came a stab of the purest hatred for Tomasso. That ridiculous boy. And just as quickly, for myself & my folly. All the things Papa had called me in Rome during those last days — from *putana* to idiot — they were the truth.

Finally, I told the driver to take me home. In Rome, I was never a weeper. Even when I realized I was going to have a baby — it took me a while, I was so ignorant — even then, I hardly wept. For quite a long time I refused to think about it, refused to believe it. Then, when it could not be denied, came a cold, sick, doomed feeling, & the sensation of pushing my way through each day as if my shoes were sinking into muck. The anguish of talking to Papa, & then my departure & the horrors of the *Asia* — I had never minded an ocean voyage before, but I was sick the entire time, & there were rats — & then winter in New Haven, when I could not leave the house, & my belly getting bigger every day.

In spite of it all, I do not remember many tears. And yet in New Haven I am so often on the point of crying, and I confess that I wept all the way back from my aunt's house to York Street, Prudence watching me with her big blue eyes. I wished I hadn't gone there at all — the sight of the yellow house, once so welcoming, brought back my headache, my crown of thorns.

Elena was out when I returned, & I was glad of that. Lately, she has been leaving here early in the day, taking her basket of sewing, saying nothing about where she might be going. I'm happy enough to watch her walk out the door, & yet it seems wrong for me to give her so much freedom. Finally, I said to her, in what I meant to be a playful way, "Where on earth can you be all day, Elena? I think you must have a secret life!"

She did not lose her self-possession. I'm sure she had been wondering when I would ask her — I must be the most indifferent mistress she has ever known. She looked at me from under her black eyebrows & said that she visits friends from her church. They sit & sew together, making bandages for the missionaries of the Congregation of the Sacred Hearts of Jesus & Mary — I think that is what she called it — who work with lepers in the Hawaiian Islands. They are mostly Irish women but there's also a woman from Milano, named Maria Reggio, with whom she is especially friendly. "We speak Italian together," Elena said. "It is very comforting."

I wonder why she bothers to tell me the unnecessary detail of the Italian woman's name, & the missionary society — it makes what she says sound somehow implausible, a lie. And yet why would she lie to me? I conclude that Elena is simply peculiar in ways that are beyond my comprehension.

"Well, that sounds perfectly lovely," I said, but I felt I should assert my authority, so I added, "I suppose you are free to come & go as you like, Elena, though there are times I wish you were here to help with Prudence. You could take her out in her carriage sometimes in the afternoon after her nap."

"When your suitors come calling?"

I didn't respond to this impertinence, merely stared at her until she dropped her eyes & said, "If you need me, you know you have only to say so."

We have not been especially friendly since that conversation, & for nearly a week now we haven't bothered to pick up our book in the evening. It is *Persuasion*, which has its longueurs & perhaps depresses Elena because it's about a woman who is past her first youth & still unmarried. We sit quietly — sullenly? — with our needlework, & I usually go up to bed early, leaving Elena free to go down to the kitchen & gossip about me with Dora.

The word *suitor* is absurd. It is *balderdash*, as Harold would say! *Flapdoodle!* And the plural must mean Mr. Cooper, whose letter I had a few days ago telling me his father — poor man — has died. He says nothing about coming to New Haven — not much of a suitor! Elena can use whatever word she likes. Perhaps she envies me. It's a ludicrous thought but I suppose compared to her I am a veritable Circe!

It's true that Harold is often here. This past Saturday he stayed all afternoon. It was a warm day — the heat has been ferocious! — & we had tea in the garden. I picked a daisy — there is a fine stand of them, I think they must be wild — and tucked it into Harold's buttonhole. He carried out the small table from the hall. I had Dora make sandwiches & put them on a plate with a wire-mesh cover, & fix us a bowl of strawberries. Harold brought butter cookies — a specialty of his aunt's cook, flavored with, of all things, lavender!

We sat there together for a contented hour & had eaten nearly everything — Harold does like to eat! — when I had to leave him for half an hour to feed Prudence. It was the first time this happened — his visits are not usually so long. When I heard her cry & saw Dora's face at the window, I didn't know what to say, so I said nothing — just said I must excuse myself for a few minutes — & Harold pulled a book from his coat pocket & held it up. "I shall return to Mr. Lane's travels in Egypt," he said. "Bread & dates & buffalo milk in the Temple of Osiris!" He is the soul of politeness & tact. The baby remains solidly present but invisible, like a closed window between us.

He & I talk often of Rome. He likes hearing about not only the monuments & the ruins and the gardens but the daily life there, what it is like to live in an ancient Italian city. He made me describe our house, & tell him where I walked & what kind of people I knew, what kind of Americans live there, what the Italians are like. And what we ate — he loves to hear about Angelina's cooking, Papa's dinner parties. I told him about the time Papa insisted that we eat only the food of the ancient Romans, & Angelina cooked a cod soup with honey in it, & a pig stuffed with a chicken stuffed with a dove, & we all wore wreaths of vine leaves in our hair & the men wore togas!

When I showed him Elena's patch of herbs & garlic he insisted on tasting them all. He made such a face when he bit into a clove of garlic. I told him that if it is cooked well it becomes entirely different, & he was curious to hear about that. Everything interests him. He has always wanted to travel to Egypt, he said, & Persia, & to see the Alps & to take a boat down the Rhine, but now it's Italy he wants to see. He has been to London, where he has cousins & which, he claims, is nothing but a bigger, older New Haven! But he has been nowhere else of interest. "If only you could show me Rome," he said, & then, "Do you know something, Lily?" & stared off into space the way he does, as if he is thinking very profoundly. (I know he is not, I know he is going to say something humorous & inconsequential, & I cannot convey the charm of this.) Then he looked at me. "If I had the chance to travel anywhere tomorrow, I would refuse it. Even to go climbing in the Alps! Even to Persia!"

I knew I was supposed to ask why, & so I did, & his answer was, "Because nothing could be more interesting to me right now than York Street in New Haven, Connecticut."

Not inconsequential at all. We did nothing but look at each other for a very long time. The day was darkening, & as I watched his face a shadow moved across it, & all I could see were his light blue eyes, shining. It was like being under a spell. And then he said, making me laugh, "You are my Persia, Lily. You are my pyramid & my castle on the Rhine & my Alp," & he pulled me close to him.

He says I have a wonderful laugh, & that so few women look pretty when they laugh, but I do. When he was gone I laughed into my dressing-table mirror & saw squinty eyes & a mouthful of teeth & could only marvel that he could like me. But he does like me.

Harold Hopkins Milgrim.

I'm sure Dora tells Elena every detail. When we first arrived, Dora had trouble with Elena's accent, & Elena of course saw Dora as nothing but a kitchen slut whereas Elena has served the haughtiest of Roman madames & signoras. But things have changed. Elena is often in the kitchen — she is nearly as good a cook as her mother — & I hear their voices over the sound of dishes clattering & pans banging. I suppose they have now become friends, as women do when they are servants in the same house — friends who talk mercilessly about their employers. It's disapproval of me that has brought Elena & Dora together, I have no doubt. A few days ago, Dora opened the drawing room door as Harold was embracing me — it was nothing, just a brief moment when there was so much tenderness between us, we both felt that it had to be expressed! Dora backed out of the room mumbling, her eyes ablaze. Is there even the smallest chance that she didn't describe this to Elena while they were chopping vegetables together in the kitchen?

Harold was displeased, & said Dora was above herself, no servant should show her feelings in that way, nor should she come upstairs with her apron in that condition. Lax mistress though I am, I suppose I agreed with him, but I defended her & said she had been with us so long, & worked so hard, & was usually so demure, & was so much like a member of the family. I don't think Harold liked this characterization of a servant, but he said nothing more. What if he knew I had wanted her to sit with Elena & me while we read aloud? He & Elena come from opposite ends of society, but I'm sure he would dislike the idea as much as she did. Which puts me somewhere between them, in the middle, neither this nor that — not a surprising idea, I suppose, but I had never seen things quite that way before, & this strange little thought has stayed with me.

Harold does not call on me on Thursdays, Dora's half-day, when I have told him it's impossible, or on Sundays, when Dora is with her mother & which Harold spends with various branches of his family. His parents have gone to the shore for the summer, they have a house in Old Saybrook, but he is particularly close to his aunt & uncle, the Ralph Milgrims, who stay in town & do good works —

he says that as if it's part of some comic story, as if "good works" were something like turning cartwheels on the Green! But they do indeed do good works. The newspaper often mentions them. His aunt Martha is forever rescuing orphans & opening charity balls & giving dinners in aid of some cause or other, & his uncle has invested in the new Alms House, where he is a director, & is also on the hospital board. Harold himself is on the board of the library. I think he needs to joke about things he considers serious.

Then for three days, I didn't see him, nor did he write, but yesterday — after I watched out the parlor window for hours — he arrived again at teatime, & we sat close to each other in the drawing room, & he said some of what I've been longing to hear. And Dora did not come in.

Harold & I don't discuss Prudence — ever — or my dismal Roman history. I asked him a question once about something from his childhood— not the happiest of times, I think, in spite of wealth & privilege — & he said, "The one thing I like about the past is that it's over."

I take this to heart. I take it to mean that my own scarlet past means so little to him he doesn't even want to know what it is. And yet it seems odd that he knows so little about me. I assume he deduces. But there are times when I want to pour it all out. He is a man of the world! He would not judge me, I'm sure.

We have had some rain, at last, & the garden is refreshed & green. I'm expecting Harold again this afternoon, & he suggested that, if it is dry, we sit in the garden & play piquet on our little table. He can make a game of piquet extremely amusing! A theme from that Busoni bagatelle keeps going through my head — what a hash we made of it! Oh, my darling Harold! He is so very good for me. With him, I am a better, merrier, almost blithe Lily Prescott. Dare I say I'm my old self?

Chapter Seventeen

The road to the Middletown Lunatic Asylum was only partly paved, and it was hot and dry and dusty, but the ride took less than an hour. Mavis, the old mare, had gone lame in the spring, and once she mended Calvin had been in charge of exercising her, but Charles knew she had not really been out in weeks, and he was hoping that Middletown and back would not be too much for her.

Chillick seemed shy with Tamsin, but she had greeted him with delight: "Sam Chillick! How many years has it been since we used to walk out to the cove and skate behind the Moseleys' farm? Remember when I tried to teach you to skate backwards? I would say that you have not changed one whit — except for the spectacles, and the whiskers, and the long trousers."

"And you have not changed at all," he said, but she cut him off.

"I appreciate your gallantry, but I've just figured it out. It has been eighteen years since we used to go skating together on Packer's Pond! If you really think I'm unchanged in eighteen years, you probably need much stronger spectacles."

He smiled. "Well, you have not changed in one respect."

"Which respect is that?"

Charles laughed. "I think we all know what he means, Tam. You have inherited Father's gift for speaking your mind at all costs."

"It's one of the things I always liked about your father," Chillick said. "And your sister, too."

"Thank you, Sam. That's a compliment I will accept gladly."

The carriage seat was not meant for three, but Tamsin squeezed in easily between them. She was certainly as small and thin as she had been as a girl, Charles thought. It was good to have her there. She talked easily about everything but their grim destination. How good it was to see the low Connecticut hills she had grown up with, and the beautiful mountain laurel, which did not grow in the desolate patch of Ohio that she knew. She told Chillick about the pleasures of keeping hens, and talked a little about her boys, and asked him about his classes at Trinity. Charles was surprised by her easiness with Chillick, and by her warmth. He had always thought of his sister not just as frank and forthright, but as prickly and difficult, with a sharpness that was something like their mother's, untinged by their father's amiability. Her years with Eli Pugh may have been disastrous, but they had softened her, too.

She did not mention Eli during the ride, and Chillick didn't ask about her husband. Nor did she mention the purpose of their excursion until they were approaching the asylum. Then she said, "I scarcely remember your little brother, Sam. I do recall your sister — Mary?"

"Yes. Mary lives with my father in New York City. You may remember that my father was an attorney in Hartford — he's now retired. He has not seen Roland since we took him to the asylum for the last time. My father pays for his upkeep, but he goes no further. My sister has said many times that she would be happy never to set eyes on him again."

"That leaves it all to you, then. I'm sorry to hear it. It is so hard to have someone — what is that wonderfully bland word we always use? difficult? — in the family. Father certainly did his duty. He visited Mother in Middletown regularly, but once he realized his wife would never be what is called cured, he would stay there just long enough to see that she could still walk and talk. All the way home, I remember, he would never say a word. It was all deeply upsetting to him."

"And to you, I'm sure," Chillick said.

"It was easier for me than for Father. Their troubles together were a tangle that went back many years. To me, Mother was just my mother. In a way, I was always glad to see her, even locked away from us at the asylum."

Charles glanced over at his sister. Her bonnet shaded her face, but he could hear the sadness in her voice. He had been struck by Tamsin's view of their mother, and by her plan to visit her. Had he been unfair to her all these years? Too much his father's son, and not enough his mother's?

There was a stream at the foot of the long drive up to the asylum, and Charles stopped the carriage and jumped down to fill the bucket for Mavis. "Father and I always did this very same thing," Tamsin said. "I wonder if Mavis remembers."

Charles resumed his seat. "She turned into the drive here as if she knew the way."

"Mother used to come out to say hello to her. I'd forgotten that."

"Mother always seemed to care more about animals than she did about people," Charles said dryly.

Tall trees shaded the drive, meeting overhead. The asylum sat on a little rise — a large, turreted brick building with a slate roof and a flight of wide, shallow steps. There was a smell of cut grass — the lawns were pristine, the gardens well-tended. The property was enclosed by a stone wall. Here and there an inmate or a pair of them walked, or sat on a bench. Charles remembered his mother's stories about one of her fellow inmates, a woman who was convinced she was Queen Victoria's long-lost illegitimate daughter. And another, who did nothing but count, far into the thousands, smiling and gesturing as if it was a conversation she was having.

"It does not look like Bedlam," he said. "It looks like a school. Or a hospital."

"It is a hospital, I suppose," said Tamsin. "A place for sick minds to heal — that is the hope, at least."

"They should call it that. Instead of the Middletown Lunatic Asylum. Asylum is a word that is meant to be benign — a haven, a place to find peace. But now when we hear it we think of insanity."

"Mother called it the *Irrenanstalt*. Everything sounds so dire and urgent in German. But she always spoke the word with affection in

172

her voice. For her, it really was a haven. Oh, Charles —"Tamsin laid her hand on his arm. "It's so strange to be here. It was fifteen years ago Father and I first brought mother up this drive. And more than ten years since she left it for good. That's the last time I was here."

"And ten years ago," Chillick said, "Roland had begun making our lives a misery with his rages, his fights, his neglect of his studies. We had given up on Yale by then, but my father still hoped Roland could be trained for something."

Charles pulled up the carriage in front of the building, and Chillick climbed down and helped Tamsin alight. "We had no idea, Sam," she said, "during our ice-skating outings, that we had this misfortune in common."

"I had no words to talk about my brother in those days."

"Nor I my mother. When I was out with my friends, I wanted only to forget what life was like at home."

Inside, the asylum was silent, cool, dim. They were met by an attendant, who, after a short wait, showed them into the office of the director of the place, Dr. Everett Maxwell, who would be with them directly. His office recalled a headmaster's study, paneled and book-lined. On the walls were gloomy oil paintings of worthy-looking gentlemen in stiff collars, and hanging over the mantel was the stuffed head of a stag. Maxwell's desk was highly polished and completely bare except for its leather-bordered blotter and a cut-crystal inkwell with a silver pen in a holder — English, Charles thought. The chairs they sat in were leather, and absurdly comfortable. Charles wondered what kind of fees the Chillicks had been paying for Roland's keep.

Maxwell strode in, took a seat behind his desk, and looked at the three of them in turn. He was a large man in a checked coat, with a shock of wavy light hair. His small eyes were not friendly. "It's fortunate that I'm free this morning," he said with a touch of reproof.

"I apologize for not making a definite appointment," Chillick said. "We came somewhat on the spur of the moment."

Tamsin introduced herself and Charles as Magda Cooper's daughter and son. Maxwell said he had been only the assistant director during Mrs. Cooper's stays at the asylum, but he remembered her well — *very well*, he emphasized, and he hoped she was still with her sister in Pennsylvania. Charles would have liked to ask if he remembered every person who passed through the doors of his asylum, or if Magda Cooper's particular madness had been especially interesting.

"You favor your mother," Maxwell said to Tamsin, and it occurred to Charles that perhaps he remembered Magda Cooper because of her beauty.

Tamsin ignored his comment. "Her doctor was Martin Jones. Is he still with you? I would like very much to say hello to him."

"Dr. Jones left our establishment a few years ago, shortly after I became director."

Tamsin raised her eyebrows. "I'm sorry to hear that. He was an extraordinary doctor. I do believe that it is thanks to Dr. Jones that my mother is able to lead a normal life. Whatever happened to him?"

"He chose to return to Europe. I am sure he is a fine doctor, but there are numerous different philosophies pertaining to the treatment of the mentally ill, and Dr. Jones and I had some small but not insignificant differences of opinion." He shrugged and spread his hands, then clasped them together in front of his cravat. "And so," he said, turning to Chillick with a frosty smile. "What exactly can we do for you, sir?"

"I had hoped to speak to Roland's own doctor, if I could."

Dr. Robert Brown, however, was not free to talk to them — Maxwell didn't say why, but he managed to imply that everyone at the place was consumed with working tirelessly for the good of the poor souls they were trying to help and could not always be available to confer with guests at the drop of a hat.

"But let us see if I can assist you," Maxwell said. "You are not planning to return your brother to our premises, Mr. Chillick?"

"My brother is still missing."

"That is devastating news." Maxwell looked sharply at Chillick, as if it he were somehow at fault. Charles tried to think if he had ever disliked anyone on sight quite as much as he disliked Dr. Everett Maxwell. "He has been gone all this time?"

"I think we all assumed he would find his way home, but it has been many weeks, and I'm no longer confident of that."

The doctor shifted in his chair. "Of course, our responsibility for him was terminated when he left our establishment. But I will say that your unfortunate brother is not in any condition to be out on his own, wandering at will around the countryside."

Chillick said. "That is obvious."

"Indeed." There was a brief pause. "And so —?"

"It has become somewhat urgent that I find him. I thought you might be able to help."

"Of course we will assist you in any way we can. But all I can do is tell you what happened here."

"That is what we came to find out."

"A bit belatedly."

Chillick flushed, but said nothing. Maxwell sighed deeply, stood up, and took from a cabinet a sheaf of papers in a cardboard file tied with a ribbon. He didn't open it, just set it on his desk with one hand spread out on it as if he could intuit its contents by touch. He seemed well acquainted with Roland's case. He said Roland had disappeared from the asylum on May sixth. By the time Dr. Brown had written to Samuel with the news, the buildings and the grounds had been thoroughly searched and he had sent a pair of attendants into the town itself. No one had seen Roland. He had left no trace — but they were almost sure he had climbed over the wall, high though it was, at a point where the stone was crumbling and might have offered a handhold to a strong and agile man. And a clever and determined one. "Usually a good combination of qualities," Maxwell added. "But perhaps not in the circumstances."

Charles slid his eyes over and met Tamsin's: how was Roland able to climb a high wall without being observed? The word *determined* especially puzzled him, and Tamsin said, "I remember from my mother's stays here that the patients who were well enough to have some freedom were, for the most part, contented. Many of them seemed afraid of the world outside these walls, and grateful to be safe within. I wonder why Roland Chillick was so bent on escape."

"The last time I saw him he seemed happy enough," Chillick put in. "He was going to help plant a vegetable garden, he said. He saw it as a great privilege, and was looking forward to it."

"The last time you visited him was on March thirteenth, sir," Maxwell said.

"I visit my brother three or four times a year," Chillick said stiffly. "I come as often as I can."

"I didn't intend a criticism. I meant simply that a great deal can happen in a month or two. Yes, it is true that we pride ourselves on the fact that our patients are, for the most part, calm and happy here, and the privileges we give them reflect that freedom. But they are also fundamentally unstable, and their serenity is not something we can necessarily count on."

"You are saying that Roland changed?"

"He changed significantly during the month of April."

"He always has trouble with the anniversary of our mother's death."

"I'm aware of that. He often talked about her, as you know. But it was usually melancholy that overcame him at those times — only melancholy. Not his mania. The agitation, the wild talk. Imagining things. This year he heard his mother's voice, and relived her last afternoon, as if its events had occurred yesterday. And he heard *your* voice, Mr. Chillick — that was something new. He seemed to be under the impression that you were a patient here at our institution, like himself. And then he — well, rather than relying on my imperfect memory, let me consult Dr. Brown's notes."

Maxwell opened the folder and shuffled through it. Charles found his gaze drawn to the stag over the mantel. Its glass eyes stared out into the room as if still startled by the appearance of a hunter with a gun. What effect would it have on a patient here? It seemed the stuff of nightmares.

"Here we are." Maxwell picked up a paper, put it down, picked up another. "More of the same, really, every day. He is increasingly agitated. His brother Samuel is sitting in the garden with him. His brother brings — cocoa? Yes, cocoa. He has been sleepless, he has a slight fever. And — ah yes — here is where it begins. In late April there was something else."

"Something else."

"Yes — it's somewhat distressing. I hesitate to speak of it in front of a lady."

Tamsin spoke up. "I'm old enough to be beyond shocking, Doctor."

"What I'm going to say is not pleasant."

Chillick burst out, "For God's sake, man, just tell us what it is!"

Maxwell sat back in his chair. "I am about to do that, Mr. Chillick," he said coolly.

"Forgive me." Chillick rubbed his hand over his eyes. "My brother — for so many years now, it has been so difficult — and it never ends, there is always something new, something appalling. Pray go on, Dr. Maxwell. I will not interrupt again."

Maxwell squeezed out a smile, then fished a paper out of the stack, looked at it, picked up another. "Well," he said. He pursed his lips and sighed. "Roland, you see, had become friendly with one of our female patients, a young woman, and I believe — " He stopped again and looked at them with something near belligerence. "You know, we don't supervise our people every minute, the ones who are doing well — that's one of the aspects of our establishment here that seems to have a good effect and helps so many of them improve. And we do not segregate the sexes except for where they sleep. They often fraternize on the grounds and in the dining room."

Tamsin asked, "Is that such a good idea?"

Maxwell raised his eyebrows. "A good idea? Why yes, in fact, it is, Mrs. Pugh. We try to be not only modern here, but forward-looking. After all, it was not so long ago that mental patients were kept in chains — even in cages. Cold baths. Restraints. Our philosophy reflects the very latest thinking, I assure you. But, as it happens, in this case, perhaps we went too far. It was probably too much freedom for a patient such as Roland. I will tell you frankly that we thought he was more capable than he actually was. Your brother could be very cunning, Mr. Chillick."

"I know that only too well." It was clear Chillick was keeping his voice level with effort. "Please. Tell me what happened."

"As you wish. It seems that Roland and this young woman were intimate. I know this is rather — I have to say they were discovered twice, in flagrante."

"You're talking about a sexual union?"

"I'm afraid I am." Maxwell turned to the folder and shuffled more papers. "They were, as I said, discovered twice, during the month of April, on the nineteenth and on the twenty-fourth. And, as it turned out, the girl was also — well, there was another man, actually a member of our staff, a very young under-gardener. She was intimate with him as well." He cleared his throat. "There may have been others."

"Good God!"

"She was removed by her family to another institution. She is a very troubled young woman, and quite — quite without inhibitions. Unfortunately, Roland was very attached to her. He took it hard when she left. And — also unfortunately — it became generally known that she had shared herself, shall I say, with more than one man. The gardener was of course dismissed."

"Dismissed!" Tamsin straightened in her chair, eyes blazing. "The man should be in jail! Taking advantage of a mentally impaired young woman!"

"That is a side issue. We are talking about Roland Chillick."

"What a god-awful situation." Chillick bent over, elbows on knees, head in hands. "I'm sorry to bring you into this, Tamsin. Charles. It is very ugly."

"Neither of us is unacquainted with ugliness," Tamsin said. She reached over and laid a hand on his shoulder. "I think it is better that you did not come here without friends."

"Very wise, Mrs. Pugh." Maxwell resumed his tiny smile, which Tamsin did not return. "It's always a mistake to try to face these matters alone. A mentally ill relative can be heartbreaking. I know you're familiar with all this. "

There was another silence, during which Maxwell's smile gradually faded. Then he said, "To continue. Roland was thrown completely off balance by this incident. And as Dr. Brown wrote to you, Mr. Chillick, and as I have already described, your brother became delusional. He began to talk about you. Or rather — he began to be convinced that you were talking to him. He kept saying that you had told him what to do." He picked up his pile of papers and flipped through them again. "*Sam is a good man. He always sets me on the right path.* He said that you agreed with him that — " Maxwell stopped again. "I hardly know how to —"

"Please go on, Doctor." Tamsin's tone was exasperated. "I swear to you that none of us will faint!"

Maxwell closed his eyes briefly, then returned to the paper in his hand. "You agreed with him, Mr. Chillick, that women are nothing but — harlots. Young women — pretty ones. Harlots, connivers, and thieves." He threw down the paper and leaned back in his chair. "You know how he would sometimes repeat things, over and over — sometimes shout them without warning."

Chillick hadn't moved. "I'm afraid I do," he said, and his voice was barely audible.

"He would say things to the women here. Of course, it offended them. Dr. Brown and I both talked to him. He was told that he would lose some of his privileges if he didn't calm himself, and so after a while he did. Or seemed to. He admitted eventually that no, it wasn't true that all women were harlots, connivers, and thieves. Just some of them."

Chillick looked up and laughed, then stopped himself. "I'm sorry. That sounds so like Roland. Trying in the midst of his madness to be reasonable. I remember the time he — " He waved his hand. "Oh, never mind. What's the use? Go on."

"Finally, he narrowed it down further," Maxwell said. He looked down at his papers. "I made a note here that on the fifth of May, during my own Monday afternoon session with him — I see each patient myself at least once a week — Roland talked at length about a woman who had stolen a ring from your mother. He mentioned this several times and said that he had talked about it with you in the garden, over cocoa." Maxwell closed the folder and tied the ribbon around it again, frowning. "That was Monday, and on the Wednesday he was gone."

You have your wish. The object is in my pocket, and I'll be home soon.

The look on Chillick's face was suddenly like that on the stag over the mantel. Charles knew he was seeing, with absolute clarity, as he was himself, what Roland Chillick had done, and why.

❧❧❧

Back in the carriage, Tamsin said, "It's outrageous that you knew nothing about what was going on here, Samuel — about your brother and the — that poor woman he was so attached to."

"It does not matter now." Chillick took off his hat and ran a hand through his hair. "What matters is that my brother is a murderer. I didn't really believe it before, but now I don't think there is any room for doubt."

"Your brother is not well," said Charles.

"Nor is Letitia Trout, thanks to him."

They headed down the drive, and Mavis took the left turn onto the road without prompting. Chillick sat dumbly, hat on his knees, staring out at the roadside. The mountain laurel made a pale backdrop for the brighter pinks of the vetch along the roadside, but Charles suspected Chillick was seeing none of it, or the huge puffs of clouds above, being pushed along by a wind they could not feel below. He could sense that, beside him, Tamsin was seething, but she was quiet too, staring straight ahead at the dusty road. What was there to say?

Charles thought about his encounter with Roland, and the letter he had written for him in all innocence. Would he have to testify if Roland came to trial? Would Roland hang, as Milgrim had said, or would he be locked up for the rest of his life? If he was returned to an asylum, it would not be to a place like Middletown, where the patients ate their meals in a communal room and were given the run

180

of the grounds, but to a prison where they locked away murderers who were also insane.

And where was Roland Chillick now? He had been missing for more than six weeks. He had a thirty-mile journey to make, he was proceeding on foot, one of his hands was badly burned, and he was mentally unstable. But he was not unintelligent. He had managed to leave the asylum grounds and get to New Haven, twenty miles away, in only a day or two. He had had a little money. Perhaps he was on the road now somewhere to the south, and was meandering slowly homeward. Perhaps he had found a way to get along.

On the other hand, Charles thought, it was easy to imagine him dead in a ditch.

They were well past Cromwell before Chillick spoke. "Well," he said, his voice weary, as if he had woken from a stupor. "That is over, at least."

Charles glanced over at him. "What now?"

"My brother must be found. I shall have to see the police. Maybe they can conduct a manhunt. Smoke him out wherever he may be hiding. Or perhaps he's not hiding at all. Roland may have forgotten the murder completely. Perhaps he thinks Letitia is with him, and that they're drinking cocoa together. Perhaps he's walking with my mother. Or me — maybe we're walking along the road somewhere having a brotherly chat about the perfidy of women."

Tamsin burst out, "The negligence of that place is appalling! Your poor brother was unstable to begin with, still mourning your mother, and then — say what you like about what went on there, but he had his heart broken, too! Small wonder he heard voices."

"But to kill, Tamsin. I thought there was nothing worse than hearing that Letitia was dead. And now I know that it was my brother who killed her. Murdered her in a rage for a piece of jewelry because he thought I wanted him to. Yes, he was mad. Yes, he should not have been given so much freedom. Yes, I should have been told of all this and taken him to a different kind of hospital entirely. A number of things should have happened, or should not have happened. But what did happen was that he lost control — what little he had — and did this horrible deed. And I know there is more to come. As you said, Charles, my brother's story is not over." He pulled out his handkerchief and blew his nose. "Ah, I don't know," he said. "Is life just a series of —?" He gestured with one hand, then dropped it wearily and continued. "I also know that, in a way, I'm to blame. I cannot get that idea out of my head. The last time I was here, in March — the thirteenth, as Dr. Maxwell took pains to point out — "

"I did not like him," Charles interrupted. "I've never liked people who use six words when one will do."

"And I've never liked people who will not take responsibility when they have made a mistake!" Tamsin said. "And that coat! That dreadful pretense at a smile! The man has no dignity. I'm thankful Mother was gone from there before he took over. I can well imagine the differences of opinion between him and Dr. Jones. The difference between a cold fish and a humane and intelligent doctor! The place has greatly changed."

"I should have paid more attention. I have been remiss, I know that."

"Not as remiss as Dr. Maxwell and his staff."

"I told Roland in March, finally, that Letitia and I were not going to marry. I think now that she was right to break it off — we were probably not really suited. But I was still angry about it the day I told Roland what had happened, and I told him that I had tried repeatedly to get her to return Mother's ring and had failed. I should not have been so incensed when I spoke to my brother. Exasperated. Call it what you will. I can see that that was the worm that made its way into his brain and did its work."

"You had no way of knowing what would happen."

"He didn't really seem to be affected by the news when I told him. In fact, he was having a good day, and I brought him home for the afternoon. If I made an application to his doctor, Roland was allowed to leave the grounds for a day, in my custody — one of his privileges, as Maxwell put it. Roland would sit on the porch and drink coffee— yes, and cocoa! I always saw to it that my housekeeper had a plate of shortbread ready for him. They never had such things in the asylum. Then he would smoke a cigar, and I would take him back. Again, I feel I'm at fault. You have seen my house, Charles. When Letitia threw me over, I thought: I will live like a monk. I'm afraid I went rather far. I stripped the house of everything that was beautiful or artistic or even interesting. Most of my mother's possessions had gone to New York with my father and sister, but I had a few things. A fancy cupboard filled with her china, and a nice old dining room table with chairs, and — well, it doesn't matter. I had it all hauled out to the barn except for what I couldn't do without. And I had the house painted white. Walls, molding, doors, window casings. You noticed, Charles, I'm sure."

"It would have been difficult not to. It does go against the prevailing fashion."

"It's no one's taste but my own." He smiled. "And perhaps a Cistercian Abbey or two."

"Or the Shaker community up in Enfield."

"Yes. I have been there. Maybe it's the Shakers I was thinking of. Wherever it came from, I found the plainness comforting, but Roland did not like it at all. He kept saying Mother would hate it. Where were the shepherd and shepherdess that used to sit on the mantel? The beaded lampshades that she went to New York to buy? The mirror with the gilt frame? We argued about it. I had to take him back to Middletown earlier than usual."

"But you cannot continue to blame yourself for what happened, Sam," Tamsin said. "I do not think it can be right to blame ourselves for things we did not mean to do."

"That may be true, and in time I may even agree, but at present — that is not how I see it."

They were not far from Wethersfield. It was still early afternoon, and Charles wondered if he should finish up the chicken coop or go to his desk and work on the writing manual. He had been neglecting it lately — it was active in his mind, but on paper it was just an introduction, some basic diagrams, and a few pages of notes.

But he would work on the coop, he decided. There had been some rain the night before, the heat wave they'd been suffering through had eased up a little, and he wanted Tamsin to have her chickens. This was not the day to think about the angles and curves of sixteenth-century Italian lettering. And first he would stop at the post office. He had a piercing desire for a letter from Lily Prescott. He had kissed her hand. He had promised to return. He had not seen her now in three weeks, and she had not replied to his last letter.

He wished Lily hadn't come into his head, because now she would not leave. Even Mavis's hoofs on the road said *Lily Lily Lily.* He began composing a letter to her in his head: *My dearest Lily. My darling Lily. Our last encounter was an inexpressible joy bliss rapture to me. Our last encounter was. I think about our last encounter every day, and hope that you. Kissing your hand was the most. Your sweet face when I left gave me hope that you will consent to. Your eyes. Your.*

They made the turn onto Broad Street, the trees arching overhead to make a welcome shade. "I thank you for driving me there, Charles," Chillick said. "And I am grateful to you for coming, Tamsin. It meant a great deal."

"Still, it was hard for you," she said.

"It's better to know. I'll go home and collect my thoughts and then talk to the police this afternoon." He broke off as they turned down Coleman Street. "Good God."

Charles slowed the horse. "Good God indeed," he said.

"Who is that?" Tamsin asked, but then she raised her hand to her mouth with a little gasp. Who else could it be?

"It is my brother," Chillick said. "My brother Roland, sitting on the porch."

Chapter Eighteen

4 July, Friday. I have not yet answered Mr. Cooper's letter of nearly three weeks ago, about his poor father. It would have to be not my usual bantering style but a letter of condolence. What can one say that is adequate to the occasion, & how can one say it? But then I had a note from him yesterday saying that he would call on me on Friday afternoon, which is today.

I woke up feeling rather ill-humored. That is a state I try not to give in to, but yesterday at breakfast Elena told me with tears in her eyes that it was the feast of St. Thomas — San Tomasso — her brother's saint, & did I know that next Sunday week will be the first anniversary of his death? I did not remember this, & do not want to, but I know that on that day Elena will expect me to do something to mark it — cry, wear black, go with her to church, at least be in a state of gloom all day.

Then last night I read a story in *Godey's* about a fallen woman, & it would not leave me. The author called her *a woman who strayed from the path of goodness and virtue.* Really, their stories are sometimes not very good, full of morals & happy endings — Elena likes them — but I read it as one might press on a bruise, to see how much it will hurt. The woman is a ninny, a governess who lets herself be seduced by her swinish employer. Already the story rings false — who would hire this simpering dunce to teach their children? But there she was, tending to her little charges & being bent over a table in the schoolroom by their father — or so I assume, it was

185

all quite vague. In the end, after too many unconvincing torrents of tears, poor stupid Alice is persuaded by the kindly housekeeper to stow her child in a home — where she is allowed to visit him on Sundays! How could she possibly object? — & go out to work among the poor, where she meets a decent & entirely implausible man, the manager of a fish cannery, who marries her & adopts the boy. I imagine her husband coming home every day smelling of fish. I imagine him reminding her every day that without him she would be lost. I imagine her tip-toeing about the house, waiting on him, afraid to let out a peep lest she wind up on the streets. We are meant to applaud this nauseating ending.

Harold came three days ago, on Tuesday, to tell me he has been forced to agree — practically at gunpoint, he insisted — to go with his parents & sisters to Old Saybrook, where he says the tedium will be made endurable only by the ice cream. They make ice cream using a recipe that was a favorite of President Jefferson. It requires cream that has been boiled with a stick of vanilla in it, & plenty of sugar & eggs, to be put into a wooden apparatus lined with ice, & there is a handle of some sort that must be turned for fifteen minutes without stopping. We often ate ice cream in Rome, but Angelina didn't make it. We could buy it from a street vendor, in any flavor, & I never thought about how it is made. Harold ferreted out the recipe in an ancient cookery book, he said. Imagine such a thing! He is a great admirer of President Jefferson.

He stayed so long that I had to go twice to tend to Prudence, & the second time it was so late in the day that she dozed off while I was feeding her, & I put her to sleep in her cot. Harold didn't seem to mind being left alone — Harold never minds anything, he is the most naturally cheerful person I have ever known and can joke about things no one else would find the humor in. When I returned we sat in the drawing room until it was nearly dark, & we did not light the lamps.

I thought that, after all this, he might send me a note, but he has not, & I realized today that Harold has never sent me a note.

I slept badly & had forgotten today was Independence Day until, late in the morning, I heard the strains of "Yankee Doodle" played on fifes and a fiddle, with drums as accompaniment. The parade was passing on Chapel Street. My great-grandfather Prescott, from Boston, died at Bunker Hill, Papa told me once, but I have never thought of myself as patriotic — in some ways I do not feel American at all, & if patriotism means loving a place, feeling completely at home there, then I suppose I am a Roman patriot! But, in spite of myself, my toes started tapping, & I decided to take Prudence out into the sunshine.

It was a very warm Independence Day. I put on my lightest dress — the blue lawn — & had Dora bring up the baby's carriage while I pinned a clean diaper on her & tidied my hair & put on a hat. Dora looked so hot & damp, I told her to come too, but she said, rather snippily, that she was in the middle of the ironing & had bread rising & could not leave. Elena had gone out, of course, after breakfast — her church was having a picnic, she said — & so I wheeled Prudence by myself down to the corner.

Crowds of people thronged Chapel Street, three & four deep, waving miniature flags & cheering. It was a sea of parasols. I squeezed Prudence's carriage into their midst — people always make way for a baby carriage — and found a place across from the college buildings. The parade was vast — soldiers, & firemen, &, I assume, various local dignitaries — men in black coats & top hats & red faces shiny with sweat, waving at the multitudes. A small army of school children marched along, dressed in red, white, & blue, singing raggedly, & carrying a sign that said 80 YEARS 1776-1856. A wagon went by bearing a grim-looking woman with a wooden axe who was pretending to chop down a saloon under a sign that read:

TIS NOW WE PLEDGE ETERNAL HATE
TO ALL THAT CAN INTOXICATE.

A group of men & women, dressed in heavy mourning, were pretending to weep into large black handkerchiefs as they followed a gravestone on wheels marked INDEPENDENCE. The backs of their coats said CONNECTICUT ABOLITIONIST SOCIETY.

I wondered if such things had any effect on people, if a woman with an axe or people looking funereal in black would draw anyone to their cause. A man called out, "Hey, you old battle-axe!" to the temperance woman, making several people laugh, & two woman standing near me looked at the abolitionists & said, "How warm they must be!" & "Imagine doing that on such a day!"

The fifes & drums had already passed, but they could still be heard. As the parade dwindled down to stragglers — including a band of collegians who, despite the presence of the temperance wagon, seemed to be intoxicated already — the crowd began to move toward the Green. There would be speeches, I assumed, & demonstrations, & songs, & heaven knows what else. Even in the overarching shade of the elms, it would be very hot, & Prudence was starting to fuss. I started back to York Street, & as I did I saw Margaret Brock, not ten feet from me, as tall & ruddy & sharp-nosed as ever. I am rather short-sighted, but Margaret is unmistak-able. She has grown even taller in the two summers since I saw her last, & she wore a vast flowered hat — pink, like her dress — that added several inches. She had never tried to disguise her height. She used to call herself the Grove Street Lighthouse. Margaret was never a beauty, but she was such good fun, & catching sight of her, I felt a great fondness for her, and for the days when we were friends.

And then she turned her head & saw me. Her eyes widened, then narrowed, & then it was as if I were a lamp post. She continued on her way, talking to her companion, a woman I'd never seen before. I stood & watched her make her way down Chapel Street toward the music, the plumes of her pink hat swaying like some rare bird, until she was lost in the crowd.

The encounter did not put me in high spirits. Margaret Brock, of all people. We had known each other since we were tiny girls playing house & dressing our dolls and walking to school together. We had told each other our deepest secrets & sworn to be friends forever. I try to imagine a reversal of our roles: Margaret suddenly, mysteriously, the mother of a child, & myself knowing she was in town, assuming she was lonely, remembering all that had been between us — & cutting her dead on Chapel Street! I know I could not have done it.

By the time Mr. Cooper came to the door — Charles, as I am determined to call him — I had worked myself into a state of peevishness, & when Dora told me he was in the parlor I was tempted to have her say I was not at home. But that seemed like something worthy of Margaret, not of me. So I washed my face & went to meet him.

He was wearing a black armband on his black coat, & his whiskers were neatly trimmed. He was shorter & somehow drabber than I remembered him, but his face was radiant.

"Charles!" I said. "I got your note. I am so very sorry about your father."

"Thank you." We stood in the parlor, with our hands clasped. "It seems a strange world indeed without my father in it."

It occurred to me that I too live in a strange world, without my father in it. But at least he is still alive. I suppose someone would tell me if he were not.

I said, "I'm happy to see you," & this was surprisingly true. "It has been — how long?"

"Five weeks," he said, & added, "To the day."

I smiled at him & pressed his hand & said, "It seems longer than that," & his face got very red, & he said, "It does." I could tell all this pleased him immensely

He did not bring his clever little desk, & I would not be having a penmanship lesson, but we went up to the drawing room nevertheless, where we used to be so comfortable. Now of course it is Harold's room. As it is Harold's garden.

We didn't sit at the table but on the couch, beside each other. I made myself not think of Harold, of where he was & what he did & whom he saw & did he think of me. "Tell me what brings you to New Haven this Independence Day, Charles," I said. "Not the mayor's speech on the Green, I assume."

"No. Nor the children's choir, which is going to sing patriotic songs at five o'clock."

"Oh dear. Well, then, I hope you will say you came here to see me."

"I did — of course." He picked up my hand again & held it, damply & tentatively. "I have thought of you so often these past weeks."

"And I of you," I said, & then was sorry, he looked so happy & eager, so I added quickly, "But you said you were here for another purpose, I think. In your note yesterday. To reconcile with old friends, was the way you put it."

He gave a short laugh. His nervousness was palpable. "Ah — yes. Dear old friends with whom I had a misunderstanding that has now been cleared up."

"I am glad to hear it."

"It was weighing on my mind," he said. "The idea that there could ever be a barrier between us grieved me."

I thought of Margaret Brock in her pink hat, & felt inexpressibly sad. I suddenly saw Charles Cooper as someone large & substantial, a man with his own complicated life that he carries with him as he does his card case, or his handkerchief. His dead wife, his dead father, his cousins in Wethersfield, his sister — he did mention a sister, back home from out West. And these old friends in New Haven. He has lived in Connecticut all his life. When he says *home* that is where he means.

I started to feel sorry for myself, a state I despise but one that I give in to more & more of late, & then I heard Prudence, from down in the kitchen where I'd left her with Dora — her voice rising into a strong wail. I had hoped she would sleep long enough for me to spend an hour or so with Charles, but it was the time of the afternoon when she was usually fed. I said, "Charles. I wonder if you would excuse me for — perhaps half an hour? I'm so sorry, I'm delighted to see you, but this is often not a good time of day for me."

The impulse to self-pity left me, & irritability took its place. The world is so full of nonsense. Why cannot I just say to a guest, "I must give my crying baby the breast"? The right to vote & to become president & to be paid fairly for work are all very good things for women, I have no doubt, but I have never heard of anyone marching in the streets for the rights of women to simply be themselves & to do what they need to do without shame.

Charles blushed, of course, but he said, "I understand that you have an infant to care for. Perhaps I'll stroll downtown & join in the singing of 'God Save the Thirteen States.' Or listen to the Mayor read the Declaration of Independence."

"Oh dear! That does not sound pleasant on such a warm day!"

I found I wanted him to stay. His presence was strangely comforting. If he went down to the celebration, he might not return for hours. I proposed that he stay where he was, & he said in his agreeable way, "Yes — yes, that would be delightful. I'll find a book on the shelf, & occupy myself quite nicely until you return."

I thought of Harold, who always had a book shoved into his pocket. But I would have thought of Harold if he never read a book in his life.

"I'll try not to be long," I said, & fled down to the hot kitchen where Prudence's screams were now tortured. Dora's sister Sue was there, & the two were sitting on the step in the doorway, fanning themselves & paying precious little attention to the baby in her cradle. It was appallingly hot from that morning's baking, & the clothes Dora had ironed were not yet put away but were draped all over the kitchen. I did not reprimand her, just told her to give Mr. Cooper some lemonade, or iced tea, & she & Sue could have some as well.

I took Prudence up the back stairs to my bedroom. We sat in the old rocking chair, & I held her in one arm & fanned us gently with the other, & she quieted down & had her milk. She was slower than usual, & kept stopping to coo, or wave her hand at my face, laughing when I caught it or patted it or touched her little nose with my finger. Oh, my darling girl! No gentleman caller, no *suitor*, no one is more important to me than you are, my Prudence, my little love.

I nearly dozed off, & I think nearly an hour went by before she had her fill. She was wide awake, & I hated to leave her, & so I crept back to the drawing room with her in my arms & looked through the doorway. Charles was stretched out with his feet on the ottoman, quite as if he lived there. He had *Harper's Monthly* opened in front of him, & was so intent on what he was reading that he didn't see me for a minute. Then Prudence made a sound, & he looked up, startled, & got to his feet.

"It took longer than I expected," I said. "I hope it was not too tedious."

"I was reading another strange tale by Mr. Melville."

"Oh — Mr. Melville. I have quite given up on him." I settled the baby in the corner of a chair, sitting up as she likes to do now, & tucked her quilt around her. "This is my Prudence Anne, Charles, whose certificate of birth brought us together."

"Ah yes," he said, but his smile was restrained & he remained on his feet, with his hands in his pockets. "The famous Prudence."

I suppose men are not like women, who always want to cuddle a baby, or hold out a finger to be grabbed, or plant a kiss on the top of its head. Charles was content to gaze from afar. Prudence looked up at him, then at me, then began to close her eyes.

I sat down & gathered in my skirts, & Charles closed the magazine & sat beside me. I had decided, while I was nursing Prudence, that I should be a bit more frank with him — more free. What had I to lose? So I said, "I should tell you, Charles, because we have said we are friends, & I have so few of them, that what you have no doubt deduced is true. Prudence is fatherless because she is the product of my folly. She is fatherless, she is all but grandfatherless, she hasn't a friend in the world, & she is blessed only in the fact that she has a mother who loves her beyond anything. Her life is my life. Everything I do is for my child."

My voice shook, & I stopped short. Why was I telling him this? I expected nothing from Charles Cooper. He is a very nice man, a comfortable man. My heart does not leap when I see his tan whiskers & mild gray eyes. And yet I wanted to say these things — to say something *real*, something that has importance for me, so that I would not feel quite so much like an unclaimed parcel, like a boot left out in the rain — like nothing.

"I am a scandal," I went on. "I have lost all my friends. I am, as they say, excluded from polite society. Even my relations have withdrawn their affection, my aunt Julia, my uncle. I am alone in the world. And I appreciate your friendship more than I can say."

He did clasp my hand & then, as if he could not help himself, he took me into his arms. I let him kiss me because, if I am a bird beating her wings against the bars, perhaps it is Charles who will be the one to hold open the cage door through which I can flee.

Chapter Nineteen

"He made a choice. It was the drunkards in New Haven or the heathens in China. Perhaps he tossed a coin. In any case, the heathens won, and my son left for China on the *Midas* in early June."

"It was the right decision, I am sure," Emily said. Bernard had decided to make a joke of it. Emily, however, was distraught and trying not to show it. "He did not have to go to Divinity School. Philip is quite pious enough, and as learned as he needs to be. This way, he will see the world, and he will be under the care of the Reverend Dudson, who has a thriving mission in Canton."

"I rather envy him, seeing China," Charles said. Sometimes a lie was not only justifiable but necessary. "Most of us are lucky to see Boston, or New York!"

"I know the experience will have a profound effect on him, whether he converts anyone or not."

"Oh, he'll convert them," Bernard poured more wine into Charles's glass, then into his own. "They wouldn't dare not convert, lest Philip harangue them to death. He will probably set records for conversions. There will not be a single heathen left in all of China by the time Philip and the rest of the Dudsonites get done with them."

"Bernard is angry, of course. And I do not blame him. Philip has been so very difficult." Emily sighed. "It grieves me to say so, but sometimes religious fervor can have an ill effect. I wish he had joined the Society of Friends when we did. I think he would have been quite different. Quakers forgive."

"I'm very glad the two of you did convert," Charles said.

He was still aggrieved that the Gaudets felt he needed forgiveness for his attraction to Lily Prescott, as if love were a failing, like a bad temper or dropping ashes on the carpet. They had thought it over carefully, Emily told him. They had looked into their hearts, they had prayed over it, and they had written, together, the letter that had brought him to New Haven. *We are too fond of you to let a lack of understanding and a failure to forgive keep you from us. We have found these faults in ourselves, and we are sorry we have wounded you, and sorry that we turned you away.*

And so he had come back. Tears and smiles all around, a few more Quaker homilies, the gratifying news about Philip, and now he was sitting with them in the dining room, with its velvet drapes and rush-seated chairs, drinking Bernard's best claret and eating Hester's roast loin of pork with red onions — Charles's favorite. The relentless benevolence even extended to the new woman in his life, the Jezebel in the purple dress. "Tell us about her, Charles," Emily said. "If you are fond of her, then we must be, too."

Charles had stayed at Lily's until the fireworks began. When he finally left they were bursting in the air over New Haven, vast celestial fountains of color and light and noise that seemed perfect echoes of the alternating jubilation and terror that seized him. The crowd on the Green let out a collective roar as each one went off. Charles walked among them almost oblivious to the display, down Temple Street to Elm and out Whitney Avenue to Bradley Street. The heat had been pushed back a little by the dark, and he was glad of the walk. He was full of the memory of Lily Prescott's hair and eyes and lips, the softness of her under his hands, her words to him, and he went over everything again and again in his mind, trying to decide what it had meant and where it was taking him.

In the drawing room at her house, he knew that his feeling for her was more intense even than what he had felt for Sophie, and that if she would have him, he would make her his wife. He tried to think rationally. What kind of match would it be for her? She was the motherless daughter of a bohemian painter who lived mostly in Europe, she seemed to have no money of her own, her father had possibly disowned her. I am neither exotic nor interesting, he thought — just a solidly middle-class nobody.

But he had money in the bank, an interest in a thriving general store, and a decent position of his own. Most of all, he could not live without Lily Prescott. He had never been surer of anything, and he cared not for anyone else's opinion. All would come right, they had only to love each other.

By the time he reached Elm Street he was sure he was being absurd. The trouble began when he tried to imagine introducing Lily and Prudence to the Gaudets. To his aunt Lottie and uncle Edward Jessup. His mother and all the Pennsylvania Legenhausens. His friends at the college. Tamsin's would be the only sympathy he could count on — or could he? Even that he was not sure of.

He had the contemptible thought that he would pass Lily off as a widow, and as soon as the idea crossed his mind — he was halfway out Whitney Avenue by then — he knew he could not marry her. He would be her friend. He would be her — he choked on the word *lover*, and cast from himself the idea that she was already fallen, she could fall again, and why should it not be into the arms of Charles Cooper? It was love he felt for her — that much he was sure of. And pity. She had told him frankly of her plight, and he knew that only a husband and a home could redeem her. And, thinking this — he was nearly to Bradley Street, the last few fireworks fizzling out in the sky behind him — the pity overflowed, and he determined that he would be the one to give her those things, and damn the lot of them! Anyone who would not accept her, he did not wish to know! By the time he reached the Gaudets he was ready to tell them everything. He would call on Lily Prescott in the morning and propose marriage. She was a paragon among women. Life had treated her harshly, but it had not dampened her spirits or her sweetness or her zest for life. She was an admirable mother and she would make an admirable wife.

Then he was at supper with the Gaudets. *We were not introduced by mutual friends, as Sophie and I were,* he imagined himself saying.

We have no mutual friends! We have no ties at all. I met her on the Green. She could be anyone — worse yet, I could be anyone, but she didn't care. It was she who pursued our conversation. None of this was either proper or usual. But I had only to look at her, the golden-red hair under her little hat, the sweet firmness of her cheek, her lips smiling at me. I fell in love with her before I knew her name. And so when may I bring her over so you can meet her? Oh—and there's her baby, too. How would Tuesday afternoon do?

When Emily said, "Tell us about her, Charles," her eyes were full of the determination to be tolerant and enlightened, and he knew that she would sympathize with Lily's plight and deplore a society that punished so harshly for such a small offense. But marriage to such a woman?

He shook his head. "It is premature," he muttered, and held out his glass for more wine.

❧❧

In the morning, before he returned to Wethersfield, Charles walked downtown to see Harold Milgrim. By now, he had probably been informed by the police of Roland Chillick's arrest, but Charles felt he owed him a first-hand account of the harrowing ride to Hartford — Samuel and Roland squeezed onto the seat beside him, Roland fast asleep and snoring loudly with his head lolling on his brother's shoulder, waking up to mutter something unintelligible, then dropping off again. He was dirtier than ever, his jacket ripped all along one arm, the shirt under it of an indescribable filthiness. His right hand was scabbed over in places and bloody in others, and still black, though whether with soot or dirt it was impossible to tell. The stench was great, but was no longer the smell of burning — only the reek of an unwashed body. Charles had kept glancing over at him. "He is fine," Sam said quietly. "He will be fine." And so he was, even when they delivered him to the police headquarters of the Hartford police and left him there — to what fate Charles did not yet know.

But Milgrim's office was closed; even Miss Mullen was not at her desk. Charles wasn't surprised — it was the morning after Independence Day, and a Saturday — but he was disappointed. He had hoped that spending some time with Milgrim and his flights of fancy — his way of making a joke of everything, as Samuel Chillick had not inaccurately put it — would give him something to think about besides Lily Prescott. Now he was only a few streets away from her and unable to get her out of his mind: Lily as she had been yesterday. The brightness of her eyes and the silkiness of her hair. *I am a scandal,* she said, and called him Charles — his name on her lips sent a jolt through him every time. *I am alone in the world. How much I appreciate your friendship, Charles.*

His fear was that he had compromised her. He had taken liberties — he had kissed her, he had mumbled words of affection. If he just walked by her house the next morning without calling on her, was he not a heartless rascal?

And yet he could not call. If he did, he knew he would have to propose marriage. If he did not, he could postpone his decision. He could see what happened: *seeing what happened* sounded neutral enough.

He knew he was being a fool, but he couldn't think of any other way to be. Most of all, he wished he had someone to advise him. He wished his father were alive — it was a difficult subject, and he couldn't imagine actually broaching it, but if he could, Matthew's good humor might have shed some light. He could talk to Samuel Chillick, if Sam's own wounds were not so fresh. He might even have confided in Harold Milgrim, who seemed a man of the world.

As it was, he advised himself: Go home, Charles. Let it be.

He turned abruptly and took a roundabout route via Hillhouse Avenue out to Bradley, avoiding the Green, avoiding the entire downtown, lest Lily be out walking. He felt like a coward and a cad, and at the same time his heart yearned for her. He would talk to Tamsin when he got home, and, having decided on it, he couldn't wait to get on the road.

Tamsin said, "What a struggle it is to get the boys properly bathed. If I were rich enough to do just one thing, I would have pipes installed in this house for hot water."

"If I were rich enough, I would move to Tahiti."

She laughed. "Oh, Charles, you would not move to Tahiti! I should think you, of all the people I know, are the least likely to move to Tahiti!"

"If I had someone nice to go with me, I might."

"Someone nice. Does that mean you have fallen in love with someone?"

He took the plunge. "Since you ask — I have met a woman in New Haven."

He told her about Lily, realizing as he did so that there was much he didn't know. And he told her that, too — that there had been an Italian escapade, the result of which was a fine healthy baby. He told her everything Lily had said to him, that she had been disowned, that her relatives had forsaken her, that she was friendless and alone — and that she cherished his friendship all the more because of it.

Tamsin frowned. "You mean that you are all she has."

"I suppose so. But I know that she cares for me."

"She has said so?"

"Not outright. Of course not. Nor have I told her exactly how I feel. But it is all there. It is between us. We both feel it."

"Lily Prescott is very beautiful?"

"She is magnificently beautiful."

"Oh, Charles." Tamsin was curled up in Matthew's big chair, her elbow on the arm and her head resting on her hand. She looked at him, saying nothing, while he looked back at her defiantly. He knew she was going to take issue with everything he had told her.

"I married so foolishly," she said. "Without a thought. I fell in love with Eli's handsome face, and with his fiddle playing. His music made me dance, Charles. It made my heart dance — that may sound silly, but it's the truth. I thought if I can live the rest of my life with the sound of this music, how could I be unhappy? I knew him three months. I know you and Father didn't like him much, and there were things about him I didn't particularly like, either. I knew he could be lazy and short-tempered. I didn't know he would be tyrannical and — well, all the rest of it. And unable to hold a job for more than a few months. And that he would play his fiddle only when he was in an amiable mood, which as time went by was not so often." She smiled. "This may sound a bit radical — next thing you know, I'll be advocating for free love — but I sometimes think people should be allowed to live together for a year, not having children but otherwise living like a married couple, to see if they are suited. And at the end of a year they could decide, and if they separated, there would be no stigma. What an enlightened world it would be."

"You will never cease to astonish me."

"You don't see that it's a good plan? If people just thought about it — if it were an accepted thing, not shocking, just the way things are — where is the harm?"

It's hard to imagine such a world," Charles said.

"That is the truth."

They lapsed into silence. Charles thought about virginity. The night they were married, when Sophie gave herself to him, her pain had been so great they had both wept. It took weeks of patience and tenderness for her to get used to it and, finally, to like it. To like it so much that now, four years later, he had to squeeze his eyes shut, thinking of her eagerness, her hands on him.

But what if Sophie had come to him after having already been loved in that way by someone else, in a romance that had not lasted? A man from whom she had willingly parted after a year? Would he have loved and desired her less?

Tamsin broke into his thoughts. "Charles — given that this is the world we live in, whatever bad decision Lily made in Italy, however she came to be carrying this mysterious baby — does it not show a sort of — lightness of mind?"

"She was an innocent, with no experience of the world, when it happened. She was practically a child herself!"

"How old is this baby?"

He counted and said, not without sullenness, "Four or five months. I know what you're going to say. And it's true, she is still very young. But she is much less young than she was a year ago, I am sure of that."

"Of course she is. There's nothing like childbirth to make a woman grow up quickly! But she is still the same person. And you have known her for how long? Two months?"

"Tamsin, I knew after two weeks that I wanted to marry Sophie!"

"Say what you will, Charles, this is nothing like your marriage with Sophie! Think of Father — what would he have advised you?"

"He would have been opposed, but he would have come to love her as he loved Sophie."

"Oh, Charles." She shook her head. "Think of your friends. Think of Aunt Lottie and Uncle Edward."

"Tam." He spoke through gritted teeth. "No more, please. Do you imagine I have not thought of all this, a hundred times? I am fond of Aunt Lottie and Uncle Edward, but I have to tell you I am even fonder of Lily Prescott!"

"Think about *fond*, Charles. Think about love. What does it mean? In a practical way. Marriage is not just about that — that excitement we all know. That passion and urgency. The feeling that if you do not see a certain person — touch a person — you will go mad."

"It's partly that."

"*Partly* is exactly right. There is so much more. Wait a year before you speak to your Lily. See her often. Wait until you have your first tiff — for you will have tiffs, of course. See her in distress, in anger, in confusion and frustration! Then decide."

"You're making it too complicated, Tam. Two people fall in love, and they marry."

"You don't think that's complicated?"

He left the house angrily and walked the perimeter of the town and into the woods to the north, where there was a trail that, if you followed it far enough, would take you to Massachusetts. He followed it for a mile and then sat on a bed of pine needles with his back against a tree. Why did Tamsin have to be so sensible? Worse yet, why did he? Wait a year. That was the right thing to do, and he knew it. And what harm would it do to wait for her? It was not as if

Lily was besieged with suitors. If only she were besiegeable! But if she were, she would not have him.

And if she did agree to have him, was blind adoration on one side and a sort of friendly gratitude on the other a basis for marriage? But no — she liked him. Her chaffing of him, the banter between them. The look on her face when she saw him was pure affection — it was something you couldn't feign. He could not imagine her telling a lie, or deliberately misleading anyone. She would learn to love him, really love him, with the passion he could sense was simmering in her. And weren't they in so many ways kindred souls? She was artistic, and home-loving. They would have more children. And together they would win over her father, and the aunt and uncle who refused to see her, and Tamsin and the rest. And if they could not — they would go to Paris or some equally enlightened place, where the small irregularities of domestic life were looked on with less priggish disfavor than in the stuffy towns of New England!

At the same time, he knew he was a jackass. She would never have him. If she did, it would be a disaster. Paris! What would he do in Paris? It might as well be Tahiti. And when he was being perfectly honest, he wondered if he could ever welcome her child — someone else's child, who knew whose? — into his life as he would his own.

And yet how could he leave her to her fate? How could he give her up? A bit of German came to him, another fragment of a poem he wasn't aware he knew: *Bei Tag, bei Nacht, im Wachen und Traum* — day, night, waking, dreaming. He could not stop thinking of her.

And why should he? He wanted a wife — this was something he knew about himself. He had loved Sophie. He would miss her and regret her death until he was dead himself. But she had been gone for four years, he was twenty-eight years old, and he wanted to live with a woman and love her properly. Was he to look among the drab females of Wethersfield, where he knew everyone and was well aware that there were no Lily Prescotts? And besides, it was not just a wife he wanted, it was his own Lily — the Lily Prescott he had kissed, whose head had rested on his shoulder and whose hand he had pressed in his own.

He sat until he could no longer stand his own thoughts, and then he walked home. As usual, he stopped at the post office. Technically, it was closed, but Zeke was sitting in front with his pipe, and he went inside and retrieved a letter for him. Charles read it as he walked slowly home. It was from his old friend William Blanchard. The name carried a cloud around it, like the block on Wall Street where his old house had stood. It was Blanchard and his partner, Jonathan Ives, whom Charles had been with at the tavern the night of the fire. But his letter was welcome news indeed:

Dear Charles,

This letter is to let you know that Jonathan and I have reawakened our idea of beginning a school of business in New Haven. Or rather, the idea has never slept, but it has taken us some time to formulate exactly what we would like to do, how the school would be run, exactly where we might locate it, and need I say, the funds to get it started. We now have investors, a site, and many plans! All we lack is a staff and a curriculum — and students, of course, but we are confident they will appear once the school does.

The school would be as we discussed before — it would provide instruction in all aspects of business education, but with an emphasis on the different varieties of penmanship — not just that which is used in the world of business, but the more artistic and ornamental types on which you are the reigning and undisputed expert. We need a director who has the highest principles combined with the greatest skill and good sense, and with the requisite experience as an educator. Your name is as high on our list as it was four years ago. I hope you will let me know when you will be in New Haven next so the three of us can arrange to meet. Near the middle of next month would do very well for us.

I trust you are having a pleasant summer, and that we can revive your enthusiasm for our scheme. With all good wishes, I am, etc....

Charles spent the rest of July at his desk with pen and paper and the notes for his writing manual, working out the easiest way to teach others the script he had devised. He was pleased with it: a hybrid of copperplate and the work of the Italian masters he admired above all. It was practical, not fancy, but beautiful — and quicker than the running hand that was taught in most schools.

"You should call it Cooper Italic," Tamsin said. "Why should you not name it after yourself, as Mr. Spencer did?"

"I would feel like a fool, is why," he said, and Tamsin laughed, but he kept thinking about naming his script, and later he had an inspiration: Connecticut Italic.

It came to him on yet another sunny afternoon as he was finishing up the chicken coop with a coat of whitewash. He had made the old structure into a snug and roomy one, elevated to keep the mice out, with sturdy screens on the windows, shutters that could be closed in cold weather, and a fenced-in pen around it.

"The new coop is a palace," Tamsin said. "My girls in Ohio were good layers, but their accommodations were primitive." She laughed shortly. "Everything on our property was primitive! The whole place could as easily have been set up in the 1450s as the 1850s."

They were driving back from Mr. Jenkel's farm out by the cove, where they had bought four laying hens. Tamsin had had her heart set on red ones, but she let Jenkel talk her into two reds and two of a handsome new breed, Barred Plymouth Rocks, which he had just acquired. Barred Plymouth Rocks loved cold weather, Jenkel said. They live forever, and sometimes their eggs are pink. The boys were enchanted, and Tamsin could not resist.

"It's good you can laugh," Charles said.

"I didn't laugh for half a dozen years, it seems. I'm making up for lost time."

Charles had wondered if Eli would provide Tamsin with some kind of support now that they were separated, as Matthew had for Magda. It seemed unlikely that Eli was in a position to do so, and the separation had not been a mutual wish — Tamsin had apparently just left, with no warning. There was no question of her going back: she told Charles she felt like someone who had come out of a cave where she'd been hiding, into the light and air. Or like someone freed from a trap. She had written to Eli to let him know she and the boys were safe. As far as Charles knew she had heard nothing from Ohio.

Tamsin smoothed down the skirt of her old pink calico dress, intently studying its tiny white flowers, and then she asked, abruptly, "Have you seen Samuel, Charles? I keep wondering about him."

The last he'd seen of Sam Chillick was when he'd taken him back to Coleman Street after their drive to Hartford. Neither of them had spoken the whole way — Chillick seemed sunk in gloom, and when they pulled up at his house he had shaken Charles's hand, thanked him, and gone inside without another word.

"I haven't wanted to intrude," Charles said. "But nor do I want him to think we aren't concerned about Roland's fate. I'll walk over there soon."

"I hope you will. It's hard to know how to act, I suppose. It's like a death in the family — maybe worse. But I'm sure he would like to know we think of him."

"Tamsin — he is not the jolliest of fellows."

She gave a little laugh. "Well, I appreciate your observation, Charles. But first of all, he is quite jolly enough when he is not worried to death about his brother. And second — surely you don't think I have my eye on Sam Chillick. I am still a married woman, after all."

"Father and Mother found a way around it."

"Yes, but Father did not take up with Mrs. Griswold when mother left!"

"Strange things happen."

"I will not even ask you what that is supposed to mean," she said, and turned away from him to look out at the passing scene which, as they neared Wethersfield, was one of barns, hayfields, meadows dotted with cows motionless in the heat. "And Charles —"

"All right, all right, I apologize. I have stuffed my foot into my mouth, as I used to do when I was twelve and you were twenty and you used to agree with mother that I was a chowderhead."

She laughed. "No, no, this is something else — something that has been bothering me all this week. I want you to accept my apology for what I said about Lily. I'm too much the big sister, but not because I think you're a chowderhead. I know full well that you are not twelve anymore."

"Sometimes I manage to be about fifteen."

"Don't be silly. You have been so kind to me and my boys. There's enough misery in this world! If you want to bring Lily home as your bride, if she makes you happy after what you have been through, I will welcome her with all my heart."

"There is nothing to apologize for. You provided me with much to think about, Tam. I was wrong to get angry."

"You should have been angrier! You are too good sometimes, Charles. Too mild." She leaned her shoulder against his. "Lily would be lucky to get you. Remember what I said. Do what you think is right. You don't need me to advise you."

They drove along in an amicable silence, and Charles suddenly felt easy in his mind. Tamsin was home, the new hens were clucking cozily in the back of the wagon with his nephews, Eli Pugh was far away, and he was pleased about the letter from Blanchard and his prospects in New Haven. Only Lily kept him awake at night. It had been so easy with Sophie — he and she had fallen into a friendship, an ease with each other that was more like a brother and a sister until, on an impulse, he kissed her for the first time — and then it was settled.

But when he thought of Lily, it was all shilly-shally: he loved her, but did he love her enough? Was he being wise or foolish to pursue her? How was wisdom defined? And how could anyone know the difference between love and foolishness?

He would see her when he met with Blanchard on the fourteenth of August, and when he saw her, he told himself, the answers would come to him.

❧❦

The next afternoon he took a walk to Coleman Street and found Samuel Chillick sitting on his front porch, smoking, his spectacles pushed up on his head. Construction had commenced again on the house across the way, and Charles took off his jacket and sat down with him to watch the work. A mason was building a short wall from Bernard's bricks, and two men were sawing boards. The smell of soil and sawdust and the rhythmic whine of the saws came to them where they sat, mixing with the smell of Samuel's pipe.

Samuel told him his brother was still in the Hartford jail, but would soon be taken to the asylum there. "They call this one a hospital — the West Hartford Hospital for the Criminally Insane." He shrugged. "They say it's a humane place. Even for murderers."

"He will not be prosecuted?"

"There will be a hearing in a few weeks. His attorney will apply what is called the M'Naghten rule, which says defendants may be acquitted if they committed their crime because of a disease of the mind — he will have to prove that Roland did not realize that what he did was a crime." His mouth tightened. "That should not be difficult. Roland is raving. He is in restraints."

"I'm sorry, Sam. My heart goes out to you."

"It could be so much worse. He could be hanged, but it does not look as if that will happen. He will be locked up for the rest of his time on earth. I had hoped he would be sent to the state prison here, but they do not take the insane. But in Hartford I can visit him, and I can hope that he will improve enough to find some satisfactions in his life. I suppose it has worked out as well as can be expected. For everyone but Letitia, of course. I went to see the Trouts. They were not very welcoming, but they were not unsympathetic. At least they didn't throw me out. They seemed so devastated, so broken, it was as if they had died themselves."

Charles had a sudden thought. "Sam — what happened to the ring?"

"The ring." Samuel shook his head and sat looking down at his pipe. "The ring that started Roland on his course of violence. It's gone. It's nowhere. Roland didn't have it on him. He had no memory of what happened to it. The ring was as alien to him as — as my hygrometer. He may have lost it. He may have sold it. Perhaps it was stolen from him. Perhaps he thought it was the devil and cast it from him into the Connecticut River. The accursed ring is nowhere to be found.

An absurd ending to a tragic tale. A tale whose narrative was set in motion by no one but myself. It is a hard thing to bear, Charles."

They were silent a while longer, watching the men across the road as they worked. Charles wished he had a pipe to smoke. There was something he wanted to say, but his habit of reticence was strong. Finally he nerved himself and said, "I was struck, Sam, by what you said on the ride home from the asylum. About blaming yourself." He spoke hesitantly. "When I said it seems wrong to blame ourselves for things we did not mean to do, I was talking about myself."

Chillick looked over at him. "You?"

"For a long time I held myself responsible for something very bad that happened — worse yet, others held me responsible, and saw it as an event that I could have prevented if only I had acted differently. But I did not act differently, because I did not know what would happen. No one could have known. It was only after it happened that I could see what I could have done differently. It's as if there are two worlds, the real one and the one that exists in our heads in which we should have done something it did not occur to us to do."

He stood up abruptly and walked to the road: the mason loaded bricks into a wheelbarrow and trundled it back to the wall. Charles had to stifle the impulse to sob. Without warning, he was in the grip of a strong emotion he could not at first identify, and then he recognized it as happiness, an extension of the way he had felt in the wagon with Tamsin. He realized that he was free at last from his long guilt about Sophie and Charlie — a release that had crept up on him slowly over the summer. He would miss his wife and child forever, but he was no longer tethered to them.

He calmed himself and turned to look at Chillick. "I'm probably not making myself clear."

"No — you are very clear." Chillick sucked at his pipe. "Perhaps sometime you will tell me what it was that happened."

Charles sat back down on the step. "Perhaps."

"I am trying to come to that same conclusion — or rather, I'm trying to strike a balance between taking some responsibility for what happened to my brother — to Letitia — and what you are

208

talking about. The perception of something after the fact — you are right — that is about a world that never existed. I tell myself that Letitia is dead because my brother is mad, and that it is absurd to think she is dead because I failed to visit him more often. And much of the time I believe that is true." Chillick went on, "Lately I've been trying to distract myself with work — something I have always been able to do successfully."

"No doubt much good work has been born out of the need for distraction."

"I believe it. I'm working on a cloud atlas, as I think I told you, a sort of encyclopaedia of the various kinds of clouds, but I've come to an impasse over the illustrations. I assumed some sort of photographic process could be used, but I've talked to an artist at the college who has done work with a camera, and he is doubtful. Clouds are so evanescent, and of course they are always moving. There is a new process that shortens exposure times for photographic images, but he says he is not yet a master of it, nor does he know anyone who is."

"I once saw a fine series of photographs of old New England churches, " Charles said. "And while you could see every detail of the buildings, the sky was a blank white space. It makes me wonder, even if you could photograph clouds quickly enough, would there be enough contrast between the cloud and the sky."

"The conditions would have to be exactly right — the sky a very brilliant blue, the clouds a pure white. And there are colored glass filters, I think, that could create some contrast. But of course some clouds, by their nature, are grayish, and the sky they appear in is often gray as well! The whole process seems impossibly complicated. Only a master could manage it — some Frenchman, no doubt, who is up on all the new inventions."

"This scene," Charles said, pointing to the men at work across the way. "The blue of the brick mason's shirt, the reds and browns of the bricks, the two men with the saws, the wheelbarrow, the green-wood as a backdrop. If only one could produce photographic images in color! We could sit here on your porch with our apparatus and make a picture worthy of a museum."

"And reproduce the blue sky with its white clouds, exactly as we're seeing it now." Samuel pointed with his pipe. "An impressive stand of cumulus that is slowly moving into a more cumulonimbus phase."

"What is it saying to you?"

"It is breeding rain."

"And when will it deliver?"

"Around suppertime. A thunderstorm. See if I'm right."

Charles smiled. "You know, when I look at those clouds, it strikes me that what you require is not a photographer, but a painter. Did you go to see the paintings by the painter Constable that were shown at the Athenaeum in Hartford? Paintings of people at work, with huge skies behind them, and every variety of cloud. Maybe your illustrations should not be exact likenesses. Maybe they should leave out some of the detail while they increase the contrast, so that they can be used more easily for identification."

"I've been thinking along those lines myself, and actually made an attempt at painting them. It seems so simple — drawing a cloud! But like most things that seem simple, it's in fact damnably difficult. Some painter — maybe it was your Mr. Constable — observed that an artist who is self-taught is taught by a very ignorant person indeed."

"I've even had lessons in painting," Charles said, "but can no more paint a cloud than I can fly to one."

"So many failed Constables in this world."

"Tamsin is the one with the talent. She could probably paint a cloud as quickly as I could write the word on a piece of parchment. And it would look like a cloud, not like some kind of baggy undergarment that has gotten loose from a clothesline!"

Samuel laughed. "I didn't know she included painting among her talents. I will talk to her."

"Come for supper. I can easily have Annie throw another potato into the pot."

"I would like that very much."

"Bring your umbrella, of course."

Chapter Twenty

5 August, Tuesday. Elena took my baby to the wet nurse yesterday. The night before, no one slept, Prue cried so. I had a fever, & spent two days in bed, feeling like death. It passed, but as a consequence my milk has dried up. Not suddenly, but over the course of several days — days on which she cried more & more, & at first I didn't know why, I was still weak & sick from the fever, & then I realized that she was hungry, she wasn't just fretful, the milk was not sufficient, & all the time E. sat there with us, like a spider, waiting to pounce on the morsel she had been waiting for with such patience. And she said even if the milk should come back, it could hurt Prudence, it could infect her with whatever is ailing me.

It is Mrs. Duffy's young sister, Mrs. Whelan, whose baby, dreadful to tell, was lost on the boat coming over & buried at sea. She has been here two months, has nursed another baby, & now will nurse mine. What was her baby's name? E. doesn't know.

Dora said we can give Prue cow's milk, if we thin it with water it will not harm her. No, E. says, I have cared for enough babies, it is too soon, they can't keep it down, it makes them sick. I know she is right about the milk. I even read it in *Godey's*. It's what everyone knows. But how I wish I had someone to advise me — a mother, an aunt, a friend! I have only Dora, who knows nothing, and Elena, who talks as if she knows everything, but — how do I know she is right? And yet the facts are undeniable. I cannot feed my child, I am almost too weak to hold her, and my head is in a muddle. I am lucky to have Elena.

But I thought we could invite Mrs. Whelan to live here & nurse the baby in my own house. Could I bear to watch this? It doesn't matter, Prue would be here, nothing else matters, I want to do what's good for her. I would bear it. I would befriend the poor woman. I could watch my baby grow. Every day she is different, every day she is more beautiful, her hair is coming in golden brown, her eyes are so blue. She can sit up so well! And she smiles when she sees me, she reaches out her arms.

E. says it is not possible for Mrs. W. to stay here. Her husband wouldn't allow it. But I can see Prudence, I can visit her in Irishtown. When I'm feeling better.

I'm still not really well, & so I know I ramble. It's too much trouble to order my thoughts. The days are so hot, & I don't know whether I still have a touch of the fever or if it's the weather. We are past July — it has been nearly a month since I wrote here last. Then I was trying to practice my penmanship as I wrote. Now it's just scribble scribble, & I have to stop to rest. I am tired all the time, & my stomach is unstable.

I could see old Dr. Punderson, who has known me since I was six, but of course I cannot see Dr. Punderson any more than I can send a note to my aunt to come & take care of me. I swallow a spoonful of Mrs. Duffy's Chinese tonic from the ugly brown bottle three times a day, before meals, but I cannot say it helps. The stuff itself is fibrous & thick, the color of stewed toads, but it tastes surprisingly pleasant, with mint in it, I think, & some sugar. So I swallow it willingly enough, & it may do some good.

When the heat isn't too extreme, I sit in the garden & work at the dress I'm making for Prue, white with a blue ribbon threaded through the hem, to wear the first day of September, which is when we have decided she will come home.

I cannot think about poor Mrs. W. Her name is Mary, she is younger than I am, only seventeen, & she comes from a town in Ireland E. doesn't know the name of, in County Cork, & she has a husband called Liam, which is Irish for William. E. says he is very handsome. They live in Irishtown, in Fair Haven, on the river, where I have always heard that pigs run in the streets, eating garbage, but E. says that is not true at all, it's part of the prejudice against the Irish. She has become very pro-Irish! She says the Whelans live in a nice little cottage, full of their relations, so crowded it's shocking, she says, but very clean. She says they are very fine people, and not as poor as you might think. Still, I suppose they need the money I'll pay them. Her husband, the handsome Liam, works for the railroad, but Mary W. has been unable to find a position, & so she puts strange babies to her breast & suckles them. At what cost to herself?

I woke this morning before dawn as if to Prue's little cries, as if my breasts were still swollen with milk & needed relief — the beautiful, drowsy time of day when I used to bring her into bed with me and doze on and off while she nursed. There is always that faint crowing of a rooster from a farm somewhere to the west. A cricket. The clop of the milk wagon. And light creeping in slowly between the curtains. The house is so still, & then come the noises that tell me Dora is up, far below in the kitchen — the kettle banging, and her voice in the alleyway talking across the wall to Mrs. Thorpe's cook.

All was as usual this morning, and then I remembered. She is such a small person, so new in this world, & yet such a part of me. The birth certificate still sits on the shelf with a neat pile of tiny caps & booties, & a cloth dog I sewed that has Mortimer's floppy ears & white-tipped tail. But the cradle was empty, & by the time my room was light & I heard E. go downstairs, I was sunk in the loneliness that will be my life for the next four weeks.

When I really want to torture myself, I think about Harold. I saw him on 22 July — it was a Tuesday, & I remember that day because Elena told me it was the feast of St. Mary Magdalene, who I know was a reformed sinner. A loose woman who bathed the feet of Jesus with her tears. Or so they say, though it sounds improbable. No one could shed so many tears. Though that is the least of Elena's nonsense.

He had been away, at the family summer house in Old Saybrook, & I had not heard from him in many days. He was full of funny stories about his family & how they blight his life. He said even the ice cream wasn't so good this year, & it was much too hot for *boules,* which they play on the lawn — there is a vast lawn, & it slopes down to the water — but his cousins kept insisting, & when it wasn't hot it was wet, & sometimes it was both.

There was of course no question of his inviting me there for a visit, to meet his family. Of course he missed me. But I am what I am. I should pray to St. Anthony — Harold is my hopeless case.

He stayed only half an hour. "Business!" he said, making it sound like a treat, a party with cake & champagne. He kissed me when he left — such a long kiss it was as if he would not see me for a long time. And in fact it has been two weeks. Nor does he write.

Without Prue, without Harold, I am more alone than ever. I went up to Papa's studio & took the miniature of my grandmother — I think it is my grandmother, I hope it is — & tied it around my neck, & I put on the silver bracelet that was my mother's.

I take my toad tonic & go up to my room early. I think it's the tonic that makes me so tired. I can hardly keep my eyes open, I cannot concentrate on a book and can hardly read the newspaper, but I don't mind. If I could sleep until Prudence comes back, I would be content. I look forward to the darkness, and I like going to sleep as much as I used to like waking up to my baby's cries. As I lie there feeling sleep come, it's as if my troubles were actually objects weighing me down, rocks I'm buried under, & I can sense them lifting away, one by one, leaving me light & free, & alone with my dreams.

Chapter Twenty-One

Charles had made up his mind before he drove to New Haven that, depending on terms, he would accept the offer from Blanchard. He would not be sorry to leave the college in Hartford, except that he had a few good friends there. He had his own ideas about how a business school should be run, and what should be taught, and how. He would welcome the opportunity to put his ideas into practice — best of all, to introduce his Connecticut Italic to the world. And, now that his father was gone, to live in the bustling city again would be a pleasure — and he would breathe the same air as Lily.

Tamsin had needed Mavis, so he took the train down, and walked from the station to meet Ives and Blanchard at the Exchange Hotel on Chapel Street. Charles was eloquent on the subject of what he wanted in a school — what was lacking in every establishment he had been associated with — and he had refined his ideas since their meeting four years before. He favored an emphasis on elegance as well as utility, a curriculum tailored to each student's requirements, an openness to new methods not only of penmanship but of business practice in general, and possibly a division for women along the lines of Mr. Spencer's school in Washington.

The two men liked what they heard. Blanchard ordered champagne, and the deal was quickly done. They hoped to open the Elm City School of Business sometime after the new year, with a small staff to begin with but with room to expand. They had leased the second floor of a new building on State Street, not far from the railway station. The hiring of the teachers would be up to Charles, and if he would use his skill with the pen to design a letterhead — "fancy but dignified" — they would like very much to see it.

"Fancy but dignified is my stock in trade," Charles assured them. He immediately saw it in his mind: a diminishing row of elm trees, and above them the name of the school, nicely flourished. "There are two teachers I will try to poach from Wethersfield. Aside from that, I will have to write letters and make some inquiries. There are one or two old students of mine who would do very well, I think." By Christmas, he said, he would have a staff in place.

He wondered at his own audacity, and hoped the champagne was not making him too reckless in what he promised. And yet if there was anything he felt secure in, it was his ability to teach penmanship and business practices, and to make others excited about them. Ives and Blanchard had no doubts about him, and so he had no doubts about himself.

All his doubts were saved for Lily — how she would receive him and how he would feel when he saw her.

As he turned the corner onto York Street, his heart was racing. He sprinted up the stone steps, but then stood there with the door knocker in his hand. His need to see her was acute, but at the same time he was afraid to knock. It was like the moment just before he had kissed her — nearly six weeks ago. He stood on the step and remembered how her voice had trembled, how he had taken her hand, put his arms around her, begun to lift her hand to kiss it, and then, instead, had kissed her lips. She had not pulled away. She had clasped her arms around his neck and kissed him again....

He let the knocker fall, and Lily answered the door herself, almost at once. Her appearance was shocking: she was disheveled, wearing only a wrapper, and her hair was down — his first thought was that she looked like a mad woman. "Charles." She drew him inside and slammed the door, her eyes panicked. "Thank God you're here," she said. "Elena has not come back, and I think she has taken Prudence. Charles, you must help me." Her voice rose. "I don't know what to do."

"Lily." He led her into the parlor. The room was dim, the drapes nearly closed against the heat. He sat on the sofa and pulled her down beside him. "Calm yourself. Tell me what happened."

"Elena." She clutched his arm with both hands, "Elena went out yesterday and didn't come back, and this morning she is not here, she has not been in her bed, and I have waited all morning but she has not returned, and now I don't know what to do, Charles. What shall I do?"

Her eyes were wild, and her face crumpled again. He shook her a little. "Lily. Where is the baby? What happened to Prudence?"

"Oh — she has been gone nine days. I have been ill." Lily put her hand to her forehead and started to cry. "I said I would not cry, I swore to myself I would not."

"Just tell me."

She looked at him piteously. "My — my milk dried up, and I was unable to feed her, and Elena found a wet nurse in Irishtown, her name is Mary Whelan, and I have missed her so badly, but it is only until the middle of September. That is less than a month. I thought it would be all right. I thought this was best for her. She cannot have cow's milk, or even goat's milk, she is too little."

"Yes, yes, I understand. Now tell me — here —" He pulled out his handkerchief and gave it to her and watched as she wiped her eyes. He tried not to think of how beautiful she looked in her distress — beautiful and a little alarming, half-dressed, her wrapper pulled loosely around her, her neck and arms bare. "What do you mean, Elena has taken Prudence? What makes you think Prudence is anywhere but with this wet nurse?"

"Her earrings are gone. Tiny gold earrings Elena got for her." She spoke through a sob. "And all her dresses are gone from the shelf, and the little dog I made, with ears like Mortimer's — these are not things that went with her to Mrs. Whelan. They are things Elena took yesterday when she left. She usually takes only her sewing basket, but she had a valise, and I asked her why and she said it was old clothes for the missionaries at her church, they send things to the Hawaiian Islands."

"Excuse me — Miss Lily. "

Dora, the housemaid, stood in the doorway, in a very dirty apron, her cap askew. Lily raised her head. "Dora — don't stand there gaping like a fish in a tank! What do you want?"

"I just wondered, Miss Lily. If I might be of service. " She spoke with some resentment, but she stood her ground. It was clear that the girl was worried. What kind of a morning could the two of them have had? It was nearly noon, and Lily had had hours of grief and panic before he arrived. "I thought I could go and get your aunt, Mrs. Tuttle, to stay with you in your trouble"

"That sounds like a capital idea." Charles would welcome another presence. "Where is your aunt, Lily?"

"Dora, you are so stupid!" She was crying again. "My aunt will not, she will not — my uncle will not allow it —"

"She is out in Westville, sir," Dora said. "On Blake Street. I know where her house is. I wouldn't mind except that this is my Thursday half-day, and I wouldn't take it, I would stay with Miss Prescott myself, but Mother is not well. She needs me and I promised."

"Charles, you must listen to me. My aunt will not —"

"You don't know what your aunt will do until someone asks her." Charles took some coins from his purse. "Here — Dora — go down to Moore's and hire a carriage and take it out to Westville. And find Miss Prescott's aunt and ask her — beg her — to help us. Persuade her that she must come. "

"I could take the omnibus coach, sir, down at the corner. It is only a nickel."

"That's all right. You may get a carriage."

"Yes, sir." She looked dubiously at the handful of coins.

"Can you do all that, Dora?"

"Of course she cannot do all that!" Lily cried. "Dora, you know nothing about this. You are a foolish, foolish girl!"

Dora tightened her lips. "I can, sir."

"I hope so," Charles said grimly. " I will stay with Miss Prescott until her aunt comes. And then you can take the carriage and go to your mother's."

"Thank you, sir," Dora said, managing a curtsey.

Lily raised her hand to her forehead, then raked it back through her hair. "Oh, this is hopeless! And your apron, Dora —"

"It's all right, Lily. Don't fret about Dora's apron."

"I will not wear my apron, Miss Lily." She spoke with dignity. "I hope I would not wear a dirty apron in a carriage to see Mrs. Tuttle."

Dora left abruptly and clattered down the steps to the kitchen. Charles turned to Lily. "My aunt will never come," she said. Her wrapper had slipped back, and she gathered it around her. "Oh, Charles, everything is in such a muddle. It's just that I've been so ill, and it has been so hot, and life goes on around me...."

"Listen to me, Lily. It will be all right. You don't know that Elena has taken Prudence. Elena could be anywhere. But we know where Prudence is. She is with a wet nurse in Irishtown. I will find the woman, and find your baby."

"And bring her back! I can't let her go again! I'll find another nurse, someone who will board here with us —"

"We will do all that. But you must remain calm."

"Elena could spirit her away — anywhere! She has taken up with these Irish women. She could take her to Ireland!"

"Lily." He put his arms around her and pulled her against him, and stroked her shoulder under her silky wrapper. "You are being absurd," he said gently, and gradually he felt her relax. Her hysteria and her disregard for anything but her feelings was worrisome — he was afraid of the kind of hysteria he had seen in his mother — but in Lily it also touched him deeply. He remembered what Tamsin had said, that he needed to see Lily in distress, in confusion. She had no one else but him to care for her, and care for her he would, no matter what. *Bei Tag, bei Nacht, im Wachen und Traum...* He bent his head and kissed her neck.

Eventually, she dozed in his arms. It was very warm in the parlor. Charles sweated under his coat and wished he could take it off, but he didn't want to disturb her. Her sleep was not peaceful — she twitched awake, he soothed her back to sleep, she woke again with a cry, dozed again. His handkerchief was balled up in her fist, and he gently pried it away and wiped his face with it, then held her loosely, alternately watching her sleep and looking at the painting over the mantel: a formal garden with an immense villa rising behind it and, in the distance, blackish-green hills, the sky above it all a vivid orange dwindling to pink. Italy, he assumed, and imagined Lily in his conception of Rome, a white marble city in the sun, full of swarthy people, slightly dangerous. Everything heightened, larger than life. "New Haven is such a tiny city," she had said. They could live in Rome, he thought. Disappear into its vastness. He looked at the painting, imagined climbing into the wooded hills, walking across the veranda. What would it smell of? What would it be like to hear little English, to speak Italian, to wake up every morning a stranger in a strange land?

He closed his eyes and held her. All he wanted was to keep her calm and happy, live with her in peace. Whatever happened, he would remember this quiet, and beneath his cheek the softness of her hair, the heat of her skull.

Nearly an hour went by before the carriage pulled up with Lily's aunt in it. The knocker woke them both. Lily sprang to her feet, went to the window, raised her palms to either side of her face, and said, "Charles! What do I look like? I must look like a witch!"

He tucked her hair behind her ears. "You do not look like a witch. And it would not matter if you did."

She looked at him wildly, then ran into the hall to open the door, Charles stood up and wiped his face again with his handkerchief. He heard Lily weeping incoherently, and her aunt's voice, gentle and firm, attempting to comfort and calm. In a moment they came in, and Mrs. Tuttle introduced herself briskly — a short, stout woman with eyes the color of Lily's.

Charles bowed and said his name, and Lily said, "Charles is going to find Prudence and bring her back."

She had regained her composure, but tears were sliding down her face. She seemed unaware of them. She held on tightly to her aunt's arm. This was the aunt, Charles assumed, who had all but ignored her for nearly a year, but she looked at him kindly enough and said she was grateful to him for helping Lily. She disengaged herself from Lily to take off her bonnet, and smoothed back her white hair, which looked as if it might once have been golden-red like her niece's.

"I do not really understand what has happened. But Lily will tell me. I'll stay with her while you —" She broke off. "You know where the baby is?"

"She is somewhere in Fair Haven," Lily said. She sat down again, and Mrs. Tuttle perched beside her. "She has gone to a wet nurse. Mrs. Whelan. Mary. And her husband is Liam, I think — yes, Liam." She spoke eagerly, as if the accumulation of detail could bring Prudence back. "She is Mrs. Duffy's sister — Mrs. Duffy is a friend of Elena's from her church."

"Elena," Mrs. Tuttle said. "Who is Elena?"

"I will tell you," Lily said. "Oh, there is too much to tell."

"Is that all you know about this wet nurse?"

"She is near the river, Elena said. A cottage."

"That's all?"

"I — I only know what she told me. I have not been well, Aunt Julia. I scarcely knew what — oh — but Mrs. Duffy is a friend of Mrs. McAlmond, who is a midwife. That may be helpful. Surely Fair Haven is not so big?"

Lily and her aunt looked up at Charles expectantly. He took a deep breath. It was not much. Wet nurses and midwives. Whelan, Duffy, McAlmond. A cottage near the river, meaning not the Mill River where he went fishing, but the big river east of it, the Quinnipiac — he had a vague idea that the two rivers joined to empty into the harbor, and that between them was Fair Haven, where they trolled for oysters. How to get to it from York Street, Charles had only the haziest idea. New Haven was a tiny city, Lily always said, but it didn't seem to him tiny at all. He had never been to Fair Haven. That part of town was no doubt a maze of cottages on the river.

Lily managed a smile that nearly broke his heart. "I know you will bring her back."

He felt ridiculous — a knight, a savior. He leaned over and gently wiped the tears on her cheeks, then handed her the handkerchief again. "I will," he said, and bowed to them both, feeling Mrs. Tuttle's eyes on him.

He emerged onto York Street, and took a series of deep breaths. *What now,* he thought. *What now what now what now....*

"Sir? Mr. Cooper, sir?"

It was Dora, in the carriage, which was still pulled up in front of the house. She looked remarkably self-possessed, and in her bonnet and cloak, quite ladylike. Charles doffed his hat. "Yes, Dora. What is it?"

"I waited for you, sir. I wanted to say something. I hope it is not presumptuous, but I felt you should know."

The driver sat holding his whip, impervious. Charles stepped closer. "I am listening."

Dora's eyes were large and terrified. She looked past him at the house, as if expecting someone to come out and hush her. "It is Elena," she said.

"Elena? What is Elena?"

"She gave something to Miss Prescott that made her sick."

Charles stared at her. "What are you saying?"

"Something in a bottle that she made Miss Lily take. She done it so the baby would go out to nurse."

"Dora. How do you know this?"

"Well — I do not know it, sir. I know nothing for sure. But it was the way Elena talked about it, the way she would smile — I cannot explain it better, sir. I just know it was bad medicine." She looked down at her hands, which were clasped tightly in her lap. "She wanted the baby," she said, in a near-whisper.

Charles gripped the carriage door. "She wanted the baby? Elena did?" He saw her nod. "Dora. Dora — whatever for?"

"She wanted the baby for herself." Tears slid down Dora's fat cheeks, and her mouth quivered. She looked up at him, then down again quickly. "I just know it. The way she would look at her."

"Dora."

"I must go, sir. I don't want to say any more. What if it's not true? I'm only saying what I think."

"I won't tell anyone you told me this, Dora, I promise. You need not fear."

"Thank you, sir, but — I must get to my mother."

"Yes, yes, of course." He stepped back helplessly. "I —"

"I can't tell you no more. But — I know it is true, sir." She wiped at her eyes and sat back, then raised her voice and said to the driver, "Please. We can go now."

"Wait! Dora!" Charles trotted alongside the carriage as it began to move. "You don't know where Elena is, do you? Or where this nurse is? This Mrs. Whelan?"

"I do not. I'm sorry, sir. I do not. I have told you everything I know." Her face looked out at him fearfully. "And maybe I do not even know it!"

Charles stood watching the carriage until it turned and was gone. Then he walked up to Chapel, and paused at the corner by the college buildings to gather his wits. It was past midday, and the street was clogged with horses, carriages, a clattering milk wagon, a plodding oxcart carrying logs, women with parasols against the hot sun, a black man with a hand cart peddling tin ware, a trio of well-dressed children with their governess, two uniformed policeman on horseback. Charles stared stupidly at the scene, hoping for inspiration. It was a desperately hot day. He felt a great desire just to sit down somewhere and think. The abrupt leap into the intricacies of Lily's life — her baby, her servants, her distress — had unnerved him. It had placed their association on a different level, but he was unsure what it was. She had turned to him as her rescuer — what did it mean? Love? Terror? Simple hysteria?

What he should have done, he thought, was get a drink of water at Lily's. He considered a stop at the Park House for a cold draft of ale, rejected the idea — thought about taking a carriage out to the Gaudets' to ask Emily for advice and a cup of tea, but knew he could not.

Then he thought of Harold Milgrim. It should not be difficult for a man who had solved cases for Scotland Yard to help him find a baby in New Haven. If nothing else, he could tell Charles how on earth to get to the river!

He walked quickly down to Park Street and up the two flights of stairs to the third floor. At the end of the first flight, he took off his frock coat, and at the top of the stairs he removed his waistcoat, too, and his hat. When he walked into Milgrim's office, he was out of breath and bedraggled.

Miss Mullen was at her desk. She had rolled up her sleeves and was fanning herself with a palm-leaf fan. Her brown hair, frizzed in the heat, was in an untidy bun, but she looked cool and serene. "Mr. Cooper!"

"Miss Mullen."

"Is this not the most vile hot weather you have ever encountered? What may I do for you? You're looking for Mr. Milgrim, I suppose?"

"Is he here?"

"He is not." She reached behind her to a shelf for another fan, and handed it to him. "Here. It will help. And sit down. Please."

He sank into a chair and fanned himself vigorously. It did help. "Where is he?"

"In Old Saybrook with Mater and Pater and, I believe, his *fiancée*."

"*Fiancée?*"

"It's Mr. Milgrim's own expression — where does he pick up these things? It's a fancy French word that means his intended. His betrothed."

Charles was startled. "He has an intended?"

"Oh yes. He has not told you?"

"I have not seen him. I had a letter from him not long ago, but he didn't mention an engagement."

"Well, it is rather recent. A summer courtship. Miss Margaret Brock, an old friend of his family. They were childhood sweethearts. Then they grew up. Now I suppose they are in their second childhood! Ever so lovey-dovey. Miss Brock is a dear girl — and quite delightfully tall," she said impishly. "Perhaps even taller than Mr. Milgrim!" Then she lost her smile. "But you are not here to discuss Mr. Milgrim's romantic pursuits. Something is wrong, Mr. Cooper. What is it?"

Charles reached for his handkerchief, remembered that he had given it to Lily, and subsided back in his chair. "Miss Mullen," he said. "Do you know Fair Haven at all? Irishtown?"

"Irishtown is what I was rescued from. I was put in the orphanage there. The Sisters of Mercy." Miss Mullen leaned forward with her elbows on her desk. Her arms were bare, as Lily's had been — it had seemed shocking and almost wanton in Lily, but in Miss Mullen it seemed completely natural. She talked to him confidingly, as if she had known him all her life. "There was a time when I had relatives in Fair Haven," she said. "My aunt, my cousins. They're gone now. My aunt died, my cousin Katie went back home, the others have scattered." For a moment she was pensive, but then she looked at him with a smile and said, "But do I know Irishtown? Better than anyone else on Park Street, I'll wager. Why do you ask?"

"A woman to whom I have taught penmanship." He wanted to say the words *my own intended, my fiancée* — what harm? were they not as good as engaged? But he found he could not. "A friend as well as a student," he said. "She is in a difficult situation. She — she has a child, a baby, who is being cared for by a wet nurse in Fair Haven. She wants the baby to return, but doesn't know where she is exactly. A servant took the baby there, and now the servant has — well, disappeared. My student is in great distress."

Miss Mullen looked puzzled. "And you? You're supposed to retrieve your student's baby? Or find the servant?"

"Both, if possible," Charles said. "I told her I would try. She has no one else." He sat back in his chair, letting the breeze from the fan cool his face. He would have liked to roll up his own sleeves, loosen his cravat, and sit there for an hour. He felt his eyes closing.

"George could take you there."

He opened his eyes. "Mr. Milgrim's assistant?"

"That very George. He is also my brother."

"Is he!"

Miss Mullen got down from her stool, shook out her skirts, and went to the door of the inner office. "George?" She looked back at Charles. "I think he's asleep. George! Wake up!" She opened the door and poked her head inside. "I need you." She left the door open and returned to her seat. "George can often be found under Mr. Milgrim's desk, asleep. He hates hot weather. He would like more than anything to be back in Ireland, which he now thinks of as a cool green Paradise. He forgets that he had nothing to eat, and that the hovel he lived in was not fit for goats, and that the little we had was not green but mud-colored. Ah — there you are. Wake up, George!"

A man stumbled out of Milgrim's office, yawning. "It's too hot," he said, squinting in the light. He resembled his sister, but was older and ruddier.

"I want you to go out to Fair Haven with Mr. Cooper. He's a friend of Mr. Milgrim. He needs to find a baby. Is that right, Mr. Cooper?"

"Yes, I'm afraid it is." Charles stuck out his hand. "Hello, George."

George shook it sleepily. "A baby? In Fair Haven? Talk of the needle in the haystack! There are enough babies down there to pop-ulate a small city. A small and very noisy city."

"This particular baby is being looked after by a woman named Mary Whelan. Her husband is Liam."

"I don't know them," Miss Mullen said. " Do you know any Whelans, George?"

"Not here, I don't. In Clonakilty we had whole streets of Whelans, Whelans of every stripe." He spoke in a rich brogue. Miss Mullen had shed hers, though Charles could sometimes hear scraps of it.

"This Mary Whelan is the sister of a Mrs. Duffy."

George frowned. "Duffy, Duffy — Duffy rings no bells this side of the great pond."

"And —" Charles tried to remember. "Mrs. McAlmond?"

"Oh — Mrs. McAlmond!" Miss Mullen brightened. "Well, why didn't you say so? Mrs. McAlmond the midwife? Everyone knows her!"

"I don't," George said.

"Oh, George, yes you do. Maggie McAlmond, she was a friend of Aunt Rosie. She keeps the rooming house next door to the Henleys, George. On Pearl Street, just behind the oyster packing place. Wake up!"

"Which oyster-packing place?"

"The big one, the one on Front Street, south side of the bridge. Come, George, you know where I mean. The place where Peter and Katie used to work. What's it called? Tierney's."

"Ah — Maggie McAlmond." George yawned again. "Yes, all right. If it wasn't so bloody hot, I'd have remembered right away. Aunt Rosie's friend. Behind Tierney's."

"Go and wash your face and pop over to Moore's and hire a trap, will you?"

"They don't usually have a trap available."

Miss Mullen rolled her eyes. "Well — hire something! A buggy, a wheelbarrow! Look lively, George. This baby must be returned to her mother by suppertime!" She turned to Charles. "Does that sound all right, Mr. Cooper? George can accompany you to Mrs. McAlmond's, and I'll bet you a doughnut she will be able to find these people, and the baby, too. Maggie knows everyone, and if she doesn't, she knows someone who does."

Charles sat up in his chair. "A minute ago I had no idea where to turn. Now it looks as if this may not be a hopeless quest, after all."

"Well — I know nothing of these Whelans," Miss Mullen said. "Nothing is certain. But it's a start."

"A pity Mr. Milgrim isn't here. The case of the purloined baby."

She and George exchanged smiles, eyebrows lifted. "We'll just have to do our best without him."

"Somehow," George said.

"Go along then, George. There is no time to waste."

Charles dug into his pocketbook again and pulled out more coins. "I'm obliged to you, George," he said, handing them over.

"It's nothing, sir." He shrugged into a gray jacket, pulled a cap out of his pocket and put it on, then took it off with a flourish. "George Mullen, at your service. Back in a tick."

When he was gone, his sister said, "Let me tell you about George, Mr. Cooper. He is a poet — which means he can be oblivious to the workings of the world. He is a dreamer, and very forgetful, and so sometimes he needs to be pushed, and pummeled, and picked on, so that he stays on track. Nor does he have very polished manners

— he may as well have been raised by a pack of muskrats. But he is a darling lad — my oldest brother, and the only one of them who wanted to emigrate. He came over with me from Cork when I was a wee thing. He was just a boy himself, but he took care of me and my sister all the way, like a mother."

"Your parents —?"

She looked at him bright-eyed. "Father was not well enough to come with us. He died in Ireland. My mammy died on the ship."

Died on the ship, he thought, and so buried at sea. He imagined a child watching her mother lowered over the side into the black ocean. "And your sister?"

"Molly. She is in Boston now, with a very nice husband and two fat babies, doing very well. All is not lost, you see, with the Mullen family." She applied her fan vigorously. "When we first came to New Haven, she found work as a cook — she is a fine cook, our Molly! But I was too young to be a fine anything, though I've learned some cooking since — "

"Your lavender cookies."

"Ah — those! It's Mrs. Milgrim's cook makes little delicacies like that! She was trained in France."

"But Mr. Milgrim gave me to understand that they were your specialty — that you could open a pastry shop if you were so inclined!"

"Mr. Milgrim will say anything if he thinks it sounds amusing. No, I could not make a batch of lavender cookies any more than I could lay a dozen eggs! I can cook a pot roast, cut up a chicken and fry it, boil a potato — nothing fancy."

"And so Molly became a cook, and you —?"

"There was nowhere for me but the orphanage. Do you know where it is? On the other side of the river just above the bridge? The Sisters of Mercy are good women, but sometimes mercy is in short supply. And who can blame them? So many rowdy Irish lads and lassies could test the souls of anyone, even nuns."

"And that is where Mrs. Milgrim found you."

"She did. Now there is a truly good woman! Martha Milgrim plucked me right out of that blighted place, and installed me at her house, and sent us to school. It wasn't just me, there were three of us, all girls she sensed had potential. Potential for what, she never did specify. 'Don't let me down, girls!' she would say. 'Promise me you will not grow up to be ordinary!' She has a deep, booming voice, and we all used to imitate her." Miss Mullen's smile showed her dimples. "But she is an angel. Everyone loves Aunt Martha."

Her hair was coming down, and she reached up and pulled a large tortoiseshell hair pin out of it. She stuck the hairpin in her mouth, smoothed her hair back, and replaced it. Charles watched her with fascination, forgetting to employ his fan.

"Forgive me," she said. "Hair is such a bother. If I could, I would chop it all off." She replaced another pin, but to not much avail. "Oh, blast." She sighed. "And so that, Mr. Cooper, is the story of my life."

"Except for how you ended up here."

"In this office? Oh, the years went by, and — well, it's too long a story to tell in the time it takes George to sprint over to Moore's. But the end result was that Aunt Martha installed me here to keep an eye on her wayward nephew. Keep him busy! Keep his brain occupied! It is perfect for him — a modern office, and a secretary, and business cards, and his swivel chair! Mr. Milgrim is mad for gadgets. He has become interested in a new machine called a typowriter. He even went on the boat down to New York to see one. Have you heard of it? It works like a harpsichord. As you strike a key, instead of a musical note, a letter is pressed to the paper, with ink. I was so sorry he didn't bring one back! But I see it in my future as surely as if I were looking into a crystal ball. Once Mr. Milgrim gets an idea, it doesn't leave him. It sticks to his brain like a thistle sticks to your trouser leg." A thought struck her. "A typowriter, Mr. Cooper." She lowered her fan. "I wonder if it will make penmanship unnecessary some day."

Charles was startled. "A machine, you say? That would make letters look like — what? A printed page in a book?"

"Well, I suppose that is the idea. It would do away with inkblots, and with scratchy pens and unreadable scrawls." She laughed. "Would that not be odd? To read a letter written by a friend, but that

229

looked like it had been printed on a press? But I suppose it would just be for letters of business. The machines are very expensive."

"It's an intriguing idea," Charles said. "It would make such a gulf between a bill of sale or a legal document, and a letter from a friend. They would be entirely different entities."

"I suppose a really wealthy person could have a typewriter, just as a business might, and the tune he played on the keys could be anything he liked. A love letter, printed out like a book."

"A sonnet, looking like it was torn from a volume of poetry!"

"How would you even know who it was from? Anyone could bang it out."

"Forgeries would abound. Fraud! Letters that could never be traced back where they came from! A strange state of affairs indeed."

"I doubt that it will go very far. But I do find myself hoping Mr. Milgrim will acquire one so I can give it a go. Can't you just see me bashing away at it, red-faced and muttering, while you sit relaxed at your desk, writing with a pen and ink like a civilized person instead of a — an ape?"

There was a shout from outside, and she put down her fan again. "That will be our George. Speaking of apes." She went over to the window, stuck her head out, and waved. "He's got some kind of open wagon. It looks like a rattle trap, but at least it will be cooler than a closed carriage."

"I'm sure it will do us very well," Charles said. He got to his feet and put on his coat.

"Oh, it's so hot for such a heavy thing," said Miss Mullen. "Keep the fan, Mr. Cooper. You will need it. And — goodness me, you'll be coming back with a baby!"

"If we're lucky."

"I wonder if I should go with you." She pursed up her lips, thinking, then said, "Better not. There's not really room in that thing for three people and a baby. You'll just have to manage."

"We shall."

"I'm sure of it. There you go, then, Mr. Cooper. Good luck!" She saw him to the door and called after him down the hallway, "Keep an eye on our George. Don't let him wander away to look at an interesting duck on the river. Or go into the alehouse down there. George can be very easily distracted by an alehouse. He says he writes his best poems when he is slightly inebriated."

Downstairs on the street, George stood by the wagon, which was low, wooden, and badly in need of paint. "This was all they had available, sir," George said. "It was this or horses, and I thought if we're bringing back a baby, horseback might not be the best idea."

"Heavens, no!" Charles said in alarm. Bringing a baby back at all was challenging enough. It was years since he had held a baby. The reality of transporting one — hungry? crying? — back to York Street from Irishtown was something he hadn't thought about. Maybe he would drive and let George hold the baby. He considered going back upstairs to fetch Miss Mullen, to beg her to reconsider. She and her brother could drive to Fair Haven, search out little Prudence, and bring her back while he sat on a bench on the Green contemplating the cupola of the Exchange Building.

But in a moment they were on their way, George driving smartly. The horse was frisky, and as they rattled down Elm Street, Charles began to think of it as an adventure. They passed through downtown and, as Elm gave way to Grand Street, a breeze sprang up, and he took off his hat to feel it in his hair.

"It's always a bit cooler by the river," George said. "I do hate the hot weather."

"Miss Mullen says you miss the climate in Ireland."

"I do on a day like today. But I haven't forgotten that rain and mist and a chill in the air even in the middle of summertime can be as oppressive as this heat."

"How long have you worked for Mr. Milgrim, George?"

"As long as he's had his inquiry business. Must be a little over a year now."

"A year? He has been there only that long?"

"Well — he had another kind of business for a year or two before it, in imports — rugs and that, from China, or maybe India. And he had a try at being a sculptor, too."

"A sculptor!"

"Oh yes, indeed. He wore a white smock thing for it, and spent day after day hacking at great blocks of stone in his father's barn. I used to assist him there, too — helping him position them, and gouging out some of them, and nipping down to the tavern for his pint of sherry. Now it's all about driving him places, or spying on people for him. But it's all the same to me. He's an easy chap to work for, and he gives me a laugh."

"Did you say spying on people?"

"For his divorce cases." George flicked the whip. "That's mostly what he does — it's what he likes best, he says."

"You mean — "

"Oh, finding out who is where, and who with, and when. Writing it all up in case it's needed in court. That sort of thing."

Charles sat in silence for a moment. "And his work with Scotland Yard?" he asked. "When did he do that?"

"Oh — Scotland Yard. He was in London visiting his cousins during the Great Exhibition a few years ago — England is teeming with Milgrims the way the river is teeming with oysters. He has three sets of cousins in London, let alone the countryside. Ireland, too — there are Milgrims in County Down, I do believe. "

"And Scotland Yard?"

George looked sideways at Charles. "Do you remember the Bradford case? The murder in London, just outside the Crystal Palace? I think by now he may actually believe he had a hand in solving it." George laughed comfortably. "I don't mean to be cheeky about Mr. Milgrim. We're all as fond of him as we can be, though everyone knows you can't count on him — he's a flibbertigibbet, as they say. But he's an entertainment, too, is Mr. Milgrim — as good as going to the variety!"

As soon as they crossed the railroad tracks and then the Mill River, the city was left behind. They passed meadows dotted with cows, a field of tall corn, a hayfield stretching up to the north, where Charles could see the familiar cliff of East Rock in the distance. Then, as Grand Street led them into the heart of Fair Haven, the rhythm of town life started up again. Grand Street had the hum of a place that used to be one thing — a sleepy oystering community on the border of farmlands — and was rapidly becoming another. The streets were crowded with people, lined with shops and houses and the white-painted oyster-packing establishments. George pointed out the brewery — Charles thought of Philip — and the big new mercantile store, the King's Hotel, the clock factory, and, to the south, the long stretch of marshland where the river met the salt water of the harbor. Many of the houses were raised up above a work area — below, in oyster season, there would be teams of shuckers working at top speed.

"It's quiet now," George said. "But the season starts up again on the first of September, and it will be bedlam. The boats line up after dark, waiting for the midnight bell, and then they're off. They darn near clean out the river. You should come down and see it, Mr. C. The crowds are terrific, and all the taverns are open. It's like a circus."

Across the Quinnipiac, on the Heights, George said, there were a few splendid houses built by sea captains and the men who had made fortunes from the rich oyster beds, but on the short streets off Ferry and Grand were the people who fished for the oysters and shucked them for packing. Here and there, a big three-masted schooner loomed up between the houses, its bowsprit hanging over the street. On the breeze came the unmistakable smell of the sea.

"My sisters and I used to live right down there," George said. "On Pierpont Street. A tenement that creaked and swayed in a windstorm like a ship — it burned down last year, and good riddance. What a hell hole that was. Not that there ain't plenty more!"

"Where do you stay now, George?"

"In a much improved situation, Mr. C." he said. "A very superior boarding house on Broadway. Me and an assemblage of Yale students who occasionally drink too much on weekends and get noisy — how those lads do like to sing! But they are otherwise quiet and studious. It's more snug than commodious, but that is what I like. And it's convenient to the office. Snooping for Mr. Milgrim is not all I do, however. I'm a bit of a jack of all trades." He slowed the horse for a turn. "Here we are at Pearl Street. You see the paving? It's topped with crushed oyster shells all the way down. Pearly indeed, ain't it?"

They pulled up in front of a three-story house facing the river. It might once have been painted gray but was faded almost to white. There were net curtains in the windows. The front yard was thick with shells, a wooden rake leaned against an overturned boat. A sign in the window said ROOMS TO LET. A very fat woman, bonnetless, her hair in a tidy bun, sat on a chair in the doorway.

George leapt down. "Maggie McAlmond! It's a treat to see you."

She squinted at him. "Is that George Mullen?" When she smiled her eyes nearly disappeared. "I haven't seen you in a year. You've become very grand."

George laughed. "Aye, in my old tweed cap that I've had since I was seventeen years old."

"That's not that long ago. How is your lovely sister, Maud?"

"Maud is twice as lovely as she used to be. Quite the fine lady, you know."

"I've heard about Maud, and I wish her the best. Tell her I send my love."

"I shall do that. How are you, and how is everyone? The harvest will be starting up soon."

"Couple more weeks, they'll be going out. They're racing the sharpies this afternoon, Jimmy and them boys." She pointed toward the water, where speeding downriver were half a dozen long, narrow boats with fat sails. "Having the last bit of fun before the season begins."

"The McAlmonds are oyster royalty," George said over his shoulder to Charles. "Harvesting, shucking, canning the little buggers. Maggie's two boys have a fleet of sharpies, and her Jimmy is a hundred-quart man. That means he's been known to shuck more than a hundred quarts in a day."

"All it takes is a nimble way with an oyster knife," Maggie said. "And a brain that is not so big it can't concentrate on the task at hand."

George laughed. "You're looking very well, Maggie."

"Get away with you, George. Tell me why you've driven over here in this wretched old wagon. Not to flatter me, I'm sure." She looked past him at Charles in the wagon seat. "And not to get drunk at the Phoenix, I hope, the two of you."

"Not bloody likely. We are here on a mission. This is Mr. Charles Cooper —"

Charles stood up and bowed. "How do you do, Mrs. McAlmond."

"We're looking for a baby," George said. "And it may be that somebody named Mary Whelan has her — Mary Whelan the wet nurse? There is such a woman?"

"Who wants this baby, then?" Mrs. McAlmond asked skeptically. "And what business is it of yours?"

"A friend of Mr. Cooper has lost her baby." He turned to Charles. "How does it go, Mr. C.? The baby was put out to nurse? But her mother doesn't know where?"

"It's not quite like that." Charles climbed down and joined George on the side of the road, crunching the oyster shells on the path to the door. A shadow moved overhead, blocking the sun, and he looked up to see a large bird — an egret? a heron? — flying low toward the river. He thought suddenly of Lily on the Green watching the birds. Poor Lily. "The baby's mother is distraught," he said. "She has been ill, and someone else had to deliver the baby to the nurse, but she knows her name. It is Mrs. Whelan. She has a husband named Liam, if that is any help."

Mrs. McAlmond gave him a sharp look. "You're sure about all this?"

"Do we look like we're here to kidnap the little bairn?" George asked. "What would we want with a baby? Her mother wants her back, is all. We are doing a good deed."

"It all sounds very curious to me. I know nothing about any baby."

Charles's heart sank. "But you know Mrs. Whelan? The wet nurse?"

"I do, sir. She lost her own tiny baby on the ship coming over."

They were silent a moment. How many died, Charles wondered, on the ships?

"And where is the poor woman now, Maggie?"

"She's but a girl. She lives on that little lane that goes down to Front Street. Drive to the end here, and come back along Front

Street, and you'll see it on your right hand. Down there near Daniel Coyle's place, George. You remember Daniel? Further down."

"And she has a baby with her, that she's nursing?"

"That's all I will tell you. You'll have to speak to Mary yourself."

On Front Street, between two rows of identical squat, shingled oystermen's cottages, was a short lane leading up from the river. The house on the right was tiny, with a narrow front stoop and a window on each side. Seagulls screamed, a contingent of small boys came yelling around a corner, and the shouts of the racers on the river carried over the water.

George tied up the horse, and they went together up to the door. George was about to knock when it was opened by a young woman — round-faced, black-haired, blue-eyed. She looked about twelve years old, except for her enormous breasts, which strained against her dress. She crossed her arms over them and frowned. "Who are you?"

"We're looking for Mary Whelan," Charles said. "She who has the baby Prudence Prescott."

"Maggie McAlmond sent us over," George put in.

The woman eyed them cautiously. "I am Mary Whelan," she said. "But I don't know why Mrs. McAlmond would send you here. I know no Prudence Prescott." Behind her, there was a cry, and the girl looked over her shoulder. "That is the baby I'm nursing now. Her name is not Prudence."

The baby's wails increased, then stilled, and after a moment a man joined them at the door, cradling a baby against his chest. He patted its back. "I am Liam Whelan," he said. He was a fine-looking man, in shirtsleeves and suspenders, with very blue eyes and a short black beard. "How may we help you, gentlemen?"

Charles looked from Mary to Liam. "This man is your husband?"

"No, sir, he is my brother."

"Ah — well, no matter. My name is Charles Cooper, this is George Mullen, and we've come from the baby's mother, who wishes her to be brought home."

The two looked at each other. "The baby's mother," Mary said. "Her name is Prescott?"

"Lillian," Charles said. The baby was large and squirming, older than little Charlie had ever gotten to be, but Charles thought irresistibly of his son. Such precarious little creatures. He wondered how old Mary Whelan's baby had been when it died on the ship. "Lillian Prescott," he said. "In New Haven."

Liam smiled at him, shaking his head. "This is not the baby you are looking for. Her name is Anna. My wife was a widow when I married her, and this is her child."

"This child is Prudence!"

"The baby belongs to my wife, sir. My wife has been in service, but she was allowed to keep the baby with her until just recently, when she was told she must put it out to nurse. She was forced to quit her position in order to be with the child, and so — she has come here. They are both here. I am taking care of them now."

Charles was beginning to feel lightheaded. Could he be mistaken? He had seen Lily's baby only once, and had paid as little attention as possible. But this one had the fat face he remembered, and Lily's wide-set eyes. The baby's ears were pierced, and in them were tiny gold hoops. What had Lily said? Elena had taken a pair of gold earrings for the baby.

George glanced at him nervously. "You're quite sure about all this, Mr. C.?"

"Of course I'm sure," he said. "I am here to take this child home to her mother, and if you do not turn her over to me, I shall have to find a policeman." A thought struck him. "If there is a bill to be settled, I will settle it, and then we will take the baby with us."

"We do not need a policeman, sir. We are not trying to steal either your baby or your money." Liam Whelan, Charles realized, was a very large man, but his face was kind and his voice was temperate, and his rough cheek was against the baby's hair. Charles had heard much about crazy Irishmen and their goings-on, but this man was as mild as Matthew Cooper.

Charles flushed. "No — no, of course not," he said. "Nobody is accusing anybody, Mr. Whelan. I am just trying to work out what's going on."

"As are we all, I think." Liam handed the baby over to his sister. "I will get my wife. There is some terrible mistake here."

He disappeared inside the house. Charles caught a glimpse of a wooden table, a baby's cot in front of a hearth, a stone floor swept clean. Mary cradled the baby in her arms, smiling down at it, and the baby turned her head toward Mary's breast, opening her mouth like a little fish.

"Oh dear," Mary said. "Soon she will start in."

George said, "Ready for a feed, eh?"

"At this age, it's just about all they know how to do."

Charles feared that in a moment she would open her dress and start nursing the child. He felt, suddenly, very tired and very hot. All he could think about was a cold glass of water — or a cold draft of ale. He wondered, fleetingly, where the Phoenix was. Beside him, George reached out and tapped the baby's nose with his index finger, and the baby rewarded him with a smile, showing a tiny white tooth. Had Lily's child had a tooth? If she had, Charles had not noticed it. The baby, in fact, had been asleep, slumped in a chair, her fat little face sunk into her quilt. And didn't all babies have fat faces? He wondered if he was on a wild goose chase. Maybe there was another wet nurse named Whelan? Maybe it wasn't Fair Haven they should be searching but East Haven, or West Haven....

A woman appeared in the doorway, with Liam behind her. It was Elena. Charles had only seen her on the Green that day — black-browed and disapproving. Without her bonnet, wearing a checked wash dress instead of deep mourning, she looked completely different. He had never seen such glossy blue-black hair, such springy ringlets. She was almost beautiful, with the long nose of an aristocrat, and golden brown eyes.

"Elena," he said in confusion. "I'm sorry, I do not know your name."

"I am Mrs. Whelan." Elena stood next to Liam, and took his arm. "This is my husband, Liam Whelan."

Charles gaped at them. "You are married?"

"We were married two weeks ago," Liam said. He smiled down at Elena. "At St. Mary's."

George let out a whistle. "Well, that's one on us!"

"And you live here?"

"We do. My wife could not get away from her work until just yesterday," Liam said. "But she is with me now. I work for the New York & New Haven railroad, and next month we are leaving for New York, where I have a better job. But for now we are here with my sister."

Charles could not stop staring at Elena, who stared back at him in defiance. "My husband is rising rapidly in the world," Elena said. "He will be a stationmaster — that is a very good position."

"But — Miss Prescott?" he asked her. "Your work is with Miss Prescott. She had no idea where you were."

Elena raised her chin. "I did not intend to stay with Miss Prescott forever." Her English was almost without accent. "This has happened quickly. I will write her a letter explaining it all."

Charles looked from one to the other — Liam so matter-of-fact, with a face that showed honest and slightly amused puzzlement, Elena proud, angry, and hopelessly deluded, or worse. "I — " he floundered. He wished he could take Liam aside and talk to him, tell him what Lily had told him, about the tonic and the earrings and the clothes for the missionaries. "I'm not sure what is happening here," he said finally. "This baby belongs to your wife's employer, Mr. Whelan. She said you had disappeared, Elena — Mrs. Whelan — and without you, she did not know exactly where the baby was, and so I came here to find her and fetch her home. Lily wants to find a nurse for her who will live there, so that she may be with Prudence. Lily, I mean." *Lily*, he kept saying. *Lily*, stumbling a little over her name. Should he call her Miss Prescott? They seemed so far beyond propriety — what did it matter what anyone called anyone else? "This is her baby," he concluded finally, "and she wants her home."

Elena looked at him without expression, her arm through Liam's, and then, without warning, silently, her eyes overflowed. It was like watching a statue weep.

Liam looked down at her with concern. "Elena?" His feeling for her was clear. Charles tried to imagine how their romance must have unfolded, the invasion of this tall, striking Italian woman into a close-knit Irish community where everyone knew everyone else, and where the heart of the dashing Liam, who had dreams beyond harvesting oysters, was waiting to be won by someone regal and exotic, a foreign widow with a baby and, no doubt, a tragic story.

"I'm sorry," Charles said. "I don't mean — "

Elena spoke through her tears. "This is my child. I am her mother," she said, but her voice wavered.

"Elena — I know that is not true." Charles reached out a hand to touch her arm, but she pulled away.

"You do not know! You know nothing!"

George emitted another low whistle. "Wheels within wheels, this is. I'm lost."

Liam said, "Elena? Is there something amiss here?"

Elena stood clinging to her husband's arm, weeping.

Charles said again, very gently, "I'm sorry."

"The baby is Anna Zanetti!" The tears ran down her face. "She had a father as well as a mother, but you would never know it. She would not speak of him. You would think it was only Lillian's. That she pulled it out of the air!"

Charles stared at her. "Who is the baby's father?"

"Anna is my brother's child. Tomasso. He is dead. I came here to be with the little one."

"Oh, good God." Liam slumped against the doorway. "Is it true, Elena? This is not your child?" She said something in Italian, and he reached out and laid his hand along her cheek. "Speak English to me. You said Anna's father was an American."

"An American?"

Liam looked at Charles. "An American she married in Italy, who died of fever on the ship. That is what — " He turned back to his wife. "That is what you told me, Elena."

She looked at him pleadingly. "I only wanted to rescue her. My family's honor — "

"You could be prosecuted for this."

"She will not be prosecuted," Charles said, hoping he was speaking the truth.

"But what you did was wrong. You know that, Elena. The priest will tell you. It was a sin, what you did." He closed his eyes, his lips moving as if in prayer, then opened them. "Tell me the truth now. I will not — it will make no difference. Just tell me. You took this baby from her mother?"

Elena's face crumpled, and she lapsed into a flood of rapid, grief-stricken Italian that needed no translating.

❧❧

Lily must have been watching out the window, and was at the door before he had climbed the steps, the angry, red-faced, wet bundle of Prudence squirming in his arms. Their passage up crowded Chapel Street had been slow and chaotic. Prudence had cried all the way, despite his attempts to calm her. People stared at them as they drove by — two men in a shabby wagon, with a screaming baby. "This is a bloody nightmare," George kept muttering, and then the two of them would burst into laughter, drawing more stares. "Sing her a lullaby," George said. "Or make faces at her — they like that. Make funny noises."

Lily was dressed and had done her hair, but she was still distraught, and she fell on the wailing Prudence with sobs of relief, holding her so tight that the baby only cried louder. Mrs. Tuttle stood by looking pained — at Lily, at Prudence's noise, perhaps at what Lily had confessed to her while they were gone — but she clasped Charles's hand in both of hers, and her thanks were heartfelt.

"We owe it all to George Mullen, really," Charles said. "He's the one who took me down to Irishtown and ferreted out the Whelans."

Mrs. Tuttle shook George's hand as well, and thanked him graciously. Charles could see her calculating as to whether she should pay him something, then deciding it wasn't necessary. He explained how they had found Prudence, leaving out Elena's revelations about the baby's father.

"So this dreadful Italian woman did steal her," Mrs. Tuttle said, her nose wrinkling as if she had caught a whiff of garlic.

"She is a sadly misguided soul," Charles said. "But she knows what she did was wrong, and she is very sorry for it." He hesitated. "Elena is married now, Lily. She is the wife of one of the Whelans. Of Liam, in fact. He is not Mary's husband, as it turns out, but Elena's."

"Elena's!" Lily stared at him. "Elena married!"

"They have been married two weeks. And they are moving to New York, where Liam has a job with the railroad."

"We shall certainly be prosecuting her," Mrs. Tuttle said. "However far she may try to flee. Even in a city like New York, people can be found and taken to the law. When that happens, we may need your assistance, Mr. Cooper."

Lily raised her head. "We shall not be prosecuting her, Aunt. I want nothing more to do with her. She is a conniver and a sneak, and I hope I never lay eyes on her again."

"We will talk it over with your uncle."

"I will not do it!" Lily said vehemently.

"We shall see," Mrs. Tuttle said, but Prudence's wails all but drowned out her words. Lily put the baby on her shoulder, patted her, talked to her softly, walked her up and down, to no avail. Finally, Mrs. Tuttle disappeared down into the kitchen and returned with a sugar-teat. Prudence alternately sucked on it and screamed, and then, whether it was effective or whether she was simply worn out from screaming, she fell asleep on Lily's lap.

The silence in the room, Charles thought, was like a cool drink on a hot day. Lily laid the baby on the sofa, then sank down abruptly beside her, bent over, her head in her hands as if suddenly overcome by exhaustion, or relief. She stayed like that for a long minute while Charles stood before her uncertainly, watching the dusty shaft of late-afternoon sunlight that lay across her bright hair and the pale stripe of her dress. He knew they should leave. His duty was done, he felt awkward in front of Lily's aunt, and the prospect of Prudence's waking up and starting in again frankly unnerved him. But as he pondered what to do, Lily straightened up and raised her head. Their eyes met and, suddenly, she rose and threw her arms around him.

"I will never be able to thank you enough for this," she said. "Ever. You have been magnificent."

"I am glad I could help you," he said, his lips against her hair. "I am honored."

She looked up into his face. More than anything, he hoped she would kiss him, though he knew this was a nonsensical idea, with her aunt six feet away and George pretending to study the painting over the mantel. And then, miraculously, she did kiss him — swiftly and softly, but a kiss nonetheless, and briefly laid her cheek against his. "You are truly my knight in shining armor, Charles," she said. She stepped back and held him by the shoulders. "Though it may look like a black frock coat with a large wet patch on the front."

Charles hadn't noticed the stain. He looked down at his coat — the patch was large indeed, and now he could detect a faint odor of urine. "What matters a bit of damp in the service of Miss Prudence Prescott?" he asked.

George let out a guffaw, and even Mrs. Tuttle produced a benign little smile.

"When she is old enough, Miss Prudence will thank you." Lily turned to George and shook his hand. "And you, Mr. Mullen. I will see that you get some recompense for this," she added, and Charles felt irrationally proud of her.

"Not necessary, ma'am," George said stoutly. "Absolutely not necessary, don't give it a second thought. I was glad to help out. She's a gallant little lass, your Prudence."

Lily beamed at him. "She is, isn't she?" They all looked at the baby, who stirred in her sleep and gave a little hiccupping sob.

"We should be on our way," Charles said.

"I suppose you must," said Lily. "I am driving with my aunt and uncle out to Westville. Uncle is on his way with the carriage."

"To stay?"

"She'll be better off with us for the moment," Mrs. Tuttle put in, as if continuing a discussion she and Lily had been having. "This young lady needs someone to look after her. She needs to get her health and vigor back."

Charles bade Mrs. Tuttle goodbye, and Lily walked him into the hall, making a humorous little face that, Charles could see, masked a touch of annoyance. He wondered how long she would consent to live under the thumb of her relatives. But in the presence of her aunt, and with Prudence returned to her, she seemed absurdly young, just a girl — a far different being from the anguished, grieving woman who had opened the door to him earlier that afternoon. The richness of her, he thought — the endless delight, like a treasure chest, like a work of art you could stare at forever and never tire of.

At the door, she took his hand. "Good-bye, dear Charles."

"Lily — may I —" He wanted to say, "May I hope?" but he could not, with George at his elbow. Instead he said, "May I visit you in Westville?"

She formed an O with her lips, as if he had said something surprising and outrageous. "Need you even ask? I insist that you visit me in Westville!" she said with a laugh, and kissed him quickly again.

He was unsteady going down the front steps. At the bottom, he took a deep breath and looked around. Here was the world, then — York Street and Chapel, carriages and carts, top hats and parasols, the same and yet completely different. The events of the afternoon had changed it forever. First the meeting with Ives and Blanchard. Then Lily, weeping and distraught. She had put her predicament into his hands, trusting him completely. She had cried on his shoulder and slept in his arms. Without a second thought, she had allowed him to take charge, and in front of her aunt she had not disguised their intimacy. She had kissed him, not once but twice. His chest was tight, and he felt close to tears.

George broke into his thoughts. "Well now! That was an adventure from start to finish, Mr. Cooper."

Charles gripped his hand hard. "I'm more grateful to you than you can imagine, George." He wondered what George had made of it all — how he would describe it to his sister. And to Milgrim? The more Charles thought about it, the less he wanted his friend to know. The day had had its farcical elements, but it was also, to him, sacred. Milgrim, he had a feeling, would blunder over the sacredness and lunge head-first for the farce. He imagined him working with the Tuttles, *Inquiries of All Kinds* put into full play, tracking poor Elena down and spying on her, seeing the whole episode as a puzzle to be solved, Lily no more than a pawn in the game.

"And George," he said. "I would be grateful if you would keep quiet about this afternoon's events. The case is still — you know — still pending, as it were. I do not know what will happen, whether Miss Prescott will decide to go to law, or what, but for now —"

George raised a hand. "Not to fear, Mr. Cooper. I will not mention it to a soul. I will tell Maud that the case was concluded satisfactorily — that is all she needs to know. And as far as anyone else is concerned —" He winked. "Mum's the word. You can count on me, sir."

George clapped on his hat and took off up Chapel Street in the wagon. Charles headed in the other direction, toward the train station. He could see flat-topped storm clouds clustering ahead of him to the south and hoped vaguely that he'd get home before the rain began. He knew he should remember the name Sam had given them — cumulo-something. But at the moment there was no room in his head for the names of clouds.

❧

"Will you join me in a glass of sherry?" Milgrim talked as he poured. "It is time we had our celebration."

"The Chillick case?"

"None other," said Milgrim. "What a team we make, Cooper!"

Since the apprehension of Roland Chillick, Charles had thought carefully about the Chillick case, running over its events in his head. First, he had heard about the murder from Emily, and it had made him think of the man on the Green. Then he had talked it over with Harold Milgrim, who assumed Sam was the killer. Then the two of them had gone to Wethersfield to "observe" Sam, after which Milgrim had agreed that Sam didn't have it in him to bludgeon his former betrothed to death. Milgrim had checked Sam's alibi. Then he had sat at his desk in New Haven and waited.

Charles had to chuckle to himself: it was none other than Charles Cooper, he realized, who had applied the ratiocination and solved the murder case. He had remembered the letter, produced the blotter, talked to Sam, realized that Roland was a fugitive from the madhouse, gone with Sam to Middletown, and then driven him and Roland to the police in Hartford. Milgrim had done almost nothing! But an entertainment he surely was.

"I have much to do while I'm in town," Charles said, "but I certainly have time to celebrate."

He was there only for the afternoon. He had come to New Haven to meet with Blanchard and to visit Lily — he had not called on her in Westville for nearly a week. He had considered staying the night with the Gaudets. Emily had written to tell him that Philip had arrived safely in China, and Charles felt a wave of relief that Philip was — he had calculated it as best he could — eight thousand miles away. He would not have minded reading Philip's letter, which would be predictably sanctimonious but also perhaps interesting. How often does one read a letter from China?

But he had promised the twins he would be home in time for supper and for one of their peculiar games of chess. The two of them played him together, working as a team, and so far Charles's only goal was to teach them the moves. Maddox insisted that a bishop would not move on the diagonal. "It is right that he should not jump, as the knight does," Maddox said. "A bishop would not jump. But he would also travel in a straight line, going directly to his destination."

"Why would a bishop do that?" Charles inquired.

"Because that is what bishops are like."

"Have you ever met a bishop?"

"You don't have to meet a bishop to know that," David put in. "Everyone knows that."

"But you must realize that this is not a real bishop. This is a chess piece."

"Then why is it called a bishop? It must be called a bishop for a reason," Maddox insisted.

"And if it is a bishop, it should go straight," said his brother, and the two boys looked at each other and nodded.

Charles was greatly anticipating their next game. He was also glad he had caught Milgrim in his office. Milgrim was looking smarter than ever, wearing a matching vest and trousers, his cravat tied in a loose bow. He was in shirtsleeves, and had flung his coat on a chair. Charles took off his own coat — the heat of the day was as intense as ever — and laid it on the chair along with his hat, a broad-brimmed one with a striped band.

Milgrim raised his eyebrows. "I say, Cooper! Is that a new hat?"

"It is. I decided to throw decorum to the winds and strike out for high style. I hope New Haven is ready for a large blue hat."

"It is most impressive! I congratulate you on your audacity. I think it might start a trend."

Charles sat down. He had in his pocket the envelope Lily had asked him to deliver to George. "I'm sorry George is not here — unless perhaps he is asleep under your desk?"

"Ha ha! You know him too well. No, our George is off on one of his excursions, I know not where."

"Well, I shall catch him another time. And Miss Mullen? I always like seeing her, but she was not at her desk."

"I gave Miss Mullen a week off. I think the situation with Archibald March is becoming critical. I hear from our George that the great man is in town, but I sense that Miss Mullen has cooled off a bit toward him — there are not quite so many letters being scrawled when she thinks I am not watching. Poor Archie!" He handed Charles a glass of sherry. "Here we are, Cooper. This celebration is long overdue. It's nearly September. But here's to us! We have dotted our i's and crossed our t's, and the Chillick case is closed!"

"Ratiocination has ruled the day."

"How very true."

Charles said, "If I may, I would like to propose a toast to you and your intended — your *fiancée*." He raised his glass. "I wish you both all possible happiness."

"I am much obliged." Milgrim drained his glass, looked at it in surprise, and refilled it. "My engagement, I should say, is another example of ratiocination at work. I have chosen a wonderfully sensible young woman — or, to put it more gallantly, a wonderfully sensible young woman has inexplicably chosen me. Margaret's father is a particularly canny fellow. He is in the business not only of paving roads, but also of making muskets at the Armory out in Hamden. Mr. Whitney's factory. So when the world is finally paved over from here to the Massachusetts border, there will always be a war somewhere he can fall back on. And I believe there is a substantial dairy farm in the family, too."

"Congratulations," Charles said. "I know you have always sung the praises of diversification and flexibility, Milgrim." He tried to figure out what it might mean to make your fortune combining the paving of roads, the making of muskets, and the milking of cows. It was beyond him. "Will you and your wife live in New Haven?"

Milgrim looked at Charles pop-eyed. "Will we live in New Haven? Why, where else is there to live? Ah! One moment." He turned and picked a book off one of the shelves and opened it to a bookmark. "Have you read what Mr. Dickens has to say about the glories of our little city? I just came across this book — *American Notes*, it is called — and was quite charmed. Listen to this, Cooper." He read aloud: "'New Haven, known also as the City of Elms, is a fine town. Many of its streets are planted with rows of grand old elm-trees; and the same natural ornaments surround Yale College, an establishment of considerable eminence and reputation.'" He looked up. "I could not have put that better myself."

"Nor could I."

"But that is not all. Listen: 'The various departments of this Institution are erected in a kind of park or common in the middle of the town, where they are dimly visible among the shadowing trees. The effect is very like that of an old cathedral yard in England; and when their branches are in full leaf, must be extremely picturesque. Even in the winter time, these groups of well-grown trees, clustering among the busy streets and houses of a thriving city, have a very quaint appearance: seeming to bring about a kind of compromise between town and country; as if each had met the other half-way, and shaken hands upon it; which is at once novel and pleasant.'" He slammed the volume shut. "Now that is writing! Sentiments that are not only true but beautifully expressed."

"Capital indeed," Charles said. "'A kind of compromise between town and country — that is a very good description of the Green." He made a mental note to pick up a copy of the book for Lily, who seemed fonder of Dickens than she was of New Haven — perhaps he would win her over.

"Of course, the man's opinions about the rest of this country are by no means quite so buoyant — it's too huge and complicated for him, and he finds the government too dithering and reactionary — but of our New Haven and dear old Yale, as you see, he has nothing bad to say."

"I'm delighted that you're staying in town, Milgrim. I shall be moving down here myself in December."

"Excellent!" Milgrim poured more sherry for them both. "Have you taken a house?"

"I have my eye on one on Orange Street, near the corner of Trumbull."

He had, in fact, seen a small house that he liked — built of brick, with narrow windows, a back porch, and a pleasant garden. Its only drawback was that it was uncomfortably close to his former address at the foot of Wall Street. He had not walked down that street since the fire, had long ago devised a system of short cuts for avoiding it on his way around town. But he had recently forced on himself the experiment of walking by the old place. He had approached with dread, marveling at how that night, now more than four years ago, remained so real to him, appearing in dreams and nightmares, and returning at random moments during his waking hours.

But the house had been rebuilt and painted a new color, and a front porch had been added, so that at first he had trouble identifying it. The horror he expected did not wash over him. He stood there for a while as he sometimes stood at Sophie's grave, thinking about her as she had been when she was alive — that is all we can do for the dead, even Emily had said so — and then he walked down to look at the Orange Street house and thought it would suit him quite well.

"One of its chief virtues," he said, "is that it's directly around the corner from the school."

"Providing you with the more austere New England version of Mr. Jefferson's situation at Monticello," Milgrim said. "Roll out of bed and — well, a block or two later you're at work."

"It will do for me."

"We shall see much of each other, Cooper," Milgrim said. "And may I express my hope that before too long you will find a sterling girl to make that house a home."

Charles finished his sherry and picked up his coat and hat. They shook hands. "Thank you, Milgrim. It is a hope I profoundly share."

❧❧

Lily was not at home. Nor was Mrs. Tuttle. Nor was Miss Flossie. The tiger cat was there, sleeping on the porch, paws in the air. Charles did not ask about Mr. Henry Tuttle. He stood with his new hat in his hand while the maid looked at him like a mechanical figure dressed as a parlor maid — how starched and white her apron, how impassive her expression — and then he left a card and departed, gloomily, cursing himself for not having written first. He had thought she might expect him and be home. What an ass he was.

He had taken a carriage out to Westville, and now he took it back downtown. As they passed the corner of York Street, he caught a glimpse of the Prescott house, with its air of abandonment and neglect. Lily had told him she would be returning there in the fall, but her aunt had looked skeptical, and Charles had the feeling that Lily would be governed by her elders, at least for a while.

Lily was as pampered at the Tuttles as their own spoiled daughter, with new dresses and a very pretty bonnet. She was more beautiful than ever — as polished and glowing as she had been when he first met her. His visits had been awkward, certainly less intimate than his visits to the York Street house — he looked back on those afternoons in the drawing room, with Lily in his arms, as a time of enchantment — but the way she looked at him was as thrilling as ever.

Twice he managed to be alone with her long enough to kiss her, and she had returned his kisses, and he had made his decision: before Christmas he would ask her to be his wife.

It was all he could do, when he embraced her, to hold back the words of love that he had rehearsed over and over. But they would keep. He could not wait a year, as Tamsin had advised: he could hear her voice saying *rash, hasty, foolhardy*, but a year was too long. Lily needed him — and God knows, he thought, I need her. But he would make himself wait, as the kind of stern test he might set himself if he really were the knight in shining armor that Lily had called him.

He dozed in the railway carriage on the way back to Wethersfield — he was not used to sherry in the afternoon — and when he woke, he thought of Lily's heart-shaped face and wide eyes, and his heart lifted. He would come down to see her again in a week, and this time he would write to her first. He began composing a letter in his head, hinting at his feelings without actually putting them into words. He would show her the house on Orange Street. She would love it, he thought — the airy rooms and the walled garden. They would have a cat — cats had made Sophie sneeze. And he would buy a marble statue for the garden — a graceful Flora, maybe — to remind her of Italy. It would be his wedding gift to her.

Chapter Twenty-Two

29 August, Thursday. The order & serenity of a well-regulated household seem marvelous to me, I have done without them for so long. Everywhere here there is the scent of prosperity. The furniture is polished, the hearth is swept, the meals are produced silently & on time & they are not dependent on herbs from the garden or yesterday's supper heated up. My breakfast comes to my room, & the coffee is hot. They have acquired quite a fine melodeon, and Flossie & I play four-hand duets when she can put her mind to it. I remember her as a gifted musician, but she is easily distracted. She has grown up to be as pretty as I knew she would be, & she already has a beau, a young man named Austin Brewster, who sits beside her on the sofa & blushes. The delight of her life is her keepsake album, with its beaded cover & blue ribbon tie, into which she pastes scraps of poems she cuts from magazines — sentimental twaddle that she & her Mr. Brewster pore over for hours. Silly young people!

My Prudence has a wet nurse, Marjorie, a pleasant woman who has a room at the top of the house. Prudence is with me most of the day, but when she cries — off she goes to Marjorie, & she stays with her through the night. Now that my breasts are no longer huge & leaking, I suppose I must say that I rather like this arrangement!

Marjorie will be here until I leave for Rome on the sixth of September. I write that date with joy.

Papa's letter was waiting for me when I arrived at Aunt Julia's. I am not sure why he sent it here — perhaps he feared I would toss it in the fire, too rebellious & angry to open it! My father remains a mystery to me. But his letter was very clear on one point: he wants me to return to Rome. When I broke the seal & opened it & read those words & broke down in tears, Aunt Julia was angry with me. "You surely didn't think my brother would let you starve to death! You did not really think he had disowned you, Lillian!"

But I did think exactly that. She called me a foolish girl. But I did not care. His letter was brief, & not very loving, though he did say *It will be good to have you home*, & signed it *Your affectionate Papa*. He did not mention Prudence. But he has booked passage for both of us on a new ship that Uncle Henry says can make the voyage to Southampton in only twelve days, and Papa will meet us there and we will take the train to Rome.

I know Uncle Henry will be glad when I am gone. And so will I. I would leave tomorrow if it were possible.

I cannot write much about Harold. I read it in the paper. As long as I keep my mind on my return to Rome, I succeed in banishing him from my thoughts. I do pretty well, I can go for long stretches without the consciousness that he even exists. But last night, minutes after I fell asleep, I surprised myself by waking suddenly, sitting straight up in bed, & calling his name with a horrible loud sob. I hope Flossie did not hear me — she is just across the hall. I hardly slept the rest of the night. Oh, I did love him. Do I still? In spite of his perfidy & deceit?

No, I will not write about Harold. I will write about the letter that was enclosed in Papa's, with its own seal. I did not recognize the writing, & when I opened it I was at first puzzled by the signature. Who was *B. Felice*, if that was what it said? The script was difficult to make out. But then I read the letter, & as I read it my heart leapt, & then sank, & leapt again — have I ever felt such confusion? *I hope I may call you Lily. I have always. I have spoken to your father. Nothing could make me happier than. I look forward to your.*

I know not what to think. Signor Basilio Felice, my father's friend, wishes to marry me. I have a hundred questions, & chief among them is: *Does he know about Prudence?* My father does not comment on the letter, merely encloses it. Oh, for a mother! Fathers can be so unsatisfactory!

253

Aunt Julia watched me read it, & by the time I came to the end, I had probably turned white, or red. I was overcome, & made some excuse & ran upstairs to my room. I have not told my aunt about it, & I think I will not. I do love Aunt Julia with all my heart, but — well, I have grown up since I was in this house last. They are dear people — even Uncle Henry, for all his testiness & his black whiskers & his endless talk of gimlets & spoon bits & plug cutters, to which Aunt Julia listens patiently, with a wifely smile. He is being so good to me. He is, I am sure, paying for Marjorie, & Aunt Julia's dressmaker is making me two new gowns, & Prudence has a stack of dresses for the voyage. But I do not fit here — I'm like a piece of unwieldy furniture they have inherited, that cannot be reconciled with the red brocade loveseat & the little tables with their ivory inlay. The longer I'm here at the big yellow house I was mooning over a month ago, the more I wish I weren't.

I can make no sense of Signor Felice's letter. *Basilio,* I shall have to learn to call him. What does it mean, that he has always loved me? Admired me, yes — I could see that for myself. But how could he have loved me? I have seen him perhaps six times in my life, & he is at least twenty years my senior, & he has had a wife, who — well, did she die, or was there some sort of divorcement? I wish I had paid more attention.

And now he loves me. Can this be true? But I admit I do not know what love is. I loved Harold, or so I thought. And Harold loved me — though I now see that he didn't. Did I love James? I thought I did, but I was so young, no older than Flossie is now. I suppose I did not, really.

And Charles? He has been here twice to call on me, & we worked at my handwriting exercises once, but I think neither of us enjoyed it. Flossie kept running in & out, & Aunt Julia despite what she calls her undying gratitude looks at him like he's a fishmonger or the man who delivers coal, & neither time did he stay long. He has a new position, which sounds very nice, as the head of a school here, but he seemed embarrassed when he told me about it, as if he were ashamed of his excitement. He kept looking at me, with his kind eyes full of longing, & he kissed me twice, and kissed my hand when he left — lingeringly, the way he does, with his lips parted and his eyes closed. And then he came again, but I was — well, there is no point, really. I do think he loves me, poor man, but I do not love him. I cannot love him, or the life he will be living in New Haven, or anything about this small, seedy, stuffy, suffocating place. In a week & a day I shall be in New York, & the next day we board the ship, & the day after that we sail away! I have a calendar on which I cross off the days. I keep it secret from Aunt Julia or Flossie. To them, I am the affectionate niece & cousin, the fallen woman who repents — I am a ray of sunshine about the house. And all I think of is flight. The cage door will open & the bird will take wing!

But what a hero he was, my scrivener! For that I will never forget him. I shall write to him. What harm in that? And he is such a dear soul.

The house on York Street is closed up again, perhaps forever. Dora has returned to the mill — happy to do so, for she can be with her mother, whose health is no better. (There is a mill dust of some kind, from the wool, that gets into people's lungs.)

It is good to lie in bed, sometimes, until nine in the morning — a pleasure I left behind in Rome. I have the familiar back bedroom where I used to sleep when I visited, the big bed with its high carved headboard, & soft embroidered linens, & the reading lamp with its pink silk shade — oh, I do love a bit of luxury. I feel young & pretty again, & bursting with health. My malaise, whatever it was, has left me. I am convinced it was Elena's Chinese toad tonic that made me ill.

And of Elena I refuse to speak! My uncle still mutters about tracking her down and having her arrested, but I will not do that. I hope I never see her again. Charles said she went to New York with that man she married. Good luck to Liam Whelan! I hope he can control her better than I could! I can scarcely look at the red holes in Prudence's tiny earlobes — I have taken the gold hoops & flung them out the window, as I am determined to fling off the memory of all that has happened. It is as if I have been under a curse, surrounded by people I trusted & yet who betrayed me. Elena married to an Irishman, Harold marrying Margaret Brock — the next thing I hear will be that Charles has proposed to Dora!

255

What a long, hot summer it has been. But it is over now. And, against all odds, I intend to have a happy life — one way or another.

Epilogue

6 September

Charles,

I so deeply regret that I was not at home when you called last week! I write this in haste from my aunt's house, just an hour before I leave. Prudence and I are going to New York by packet boat, and then sailing to Southampton, where my father will meet us. You will be glad to know that he has written to beg me to return to Rome. I cannot tell you how his letter gladdened my heart! I am not sure how long I will stay at my father's house, but I am overjoyed at our reconciliation. Charles, I shall think of you often while I am there, and will write and tell you when I shall be returning, once I know it myself. Everything is uncertain. For now, I am looking forward to the voyage with Prudence, and with her grandfather to greet us at the end of it! Be well, my dear Charles.

Affectionately, your friend,
Lily Prescott

September the 7th

Dear Tam,

I am writing with the sad news that your Eli is no more. He died on Sat. night, & Rev. Singleton knew you could not be coming to bury him, so I & Martin & the Nashes & John Miller took care of it. The way of it was that Eli & Martin were out by the pump & that troublesome Sally kicked him so that he fell, & what did he do but crash into the wheel they were repairing & the broken spoke was sharp & gashed his leg, a lot of blood. He & Martin cleaned up the cut & he went back to work. But that night before they quit he begun to feel sick & feverish & so he went to bed, & Martin got him some whiskey too, but the next day Martin went over & he was still abed, & it wasn't the drink, it was a bad fever, & Eli's leg was swelled up double its size. We sent our Jim for doc Hayes over in town, but he didn't get there until night & by then E. was hotter than a stove top & raving, & the doc said it was too late even to take off the leg, it had spread too fast, it was blood poisoning. So he died. I'm sorry for your loss, Tam, & for the boys. He was a good man, just a drinker. Rev. S. said some prayers & there was quite a turnout & he's buried in the plot over by Millers. I told the rev. I would be writing to you, & he sends condolences & we all hope you are well, Tamsin. The horses will go for debts, Martin says. Drop me a line when you can & say what to do with the cabin & all that is in it. The hens are laying well. Believe me your sincere friend,

Nancy B.

October 14

Dear Charles,

Well, Mother has completely charmed my sons, with — guess what! *Geburtstagskuchen!* They were seven on Saturday, & we had a raucous celebration, with candles & presents & Aunt Mina's home-made wine. (I'm sure you have had some, so I shall not describe it, & in fact am not sure I could.) So many Legenhausens & Gruenewalders & a few von Schmelings & Zimmermanns & even a pack of O'Doyles — you didn't tell me that Uncle Stan's brother Otto's wife's sister married an Irishman! I am both happy to see them all & completely exhausted by them. I am often introduced to strangers as the Widow Pugh, which makes me feel about 70 years old. Mother wept with me over Eli, whom of course she never met. I was going to remind her that she did not come to my wedding or write to me for eleven years, but she seems to have forgotten all that, & so I shall forget it as well. She has called me a ninny more than once — I like to think she means it affectionately — & has referred to you as both a noodlehead (*nudelkopf* was what she was thinking, I'm sure, but she wanted to be sure I understood her) & a dunce, though I think she was willing to take that last one back when I told her you are going to be head of a school! You really should come down for a visit on your birthday, & she will make you a you-know-what. I think she misses you. It's something about the way she says noodlehead — as only a mother can. Both Mother and Aunt Mina look remarkably young — no wrinkles! I suppose it's the luck of the L's or perhaps Aunt M's wine, which they do drink plenty of, heaven help them, but on the other hand, if you never laugh, you never get laugh lines. Yes, yes, I know my penmanship is deteriorating sadly, but I am tired, & and this letter is long, & if you think what I've been through since I arrived here I know you will exercise brotherly forbearance. Write & tell me the news. I hope you have finally heard from Lily, and that she and the baby arrived safely in Rome. Tell Annie that I miss her dreadfully. I have written to Samuel myself, with the good news that I have captured a perfectly tufted altocumulus cloud directly over the Gruenewalders' barn (and just escaped a thunderstorm). We are leaving Saturday week and will be home on the 25th. Sam will meet our train in New Haven, so you need not stir. Davey and Maddy send their love, as do I.

Tamsin

❧⁕☙

Villa Fraguglia
Roma
October 1856

Dear Charles,

Here is my promised letter from Rome, rather later than I hoped. I have had no time to write, so much seems always to be happening, and no time to practice my penmanship and do justice to your excellent instruction. I have quite slipped back into my old ways!

I arrived safely, as you can see. The voyage was swift and without incident, and made easier by the knowledge that I would see my beloved father at the end of it. It is a great joy for me to be reunited with him, and with the city I love so well. Both Prudence and I are thriving. New Haven is a dear old place, but it is as if the air here is purer. I can breathe! I am not sure when I shall return. I will tell you honestly, Charles, that I may in fact not return, and that my life may soon be taking a direction I had never foreseen.

But I wish you well — more than well, I wish you the greatest happiness! I will never forget your goodness — you were the one rock I could cling to in the rough sea of my return to New Haven. I hope you will always think of me with kindness and affection, as I do you.

Yours sincerely,
Lillian Prescott

❧❧

22 Orange Street
New Haven, Connecticut
Saturday, October 19th

Dear Tamsin,

I am glad to hear that, though your head may be in the clouds, you are holding your own in the midst of the Teutonic branch of the family. Your letter almost made me miss them. I shall write to Mother and perhaps plan a visit after the spring term. My own birthday will no doubt be spent not eating cake but hard at work. I have devised an ambitious curriculum and am scrambling to assemble a staff to implement it. My office at the school has been set up, with rather dramatic velvet drapes on the windows and a large mahogany desk, behind which I sit in regal splendor interviewing teachers and students. The work has produced an avalanche of records, documents, and notes, which must be kept track of, and I find myself unexpectedly enjoying the process of figuring out ways to do that. I have devised an ingenious filing system, using different colored labeling, which I would describe to you except that it would surely send you straight to sleep. But take my word — though Mother would not believe it — it is brilliant!

At the same time, I have been moving into my new house, which is presently a bit underfurnished. It contains a kitchen table and an ancient bedstead from our barn, a set of chairs and some china that Emily and Bernard gave me, a cuckoo clock left behind by the former owners, and a sumptuous brocaded armchair that was a gift from Aunt Lottie and Uncle Edward, into which I am grateful to slump at day's end. Someday the house will really feel like a home, but right now it sometimes echoes strangely and, to be honest, sadly.

Which brings me to my only real piece of news. Lily has written me from Rome to say that she will probably remain there. She does not say this outright, but it is lurking between her words, and I know that it is true. She can, as she puts it, breathe there, as here she could not — and though you may call that an extreme flight of fancy, I believe I know what she means. I think I know now too that my feeling for her was a dream. It was a dream that seemed to me beautiful and even, from time to time, attainable. But that is the nature of dreams, I suppose — they seem quite real while they are happening.

I have had her letter for nearly a week now, and have read it over many times, and the first pangs of regret have died down. I try to keep some of Father's spirit with me — the joy that he took in the ordinary ways of the world. I do not forget that the world, in spite of everything, is a good place, Tamsin — and it is very wide.

Please give my love to everyone — yes, to everyone! I look forward to your return.

Charles

❧❧

Hotel Stuyvesant
New York, New York
2 November 1856

My dear Cooper,

You have probably already heard from the grapevine, of which George and Maud Mullen are the sturdiest tendrils, that I have closed my office in New Haven and am off to fresh woods and pastures new — in short, the obligatory year-long honeymoon tour of what is fondly known as the Continent. (Can there be more than one?) We are situated very comfortably in New York, and will sail to Southampton on 2 December, arriving I hope before Christmas, which we shall spend sponging on my cousins in London. Then it's onward to points east. I have a great longing to go to Italy, especially to Rome, to toss coins into fountains and picnic in the Coliseum, and also to Constantinople, but the rest of the itinerary is up to my bride.

And who knows? I continue to crusade against a foolish consistency
— I may perhaps never return to our fair city! Scotland Yard may call.
Or perhaps I shall set up in Paris and work for the Sûreté. Or follow
in the footsteps of M. Dupin as an independent ratiocinator!

All this is highly unlikely, of course. I am a loyal New Haven lad,
and cannot really imagine a life elsewhere. Still, it may be a while
before we meet again. May you thrive and prosper in the interim!

Your friend,
Harold Hopkins Milgrim

The Elm City School of Business
94 State Street
New Haven, Connecticut
4 November 1856

Dear Miss Mullen,

I hope you will not mind my saying I have thought of you often
since I saw you in New Haven and we took our very pleasant walk
together. I heard this week from Mr. Milgrim that he is closing
his business here and embarking on an extensive European tour. I
assume that, as a result, you are now without employment. Would
you consider taking a position as my secretary? As you know, I have
become the director of the Elm City School of Business — please
note the grand letterhead — and I will naturally require a secretary.
If you walk down Chapel Street to State and turn right, you will
see the building in which the school will be housed — the rather
imposing brick structure second from the corner. The duties will
probably not be very interesting, but they will be light, and you will
find the salary suitable, I think, for someone with your experience. I
look forward to talking this over with you soon, and have high hopes

that this will be the beginning of a long and fruitful association. Perhaps I could call on you this week?

Your sincere friend,
Charles Cooper

P.S. You may be glad to know that, improbable though it may seem in one dedicated to penmanship, I am contemplating the purchase of a typowriter. If I am to run a business school, I must not refuse to acknowledge that the world is changing rapidly. First the typowriter — then who knows what?

Author's note

I'm indebted to Katherine Florey and Becky Kraemer for planting the seed that grew into this book; to Margrit Diehl, Linda Roghaar, Jane Schwartz, and David Wilk for helping it thrive; and to Karen Kleinerman for her cover design.

For assistance with research, I wish to thank the librarians at the New Haven Museum and Historical Society, and I am particularly grateful to Rachel Quish at the Wethersfield Historical Society.

The Writing Master takes a few historical liberties. I christened two nameless Wethersfield streets, introduced baseball to Yale perhaps a year or two early, constructed a mill in Westville that never existed, and added a fictional orphanage to the colorful history of Fair Haven. Any errors or anachronisms are inadvertent and all my own.

CPSIA information can be obtained at www.ICGtesting.com
Printed in the USA
LVOW10s2215230713

344344LV00010B/385/P